Buried Sins

To my dear friend Betty Holmak, Thank you for a wonderful friendship throughout the years. God Bless, Mary

A Fictional Novel

by

Mary Elizabeth Gaines

Mary Gaines Books

Buried Sins

© 2018 by Mary Elizabeth Gaines

Published by Mary Gaines Books

First Printing March 2018

Printed in the United States of America

All rights reserved. No part of this publication may be reproduced, stored in a retrieval system, or transmitted in any form or by any means (i.e, electronic, photocopy, recording or otherwise) without the written permission of the copyright owner/author.

Library of Congress Cataloging in Publication Data

Mary Elizabeth Gaines, 1950 –

Buried Sins

Mary Elizabeth Gaines

ISBN 978-1-7320026-0-9

This is a work of fiction. Shelbyville is an actual town in Middle Tennessee, and Pope's Café and other establishments mentioned are well-known local businesses. Names, characters, various other places, and incidents either are the product of the author's imagination or are used fictitiously, and any resemblance to actual persons, living or dead, events or crimes is entirely coincidental.

This Book is Dedicated to

My Husband, Soul Mate, and Life Partner,

Samuel Gaines

I am thankful for the many blessings bestowed

upon me by God, Our Heavenly Father.

This book would never have been written without

His spiritual guidance and inspiration.

- Mary –

TABLE OF CONTENTS

Prologue 9

PART ONE – THE FAMILIES

Chapter 1 13

Chapter 2 23

Chapter 3 35

Chapter 4 47

Chapter 5 59

Chapter 6 63

Chapter 7 69

PART TWO – TERROR TAKES THE TOWN

Chapter 8 83

Chapter 9 95

Chapter 10 107

Chapter 11 115

Chapter 12 127

Chapter 13 137

Chapter 14 145

Chapter 15 153

PART THREE – REVENGE & OTHER LIFE LESSONS

Chapter 16 165

Chapter 17 177

Chapter 18 187

Chapter 19 199

Chapter 20 213

Chapter 21 223

Chapter 22 233

PART FOUR – CORRUPTION, COVER-UP, & CONFIRMATION

Chapter 23 241

Chapter 24 253

Chapter 25 261

Chapter 26 267

Chapter 27 281

Chapter 28 293

PART FIVE – VENGENANCE IS MINE

Chapter 29 307

Chapter 30 317

Chapter 31 325

PART SIX – RECONCILING THE PAST

Chapter 32 341

Chapter 33 353

PROLOGUE

1955

The putrid, rank smell of rotting flesh permeated her whole being. She was surrounded by death. She opened her eyes and terror overtook her.

All she could see was total darkness. Her body was in a contorted position with her knees at her chin and her wrists duct taped together beneath her thighs. She tried to move, but her ankles were bound with the same strong tape. She was in a fetal-like position and every part of her body screamed with pain and discomfort. She felt warm blood flowing down her throbbing right hand.

As she tried to wiggle into a less strained position, she realized she was hopelessly stuck. She couldn't move an inch in the restrictive space. Her lips were somehow sealed shut, probably with the same strong tape that tied her hands and feet. A muffled and pitiful scream stuck in her throat as she attempted to alert someone—anyone—of her horrid predicament.

She felt weight above her as if something was holding her down. A glimpse of faint light beamed above her as she felt more weight being heaved on top of her head. She wiggled with all her might, but to no avail. Instead, the light disappeared quickly as she was plunged into total darkness once more. She whimpered with fear and dread, not understanding what was happening to her. She feared the worst.

Tears rolled down her cheek as she struggled for a breath. She prayed for a small whiff of clean air through her unobstructed nostrils, but her prayer went unanswered.

Suddenly the light around her appeared again, but she was unprepared for what happened next. As she tried to breathe deeply, she inhaled a splash of liquid. The horror she felt at being confined with death escalated to a terror so deep she thought her heart would explode. She whined and tried to scream again but no one answered her plea for rescue.

Cold liquid rose around her sweating body. She felt buoyancy and panic simultaneously. She silently called her mother's name as she prayed for deliverance. She prayed for her young soul and for her salvation. But mostly she prayed for a swift end as the frightful, wet darkness engulfed her and she could breathe no more.

Part One

The Families

CHAPTER 1

2001

She tried to scream, but nothing would come out of her mouth. The dark silhouette was moving toward her and she braced herself for what she feared was coming. She clawed at the ground, trying to force herself backwards from the towering image, making a slow motion crab-like retreat from the inevitable horror. Again she tried to scream but her throat was dry. Instead, her pitiful voice came out in the form of a whimper. The closer it came, the louder she heard her pounding heart beating in her head. She closed her eyes tightly and braced as she took what she believed to be her final deep breath.

Please don't hurt me ... please leave me alone...

"Dixie, you've got to wake up! The Atlantis Resort radioed the yacht that you have an urgent phone call from the states. The caller is holding for you. Come on, honey, get a move on," Brax Edwards urged his sleeping wife as he gently shook her shoulders.

Startled, Dixie Carter Edwards opened her eyes to see her deeply tanned and handsome husband leaning over her bedside, a look of urgency in his usually smiling face. She clutched the sheet to her bosom as she struggled to detach herself from the night terror. Trying to focus on the apparent crisis unfurling, she simply gave him a wide-eyed silent nod.

"What...what's this about, Brax? I'm not expecting any calls," Dixie said as she tried to shake the nightmare from her mind. She still wasn't awake enough to fully comprehend what her husband was trying to convey. She glanced at the alarm clock that showed 7:35 a.m. in red glowing numbers.

"I don't know, babe. I don't know what could be so urgent that would warrant anyone calling the hotel. If it was a family matter, your cell phone would have been ringing nonstop," Brax remarked as he again tried to urge her to move.

Dixie scanned the stateroom for her cell phone, finally spying it on her bedside table. As she picked it up to check for missed calls, she realized the phone's battery had run down overnight. The screen was black and wouldn't revive. She had forgotten to plug her cell in the charger the night before. She frowned at the useless phone and threw it across the bed. "Oh God, Brax. The cell phone's dead."

For a split second, Brax glimpsed the little girl who still lived inside of his fifty-six year old wife. Her facial expressions had quickly changed from confusion to anger, then anxiety to fear. She looked like an upset child with her tussled hair framing her big brown eyes and her heart-shaped face.

"I'm sure it's nothing, babe. It's probably just your sister wanting to hear your voice or tell you about something that happened at work. You know how Dollie is. She's impatient as hell. I'm guessing she just jumped to "Plan B" when you didn't answer your cell phone at her command." Brax grinned, trying to relieve some of Dixie's tension.

"Yeah, Brax. I hope you're right." Dixie moved to the side of the bed. "I'll be ready to leave in five minutes. Just get out of the way and let me focus on getting dressed," she said in her normal voice, no longer appearing to be affected by her startled awakening from the bad dream.

* * * * * *

Brax sipped from a steaming cup of strong coffee as he waited for Dixie to come out of their stateroom. He was curious about the beckoning phone call, but he had other concerns on his mind.

He was an investment and financial advisor who worked three months out of each year exclusively in the Bahamas. For the past eight years, he and Dixie had spent March through May on a leased yacht anchored about a quarter of a mile off Paradise Island.

Their annual business/pleasure excursions had been lucrative for the most part, but the past two years had shown a decline in Caribbean investment opportunities. He wasn't certain how many more of these company-sponsored jaunts would be in their future unless business dramatically picked up. He tried not to reveal his financial concerns to Dixie, but he knew it wouldn't take her long to figure the money situation out. She was very intuitive, and she could read him like a book. It was hard to keep secrets from his wife.

* * * * *

Dixie and Brax were ferried from the yacht by water taxi to the dock of the Atlantis Resort. They hurried through the lush tropical grounds toward the lobby entrance. Once inside the palatial structure, they were greeted by the concierge who eagerly awaited their arrival. He motioned for Dixie to take a seat in an overstuffed chair in a secluded section of the lobby. On the coffee table was a telephone, along with pastries and coffee. As Brax poured coffee for them both, Dixie reached for the telephone.

"Hello, this is Dixie Edwards," she said with a raspy voice. She reached for the coffee Brax had poured for her and tried to clear her throat.

"Hey, Dixie, is that you?" the female on the other end of the line asked. Recognizing her little sister's voice immediately, Dixie smiled faintly. It had been a while since she had heard from Dollie. Brax was right about Dollie's impatience.

"Who else would it be? You summoned me, remember?" Dixie laughed into the phone.

"I tried your cell phone, but it went straight to voicemail. When I tried the hotel, I didn't realize they would put out an 'All Points Bulletin' on you. I was gonna try to get a message to your meathead husband, but I didn't realize you were so important the hotel would fetch you from the ocean."

It had been a while since Dixie had heard her husband called "Meathead" by anybody but her father. Ever since their Daddy heard it from Archie Bunker, he chose this affectionate nickname for his son-in-law.

Another smile crossed her lips, as she responded curtly, "Well, MEATHEAD was on the boat with me. He hadn't left for his office yet." Dixie chuckled for a moment and then asked, "So what's so important that couldn't wait a few hours? Did you get a promotion?"

Dollie paused and then sighed. "Are you sitting down?"

"What do you mean am I sitting down? Of course I am. I'm in a hotel lobby, for Pete's sake. What's the matter?" Dixie's fears were once again resurrected . "Is it Mama?" Dixie's heart began to beat faster while she waited for the answer.

"No, it's Daddy." Dollie paused to carefully phrase her next words. "He had a heart attack this morning and he died at the hospital." Dollie paused again, trying to force herself to speak calmly. "It was sudden and he didn't suffer. Mama is all upset, and she needs you here with us." Dollie's voice was starting to tremble, and she tried to focus on reigning in her emotions.

Dixie sat there in stunned silence for more than a few seconds. Through unexpected gasps, she finally said, "I don't know when I can get there considering this little island's airport schedules, but I'll get there as soon as I can... just as soon as I can get a plane ticket home." She looked at Brax as tears pooled in her eyes.

After they disconnected, Dixie stared at Brax in disbelief. He had overheard enough of the conversation to piece together the gist of the message. While Brax was envisioning an interruption in his schedule—last minute appointments he would have to miss and potential deals lost--Dixie was thinking about the past. Her mind was flashing scenes of "Daddy memories," both good and bad.

She knew when she got back to her Tennessee home town all those memories would resurface in high definition. She wasn't sure she could go through this ordeal without alerting Mama to her mixed feelings about Daddy's past behaviors and his chosen lifestyle. Mama had always been like an ostrich, with her head in the sand instead of dealing with whatever unpleasantness was around her.

Dixie thought of the mental anguish her mother must be in now that her father had passed. She didn't want to add to her mother's suffering. She thought selfishly, *Not me, I won't tell her anything. If she hasn't figured this stuff out already, far be it from me to be the messenger now.*

* * * * * *

 Two days later, Dixie took her seat in the first class section of the Delta flight from Nassau to Atlanta. Once settled in her window seat, she discretely reached into her small purse and retrieved a medicine bottle full of little pills. Already having been given water with lime, she didn't hesitate to toss a Xanax into her mouth and chase it down with the sparkling water.

She had arranged her flights as carefully as possible, choosing a flight to Nashville that would arrive in early evening. Driving to Shelbyville, Tennessee, from the airport would take at least another hour, and she wouldn't make it to her mother's home until after dark. She prayed that before bedtime there would only be enough time to have a quick dinner and some superficial talk about Daddy's death. She didn't think she could tolerate having to listen to woeful discussions about the late Corbin Carter. She wasn't ready to endure the excruciating process of digging up old memories, either. She couldn't do that tonight with Mama. Not before privately talking to her younger sister, Dollie.

* * * * * *

Although it was warm in Nashville for May, Dixie felt the briskness of the light breeze piercing the airplane skywalk. It was a nice change from the hot tropical climate from which she came.

Riding down the airport escalator to the baggage claim area, she spotted her only sibling holding up a sign with a single word—"DIXIE"--exaggeratedly printed with a red magic marker. *No expense was spared*, she thought with a smile. The sign was drawn on the back of a used piece of notebook paper. Smiling with pools of tears in her eyes, Dixie sprinted down the remaining escalator steps and ran into Dollie's arms. They embraced, holding on to each other as if each would be the other's only human savior. Finally, they broke apart and headed to retrieve Dixie's bags that had already circled the baggage conveyor at least once.

They were eager to collect the bags and get to the car. Both of them were exhausted— for different reasons—but tired nonetheless.

* * * * * *

As they traveled the fifty miles toward Shelbyville, Dollie hesitantly began the conversation detailing their father's death.

"Well, where do I start? Daddy was in his driveway last Tuesday morning trying to get a big lawn mower loaded on his trailer. He apparently grabbed his chest and fell backwards. His face was already blue when the paramedics got there, and on the way to the hospital he was pronounced dead. Mama is going crazy wondering what she could have done to help him if she'd been there. Of course, there wouldn't have been anything she could have done." Dollie sighed and took a deep breath.

Dollie then continued her story. I couldn't get to Mama from Knoxville until hours later. She called me at work and left a voicemail. By the time I heard it, it had been nearly three hours since she'd left the message. She was crying and trying to be strong at the same time. I hated hearing her like that. I wish you could have been here sooner, but I know you couldn't." Dollie kept her eyes on the road ahead while Dixie looked out the passenger side window.

"Mama said you were always the strong one. I haven't cried yet, though. I guess I was just waiting for you to get here to take over being strong and let me cry it out." Dollie smiled a troubled smile.

The only response Dixie could muster was, "I know, Sis. I'm sorry too. "

The drive was easy, almost routine. They had both made this trip numerous times throughout their lives. They rode in silence until the conversation took a turn in an unpredictable direction.

"I'm afraid you and I have to be strong together for a little while longer," Dixie said with a grim expression.

"What?" Dollie said with a tone of surprise.

"You and I need to go somewhere private and talk. We can do it tonight or wait until sometime tomorrow, but we have to do it soon. I know we'll have to take care of funeral arrangements and all the necessary other things that will be involved, but we have to have this talk first."

"Why? What's more important than getting through Daddy's funeral?" Dollie inquired, with astonishment replacing the surprised look on her face.

"We've got to discuss some things that happened years ago in our family, that's what. I have things to tell you that you probably never knew, and Daddy told me a long time ago to do this right after he died. I promised. He told me to open his safe deposit box at Peoples Bank. To tell you the truth, until we open that box I don't believe either of us will know the full story he wants told. There's stuff in there that is supposed to fill in some blanks. You've got to trust me on this, Dollie. I've been dreading this for years."

Dollie started to open her mouth, but Dixie interrupted her. "We aren't going to talk anymore about this until we get his final papers out of his lockbox and we've learned the whole story. We have to get this done before we leave town again."

Dollie could only stare ahead through the windshield as she processed this newly added task to their plans for the coming days. Sighing, she muttered, "Okay," and kept focused while she drove the Lexus SUV east on Interstate 24 toward the Shelbyville exit. Once on Highway 231, the drive was only about 25 minutes to their mother's home. Dollie wanted to ask more questions, but Dixie had made it perfectly clear that the discussion was over.

In a diversionary attempt to battle the silence, she turned on the SUV's Sirius radio station and listened to music from the 1950s. When Fats Domino's *Blueberry Hill* came on, both sisters silently cried as they listened to their deceased father's favorite song.

* * * * * *

When they pulled under the aluminum carport next to Mama's old minivan, they both exhaled with relief. Giving each other looks of encouragement and faint smiles, the sisters simultaneously exited the SUV. Both were harboring heightened emotions and anxiety. Neither could guess the state of mind Mama would be in or what they'd have to face in the next few hours.

Just keep it together for a little while longer. If it gets too intense, beg off for the night and blame jetlag or something. They are going to need you to be strong and in control over the next few days. They'll put you in charge of everything, like it or not. They always do. Just hold on, Dixie mused as she mounted the steps to the front door.

Opening the aluminum storm door and entering their mother's mobile home was a familiar gesture for them both. Whenever Mama knew they were on the way, the door was unlocked. When she was alone, there was no burglar who could silently penetrate the multiple deadbolts and other locks she had installed on her front door. She was very cautious, and rightly so, because it was no longer safe for anyone to live alone in Shelbyville. The crime rate had skyrocketed throughout the years, and the town wasn't the same one the family had once known. Leaving doors unlocked and unattended all day was a thing of the past. People had mysteriously disappeared through the years; robberies, rapes, and murders were at an all-time high.

"Is that you, girls?" Mama called out as she came through the living room area to greet her daughters. "My girls are here," she mumbled to herself.

Tearful and saddened, the three women huddled together and hugged out their hellos.

"How are you, Mama? Have you eaten today?" Dixie asked. She held her mother at arm's length and surveyed her frail body.

"I ain't been hungry for days. I think I lost about five or ten pounds already, but I could stand to lose a few more, anyway. What about you girls? Y'all want to eat something? I got a sweet potato pie here that your Aunt Tess made, and her church sent over some casseroles, too. I can fix y'all a plate. You know how good your daddy's sister cooks." Mama made a move toward the kitchen, but turned in her tracks when she heard no response from either of her daughters.

"Mama, why don't we just skip having supper? I don't think any of us feels like eating right now. We'll scrounge up something later if we get hungry. Why don't you go rest awhile? We girls have some things we need to catch up on, and we could all use some down time. The next few days will be real busy for all of us, and we're gonna need our rest." This was spoken with light authority by Dollie, who could persuade Mama to do most things through verbal manipulation and her pitiful expressions. She was powerful like that.

Mama looked at the clock. It was already past 7:30 p.m., and her day had started in the wee hours of that morning. She didn't want to admit to herself, let alone to her girls, exactly how exhausted she truly was. Pondering her alternatives, she knew Dollie was right about getting rest while they could. The next few days would be hard on all of them. She gave each daughter another long hug and turned toward her bedroom.

As Mama moved down the narrow hallway, her gentle but defeated voice could be heard. "Y'all know where to sleep. The bedrooms are ready for you. Get whatever you want out of the 'frigerator and help yourself to anything that's in there. If I can't sleep, I'll get back up and watch some television. Night, girls." And with that, she closed her bedroom door and, once again, felt alone even though her daughters were less than 30 feet away.

* * * * *

Within 20 minutes of her departure from the living room, Mama had finished her nightly bath. The loud water pipes had stopped rumbling which was a signal that Mama was now in the process of putting on her nightgown. After another ten minutes passed, the girls figured Mama had situated her head comfortably on her pillow. Confirmation came when Dollie tiptoed down the hallway toward Mama's room and heard her low soft snoring through the door.

Believing that they now had unlimited private time as long as they could stay awake, Dollie and Dixie crept toward the other end of the mobile home to the farthest bedroom from Mama's. They shut the door and looked at each other for what seemed like forever before the silence was broken.

Dixie started, "Are you settled in, Dollie? Are you ready to start this?"

Dollie sprawled herself across the double bed and nodded. She took a drink from her Diet Coke and fixed her eyes upon her sister.

Dixie began, "This is every bit of history I know that could help put all this in its proper perspective. This is gonna take a while. Some of it will just be to let you know what I've been told in the past about the family and some of the things that happened years ago. But some of what you hear might be shocking. Let's just concentrate on getting through this tonight, and tomorrow we'll tackle the safety deposit box and funeral arrangements. "

Dixie looked sadly toward her little sister. "Daddy wanted me to do this, remember that. If it were up to me, I'd leave all this stuff buried."

Dixie paused, rubbing her forehead with both hands as if she had suddenly felt the stabs of a torturous migraine headache. Seconds later she abruptly looked up and faced her innocent sister. For a brief moment it seemed as though she was transporting herself to another place and time--a much darker and more threatening world. She raised her chin high, and as they both made direct eye contact, she straightened her posture and muttered, "Lord, help me get through this."

As if trying to gather her courage to jump off a cliff or dive into a cold swimming pool, Dixie took a deep breath and exhaled loudly. "Okay, here goes."

CHAPTER 2

The Carter Family

1950

As she would so often do in the years to come, the young girl awoke startled and with a cold sweat forming on her forehead and upper lip. The small child thought that the family home on Lipscomb Street was about to blow up at the seams. The windows were rattling, and she thought the 4-room house was collapsing and the ground beneath it was quaking. She sat upright in her bed and frantically glanced around her dark bedroom to survey its condition.

The girl rubbed her sleep-matted eyes and listened more closely. She instantly recognized the source of her untimely awakening. It wasn't a storm or the earth moving beneath the house. Instead, it was extremely loud music coming from another part of the small clapboard rental home.

It was the sound of the Grand Ole Opry on WSM out of Nashville, Tennessee, some fifty miles away. On that brisk autumn night in 1950, Hank Williams was crooning sorrowfully through the speakers of the huge Zenith floor model radio that was kept in her parents' room.

"Why don't you love me like you used to do ..."

Barely five years old, Dixie eased herself from her twin bed and tiptoed through the darkness out of her tiny room. She felt the coolness of the linoleum floor on the balls of her feet as she crept through the darkness. She quietly navigated the small area between her room and that of her parents', stopping at their threshold. Her tiny silhouette was unnoticeable, framed by the bedroom doorway. Being perfectly still, hoping her Mother would see her standing there, she looked back and forth between her parents' bed and the monstrous, blaring radio in the far corner of their room:

"My hair's still curly and my eyes are still blue ..."

She remained unseen and unheard by her parents—mostly because of the darkness and high volume of the broadcast. Dixie ventured a step past the threshold and held her stance for what seemed like forever to her young mind. Still ignored, she decided to speak up—even yell, if she had to---and hope the disturbance didn't upset Daddy. Depending on whatever mood he happened to have been in that day, she couldn't be sure if her intrusion would provoke his sympathy or rage.

"Mama, I can't sleep. It's too loud," she whimpered, barely heard above the country melody.

Dixie waited. Mama and Daddy seemed to be totally absorbed in the Hank Williams song. She took a deep breath and raised her voice. **"MAMA…. I CAN'T SLEEP… IT'S TOO LOUD!"** she exclaimed pitifully, almost scaring herself with her own intensity. She started to cry.

Like a flash, Mama sat straight up in bed. Through the shadows, her white cotton nightgown emphasized the obvious contrast to her tanned olive complexion. Mama turned her face abruptly toward the door where her only child stood. "Oh, Dixie. Come here baby and lay down next to me. We didn't mean to wake you up," her mother reassured her, outstretching her gentle hand toward the sobbing child.

Daddy said nothing, but let out an audible sigh. He unwillingly scooted over to his left until he was almost at the edge of the double bed.

Simultaneously trying to keep the peace with her husband and calm her upset daughter, Mama gingerly got out of bed and padded toward the upright cabinet Zenith radio, lowering the volume ever so slightly. Since Daddy was deaf in his right ear, it was always a balancing act when the family listened to any home radio shows or broadcasts in the car. She motioned for Dixie to get in the center of the bed.

Nestled between her Mama and Daddy, Dixie laid her small head on the edge of Mama's pillow and turned to face Daddy, who looked at her and slightly smiled. Dixie wiped her tears from her cheek, smiled back, and touched his cheek with her small hand. Daddy moved his head slightly so that he could kiss the palm of her hand. Satisfied that all was now well with the family-- and considering there was still another hour left of the Opry—he turned his head away from the child's face to concentrate on the music and memorize the words to his favorite songs. As far as he was concerned, Dixie could be dealt with by her mother.

Mama, lying as comfortably on her side as she could, wrapped her right arm around the little girl destined to be a "Big Sister" to the baby currently kicking in her belly. Her thoughts wandered to what the future would hold for her and the children. She had no illusions about where she stood in her husband's life or the priorities he placed before her. She tried to settle her thoughts just as she had calmed her child moments before. She snuggled as closely as she could to Dixie, taking comfort in the love that her child—and God willing, the second one—would bestow upon her.

There was a warmth in little Dixie's heart now, lying between the two people on whom she depended for everything, including approval and affection. The now pleasant country music was soothing to her young ears. With her back against Mama's very pregnant belly, she strained in the darkened room to watch Daddy lip sync the words to Leon Payne's popular song, "I Love You Because."

> "I love you for a hundred thousand reasons,
>
> But most of all I love you 'cause you're you."

But, as Daddy silently followed along with the song's words, his expression changed into one of a love forsaken boy. It was as though he had been telepathically sending a very personal message to someone in his imagination.

Feeling secure once more as she lay between her parents, Dixie slipped into a peaceful Saturday night sleep. Mama fell asleep, too, but only after the Opry was over and Daddy started snoring. It had been an anxious day and night for Mama, but no major life decisions would be made until after a good night's rest. Holding her beautiful daughter closely, she slept through the night, albeit with interspersed dreams of abandonment.

* * * * * *

When the early morning sun beamed through the sheer window curtains, Dixie's mother, LorAnn Carter, was wide awake. The bed was still occupied by the sprawling young Dixie, but LorAnn's husband Corb was nowhere in sight. Slowly so as not to wake her child, she untangled her legs from the worn sheet and thin quilt that Dixie was still clinging to in her deep slumber; then she carefully got out of bed.

"Wonder where Corb went so early? Probably meeting that woman somewhere in town," she thought as she stepped toward the bedroom window that overlooked the drive way. She peered between the curtains to discover his old truck still parked in the exact spot where it was the night before. If he was meeting someone, he left on foot or else the woman had a car.

Just then, she heard a commotion in the front of the small house from the direction of the kitchen. Initially fearing an intruder, LorAnn was frozen in place until the familiar sounds of cracking eggs and sizzling bacon jarred her back to reality. Now she smelled the coffee, too.

"Corb, what are you doing in here?" she asked as she made her way from the bedroom to the small kitchen, less than 20 feet away from where her feet had hit the floor just a few minutes before. "I know you don't like cookin'," she said with a lilt of surprise in her voice. LorAnn's thoughts flashed to a time when a newly married Corb tried to make eggs and biscuits for her right after they were married—the honeymoon period, they call it. Momentarily, she felt a bit of optimism for the state of her marriage.

Corb looked at LorAnn, shrugged and simply blurted out his train of thought. "I woke up early and I been thinking a lot. LorAnn, you know I wouldn't just up and leave you and Dixie and the new baby all helpless. I know we got some things we gotta work out, but I never want you or the kids to suffer on my account. I'm gonna do my best to make sure of that."

LorAnn's expression changed from surprise to a softened, more relaxed smile. Corb broke eye contact, turning back to flipping bacon. After a pause, he said, "But, I don't know exactly *how* to be any good help either, given the way things are between us. I was thinking maybe I could stay at my Ma's for awhile, you know? Stay with her and Stan till this is all figured out. Maybe my Ma can help me think this through. How would that be?"

LorAnn's smile disappeared as she held back her tears in a valiant effort to maintain her dignity and pride. Now without the anticipated reassurance that her future was to continue with her husband by her side, she simply looked at Corb and replied, "You do what you have to do but you wait till after this baby is born. You better not leave me here alone to face childbirth with another youngun' hangin' on my coattails. That's too much. If you didn't love me, I wish you'd of told me a long time ago before you got me in this shape." Stoically and with head held high, she turned and exited the kitchen with the best posture a 39 weeks' pregnant woman could manage.

Out of Corb's sight, she made her way to the small bathroom. LorAnn closed the door, locking it behind her. He wasn't going to get the pleasure of seeing any more of her tears... at least, not today. Besides, Dixie would wake up any minute and she had to pull herself together before then.

* * * * * *

Corb Carter had just undertaken the hardest thing he'd ever done in his entire life. Telling his wife, LorAnn, that he was going to leave her and the family—especially with her being pregnant—was like talking through a mouth full of marbles. He couldn't believe he had actually had the nerve to spit it out, but now he felt relief in having the words out in the open. LorAnn took it better than he'd thought she would, too. She didn't throw a fit or cry hysterically. He hoped that it was finally sinking in to her that they would be better off going their separate ways.

As LorAnn exited the bathroom to check on a stirring Dixie, Corb was purposefully walking toward his Ma's backyard directly behind his own property. The rear of both houses faced each other, the distance being less than 50 feet between their respective back doors. Stan Rogers, his Ma's husband of some fifteen years, had recently stomped down part of the property boundary's wire fence to create an easement between the houses. This was created so that Dixie could easily visit with her doting grandparents who spoiled her with love, affection, and candy.

Corb slipped over the trampled fence and walked toward the Rogers' back porch steps, fashioned out of used cinder blocks. He could see their wooden back door was propped open to allow the brisk autumn air to cool the kitchen area. As he mounted the porch and pulled open the screen door, he knocked lightly but only as a courtesy before walking in.

Corb observed his step-father, Pap Stan, reading the morning paper at the red Formica dinette table. With coffee mug in hand, Stan glanced up at Corb, but uttered not a sound. Stan returned his full attention to the newspaper as his wife entered the kitchen.

Without making eye contact with her son, Ma moved directly to the stove and poured herself some coffee from the simmering aluminum pot. Clasping the hot coffee mug with both hands, she settled into the closest of the red and white vinyl padded chairs at the dinette. "You want some coffee, Corb? We already ate breakfast, but I can make you somethin' if you're hungry."

"I ain't hungry, Ma," Corb remarked as he pulled out a chair and seated himself across from his mother. "I came over here to see if you would talk to me about some stuff I gotta deal with about LorAnn and Dixie. I got myself in a mess, and I don't hardly know what to do."

Pap Stan rose from the table, silently signaling that he didn't want to be a part of this conversation, and in his low, deep voice mumbled "I'm going to the toilet, and then I'm goin' to the diner to check on things. I'll see y'all later."

Coincidentally, at that very moment LorAnn and Dixie were sitting at their own small wooden kitchen table—LorAnn only drinking coffee with tear-pooled eyes, and Dixie ravenously raking eggs into her mouth and chasing them with chocolate milk. The girl casually asked the whereabouts of her Daddy, and LorAnn comforted her with, "He'll be back in a little while."

A pacified Dixie continued gulping down her breakfast while LorAnn silently prayed she hadn't just lied to her daughter.

* * * * * *

Corbin Lee Carter was born in the fall of 1922, an identical twin to his brother, Joseph Alvin Carter, who tragically died a few weeks after birth for reasons still unknown. Corb, as he liked to be called, had only one living sibling-- a sister who was a little more than a year older than he was. Since Corb's birth and the loss of his sickly twin, Tessie Carter had developed a protective nature toward her little brother. Sometimes she picked fights with him just so he would be more prepared to defend himself if ever bullied by someone bigger. They made a good team, and their bond was tight.

Viv Carter, called "Ma" by both Corb and Tessie, was a fierce looking heavyset woman who unintentionally intimidated most people who didn't know her true nature. She had a quick wit and a sharp tongue, just the kind of person it took to usually keep her husband, A.J., in his place. Depending on his mood, A.J. generally followed his wife Viv's cues and kept his temper in check, but on rare occasions his ire would overtake him. It was on those occasions that Viv would herd their two children into another part of the house or would take them outside to play. It usually took a shot of whiskey or a long nap to snap A.J. Carter back into civility. When the kids were older, she believed they had learned to steer clear of A.J. when he acted out.

On one spring afternoon in 1933, A.J. started an argument with Corb, who by then was a twelve year old boy who had inherited much of his father's temper. When A.J. started pushing Corb out the door, demanding that the boy go buy him some whiskey from the bootlegger down the street, Corb finally physically and verbally pushed back. Knowing that hard liquor only fueled his Daddy's rage-- plus knowing his Ma would not approve—Corb finally stood up for himself and refused to run the errand.

By now the two were standing on the four foot high front porch. A seething A.J. grabbed for a broom handle leaning next to the front door. Livid with anger, A.J. drew it back with wrath, and knocked poor Corb's head across the right ear with such force that it launched the boy off the porch into the middle of the dirt yard.

Corb was stunned as he held his wounded head and now permanently deafened ear while his father continued to yell at him to get up and get going. Wiping the blood flowing down his cheek, he tried to stand but managed only to sit back down in the dirt, terrorized by the wild man ranting from the elevated podium of the porch. "If you don't get off your ass and do what I told you, I'll knock your other ear off and really give you something to cry about!" A.J. yelled at his dazed son.

Ma and Tessie heard the commotion from the rear of their shotgun house, and Ma told Tessie to stay put until she figured out what was going on. By the time Ma made it to the front door the damage was done.

When Ma realized Corb had been brutally attacked by his father, she immediately turned her big-framed body toward her drunken lunatic of a husband. He expected a verbal lashing from Viv, but this time her fist connected with his high cheekbone, knocking him backwards. He never saw it coming. He fell over the porch rocker and landed on his rear as Viv sneered, "Old man, you better get your lazy ass out of this house before I go get the gun and splatter your worthless guts all over the yard, you sorry bastard."

Stunned, A.J. slowly stood up, righted himself, and said nothing as he turned on shaky legs to enter the house. Without protesting, and in an attempt to save his hide from his furious wife, he packed his few belongings and got the hell out.

Two years later, a divorced Viv Carter married Stanley Rogers, a Godsend of a man to all the family. Stan, a long time bachelor, took his wedding vows very seriously, making him an eager-to-please husband, something Viv had never experienced. Also, to the kids, he was a much welcomed replacement for their tormenting father. Stan asked Viv to do all the disciplining of the children, and she gladly agreed that it was her place to do it, not Stan's. Everything was so different now...so much more serene.

For the very first time, the kids were happy and so was Ma. It didn't matter to them that Stan was a highly successful bootlegger-- in fact, he was the very man that A.J. demanded Corb go to for liquor on the day A.J. beat Corb deaf in his right ear; the same day that Ma sent her first husband packing. Nevertheless, Stan was a sympathetic man who made a good living and never once yelled at or struck anybody. Stan was now a contented family man who had grown to love his step-children as much as he loved Viv.

* * * * * *

After Stan left Corb and Viv alone in the kitchen, the mother and son sat in silence for a short time while Corb tried to collect his thoughts.

"Ma, I can't keep doing this. I can't stay married to LorAnn. I just ain't happy the way things are." He sighed loudly as Ma took a sip of coffee from the heavy restaurant-style mug, excess inventory from their diner situated right off the city square.

"Ma, what am I gonna do?" He looked at his Ma with tears brimming in his eyes. "I love somebody else."

Viv held back her growing disappointment with her only living son. She tried to hold her tongue as she queried, "Boy, what have you done?" Viv loved LorAnn, even if she was a little more timid and submissive than she ought to be. Viv adored Dixie, too, and had been guilty of intentionally keeping the child over night too often because she knew LorAnn wouldn't know how to gracefully refuse. "Have you gone and done something you're gonna regret, Corb?"

Considering the hardships that she had endured in the past 47 years of her own struggling life, Viv was having a difficult time understanding why Corb couldn't find happiness in the way things were with his family. But, she had to maintain her composure and allow him to provide his explanation. If he sought her advice, surely she had some leverage to steer him away from any potentially wrong choices.

Corb shamefully looked at his hands, wondering how to go about admitting his two-year extramarital affair and still keep his mother on his side. He leaned forward and cradled his forehead in his hands. With eyes closed and a look of pained grief overtaking him, Corb felt tears rolling down his unshaven face.

Rising only to refill her coffee and get some for Corb, she placed a steaming mug in front of him and settled back down in her chair. Without further comment, Viv patiently waited for what her son had to say.

* * * * *

Corb wasn't really what you would call a "ladies' man" or anything like that, but he was handsome enough. He was only 5'9" but he made up for his lack of towering height with a charismatic smile and twinkling eyes. He turned the ladies' heads easily enough, and could keep their attention with his boyish charm and quick wit.

In the spring of 1942 he joined the U.S. Army as a 19-year old private. It was the thing to do, after all, if a man was a true patriot during this troubling time of war; but unexpectedly, he was medically discharged near the end of his basic training stint at Camp Forrest in nearby Coffee County. Apparently, in an effort to meet the enlistment quota for able-bodied soldiers to ship overseas, Army doctors had neglected to test Corb's hearing. When his disability was discovered, the Army reluctantly sent him home.

Overall, he had never dated anyone for long periods of time; he had a one-night stand here and there, maybe more. But Corb didn't meet "The One" until he saw a lovely young lady sitting on the hood of a car parked near the popcorn stand on the Shelbyville square. Instantly, he knew he wanted to marry that girl.

It was shortly before his twentieth birthday and a few days after his military discharge that Corb met Lora Ann "LorAnn" Hudson, an innocent girl from a rural section of the county. He learned later that she had a good paying job at the Rubber Mill, one of the largest employers in Bedford County. That was an unexpected bonus that made LorAnn even more attractive to Corb.

As time passed, Corb continued to court LorAnn, never daring to strain their relationship by pushing intimacy on his wholesome fiancé. They dated for a couple of years and abstained from sex, but they indulged in plenty of kissing and hugging, always stopping on the verge of hormonal fulfillment.

Corb became more eager to make the big commitment and reap all the benefits of marriage. LorAnn was happy and more than ready to make the leap. So, in March of 1944 the two traveled to Huntsville, Alabama for the nuptials, and returned the same day to the newly rented Lipscomb Street house that they still occupied six years later.

Even though Corb struggled to be a good husband and provider to LorAnn, he was only 22 years old when he married her, and just a year older when Dixie was born. Married life hadn't turned out to be the blissfully erotic and fulfilling experience he had imagined. Being grounded didn't come easy to him; it was work.

Corb became a trained carpenter, holding down a lowly position in a local cabinet shop, and doing odd woodworking jobs on the side for meager extra pay. He was also an excellent mechanic, occasionally taking on extra motor repair work for the Stewart-Potts car dealership. He could build or fix anything, but he wanted to be more than just a common laborer.

Corb wanted a better job with better pay. He wanted a wife who saw intimacy as something more than a way to make babies. He wanted respect. He wanted excitement—he wanted passion.

He wanted to be someone else.

CHAPTER 3

The Carters & The Tuckers

1950

While Corb silently wept in his mother's kitchen, LorAnn and Dixie were cleaning up the mess Corb had made making breakfast an hour earlier. As far as they knew, Corb hadn't eaten a single bite. Dixie wanted to save the scraps for her Daddy, but LorAnn put the uneaten food in the trash. She was still mentally bruised from the morning conversation. But since her Daddy was subject to frequent and unexplained absences from the house, Dixie had no idea there was anything wrong between her parents. To Dixie, that morning was the same as every other morning had been. However, LorAnn saw it as the beginning of the end of her life as she knew it.

Viv didn't try to pressure her son to talk, thinking that he might just cry out what was bothering him. She sat there tolerantly, waiting for Corb to settle down.

"Ma, I can't keep going on like this. I can't keep pretending I'm happy when I'm not. I ain't made nothing of myself, no matter how hard I try. LorAnn won't understand that it's not about her or Dixie. It's about me and whether or not I'm going to stay miserable forever if things don't change. I dread waking up every morning knowing the day is gonna be just like every other awful day has been for me. Oh, Ma."

Corb caught his breath from holding it so long trying to spit out everything at once. "And what about my little girl? I can't even be a good daddy to Dixie--or the new baby-- if I don't have my mind right. Ain't that right, Ma? Am I just going through something?"

Tears overwhelmed him again, causing him to search his pants pocket for a cloth handkerchief to blow his now dripping nose.

"Or am I just a bad person? Maybe I don't deserve anything good." He gazed up at his Mother with watery eyes, looking for reassurance that his extreme emotions were within the spectrum of normal behavior.

Ma was confused by Corb's outburst. *What in the Sam Hill is this boy sayin'? What's makin' him think wild thoughts like this? This ain't like Corb—I thought he had his head on straight, but guess I was wrong. Whatever's coming ain't good ....*

Viv's thoughts were bouncing all over the place. Before she responded to her desperate son, she had to choose her words carefully to avoid getting him all worked up again. She tried the gentle approach:

"Look Corb. None of us can call ourselves happy—what is "happy" anyway? You make the best of your life as it's been handed to you, and you **live** it. We find minutes of joy every day. There's bad that happens to us every day, too. But you gotta take those few minutes of good and weave 'em together to see that overall, each day is more good that it's bad. Your life **is** good. You got a loving wife, a precious girl, another baby on the way—you make a good living and you ain't suffering. You got a roof over your head and food on the table. What are you missin', son?"

Corb blew his nose before solemnly answering, "Ma, I'm missin' out on living with the woman I love."

Viv slowly rose from the table. Thinking she was leaving the table to refresh her coffee, Corb turned his head and looked upward toward his Mother's looming figure. But Viv didn't move from her spot. Standing in front of her vacated chair, she leaned over the table toward Corb. Her round ice-blue eyes peered over the top of her bifocals, and locked eyes with her son. "Corbin Lee Carter, you're a damn fool. You better start thinking with your head and keep your pecker in your pants from now on." With that, she slapped Corb so hard that his chair scooted backward an inch on the slick linoleum floor.

Viv continued her rant. "You ungrateful son of a bitch, you're just messing up your life layin' around with that whore. Yeah, I know who she is, and so does everybody else in this town. You better straighten up and fly right or you're gonna lose everything, and then don't come talkin' to me about how to be "happy." You got everything you ever wanted right over there in that little house. Get your ass over there and act like a man. Do your duty. You made your bed, now go lay in it. Don't you ever come whinin' to me again about how you ain't happy."

She took in a breath and started in again, "AND you better watch your step, Mister. Ain't nobody gonna bail you out of any mess you make just cause you think you're in love with a tramp. Get it together and act like the man I raised. Go take care of your family and leave that trash with her dim-witted husband where she belongs."

The berated Corb rose from the dinette chair and briefly locked eyes with his angry mother. Mustering all the nerve he had, he moved from the chair to the screen door without looking back. He left Ma's house more confused and hurt than he had been when he first came through that screen door.

Instead of using the well trodden path to his own back door, he diagonally bypassed the clapboard house he shared with LorAnn and Dixie. With determination, he hurriedly paced down his driveway toward the main thoroughfare beyond Lipscomb Street. He kept moving toward Elm Street. He didn't know where he was going, but he had to find a way to contact his "girlfriend," Nell Lambert. He needed to see her, badly. He needed to see her NOW. Lord, he just **needed** her.

* * * * * *

Corb found his way to the Red Ace gas station across from the Shelbyville High School building, only a few blocks from the house. Right inside the front door was a red and white Coca-Cola cooler with a multitude of different cola choices standing at attention in the frigid water. He picked an RC Cola, opened it using the side mounted cap opener, and listened to the bottle top drop with a "clink" into the almost empty metal bin. He picked up a package of salted peanuts and funneled them through his hand into his RC Cola. Looking around, he spotted the telephone in the corner, and asked the clerk if he could use it for a minute.

With the clerk's approval, Corb dialed Nell Lambert's house. In his current depression, he would risk her husband answering the phone. He waited patiently as the phone rang at the Lambert house, but no one answered.

Disappointed and frustrated, Corb then dialed the number of his brother-in-law, Troy Tucker, who was married to LorAnn's older sister, Roz.

Troy was fighting similar demons as Corb's—he had an extramarital affair going on, too. As far as the two men knew, they were the only ones who knew any of the details about what each had been doing.

Troy answered the phone on the fourth ring, just when Corb was about to hang up. When Troy realized Corb was the caller, he perked up. He figured Corb was going to propose a little Sunday afternoon fishing or maybe he wanted to go riding around town together to pass the time. Who knew... maybe they could double date on the back roads if the details could be squared away. "Corb, what are you up to today?"

Corb swallowed his drink and chewed on two peanuts that had ridden the wave of cola into his mouth. "Troy, I'd like to go somewhere and talk, just the two of us. I'm in a mess and gotta make a big decision. Troy, I need some help. I don't know who else to turn to. "

Since Troy had no afternoon plans, he saw an opportunity to drop off his wife at the Carter house for a sisterly visit while he and Corb made the best of the possible open afternoon. He laid the phone down for a minute and sought out Roz to see if she wanted to go visit her sister. Unsurprisingly, she agreed, so Troy told Corb he would drop Roz at LorAnn's in fifteen minutes and then pick up Corb.

Within 20 minutes Troy pulled into the Red Ace parking lot and parked near the side of the building. Corb rushed to the brand new 1950 Chevrolet, opened the door, and hopped onto the leather seat.

While Troy was adjusting his mirrors and the side air vents on the car window, Roz was just sitting down in the living room on her sister's worn sofa. Little Dixie was trying to sit as close to her aunt as possible. She wanted to show her Aunt

Roz what she had been coloring that day. She also had some paper dolls with different paper dresses she was anxious to model.

Soon after indulging Dixie with her complete attention, Aunt Roz remarked, "Did I just hear your Granny Rogers calling your name, sweet girl? Do you think maybe you should check to see if Granny or Pap Stan needs you to help with something?"

LorAnn smiled at Dixie and told her to go over to Granny Rogers' house and play for a little while, but come home if she got in Granny's way. Dixie eagerly picked up her crayons, blank paper, and her paper dolls with their partially ripped paper clothing. Holding all her treasures close to her chest so as not to drop anything, Dixie ran out the back door, shouting "Granny Rogers, Granny Rogers … I'm coming to play with you."

LorAnn watched through the glass panes of the back door and saw her daughter safely ushered in to Corb's mother's house for play time and treats. Knowing she might have an hour or two to privately visit with her sister, she sat back down in a side chair and faced Roz who was sitting on the couch.

"If I didn't know better, I'd think you've been crying. You look lost. Something goin' on with you and Corb? Has Corb hit you? Is the baby all right?" Roz waited for LorAnn to give her some hint as to what was happening that caused LorAnn to look so frail and dejected.

LorAnn relayed to Roz all that had transpired the day before and that morning, and the terrible mood Corb was in when he left the house.

"I know he's been seeing some woman, but I'm not sure I know who it is. Nobody will tell me anything, but I know all the signs. He leaves early, skips lunch at the house more often than not, and he comes home late. He don't want to touch me or even kiss me anymore. I know I'm fat and ugly and pregnant, but he won't even kiss my cheek. He leaves out of the house sometimes and don't tell me where he's goin'. He comes back hours later. I know what this is, I'm not stupid, but I am scared to death. I don't know how I can take care of two youngun's by myself, and I can't ask Corb's mother to help. That ain't fair, either. They got a diner uptown they have to run, and they don't have much free time except on Sundays. Besides that, I gotta go back to work at the Rubber Mill after the baby comes, and who is gonna keep the kids then? I don't make enough money to pay a babysitter to watch two. I don't know where to turn." With that, she broke down again and sobbed into the apron she still wore from cleaning the kitchen.

Roz moved from the center of the couch to the arm of the chair where LorAnn was sitting.

"LorAnn, you gotta stop feeling scared or feeling sorry for yourself 'cause that ain't gonna do no good. Think about the positive side to all this: you got a job and a family. So what if you lose a husband in the deal. He's a piece of shit anyway. If what I hear is true, he's running after that floozy Nell Lambert. I'd bet you my own paycheck that she'll stop having anything to do with Corb once she thinks he wants to break up her marriage. It's happened before with her and more than one guy at the Rubber Mill.

"That woman don't want Corb. She just wants him to show her a good time. Her husband makes more money in one week selling aluminum siding than Corb makes in a year at his cabinet-making job. She ain't planning on struggling with a lower life style. Trust me, LorAnn, Corb will be crawling back to you with his tail 'tween his legs when she lowers the boom on him. It ain't gonna take long." Roz chuckled, and saw a hint of a smile creep across LorAnn's lips.

"Don't forget this, either," Roz continued. "You the one holdin' all the cards, dear sister. That would be alimony and child support. Corb ain't gonna part with the biggest part of his money and give it to you to spend anyway you see fit. No, sir, he has to be in control." She laughed and lightly punched her brooding sister's arm.

"Girl, you may have to wait a few weeks to hold up the victory flag, but you got all the guns. Anyway, his mama over there would rather kill him dead than have him hook up with that tramp and then leave his wife and legitimate kids all by theirselfs. She'd beat him every step of the way back here and make him do right by his family. That woman's scary." That broke the tension in LorAnn's face, causing her and Roz to fall back chuckling in their seats. Finally LorAnn began to realize she may have more control that she thought.

Nell—Nell Lambert. Lord, she has a bad reputation. I've heard about her....

LorAnn let those words settle in her mind. There might still be a way to mend what was broken if Corb would only come to his senses.

* * * * * *

As the Chevy's radio blasted out Patti Page singing *"The Tennessee Waltz,"* Troy and Corb drove toward Unionville on Highway 41A. There were plenty of back roads through the area that provided spots where they could pull over and talk-- uninterrupted. They happened to pick an area by a small spring-fed creek that had just enough room to park the car and find a cool and comfortable sitting spot under the shade of a large oak tree.

After lighting a short cigar, Troy retrieved a small cooler from the trunk of the car and took out a beer. He ambled toward Corb who had seated himself on the ground with his back against the massive tree trunk. Corb appeared to be daydreaming about something as he absent-mindedly swirled the remaining soda around in the green-tinted glass bottle.

Troy stood next to the tree, clad in overalls with a white tee shirt underneath, which made him look like a farmer who had come to town for church. He wasn't a farmer though, and he didn't wear overalls for working. Overalls were his comfort clothes of choice. He could put his chewing tobacco in the bib pocket, and keep his cigars up there, too, not to mention all the other benefits he would tell you about if he was asked.

Since Corb hadn't said a word since they got out of the car, Troy decided to move things along.

"You will never guess who I poked last week. Go on… guess! You'll never guess," he smirked with a triumphant look on his face. Corb just shook his head and shrugged his shoulders.

Troy couldn't contain his excitement any longer, and he blurted, "The preacher's wife! I poked the preacher's wife! Hah, hah, what do you think about that, huh?"

Corb was stunned because he knew the preacher's wife well. Never would he have suspected that she would be open to backsliding, and especially not with

Troy. Apparently the woman had no sense. Troy looked like a Marlon Brando reject, fat round belly, and greasy curly hair. He wasn't much taller than Corb, if any, but he wanted to be a rebel like Marlon Brando or James Dean, maybe.

"Well, good for you, Troy. I congratulate you on surprising the hell out of me and probably her, too." The words came out of Corb's mouth, but there wasn't much feeling in them.

"Excuse me for getting excited, Corb. Shit, I thought you'd think that was a pretty good prize."

Corb sighed and once again began to swirl the remaining peanuts around in the almost empty RC Cola bottle.

"Troy, you remember I been tellin' you bits and pieces about having a special thing going with a lady friend for around two years now." Troy nodded his head in agreement.

Corb continued, "And you know I been tryin' to keep who she is a secret from you and everybody else, right?" Again Troy nodded.

"So, now I am so mixed up with all my feelings, I don't know what I'm supposed to do to be fair to everyone and still be fair to me. You ever feel like that?"

Troy studied for a moment and said, "Can't say that I have. I'm a selfish son of a bitch, myself." Troy's smile showed all of his perfectly white teeth.

"Well, I'm ready to give everything up and go off with this woman that I love. Forget LorAnn, Dixie and the new baby, just live my life and be happy."

Troy stopped smiling and stared at Corb as if he had just declared he was a visiting alien from Mars. After he studied Corb's demeanor for a few more minutes, he realized Corb was earnestly trying to get advice because he truly didn't know what moves to make next.

Again Troy tried to smile and calmly said, "OK Corb, we're gonna talk through it all, and I hope by the time we're finished you will know what's right . It should be easy to plan your next move when everything's laid out on the table for you to consider."

"OK, Troy. I trust you with my secrets and I trust your judgment. I want you to know it all. You're the only real friend I have who understands any of this." Corb relaxed a little.

* * * * * *

Corb repeated the same story he was trying to tell Ma, but this time he gave Troy more detail, talking more about how his happiness depended on Nell, not LorAnn and the kids.

Listening intently for the last half hour or so, Troy didn't interrupt for clarification or to make random comments. He just let Corb get everything out; then they both sat silently, contemplating the situation for a few more minutes.

"You want me to honest with you, don't you Corb? You don't want me to hold back nothing, right?"

Corb nodded and emptied his RC bottle of peanut pieces and brown syrupy liquid.

"OK, I want you to look at all sides of this situation. Let's say you leave and go knock on Nell's door. How do you know she'd walk away from Bill and go with you? And you know she'd have to bring her kid. Do you even know that kid? Think you wanna be her new daddy?" Troy looked at Corb intently.

"I've seen the girl's picture, but I reckon her real daddy don't give her much attention anyway. And, yes, I think Nell'd come with me. She complains that Bill can't satisfy her, first of all, and he's so whipped he'll do whatever she tells him—or what anybody tells him, for that matter. She says she don't love him, and the only reason she stays is because he is gone a lot for work and he brings home a big paycheck."

A smile crossed Troy's face. "So you're saying she wants to screw around with you and still get to spend her henpecked husband's paycheck?"

"That ain't what I meant and you know it." Corb answered indignantly.

"Well, she ain't gonna be getting any big paychecks from you, old boy. By the time you pay LorAnn some alimony and child support for two little ones, you'll be asking Bill for a loan just to be able to take Nell to the movies. Have you really thought all this through?" Troy was acting somewhat superior and it was beginning to irritate Corb.

"Yeah, I've been doing a lot of thinking. Course I have."

Troy responded, "Well, try to think of this while you're at it: that woman's got a bad reputation around town for wanting to have fun and wanting to mess around with different people. How do you know that would stop with you if you married her? Has she even told you that she loves you and wants to run off and settle down? Or, is this just your bright idea?"

Now Corb was beginning to get a little riled. "I know about her reputation, but that was before 'us'." She just ain't happy where she is."

Troy reached in his bib pocket and pulled out another cigar. He chewed on the end a while before attempting to light it. "I don't think she'd be any different with you than with her other flings. I heard she had one guy at the Rubber Mill ready to take her off with him to Florida, and she told him to get lost. Said she liked the freedom she had when Bill was gone, and she wasn't gonna give it up for the likes of him. Did you know about that, Corb?"

Looking surprised at this bit of information, Corb said simply, "No."

"Yep, that was maybe 3 years ago, probably not long before she took up with you, I'd say." Troy wasn't pulling any punches. "You know, you'd be labeled all over town as a deserter and an all round sorry man to up and leave your pregnant wife and kid. And after Nell drops you, I'd guess your chances of ever making anything of yourself in this town might be a lot harder with that hanging over your head. You could avoid that bad stink if you'd just stick it out where you are. If it was me, I'd just get some on the side wherever I could—might be Nell, might be somebody better who comes along—but I wouldn't leave the family just yet. You're still young and you can start saving some money for when you want to leave later. And by then, you might not even want to leave. You can have the best of both worlds without all the hassle, if you know what I mean." Troy puffed on his now-lit cigar, the expression on his face reflecting how wise he thought he was.

Corb looked even more confused, but nodded agreement. He was beginning to realize why Ma was so angry. The things Troy said about Nell's past would make other people wonder why *he* was dumb enough to run after her. If he didn't care about what people said, that was one thing. But the fact that Nell wanted Bill's big money might be something else to consider. Corb wouldn't be able to give her anywhere close to the money she had now. That problem could lead a person like Nell to look elsewhere for another big spender. He didn't know if he was stupid for being in love with her, or just plain stupid for having the affair and getting in this spot.

Corb decided he had to have a serious talk with Nell to find out what their relationship really meant to her. What would she give up to have Corb? Now, he wasn't sure. But he was sure of one thing: He wasn't going to rule out anything until he made her admit her true feelings, too. He wanted to look her straight in the eyes when she answered his questions.

Of course, he would have to make peace with LorAnn tonight and try to get her back to her passive state. Certainly he wouldn't be blurting out anything else about leaving or staying over at Ma's. LorAnn didn't need any undue stress with the baby due any time now. He was going to act like everything was peachy keen, and hope whatever happened in the next few days would be the right and fair thing for everybody concerned.

* * * * *

That evening when LorAnn and Corb sat in the living room listening to the radio, they both were on edge about similar concerns. Neither spoke of the recent upsetting conversations, but rather, they acted as if nothing had happened. Little Dixie played with a wooden train in the floor near her parents' feet. Corb read the Sunday newspaper that Pap Stan had read and discarded. LorAnn flipped through a magazine that Roz had left with her that day.

Even at bedtime, everything was tranquil—except for the tormented thoughts of the two apprehensive adults. And once again, after a few hours' sleep, Little

Dixie woke up screaming for her mother, as she endured another night terror complete with cold sweats and a resultant fear of sleeping alone.

CHAPTER 4

Heartache and Heartbreak

1950

The next morning, Corb tried to sneak out of the house without alerting the sleeping LorAnn. He thought he was successful, but subconsciously he didn't care if LorAnn was aware of his departure or not. His chief mission that day was to try to see Nell before he had to punch the clock at the cabinet shop.

He knew Nell would get her daughter fed, ready for school, and walk her to Elm Street before allowing her to make the rest of the one block trip alone to the Tate Elementary School. Nell wouldn't walk back home until she watched the little girl safely enter the school gate, knowing the first grade classroom was just a few steps away.

Keeping in mind which areas to avoid for public observation, Corb took to the backstreets to see if he could get a glimpse of Nell on her morning journey. He parked on the side of the road near the Coca-Cola plant, expecting her to walk in that direction as she took the shortcut home. If all went as planned, he would pick up Nell, take her somewhere private, and ask her the questions he had contemplated all night.

Sure enough, he spotted Nell as she turned from waving goodbye to her daughter, who threw her Mother a kiss while skipping toward the school's entrance. Satisfied that her day was now her own, Nell picked up her pace as she prepared to stroll the few blocks to her Morton Street home.

* * *   * * *

Nell almost always got second glances from men, but no one would call her a beautiful woman. She was above-average in looks, for sure; but, she didn't have above-average intelligence. In fact, she was more aptly described as a dumb brunette. Nell Lambert laughed too loudly, talked too much and too fast, dressed to reveal her well-endowed bosom, and usually flirted more than she really meant to do.

To Corb, she was alluring, enticing, and effervescent. Everyone else thought she was a sorry excuse for a wife to her hard-working, dedicated, but mousey husband. Even though she had already been married several years before she got pregnant, locals wondered if her husband actually sired the baby. They speculated about who the poor guy could have been that knocked her up.

Normally Corb was a good judge of character and, under other circumstances, probably would have been able to peg her for the kind of person she truly was. But, as he had told his Ma, he was "in love." He was blind to anything about her that could have been an unappealing or negative trait. He thought she was a sadly misunderstood person; therefore, he thought they had everything in common.

* * * * * *

When Nell spotted Corb's familiar old truck, she grinned with all she had and dashed up to the driver's window.

"Hey handsome! Where you goin'? she playfully asked while giving him her most seductive look.

"Hi, Babe. I was wonderin' if you might have a few minutes to talk? Make some plans for later or whatever?" Corb was attempting to hide his true mission behind the façade of an eager lover, but he wasn't a very good liar. Then again, Nell wasn't a very insightful woman.

"Sure, hon. Why don't we go back to my place. Bill left last night for Nashville and I'm there all by myself for the next couple of days, at least while Annie's at school. I got some coffee and pancakes left over if you haven't had breakfast." Nell opened the truck door and climbed up on the stained cloth seat.

Corb started moving forward, aiming his truck indirectly toward Morton Street. He made a loop so as not to be seen driving directly to Nell's house. He eventually arrived at a market about a block down from the Lambert's house where he told Nell to go on ahead and open the back door. He would soon follow on foot after he bought some gum at the store and parked the truck near the rear of the building.

*** ***

When Corb opened the back door of Nell's house, he saw that she had already poured him some coffee—black, just like he always took it—and had set a plate for him at the head of her table. He nervously sat down at the chair she had partially pulled out from under the table for him.

He watched her take her seat alongside him. She scooted her chair as close to him as she could manage. She propped her chin on the palm of her hand, resting her elbow on the table top so she could gaze closely at Corb's face.

Nervously, Corb pushed the plate out of the way, signaling that he didn't have breakfast on his mind. He stared into her eyes for what seemed like minutes, then leaned forward and kissed her on the forehead. He then rested his forehead on hers and uttered the words he had held back for so long.

"I'm in love with you, Nell. I think I have been for nearly the whole time we've been together."

Not acting the least bit surprised, Nell simply stated what she thought: "I know, Baby. That's so sweet." She leaned back a little in her chair, breaking their head-to-head connection.

"You sure you don't want pancakes? They're still warm." Nell acted as though Corb's declaration meant nothing.

Corb looked puzzled, and shook his head. "Nell, I want *you*, don't you understand that?"

Thinking that she understood fully what he meant, Nell stood up and started to move toward the bedroom. Corb stopped her by grabbing her elbow. "Dammit, Nell. I don't want to have sex, I want to know if you feel the same way as I do."

Nell jerked her arm out of Corb's grip. Her brow wrinkled. "If you're asking me if I love you, I suppose I care a lot about you, but I wouldn't call it being in love. You're making this whole thing bigger than it oughta be. I thought we were just having fun, having a few laughs and making each other happy. What is it you want from me, Corb?" she questioned as she moved backwards a step.

Corb sighed, "I want us to be together, that's all. Always together. Forever."

Nell didn't hesitate to explain her situation. "We are together right now, Corb, and it's the best we can do. If you thought I was looking for another husband, you thought wrong. I just want to keep my little house together with my family and my freedom and enough money to occasionally enjoy myself. I like the way things are, and I'm not about to change anything, not for you or anyone else."

For a brief moment, he flashed back to the conversation he'd had with his brother-in-law Troy the previous afternoon. Nell had done everything Troy had predicted: she was refusing to leave the security of her unsatisfying husband for any man, not even Corb . He mentally counted—was he the second, third or fourth fool who had fallen for her seductive ways? His head was spinning and he now saw himself as a man in purgatory: not necessarily in hell, but he sure wasn't in heaven. He was hurt, but now he was also very angry.

Corb sneered and said, "Well, if that's how you really feel, I think it's time we stop this craziness. I'm outta here." Abruptly he turned and left through the back door the same way he'd arrived. He sprinted toward the corner market where he had parked his truck, and jumped in it as soon as he could get the creaking door open. He peeled out of the parking lot, attracting more attention than he wanted. His eyes were clouded with moisture, making it difficult to focus on the road ahead.

"That Bitch," he said aloud, slamming his palms on the steering wheel as he careened on the narrow road. "Why couldn't I see she was just a whore?" he ask himself, while starting to take another silent inventory of his feelings.

Corb only focused on Nell's availability, not her morality. If he had, he would also have had to examine his own. That aspect was better left alone and faced only when it couldn't be avoided, like now. He guessed he really was no better than she was, when it got right down to it.

Of course Nell was well aware that Corb was married and had a child. LorAnn was almost ready to deliver another one, and Nell knew that, too. Nell wanted his attention and affection badly enough, but apparently she didn't want to wreck his family—or her own. She was just looking to have some rough and tumble sex and a few entertaining evenings, always intending that they would go back to their respective homes and resume real life. Besides, she had a child to consider, and she wasn't going to sacrifice her little girl because of some over-zealous lover. That was crystal clear to Corb now, and he cursed himself for being so blind that he hadn't seen it before.

Now that his eyes were opened—his hopes dashed, his heart broken--he was resigned to make a go of being a better husband and father. He had to control his destiny. He'd try to do it right this time. He'd try to be devoted, and make a noble effort to please his wife, daughter, baby *and* his Ma.

And now he was going to be a better employee, too. He would do so well that eventually he'd own the damn cabinet shop. If not that, he'd get something better. He was going to find a way to redeem himself to everybody he had disappointed. Larger than all that, he had to prove to himself he was worth something.

Yes, today Corb Carter was going to turn over a new leaf and become a model family man, employee, and citizen of Shelbyville. LorAnn would be overjoyed at his change of heart; and if she could manage to forgive and forget, she'd act like the same sweet woman he'd married and everything would start falling into place again. Thank God for second chances, assuming LorAnn would give him one. He silently prayed that she would.

* * * * *

That afternoon, Corb asked his employer if he could possibly leave an hour or so early. He explained that his wife had been sickly and was expecting to deliver their second child very soon, maybe even early. When the sympathetic boss agreed, Corb phoned LorAnn and told her to have supper ready a little earlier than usual.

After he clocked out at 3:00 p.m., Corb made a special stop before heading home. When he walked into Mary's Florist Shop, the proprietor greeted him by name.

"Hello Mr. Carter. Good to see you again. You needing another funeral arrangement? Got some lovely ones already made up if you want to take a look." Ms. Mary had been the florist the entire Carter family used on occasions when their loved ones passed away. "I got a delivery already going to Gowen-Smith Funeral Home today, assuming you're mourning the same loss as the Crowell's."

Corb politely smiled as he answered, "No ma'am, I just wanted a little something to take home to the wife. Her birthday's tomorrow and she's also pregnant with our second baby, so I want her to feel special."

Ms. Mary thought for a minute, snapped her fingers and said, "I got just the thing in the back. Gimme a minute to get it."

She left Corb standing there. While he waited, he touched several bouquets and arrangements, smelling the scent of fresh flowers that usually caused him to sneeze or made his nose start running. Before he breathed in too much, she returned promptly with a small heart-shaped piece of pottery filled with African Violets. It had a red bow stuck in its center with "I Love You" printed all over the ribbon. Corb smiled and told Ms. Mary it was just right for his LorAnn, never mind the cost.

He left the florist's and then stopped by Day Brothers grocery store for some milk and bread, plus a few other grocery essentials that he knew they needed. He also picked up a Whitman's Sampler just to complete his gift ensemble for LorAnn. He hoped the flowers and the candy would put her in a forgiving mood for the way he had been treating her lately.

* * * * * *

LorAnn had fried pork chops and was mashing potatoes when Corb pulled in the driveway. There was already a skillet of cornbread warming on the stovetop, and collard greens were simmering on the back burner.

Dixie ran to the back door to wait for her daddy's entrance. LorAnn smiled, wishing she felt as excited about seeing Corb as his daughter did. She expected his early arrival to be the prelude to a long evening of sobbing and discussing how he could leave them but still be supportive.

Before Corb made it to Dixie's raised arms, LorAnn felt a painful pull in her lower abdomen. She waited a few seconds and, feeling nothing more, continued preparing the potatoes. By the time Corb was standing next to her in the small kitchen, she felt another hard cramp. While Corb was handing her the beautiful flower arrangement and candy, her face contorted with pain. Involuntarily, she bent over abruptly and grabbed her stomach, knocking the gifts out of Corb's hands and onto the floor.

As her water broke, the fluid spilled onto the linoleum where the shattered heart-shaped flower pot lay in pieces. As loose dirt from the uprooted plants swirled around in the creeping fluid, LorAnn's tightly squinted eyes opened enough to realize that Corb had brought her a peace offering. She smiled as much as she could while anticipating the next imminent labor pain.

"Corb, I think we better clean this mess up later. Turn off the stove and get Dixie over to Granny's. I got a bag packed already, but we need to be leaving for the hospital now."

Corb didn't wait for clarification or further instructions. He turned off the stove, and told Dixie to go get her pajamas, grab her stuffed bear, and meet him at the back door.

While LorAnn was putting on her coat and clutching her overnight bag, Corb was leading Dixie to Granny's and Pap Stan's house. The Rogers met the two at the door; and, upon realizing the urgency of the situation, offered to go to Corb and LorAnn's house and make sure the kitchen was cleaned up. Afterwards, they would close up the house and plan for Dixie to spend the night with them.

Nodding with much appreciated agreement, Corb left them all standing on their back porch and ran as quickly as he could to meet LorAnn, who was by now slowly waddling toward the truck.

"Can you walk? Do I need to move the truck closer?" Corb excitedly babbled as he took her left arm.

"I been through this before, Corb. It may be coming on a little faster for just that reason. But I'm fine and nothing's gonna happen before we get to the hospital." LorAnn's words provided some relief to Corb who was already planning to speed through the city streets, running any stop light that warned him to slow down or halt.

"Don't drive crazy, Corb. We got time." LorAnn reassured him, as she held her spasming belly. She tried not to audibly gasp as the pains kept coming regularly.

Corb glanced at his watch, realizing that it was just a little after 4:00 p.m. If he hurried, he could avoid the usual business traffic and arrive at the hospital in less than five minutes. He floored the old truck, making it sputter as it picked up speed.

When they got to the intersection of Main and Madison, luck was with them as they sailed through the intersection on a green light. On their left, Corb and LorAnn both noted that The Rebel Maid Restaurant hardly had any drive-in business at that time of day. That was a signal that the local businesses hadn't yet released their workers for the day. Otherwise, the parking lot would have been full of those hungry off-the-clock customers who wanted to grab a quick bite, or maybe take home something special for the family as a dinner treat.

"Hurry, Corb. I don't know if I can stand this much longer. Hurry please …. But be careful!" LorAnn was beginning to feel somewhat frantic. She was afraid she might deliver the baby before they could make it the few blocks to the hospital door.

"Try to hold on for two more minutes, LorAnn. I can see the building right up the street. Try to keep that baby in … cross your legs tight or something." Corb was anxiously looking back and forth between the road and his suffering wife.

He made the turn into the hospital driveway on two wheels, or at least that's what LorAnn thought as she held on to the door and the dash trying to steady herself. Corb pulled as closely as he could to the emergency entrance and leaped out of the truck. Leaving LorAnn behind, he ran inside and screamed, "She's having the baby now. Somebody help her!" The nurses in the lobby stared at the lone man with confusion. Suddenly realizing LorAnn was not right behind him, he turned and ran back out the door. As his distressed wife was about to reach the entrance, Corb exclaimed, "Where were you? I was in there, but where were you?"

"I thought you forgot me and I was just trying to get inside by myself. I'm slow moving, if you haven't noticed lately." She gave him a stern look and said, "Here, take my bag and I'll go in by myself, thank you. Good grief, Corb."

LorAnn straightened up and tried to walk unassisted, but another labor pain hit her just as she reached the open door. She cried out in pain, and this time the nurses saw her through the glass panes. They rushed toward her with a wheelchair and whisked her to another part of the hospital, leaving Corb to answer all their questions and fill out all the paperwork. The big black rimmed, white faced clock over the reception desk indicated it was 4:14 p.m.

By 4:30p.m. on Monday, November 20, 1950, LorAnn gave birth to the second child of the Carter family.

* * * * * *

Corb hadn't been allowed to see LorAnn yet—the doctor said she needed some rest—but he had been staring through the nursery window at his newborn daughter for almost an hour. She was so tiny, only seven pounds or so, and she had black hair. He hadn't seen his new daughter's face up close, but he knew she would be beautiful like Dixie. He was proud. He was relieved. He believed the birth of this baby was a sign from Above that his life was with her, her sister, and especially her mother. It was his destiny. It was preordained. It was a miracle.

While he was waiting for Dixie to meet him at the door to go to his Ma's house, he picked through the spilled mess on the floor to retrieve the red bow from the destroyed flowers. He had stuck it in his pocket when he grabbed Dixie's hand to leave the house, not really stopping to reason why he even made the effort to retrieve it.

Now, as he was being led by the attending nurse to LorAnn's room, he took it from his coat. As he entered LorAnn's room, he held the bow out in front of him as he approached her bed.

LorAnn smiled at her husband, and as he handed her the bow, happy tears streaked her pale cheeks. He pulled a chair up to the bedside and held her hand.

"LorAnn, honey, I have been a fool. But I've changed, I promise. If you will still have me, I'll be yours forever. All I want is for us to be a complete family. I want to take care of you and Dixie and that little baby sleeping in the nursery. Will you let me stay with you and the kids, LorAnn? Will you give me another chance?"

These were the words she had been hoping to hear and now she could hardly believe Corb was saying them to her—pleading with her to let him stay and be a loving part of the family. She looked at the bow he had handed her and read the words printed there. "Do you love me, Corb? Really love me... and our babies too?

Corb started to get choked up, but he leaned over and kissed LorAnn for the first time in months. "Darlin', just read the ribbon there in your hand. I do love you, and I will always love you...always," he convincingly said during a moment of engulfing emotion. LorAnn managed to smile, showing off her new maternal glow and her renewed confidence in her marriage.

Corb kissed her again, and continued to hold her hand. He had forgotten all about a similar proposal he had made earlier in the day to a most undeserving person. Somehow that didn't seem real to Corb anymore.

"Thank you Lord," LorAnn mumbled as she nodded off to sleep again.

"Amen," was the response offered by Corb as he peacefully monitored the rhythmic breathing of his exhausted, dozing wife.

CHAPTER 5

The Nurse

1950

The nurse wore a starched white dress, complete with white stockings, sensible white shoes, and a white belt. Her steel gray hair was adorned with a little white nurse's cap with an oversized red cross boldly printed on its front center.

She was the epitome of medical competence and efficiency. Miss Edith Ruth, who some jokingly called "Babe" just to get her agitated, was very serious about her professional responsibilities. Her bedside manner could have been much improved, but her nursing abilities were beyond reproach.

She was in charge of the hospital nursery where the Carter baby had been kept since her birth the night before, fifteen hours earlier, to be exact. Miss Ruth knew the baby's mother hadn't seen the infant since Dr. Farrar held it up for viewing a few seconds after delivery. But this didn't bother the spinster nurse.

Having no maternal instinct of her own, she unemotionally thought of a production line when dealing with the tiny nursery inhabitants. She never became attached; she only wanted to efficiently move the newborns in and out of the nursery, maintaining their health and comfort until the little nuisances could go home with their parents.

As Miss Ruth leaned over the wooden cart where the awake and wiggling Carter girl lay, she gazed at her cherubic face for a few extra seconds. The nurse caught herself smiling as she watched the baby's eyes trying to focus, moving directly toward Miss Ruth's black-rimmed glasses. Coincidence or not, it appeared that the baby intentionally found Miss Ruth's eyes and happily cooed.

Surprised that one of the nursery babies seemed to be content in her presence, Miss Ruth tenderly picked up the happy bundle and held her closely to her chest.

She gently swayed to an imaginary lullaby and watched with fascination as the infant started to nuzzle her for feeding.

"Oh, my. We'd better get you to your mother," Miss Ruth whispered, as she turned toward the door. Trying to appear unaffected, but now harboring newly evoked maternal emotions, she proceeded to take this tiny bundle to LorAnn Carter.

* * * * * *

A soft knock on her door alerted LorAnn to Miss Ruth coming through the door holding the infant. Sitting upright in her bed, LorAnn instinctively reached toward the blanketed bundle, eager to inspect her baby from head to toe.

"Mrs. Carter, I noticed on your chart that today's your birthday. Looks like you got a nice gift with this little one," remarked the usually business-like nurse.

LorAnn was stunned that Miss Ruth made such a personal remark. She had not been overly friendly to LorAnn before.

"I'm real blessed with this little baby doll, but I sorta wish she could have waited until today to be born. I got my birthday present a day early, though. That's all right by me," LorAnn agreed, as she nuzzled her face against the baby's soft cheek.

"She's had some formula during the night. You were so worn out, we didn't want to wake you to try to breastfeed. If you want her to stay on the formula, I'll go get another bottle. If you want to try feeding her yourself, I'll leave you alone so you can have some privacy." Miss Ruth resumed her matter-of-fact demeanor.

"I didn't have any luck breastfeeding my first girl, and I doubt it'll work any better this time. She can have formula if you don't mind fetching another bottle. I want to give it to her myself if that's all right."

With a quick nod, Miss Ruth vanished from the room and reappeared momentarily with a fresh bottle of condensed milk cut with water.

"Oh, by the way, Mrs. Carter, have you decided on a name yet? We'll have to have that settled before you're discharged in a couple of days."

LorAnn studied the hungry child in her arms. "She looks like a little "baby doll" with that black hair and big eyes. I'd like to call her something like that, but I guess it don't sound right when you say it out loud."

Once again Miss Ruth said something totally unexpected, considering how uninvolved she generally was with the parents and babies who passed through the hospital. "Maybe you could call her Doll – or Dollie, maybe. That's a pretty name and it fits her."

"Thank you, Miss Ruth. I like it, and I bet her daddy will, too," LorAnn agreed.

From that moment on, the infant became known as "Dollie" to LorAnn and all the attending hospital staff members. During evening visiting hours when LorAnn told Corb what she had been calling the baby all day, he agreed that it was a very fitting name.

Dollie Evelyn Carter not only had a befitting name, she had two extremely proud parents—and one proud nurse who had never suggested a name for *any* baby during her thirty years in the nursing profession.

Perhaps Dollie truly was destined to make a positive impact on the family.

Until she became an adult, she would never fully grasp how her timely birth changed the direction of the Carter family's future.

* * * * * *

When LorAnn was discharged from the hospital early on Thursday afternoon, she left behind a smiling and waving Miss Ruth, still observable in the rear windows of the ambulance as they left the parking lot.

It was Thanksgiving Day, and LorAnn had declined the hospital's institutional holiday lunch. She and Corb would also forego the usual Thanksgiving Day gathering at Granny and Pap Stan's with the rest of the Carter family. The parents needed time to get home, get settled, and introduce the waiting Dixie to her new baby sister. Granny was going to send a plate of turkey, dressing, and all the fixings for Corb and LorAnn later in the day. Dixie had been invited to stay at Granny's to eat with them and play with her cousins after she met her new sister.

When LorAnn entered their home through the back door, she was pleasantly surprised at the spotless house. There were freshly-baked casseroles in the refrigerator and the bed had been made with fresh sheets, turned down for LorAnn's anticipated need for rest.

She looked with satisfaction at how nicely Dollie's new baby bed fit in the corner of Dixie's room. She was pleased that Corb—and Viv and Stan—had taken the time and effort to make her homecoming so easy.

She suddenly felt another wave of emotion overtaking her, realizing just how much Corb was trying to show her his refreshed attention and concern. If having a baby was the foundation for security in a marriage, she wouldn't object to having a house full of kids.

* * * * * *

Dixie had been anxiously awaiting the ambulance and her daddy's truck to pull up in the Carter's driveway. She peered through Granny's back screen door and finally saw her daddy drive up, get out of the truck, and walk toward the arriving ambulance that her mother and new sister had been riding in.

"Granny, they're home! Let's go see the baby!" the young girl exclaimed. Granny, who was in the middle of basting the almost-done turkey, told Dixie that they would go together to greet the baby as soon as the turkey was back in the oven. Dixie impatiently tapped her foot while she watched Granny slowly creep toward the open oven with the large bird sizzling in the heavy roasting pan.

With the oven closed and her apron off, Granny took Dixie's small hand and rushed out the screen door. As they made their trek toward the Carter home, Granny Rogers contemplated all that had transpired in the last few days.

We all have a lot to be thankful for today. This baby couldn't have come at a better time.

CHAPTER 6

Thanksgiving Friday, 1950

Thanksgiving Day was traditionally slated to be celebrated with Corb's family, but the Friday after belonged to LorAnn's family, the Hudsons.

On "Thanksgiving Friday," as the family referred to it, everyone was supposed to bring a large covered dish and/or dessert to a designated gathering place. Each year the responsibility for the turkey or ham was rotated to a different family group. This year, LorAnn was given a free pass on bringing a dish. Her only required contribution was to bring the newborn Dollie and five-year old Dixie.

* * * * * *

For the past three years, the Hudson family's "Thanksgiving Friday" gathering had been voluntarily hosted by Roz and Troy Tucker. Their quaint home on Fishingford Pike had several spacious interior rooms, plus an extra half acre behind their house which allowed all the cousins to run loose and play games outside.

Conveniently located to the left and back of the house was an unattached garage with a spotless concrete floor. The building was easily converted to a temporary dining hall, spacious enough to accommodate the large crowd of Hudson family members.

Troy had already set up the long folding tables, and Roz had spread tablecloths over the horseshoe-shaped set up. Folding chairs were plentiful, and the decorated room appeared to be almost ready to receive their soon arriving guests.

While Roz was setting places for dinner, Troy moved toward his built-in workbench to turn on the tabletop radio. It had been installed in the garage to keep him company when he worked on his car or motorcycle. Immediately, the air was filled with Bing Crosby's soothing voice as he sang, *"Dear Hearts and Gentle People."*

Still thinking about how Corb had tried to pour his heart out to him less than a week ago, he turned toward Roz with a questioning expression.

"Roz, you think Corb and LorAnn are gonna do all right now that the baby's come?"

His wife didn't hesitate to reply, "Yeah, I do. I think they might've had some trouble, but I'm thinkin' this baby gave 'em both a new outlook on life." Roz continued arranging the silverware on the cloth napkins beside each plate, never once glancing at her husband or acknowledging any concern.

Except for Bing's singing, there were no more words being uttered. Instead, they both kept their thoughts to themselves, each assuming that the other didn't have the complete picture of what had transpired between Corb and LorAnn a few short days ago.

* * * * *

As soon as the car stopped and the car door could be safely opened, Dixie jumped out and raced to the Tucker's backyard to join her cousins who were still young enough to play with her.

Inside, the house was crowded with various relatives drinking coffee, sweet iced tea, egg nog, and Coca-Cola. When LorAnn and Dollie entered the door, the house noise faded to a silent pause; then everybody started speaking up at once:

"Let me see my new niece?" "Can I hold her?" "Is she asleep?" "How many days old is she?" "Is she a good baby?" "She has blue eyes! Will her eyes change to brown?" "Can I see her face?" "Can you pull back the blanket?"

The questions and comments were a barrage, and LorAnn couldn't answer quickly enough; neither could she move out of the center of the tight huddle of baby admirers. Roz wedged herself through to stand by LorAnn and took the baby out of her arms, turning around the huddle to bark instructions to the family.

"Okay, everybody, there'll be time enough to play with this baby. Right now I need you to all pick up a food dish or two off of the kitchen table and follow me out to the garage so we can get the buffet set up. LorAnn, you stay here for a few minutes and get the baby settled. We'll figure out everything else. "

The Hudson clan dispersed at Roz's command and within 15 minutes, all the ham, side dishes, breads, desserts, and various drinks were laid out in buffet formation on the now-cleared and cleaned workbench. It was time to eat. The family members converged on the makeshift buffet and took their heaping plates to the big table for feasting.

LorAnn, who was seated next to her twin sister Dora, was determined to be in a good listening mode that day. Dora, who had a knack for saying the wrong things at the wrong time, inappropriately started talking about how their mother used to make them do her chores while their mother just laid around the house. Dora continued to expound on the bleakness of the world, including how the hardships of post-war survival still affected so many. She found fault with the government, the state, and the city without providing any logical bases for her opinions. Dora even went so far as to chastise children growing up in the "current state of affairs" as being spoiled and soft.

LorAnn only smiled and pleasantly nodded, trying to suffer through Dora's nonsense and snide remarks. She thought of her own Dixie who was born in 1945. Dixie didn't appear to be overly spoiled or soft. In fact, she was very independent for her age, and did many things around the house to help LorAnn. But today LorAnn didn't want to argue with Dora. They'd spent too many years during their youth doing that. For LorAnn, it was as unpleasant then as it was right now.

* * * * * *

Around 5:00 p.m., the meal was finished, the cleanup was over, and the leftovers were spread out on the kitchen table for late grazing by anyone who still wanted a taste of a special dish. There were only a few people going in and out of the house, because almost everybody was sitting in the folding chairs now scattered throughout the back yard. There were groups of conversations going on in different areas of the yard, but some people were group hopping—going back and forth between different clusters to participate in the various stories being told.

LorAnn and Corb were holding hands, with Dixie on her daddy's knee and the baby nestled in a laundry basket set between her parents' chairs. Troy had been trying to get Corb's attention all afternoon, but for some reason eye contact never seemed to work. Troy pulled a chair up next to Corb and tried to whisper in Corb's ear: "Tell me what's happening. I been worried about you, brother."

Corb stared straight ahead and didn't answer right away. In a few seconds he said directly to LorAnn, "I'm gonna look at Troy's new motorcycle for a minute. You be all right here by yourself with the girls?"

LorAnn smiled as Dixie moved instinctively to her Mama's lap, and glanced down at the sleeping Dollie in the basket. Looking back up at Corb, she let go of his hand and answered, "Yeah, you go ahead. I got plenty of people here to help me if I get in a bind with the little ones."

The easy smiles they exchanged were genuine.

* * * * * *

Troy led the way toward the rear of the garage to an old tool shed he no longer used. He stepped inside and turned on a flashlight.

"I thought you were gonna tear this thing down," Corb said as he brushed a cobweb off his shoulder.

"Well, I was 'til I got a real good idea, and I thought you might lend me a hand with it. You did go to the Vocational School to get proper training as a carpenter, with a certificate and all—I've seen it hanging on your wall.

"When it's done, this might be a place we both can use, if you understand what I'm trying to say. By the way, since you're here with LorAnn and all happy, I am gonna guess you and Nell called it quits." Troy raised one eyebrow, grinned, then winked.

"Nell was what you told me and worse. We're through now, so let's stop talking about it."

Corb shifted his attention back to the shed. "You are one crazy son of a bitch, Troy. I gotta admit, you got me on this. What are you gonna really try to make out of this falling down shed?" Corb chuckled at how gullible he'd been.

Troy shifted his pitch to Corb, trying to tailor his presentation to a topic Troy thought Corb might be able to relate to. "Corb, you got it all wrong, man. I think I can convince Roz that I'm getting it in shape to keep the motorcycle in here during the winter. But, I'll have plenty of extra room for a small cot and maybe a lockable toolbox to keep stuff in. You know, tools but NOT tools? I can use this shed to look at my dirty magazines and hide just about anything out here I want to...or bring a friend here when Roz is working, maybe? Troy paused, uncertain of what Corb was thinking. "You could use it, too, if you ever decided you might want to."

Corb looked down at his feet, kicking a rock with the toe of his boots. "I think it's a shitty idea and I don't want no part of it. I know you ain't dumb enough to bring some woman here, right in your back yard. You're an idiot! " Corb said sternly.

"Okay, forget that last part, it was a joke. Would you help me make a sturdy shed out of this, or start over if we have to? I swear I'll keep my motorcycle in it. That'll be its main purpose. What'd you say to that?"

Corb looked at Troy, thinking how much his face reminded him of an anxious little boy. He had a way about him that made you want to trust him, but Troy was a tad menacing, too.

"Okay, Troy. You get the lumber and I'll bring my tools when you're ready to start. Maybe I can work on it a couple of hours tomorrow or Sunday afternoon, depending on how LorAnn's doing."

"That'd be great, Corb. That'd be real great." Anticipation was plastered all over Troy's face as they walked to the other side of the backyard to join their wives.

CHAPTER 7

Winter 1950 - Fall 1954

Before leaving the "Thanksgiving Friday" celebration, LorAnn made the rounds with the baby and Dixie, saying goodbye to each of her siblings and their spouses. She also didn't want to get stuck alone with her twin sister all afternoon, either. It was better that she move around and work the crowd as long as she could, rather than be an easy sitting duck for Dora's incessant prattle.

The adult twins didn't look alike, and they certainly didn't think alike. They didn't have much in common except their parents and siblings. If they had been strangers, it would have been doubtful that either would have chosen the other as a friend. Unfortunately, it seemed the rest of the Hudson siblings felt that way about Dora, too.

Not that Dora was weird or anything. It was just that Dora seemed to be a different person now. It was difficult to explain the exact change in her twin's personality, but LorAnn thought she knew Dora better than anyone. They were fraternal twins, after all.

LorAnn believed Dora's fragile mental health started its initial decline two years before when her first and only baby was born dead. She wondered how Carl, Dora's husband of five years, was holding up under the circumstances. He didn't appear to be affected by the loss of the baby or Dora's change in attitude. LorAnn hoped Carl's indifference didn't stoke the fires of Dora's apparent mental issues.

* * * * * *

The multitude of aunts and uncles kissed the baby and hugged Dixie, and at last the Carters made their trek home. Happy but relieved that the event was now behind them, they looked forward to resuming their "new" normal routine.

"You have a good time today, LorAnn?" Corb asked as he maneuvered through the rural roads. Sighing deeply, LorAnn replied, "As good as I could, I guess. I'm glad to be going home, though. I know these young'uns are wore out." They rode silently until they were almost to Lipscomb Street.

LorAnn asked, "Corb, what was Troy talkin' to you about tonight? Y'all were out looking at the motorcycle for an awful long time, I thought."

Corb grinned. "You know Troy, always tryin' to get somethin' for nothin'. He wants me to help him get that old tool shed into shape so he can put his motorcycle in there during the winter. He wants me to build it and he'll take all the credit," he chuckled aloud.

LorAnn smiled, thinking Corb was right. Troy always had a habit of trying to build himself up. He would definitely show off a newly built shed and then claim how hard **he** worked on it. He wouldn't hesitate to say how much it cost, either.

"You gonna help him? I mean, you gonna do it for him?" LorAnn suspected she already knew the answer.

"We'll see, but first I need to figure out what's in it for me." Corb patted LorAnn on the hand as they pulled into their gravel and dirt driveway.

* * * * *

As expected, Corb did all the work while Troy did all the bragging about the new shed. The two started working early on Saturday, and Corb had the renovated shed almost finished by Sunday night. He even threw in some little "small hidey holes" in the walls, at Troy's request, and loosened an imperceptible floor board just in case a future need arose for another secret nook.

Roz, who stayed inside the Tucker home during the entire weekend, had no interest in anything outside of her own domain. The garage, yard, and any outbuildings on the property constituted Troy's realm. Anyway, she was happy to have the time to herself to read her magazines or talk on the phone.

Roz apparently wasn't interested in whether the two workers had anything in their stomachs. As a good host might have been inclined to do, Troy never offered to get them anything to eat, either. Corb finally announced he needed a break, drove down to the intersection, and stopped at Bart's store. He picked up some cheese and crackers and an RC Cola. He figured Troy was in his own kitchen by then, looking through the refrigerator for his lunch.

Corb wasn't going to take any food or drink back for Troy. It was a matter of principle. Corb believed if he was helping his brother-in-law for free, the least Troy could do was feed the help. Then again, Troy said himself that he was a selfish son of a bitch, and by George, he kept on proving it.

* * * * * *

Meanwhile, Mr. and Mrs. Carl Brown woke up late on Saturday morning. A smiling Carl turned over on his side and surveyed the profile of a sleeping Dora. Lately, propositioning her for lovemaking was tricky; he never knew how she would react. Carl tenderly rubbed her shoulder, but she made no move. He then whispered her name, and her eyes fluttered. She looked at him with disgust and simply uttered, "For God's sake, get away from me," and moved her body as far away from him as she could.

Carl was a maintenance employee of the Bedford County School District, but his job duties tended to lean more toward the janitorial side. He had worked at the high school and adjacent elementary school for nearly ten years, and was a trusted and loyal employee. It made him happy to be around all the educated staff and bubbling students. It was a pleasant change from home.

Carl Brown and Dora had been together for more than seven years if the total included the two years they courted before they married. With that much history between them, he thought he knew almost all there was to know about her. Apparently, he had no idea how deep her dark side could plunge.

However, Dora's mother was infamous for her temper and surly disposition. Sometimes Dora sounded just like her, and unfortunately it was happening more frequently. On "Thanksgiving Friday," he was relieved Dora's mother (Ma Rose) was visiting with her only living sister. Dora and Ma Rose would always start bickering every time they got together, and Carl absolutely hated it. At least this holiday was much calmer without those two surly women together, provoking each other.

Carl often wondered what life would have been like had he met the other twin sister first. LorAnn was nothing like her mother or her twin, and lately that appealed to him more and more.

* * * * * *

By the following weekend, the shed was finished, baby Dollie had adjusted to her new surroundings, and Dixie had made herself a temporary residence at Granny's and Pap's house.

Dixie spent most days at the diner, entertaining her grandparents and sometimes a select few of their customers. She was an animated chatterbox who never met a stranger. Her personality seemed to spark when she was with Granny and Pap, but when she returned to her parents' home she resumed a more reserved nature. Pap Stan noticed it first.

"You think it's good for us to be keeping Dixie so much? Looks to me like she gets real unhappy when she has to go to her house. We don't need to start nothin' that can't last." Stan remarked.

"Old man, you're tryin' to make trouble where there is none. That girl is fine. Let her enjoy the attention we can give her right now while her folks are trying to patch things up. Anyway, she loves to be with us, and we love havin' her. When LorAnn starts back to work at the Rubber Mill next month, they're gonna need us more than ever to help out with watching Dixie, maybe the baby too. They hadn't said nothin' about it, yet, though. And don't forget Dixie'll start first grade in September, so let's just hush about all this now. Let's just let it ride out for a while till Corb and LorAnn figure out how they want to handle things." Viv waved her hand in the air as if the discussion was ended.

A man of few words, Pap just grunted his response and went to bed.

* * * * * *

Granny's wish to have Dixie in her charge came true when it was time for LorAnn to resume her second shift work schedule at the Rubber Mill. Her return to work date would be Tuesday, January 2, 1951.

With Corb going in at 7:00 a.m. and getting off at 4:00 p.m., versus LorAnn's Rubber Mill shift running from 3:00-11:00 p.m., there was little time for the spouses to see each other. The shift overlaps also made it difficult to get Dixie back and forth from school. There certainly wasn't any obvious solution for the newborn Dollie's fulltime care.

Granny offered to walk Dixie to school every morning, understanding that the first grader had to be in her classroom at 8:00 a.m. Pap volunteered to open the diner by himself, dealing with the early customers as both server and cook. Granny would join him by 8:30 a.m.

In the early afternoon, Pap would leave the diner to pick up Dixie from school and take her back to the restaurant. She would be happy there until her Daddy would join her after work. If they wanted, the two could even get a quick bite of supper at the diner and then be on their way.

That took care of Dixie, but there was still no one to help with baby Dollie, who would need constant supervision throughout the day. All family members had full-time jobs, so the obvious solution was to hire an all-day sitter.

* * * * * *

Thumbing through the classified section of the local newspaper, LorAnn discovered someone had placed an ad searching for a job taking care of infants or young children. She didn't recognize the phone number, but she called on an outside chance that the applicant might be a skilled person with good references.

When the lady answered the phone, LorAnn thought she recognized the voice but couldn't quite place where she had heard it. She went on to introduce herself as LorAnn Carter, mother of a 5 year old and a 3 week old newborn.

"Mrs. Carter! I was your nurse, Edith Ruth! I bet you're calling about getting help for your new baby. She is such a precious child, one of the prettiest and sweetest we've had in the maternity ward for a while."

Taken aback by the caller's identity, LorAnn wasn't sure how to proceed. She continued their phone conversation as if she remembered Miss Ruth to be a gracious and pleasant person, not the stern nurse without bedside manner.

"Miss Ruth, do you still work at the hospital? After all, we need someone who can be here at 7 o'clock in the morning until 5 o'clock every day."

Miss Ruth responded with a lilt in her voice, "I resigned the hospital a week after you left. I've always had differences with the way they run that place—sloppy, not following all procedures and policies, and not having the guts to call out people when they are making mistakes. I believe people should learn to do a job right the first time, and others shouldn't have to go behind them to clean up their messes. So, with enough money in savings and a good bit of an inheritance left over from my parents, I decided why not do something I know how to do, but be my own boss while I'm doing it. Makes perfect sense to me."

LorAnn felt a little baffled, but asked the obvious question: "I don't know if we can afford you, though. You're a trained nurse and all. We just need someone to take care of baby Dollie while Dixie is with her grandparents, or both of the kids later. When Dixie starts school in the fall, we'll need someone to take care of them both for the last couple of hours of the day until their Daddy gets home from work. I'm going back to work at the Rubber Mill after December's over, and I don't have anyone to look after Dollie."

LorAnn was speaking so fast her words and thoughts were running together. A confused Miss Ruth tried to clarify: "Let me see if I understand. On January 2nd, after the New Year's holiday, you need someone to take care of the baby full time. By next September you will need someone to continue to do the same thing for the baby, but add a first grader for the last two hours of each day. Both children are to be released to their father when he gets home from work. Is that right? Are there any other responsibilities your sitter would be required to assume?

LorAnn studied a few minutes and asked a simple question: "How are you at cookin?"

A widespread grin stretched across Miss Ruth's face as she answered, "I love to cook. Would I need to make an evening meal for your husband?"

"More like a lunch plus supper. Would that put you out too much?" LorAnn questioned.

"If I get to eat, too, then I think that works well. It'll save me money in the long run to have two out of three weekday meals at your house. She was happy with the request, but didn't want to do any housework. She hoped LorAnn didn't expect that, too.

"Well, I'd like to have you with us if your pay isn't too high. Why don't you let me know how much it would take for you to start out with us...on trial, you understand.

Miss Ruth smiled on her side of the phone. She remembered the precious, angelic Carter baby with whom she seemed to have a unique connection. She would love to watch the child grow up. She would love to teach her profound things that she might not get through schooling or from her uneducated parents. She realized that she wanted to be a part of the child's life and watch her discover the world. It was as if this job was meant to be.

Miss Ruth gave her a proposed salary number that LorAnn expected to be much higher. An elated LorAnn couldn't disguise her happiness when she realized it was an amount they could afford.

They sealed the deal right then, and LorAnn couldn't wait to tell Corb that their babysitting worries were over.

* * * * * *

By the end of January, 1951, the households were beginning to settle in for a new year of fresh beginnings.

LorAnn returned to her second shift job at the Rubber Mill on January 2nd. At the cabinet shop, Corb received a meager wage increase in honor of the Carter's additional mouth to feed.

Miss Ruth showed up early at the Carter house every morning at 6:30, eagerly anticipating the day's new adventure looking after Dollie and the other Carter family members.

Dixie was adjusting nicely to spending every weeknight with Granny and Pap, only seeing her parents a few minutes each day except for weekends. She still harbored some jealousy toward the attention given to the new baby, but that seemed to subside when she was with her grandparents.

Troy worked the first shift at the Rubber Mill and had his afternoons and late evenings free (as did Corb). He actively began furnishing his motorcycle shed with an old cot, a bookshelf, and various small comfort items. He also brought in a rolling red tool chest with several drawers suitable for storing his motorcycle tools and secret erotic books and paraphernalia.

Roz continued to work the second shift at the Rubber Mill, often taking scheduled breaks with LorAnn. Based on the sisters' exchange of daily information, Roz and Troy seemed to be rocking along nicely, with no blips or concerns in their daily life.

Carl was a welcome sight at the schools when Christmas break was over. There had been an undiscovered frozen water pipe in one of the bathrooms in the closed High School building over the holidays. Being extra busy meant he didn't dwell on his sinking relationship with Dora.

Dora, however, was beginning to rethink her future, which also included Carl's. She thought about trying to have another baby, but was afraid of the same awful outcome she had already experienced. If Carl would agree, she believed she had convinced herself she could handle the risk.

Ma Rose became seriously ill and eventually had to move in with her eldest daughter, Annie. For awhile, it was a comfortable arrangement until Annie's husband got fed up with the old lady's smart mouth. Ma Rose was going to have to move in with another of her children before too long, but the question was which one would take her.

But the best new beginning was Corb's new-found commitment and affection for Dollie. When he looked into the baby's blue eyes, he felt an overwhelming sense of pride and love. He had been too busy trying to make a living when Dixie was born to have made this kind of connection with his firstborn. He would make up for it with Dollie if the Good Lord was willing. He certainly didn't need any other outside diversions or stray thoughts to keep him from this objective. Being a devoted father and faithful husband was his new goal in life.

* * * * * *

The next few years zoomed by. Corb and LorAnn were still maintaining the same routines they had put into place years before. Life in the Carter household was certainly humdrum, but the children were flourishing and they hardly noticed.

Granny and Pap Stan were able to convince the proprietor of the neighborhood store to sell his business and property to them at a reasonable price. They had been successfully running the store on Cooper Street since April of 1952. Since the rear rooms of the shotgun building had been converted to a small apartment for Granny and Pap, it became more convenient for Dixie to spend a great amount of time there with her grandparents.

In May of 1952, the Carter family relocated to a larger home on Union Street. Granny and Pap no longer lived as close to them as before; however, the grandparents visited often. During the school year, Dixie adjusted her schedule for staying at Granny and Pap's to occasional weeknights, but she spent her entire weekends with them at their Cooper Street store/home. When school was not in session, she spent her weeks with her grandparents and weekends with her parents. It worked out well for everyone.

During 1952, both Corb and Tessie's husband, Buck, were hired by the Shelbyville Department of Public Works. Buck hired on with the road crew; Corb became the Assistant Superintendant of Public Works. Corb's duties were to help the Superintendant supervise the entire road crew and the other functions of the Public Works Department. This was quite a promotion for Corb.

Dora was successful with her second pregnancy and in 1952, she gave birth to a son, Arthur Steven Brown. "Miracle Baby" Stevie was the twentieth grandchild to be born into the Hudson clan. Dora and Carl were now back on track, and Dora seemed calmer and happier than ever as a new mother.

Troy and Roz finally agreed to take in Ma Rose in late 1952, about the same time Dora was delivering her new son. They prepared their extra front bedroom as a suite for Ma Rose. Troy warned the surly old woman to keep her snuff spit cans off the floor which was all Troy ever said to her in a reprimanding tone. Otherwise, they went on with their lives as before.

In the fall of 1954, Dixie was nine and a half years old, and was in the fourth grade at Central Elementary School. She was a bright student who loved to read, but she was also a pretty good athlete. She could run faster than any of the boys on the playground. She was smarter than those boys, too.

Dixie still thought her baby sister was a spoiled brat, but she loved her anyway.

Dollie, who was nearly four years old by then, was still capturing her Daddy's heart and constant attention. Every day when Corb walked through the door, he would pick the child up, throw her in the air, and hug her tightly when she landed in his arms, giggling and laughing. Corb often said the child "loved everybody" and "would run to anybody's arms" when she was invited. He beamed when he talked about both of his children.

The other Hudson and Carter siblings were consistently maintaining their nondescript lifestyles, as well.

In some ways, an unsurprising and routine life can equate to "no news is good news." Subconsciously, that's the outcome we all try to achieve.

However, "routine" should never be mistaken with "ignorance is bliss."

* * * * * *

For the small city of Shelbyville, the usually "blissful" times started to change for the worse in the fall of 1955.

It was then the dreadful "Parent's Worst Nightmare" became the mantra for so many unsuspecting and heartbroken families.

Part Two

Terror Takes the Town

CHAPTER 8

Fall 1955

The brisk autumn breeze felt refreshing to her warm face as she got out of her car and trudged toward the high school gymnasium. Coach Mildred Barnes had scheduled that Friday afternoon's cheerleading practice inside on the gym's mezzanine rather than on the usual outdoor area, the football field sidelines. The change in location was merely to benefit her and not the cheerleaders. She was certain the girls would be displeased since they all enjoyed performing for the practicing football team, especially the handsome quarterback.

Suffering with her annual nasty cold, the stout coach was stuffy-headed and believed she had a slight fever. So far, she had managed to make it through most of the day's schedule without feeling any worse. Once she had this practice behind her, she could go home and drink a hot toddy, and perhaps go to bed early and stay there throughout the weekend. In fact, she was considering shortening the one hour practice so she could leave fifteen minutes early-- if she could swing it. With every minute that passed, her body was getting more and more achy and weak.

Opening the heavy glass doors of the gym took all her effort. Inside the lobby, she inhaled deeply, and looked at the flight of steps she would have to climb to get to the upper practice area. Trying to minimize her aches and save her energy, she avoided the stairs and instead walked through the double doors ahead to enter the main floor playing area. She looked up at the mezzanine to see her squad already practicing and chattering away.

Mrs. Barnes stepped up on a lower bleacher seat and blew her silver whistle. The sound reverberated throughout the large open area to such an extent it echoed for a good fifteen seconds. The busy girls stopped in the middle of their practice/socializing and turned their attention to the source of the auditory interruption.

"Girls, time to get busy and end this week's sessions. Next Friday you'll be cheering at this season's first game, and you need to be ready," the Coach barked at the scrambling girls.

"It's 3:30 now, so line up next to the rail so I can see you, and we'll do roll call." Eager to please, eleven girls lined up for Mrs. Barnes to verify attendance. When she got to the last attendee, she asked the whole group a question, "Where's Wendy Wilson? Has anyone seen Wendy today?"

All the girls were chattering, shaking their heads, and one young lady spoke up, "Coach, I have final period with Wendy and she was in class. Maybe she went to the football field thinking practice was supposed to be there. Maybe she didn't know you'd changed it to indoor practice."

It was quite possible Wendy somehow didn't get the notice of the practice location change. Perhaps they should wait another ten minutes before starting just in case Wendy was trying to make her way back to the gym from the football field. They all agreed that was the right thing to do, giving Coach Barnes a little extra rest, and the girls would get a little more social time. They were not complaining about the delay.

By 3:45 p.m., Wendy still had not shown up for practice. Knowing Wendy would never skip practice unless she was sick or an emergency had arisen, Coach Barnes felt uneasy about the whole situation.

At 3:55p.m. Coach Barnes contacted the school principal from a phone in the football coach's office off the lobby.

"Mr. Phillips, this is Mildred Barnes. I'm in the gym with the cheerleaders, and one of our girls hasn't shown up for practice. It's not like her to skip. I understand she attended her final class before practice, and she seemed fine, certainly not sick. Perhaps you could call Wendy Wilson's parent's house to see if she decided to go straight home? She may have decided to start her weekend early, but I doubt that. I have a bad feeling about this, and I just want to be sure the young lady is all right."

Mr. Phillips smirked on the other end of the phone. Of all the days to be making a call to a parent, this would have to be it. He also wanted to leave early to meet several of his friends at the Hotel Dixie for their monthly Friday night gathering.

He assumed the child probably just walked home with a friend or something innocent like that. He surmised that within thirty minutes this mystery would all be resolved, and he wanted to avoid upsetting her parents if it wasn't truly necessary.

"Coach Barnes, I am sure everything is just fine. She probably ran into a friend and just decided to skip practice for the day. They all do it, now and then. I'm sure she's no different. Wendy's from a good family and she's been raised right. She wouldn't want to worry her parents, so I'd expect her to be home any minute." Principal Philips commented.

His unconcern made Coach Barnes feel as if she was being dismissed from the phone conversation, but she went on, "Mr. Phillips, I think we would all feel better if you would just make the call. If something is wrong, the parents need to know what's going on as quickly as possible. If there isn't anything wrong, you'll still be praised because you are a devoted principal looking out for all the school enrollees," Coach Barnes explained.

The Principal, who felt more like a receptionist at the moment, said "All right, I'll call. But go ahead and release the other girls to go home. On the off chance something is wrong, we'll need as few people around as possible if the police come here to investigate.

"Okay, but please let me know what the parents say. I'll wait here until you call," an anxious Coach Barnes stated. By now she had forgotten about how sick she was, but she was quickly realizing that feeling fearful trumped feeling sick *any time*.

* * * * * *

When the Principal called the Wilson household to check if Wendy was there, he was disappointed that no one at the house had heard from Wendy since she left for school that morning. On a normal practice day, she always made it home by 5:00 at the latest. She still had time to make it. Wendy's mother promised the principal that she would call him the minute Wendy walked through the door.

When that call ended, Mrs. Wilson then called her husband and repeated the phone conversation she had just had with the principal. She asked him to come home immediately from work.

As promised, Principal Phillips called Coach Barnes at the gym to relay the information he had gleaned from Wendy's mother. He told the coach to go home and take care of her cold; he'd take it from here.

* * * * * *

By 6:00 p.m., Wendy had not arrived at her home and she had not tried to contact her family or friends, as far as anyone knew. Principal Phillips and Wendy's parents talked again by phone, and all agreed it was time to contact the Shelbyville City Police.

The Chief of Police took the call at 6:10 p.m. and listened to a concerned Principal Phillips explain the events of the day that led him to believe a child may have been abducted near the school property, even though no witnesses had come forward about any suspicious activity.

Police Chief Arnold Taylor, with a twenty-five year career in law enforcement under his belt, had heard similar stories before. Every one of those cases had resulted in a child visiting someone without informing their parents, a relative picking up the child and running errands before taking the child home, or various other similar scenarios, none of which ended with an actual kidnapping or worse. Thinking of the trend, he believed this matter might not be as serious as the parents might believe.

The Chief knew this was going to be a long night and strict adherence to protocol would be required. Since the child had been missing for only a few hours, the family had not yet officially filed a missing persons report. All that would have to be handled quickly. The Chief would ensure the police would do as much as possible while the official report was being filed by the family.

Chief Taylor instructed Principal Phillips to stay at the gym and he and some detectives would be right there. The Chief mentioned that after Principal Phillips cleared up some official details, perhaps he might be needed to accompany the detectives to the Wilson home.

* * * * *

By 6:30 p.m., two police unmarked cars and a solid black 1955 Chevrolet sedan pulled up in front of the high school gymnasium. A single red flashing light was turning on the roof of each car, painting an eerie red tint through the shadows of the early evening. Even though the cars approached without sirens blaring, the attention drawn by the red flashing lights was enough to lure rubberneckers from their nearby homes and businesses, standing at a safe distance but watching all that could be seen from afar.

The Chief and two detectives exited their cars and approached the main double door entrance to the gymnasium. Principal Phillips, who had been waiting in the gym's lobby for their arrival, unlocked the doors and ushered the three inside. He led them to the bleachers on the main floor—to the same place Coach Barnes took roll call less than three hours before—and requested they all sit down there. The Principal stood as if he were about to conduct the meeting, but after a few minutes of silence he timidly sat down, too. He looked deflated. He clearly was not in charge.

"So start at the beginning and tell us what happened," Chief Taylor said with no emotion in his voice. Principal Phillips started to open his mouth, then shut it quickly. When he gathered his thoughts, he said, "This afternoon Coach Barnes, who works with the cheerleaders, called me and told me one of her girls didn't show up for practice. At her urging, I called the girl's mother to determine if the student, Wendy, had arrived home yet. Mrs. Wilson said she hadn't heard from her daughter since she left for school this morning. We talked again at 6 o'clock and Wendy still hadn't made it home. We all agreed that this was out of character for Wendy, so we thought the police should be called."

One of the detectives, who had been silent up until this point, cleared his throat and said, "I am Detective Brian Martin, sir. Is Coach Barnes here at the gym? We'd also like to talk to her, if you don't mind."

Almost defensively, Principal Phillips replied, "The woman has a nasty cold and had a slight fever when all this happened. In fact, the cheerleading practice had been moved indoors here at the gym today to accommodate Mrs. Barnes' illness. I told Mrs. Barnes to go home and take care of herself. If you need to talk to her, we can telephone her or you can probably catch her tomorrow at home."

Detective Martin sighed. "We'll talk to her later, then. No need to bother her tonight. But I still have a few questions. Do you have witnesses who saw the missing girl in the last class before she was scheduled to report to practice?"

The Principal wished he hadn't sent Mrs. Barnes home. He only knew the basics that Mrs. Barnes had told him and not really much else. "Mrs. Barnes said Wendy was seen in her last class and she seemed fine. I don't know who told the Coach that, but I would guess it was a member of the cheerleading squad."

"You said the practice had been relocated today?" Detective Martin inquired.

Again, the Principal didn't know anything more than the basic facts. "I know they usually practice along the sidelines of the football field, and they practice the same time the football team does."

This time, the junior detective, Lt. Harry Woodson, spoke up, "Do you know if she had a boyfriend or someone else she might have been enticed to leave the school premises with?

The Principal was feeling useless. "I'm sorry, I don't know. Her parents might have some ideas, or maybe the other cheerleaders might know something. That kind of information isn't usually shared with the teaching staff."

The Chief of Police stood from the low bleacher seat, closed his notepad, and started walking toward the door. He turned and motioned for the two detectives to follow him.

"Do you need for me to go with you to the Wilson's house?" Principal Phillips asked politely.

"I don't think that will be necessary. Thank you for your time. We'll be in touch," Chief Taylor stated as he pushed open the heavy double doors and they disappeared into the lobby.

Principal Phillips was left sitting alone on the bleacher like a lonely kid who nobody wanted to sit beside at a ball game. He got the distinct impression that the police were not pleased with the way he handled this mess.

* * * * * *

By 7:00 p.m. the police caravan had pulled up in front of Wendy Wilson's home on Woodbury Street, just a few blocks from the Central High School property. Again, their red flashing roof lights were circling, but no sirens were on. And once again, all the neighbors came out on their porches or stoops to see what was going on at the Wilson's.

Detective Martin knocked on the screen door, even though he could see Mr. and Mrs. Wilson sitting inside on a couch just a few feet away from the door. Mrs. Wilson called to them to come in.

The Chief and the Detectives entered the room, made their introductions, and sat down in the living room. Detective Martin started the questioning. "Mr. and Mrs. Wilson, I'm sorry we are here under these circumstances, but we want to do everything we can to ensure your daughter returns home safely. But first, we must ask if you have any idea where your daughter might be?"

Mr. Wilson answered, "No. She should have been home from cheerleading practice over an hour ago. The principal called and said she missed her cheer practice, too. It ain't like her to go off somewhere without asking first. We don't know where she is, I swear."

Detective Martin made a few notes on his pad. "So, you wouldn't know if she had made other plans that neither the school nor you would be unaware of?"

Mr. Wilson was becoming agitated. "If I knew she had other plans, I'd know where she is, right? Nobody knew if she had other plans. I tell you, this is not like Wendy."

Detective Woodson commented, "We have to rule out that she may have voluntarily left on her own, without enticement or assistance. Could that be the case? Or were there perhaps some issues she may have been going through at home that would make her want to leave?"

Mr. Wilson looked as though he had been slapped. "Exactly what are you saying, Detective? That we abuse our daughter in some way?" The look on his face changed from shock to outrage. "Our daughter has everything she ever wanted—probably more. We give her everything. Everything! We did without ourselves to give her what she asked for. And we never ever hit her. We don't believe in that kind of thing. Why would she want to leave here for *any* reason? She always said she wished there was a university closer than the one in Murfreesboro because she didn't want to move away from home for college. Wendy and her mother are real tight, like best friends. That child has it made here."

Looking up from his notepad, Detective Martin asked another pointed question: "So, she is fifteen years old now, I believe. Do you allow her to date?"

Mrs. Wilson answered this question. "We let her go to chaperoned school parties with other girls, and there were boys there. As far as I know, she hasn't met a boy that she would even like to date. But, we've always said she could date when she was 16, and no sooner." Mr. Wilson nodded in agreement.

Chief Taylor wanted to know if Wendy had a best friend that might be helpful in understanding where Wendy might be. Mrs. Wilson told him he should talk to Brenda Crosslin, another cheerleader who often telephoned Wendy and sometimes studied with her.

After asking several other routine questions, the three officers asked for pictures of Wendy. Meanwhile, the Wilsons were instructed to reach out to the police if they thought of anything else pertinent, or if Wendy happened to come home. For now, they would send a team out for a routine search of the immediate area where Wendy was last seen.

The policemen instructed the parents to file a formal missing person's report. They also suggested that they check with local hospitals to see if their daughter might be in the emergency room, or call a few friends to learn what they could from them. Otherwise, they should get some rest and perhaps Wendy would slip in after dark.

You never know these days what kind of trouble kids will get themselves into, thought the Police Chief, but he didn't want to share that with the worried Wilsons. *For the most part, 1955 has been a calm year in Shelbyville for the police, but this case concerns me.*

Mrs. Wilson started to cry as Mr. Wilson wrapped his arms around his broken wife. The three officers left in their separate cars and drove off in search of Wendy.

* * * * * *

Of the many people subsequently interviewed who knew the missing girl, Carl Brown was the most surprised to be questioned. He was approached by two plain clothed detectives on Monday afternoon after Wendy had vanished the past Friday.

Detectives Martin and Woodson made their way through the hallways of Central High School to find Carl cleaning up the library on the empty second floor. When Carl finished emptying the wastebasket near the Librarian's desk, he glanced up to see two shiny detective shields in front of his face.

"Mr. Carl Brown?" asked Detective Martin, even though he already knew he was Carl.

"Yes, sir. Can I help you with somethin'?" Carl responded, thinking perhaps the policemen were looking for some of the administrative staff.

"We'd like to ask you a few questions if you don't mind, sir," chimed in Detective Woodson, motioning toward a nearby library table with four vacant chairs. "Could you sit with us for a moment, sir?"

"Yeah, sure. What do you need to know from me?" Carl asked, trying not to look nervous.

"Mr. Brown, we have been told by several people that you were the last known person to speak with Wendy Wilson before she disappeared last Friday. Would you tell us what you talked about?" Detective Martin asked while Detective Woodson pulled out a notepad and pen.

"Nothin', really. She always talks to me when she sees me around the building. She's a nice girl and is real friendly to everybody." Carl paused, but could tell the officers were looking for more detail.

Clearing his throat, Carl continued. "First she showed me some silver bracelet she said she got for her birthday. Then, she said she was going to her practice—you know she was a cheerleader—but she didn't say where it was at. She asked me to wish her good luck, 'cause she was takin' a shine to the quarterback, and hoped he'd ask her to go to some school thing, maybe Homecomin' or somethin'. Anyway, she was saying she'd have to get her mom and dad in a good mood to let her go 'cause she wasn't old enough for a real date. I told her I bet she could get 'em to let her go if she gave 'em that sweet little smile she had. She shrugged, and then she left. I didn't see her after that." A saddened Carl looked down at his hands in his lap. "I hate she's gone. She was real nice."

The two detectives exchanged quick looks as Detective Woodson started to talk. "What do you mean, you 'hate she is gone'—she 'was' nice? Does that mean something to you, Carl?"

A startled Carl quickly looked back and forth between the two officers. "No, it don't. I was just sayin' she was nice and she ain't been here today. I always thought she spread a little sunshine in this place. "

"She 'was' nice. You're using past tense, sir." Detective Martin observed.

"Y'all are twisting my words and tryin' to trick me up. You know what I mean. I wouldn't hurt her or anybody else. I ain't that kind of mean person." Carl was stunned at their insinuations.

Detective Woodson continued the questioning. "So, Carl, where were you when Wendy stopped to talk to you last Friday?"

Carl didn't hesitate with his answer, "I was mopping the first floor hallway, down near the steps. She came down the stairs from the second floor and stopped to show me her bracelet, like I told you."

"How long did you talk to her, Carl?" Detective Martin asked as he scribbled on his notepad.

Carl thought for a minute, then answered, "Couldn't have been more than a couple minutes. She was in a hurry to get to practice, she said."

"Did anybody else see you talking to Wendy?" Detective Woodson inquired.

"Well, I didn't see anybody around, but you never know. Could have been. She wasn't there for that long, then took off down the stairs toward the basement doors. I figured she went out to catch up with them other cheerleaders. She said she was afraid she'd be late for practice," Carl recalled.

"And what time was it that you saw her go down the stairs to leave?" Detective Martin asked.

"Well, I always try to start my mopping after the second bell so there's no foot traffic to mess things up. It had to be 3:30 or a minute or two before." Carl was hoping the detectives would finish soon. He didn't have enough control over his emotions to keep from blurting out something offensive to these two "holier than thou" cops. Besides, he'd told them everything he knew.

The detectives rose from the table, leaving Carl peering up at them from his seated position. "Stick around town for a while, Carl. We may need to talk to you again," Detective Martin commented as he and his partner abruptly turned to leave through the library's double doors.

* * * * * *

For more than three months, the Shelbyville Police force tracked every lead and interviewed dozens of people in the hopes that they could locate Wendy. Almost all of her sophomore classmates were questioned in an attempt to learn about Wendy's social lifestyle. Relatives and neighbors spent endless hours in police interrogation rooms. Flyers with Wendy's cheerleader picture were distributed to local merchants for posting in store windows, and every utility pole that had space reflected Wendy's freckled face on a piece of wind-torn paper.

By January of 1956, Wendy's disappearance had lost its shock-value with the city's general population. Only her parents were left in limbo, not knowing whether to mourn or remain hopeful for some kind of closure. The police slowly started putting less effort on the dead end Wilson case and more manpower on the everyday police work that had backlogged during the active investigation. The Wilson case was open, but it was unofficially deemed a cold case by the overworked police department.

Eventually, the town and the police force moved on ... but Charles and Allison Wilson would never get past Friday, September 9, 1955.

CHAPTER 9

1955

On the same September morning in 1955 that Wendy Wilson was saying goodbye to her mother for the last time, Troy Tucker was calling in sick at work. He had been suffering with intermittent stomach cramps on and off all night long.

When the alarm went off at 6:00 a.m. that Friday morning, Troy found himself wishing he had a few more hours to get his stomach settled before he had to go out in public. Besides having occasional bouts of nausea, his bowel movements were being unpredictable, too. He was miserable and grouchy.

Lying in bed next to Roz and watching her breathe, he silently hoped she didn't catch whatever he might have. She had only been asleep for maybe three hours, coming to bed as soon as she wound down after her 11:00 p.m. shift ended. He knew she wouldn't be up until sometime close to noon. He lay there in silence and watched her chest rise and fall under the light blanket.

Staring at her now, she didn't look anything like the vivacious woman he married some twenty years before. She looked tired and worn, but most of all she looked older than her 38 years. His mind wandered to happier times, but snapped back into reality when the alarm unexpectedly went off a second time.

Before rising, he mentally justified calling his supervisor and declared himself too sick to leave the house. Troy didn't want to spread it around the Rubber Mill, either. Besides, he could use the time to catch up on a few things around the house, provided his bodily functions cooperated. Thus, he made the call to his supervisor and went back to bed.

* * * * * *

Ma Rose, who had become a permanent resident of the Tucker household in 1952, stayed in bed until 9:00 a.m. every day, without fail. She had always been a creature of habit and she was a slave to routine. She heard Troy's alarm go off twice, wondering why it didn't stop after the first time. She listened for the sound of water running in the bathroom, but Troy's usual morning rituals were not in operation. She wondered if she should try to get up and check on Troy, but she decided against it. She didn't like the man, anyway. She settled back in her bed and stayed there reading her Bible until the appointed time to start her day.

* * * * * *

By mid-morning, Troy seemed to have conquered his battle with his digestive system. He had taken a stiff dose of Pepto-Bismol and, for now at least, he felt almost normal.

Ma Rose was sitting at the breakfast table watching him amble through from the bedroom to the kitchen. Without acknowledging her presence, he reached for the percolator and poured himself a cup of coffee, believing that it could provide magic medicine for any malady.

"You takin' the day off?" Ma Rose asked without looking in his direction.

"Yep. Don't feel good," was the only response Troy supplied, looking out the kitchen window at the garage and shed area.

"You contagious?" Ma Rose wanted to know.

"I don't know. Just don't come near me and you won't catch nothin'," Troy snapped.

"Go to hell, you jackass," came out of Ma Rose's mouth before she even realized what she had said.

Troy laughed and said, "Save me a place when you get there, you ancient biddy." As he opened the door to exit the kitchen, Troy smiled broadly, winked at her, and blew her a kiss. He knew it would get her riled, and that was his objective.

When he was safely out of her sight, Ma Rose stuck her tongue out at Troy when the door closed behind him. She couldn't stand that man. She didn't know what

Roz ever saw in him. Nobody else liked him either...just ask anybody who really knew him. With that, she spit her snuff juice in a tin can and set it down on the floor beside her chair. She didn't care if she knocked it over or not. Troy would just have to deal with it. Jackass.

* * * * * *

Facing Fishingford Pike from the Tucker's front door, the house on his left had been occupied by the Swing family for at least the last ten years. Their houses were far enough apart that they didn't have much contact, except waving as one or the other passed by or walked out to the mailbox. That was the way Troy liked it. He wanted to be the only one who knew his business, and nosy neighbors could be damned.

The residence on his right housed a middle-aged man and his nearly blind wife, plus a mid-twenty year old bachelor son who most people labeled as "retarded" or "not right in the head." They had moved in last year when Jake Morton lost his beloved wife to a heart attack, prompting the widower to sell the homestead to the first buyer who approached him.

Ever since the strange family moved in, it was obvious that the old man wanted to know everything about the Tuckers' personal business. Both Roz and Troy tried to avoid lengthy conversations with him, but sometimes it couldn't be helped.

* * * * * *

Marvin Morgan was a 45-year old busybody who didn't have enough of his own business to take care of, so he liked to meddle in everyone else's—or so said Troy. Probably feeling his solitude more than anything, Marvin always tried to make friends, but he was too pushy and a little too opinionated to capture anyone's long-term attention. Marvin was a part-time Animal Control Officer with the County, and picking up road kill for a living certainly didn't attract friends. He was a very hard person to get to know; none of his potential friends ever stayed around long enough to learn to like him.

Geraldine Morgan had been legally blind since 1947 when a manufacturing plant accident caused chemical burns that injured her eyes and part of one ear. She was scarred badly about her face and was totally blinded in her right eye. Her left eye had retained enough vision that she could make out shadows, but no details. Even the large financial settlement she received from the company didn't make up for the fact that she was left legally blind. She was a pitiful woman who tried to be as independent as she could under the circumstances, but she was depressed most of the time. She never wanted to be dependent on anybody, but here she was smack dab in the middle of it, killing it.

The adult son living with them made lots of racket with his small motorcycle as he raced it up and down the road several times a day. Rocky Morgan was reckless with a serious lack of common sense. Rumor was he dropped out of school in the seventh grade because he wasn't smart enough to keep up with the other kids. That seemed plausible, based on the crazy road antics he pulled for attention.

So these three neighbors, through no fault of their own, ticked off Troy every time they came outside to sit on their front porch which faced Troy's house and sound carried easily between the two houses.

After a while, Troy began to think all three sat outside just to hear what was going on at the Tuckers. Every time he thought more about it, he became increasingly paranoid. As the days and weeks passed, Troy became more agitated. He and Roz even tried circumventing their own front yard as much as possible in hopes they could avoid the Morgan's' constant spying.

On this particular morning, however, Troy was already in a bad mood because of his indigestion concerns, having to miss work, Ma Rose's snarky comments, and all the things he wanted to do outside that were probably going to be either hampered by his stomach's instability or monitored closely by Marvin Morgan and family. He was going to have to address this business with his neighbor and nip it in the bud. He might as well be prepared for it today.

* * * * * *

Walking toward his backyard shed, he tried to swing as far away from the boundary wire fence as possible so he wouldn't be forced to acknowledge the Morgan family gathered on their porch. The garage's west side was only about three feet from their property line, of which the Morgans generally stayed clear. The only time they came near the fence was to retrieve firewood from their stockpile which was situated on their own land, against the fence, and about half way down the side of Troy's garage.

From the side of Troy's garage and further back, the wire fence was covered with wild vines and various weeds that partly provided a privacy shield. But from the garage front to the road, the fence row was clear, giving the Morgan's a direct view of the Tucker house and yard. Secretly, Troy wished he had the money to build a six foot tall wooden fence to hide the Morgans' homestead from his view. Maybe Roz would be agreeable to that if she started to feel increasingly uncomfortable with the strange family.

* * * * * *

When Troy stepped around the back of his garage, he quietly made his way to the shed. He glanced around to ensure he had privacy when he moved an oil can to retrieve the key underneath. He had padlocked the shed door a year after it was built just in case someone decided his motorcycle might be worth stealing. He removed the lock and dropped it on the ground, and entered his private domain.

The shed was about 10 ft. x 10 ft., bigger than some rooms in new houses nowadays. His beauty of a motorcycle was parked along the right side wall beneath a salvaged window Corb found somewhere. The Hog had lots of chrome, lots of power, and an extra long seat so that passengers could be comfortable riding behind him. It had fringe on the bulky black saddlebags that tended to accentuate the bad-boy look of the big machine. He loved the feeling of power between his legs, and that always put him in the mood for a sexual encounter.

He wished he knew some sultry woman who was available that day. He'd call her up and summon her to the shed, then have his way with her until she screamed for him to stop. His urges for sex were mingled with his disgruntled feelings toward his neighbors and the terrible way his day had started. Maybe blowing off a little steam with a good looking woman would help him get his temper back in check.

Since it would be several hours before Roz left for work, Troy was content to pull out his erotic magazines from the bottom drawer of the rolling red tool chest. He chose the one with the most pictures and propped himself up against the left shed wall, facing the motorcycle. It didn't take him long to get inspired enough to release his tensions and reach the satisfaction plateau he was seeking.

* * * * * *

While Troy tried to find a comfortable napping position on the small cot, Rocky Morgan became curious about why his neighbor had been in the motorcycle shed for so long. Rocky had watched him walk through the back yard going toward the building, and hoped he was going to bring out the big cycle. He waited by the fence row for a long time while Mr. Troy was inside.

Earlier when Troy walked toward his shed hideout, Rocky had stealthily followed along the fence line. Unobserved, Rocky peered through the tangled weeds, watching Mr. Troy move a can of oil before entering the building. As Rocky stepped to his right (back toward the edge of the garage) he tried to see through the grimy window panes a few feet away. Surprisingly, he had a pretty good view of the black shiny Harley-Davidson that was parked inside, but he couldn't see beyond that. Rocky stayed frozen in place, staring in awe at the Hog for fifteen or twenty minutes before he decided what he should do next.

The side of the shed was inset from the rear edge of the garage by about five feet, so Rocky couldn't touch the wall or window to knock from where he stood. Unless he crossed the fence, he couldn't get to the door, either. Finding himself in a dilemma, he loudly yelled, "Mr. Troy, Mr. Troy. Are you still in there, Mr. Troy? It's me, Rocky, Mr. Troy. Please answer Mr. Troy."

Believing that surely someone must have been hurt or something terrible had happened, Troy rapidly stood at attention and wiped the drowsiness from his eyes. He burst out the door and found Rocky leaning into the wire fence. There were vines and leaves smashed all over his body, but he didn't seem to care.

"Hi, Mr. Troy. It's me Rocky. I wanted to see your motorcycle up close. It's not little like mine, but I bet I can drive it. You want me to show you, Mr. Troy? I can drive real good. My mama says so. My daddy don't care. He just gets mad. You remember me, Rocky, don't you Mr. Troy?"

Troy shifted into anger mode, but the boy-like innocence--even at his advanced age--tugged at Troy's black heart. He tried counting to twenty to calm down before he answered. Finally, when he thought he had himself under control, he spoke to the mentally-challenged young man.

"Rocky, what are you doin' back here hollerin', son? You're not supposed to do that. You scared me with your damn loud screamin'. I was afraid you got hurt. Now go on back in your house and tell your mama what you did out here, and I bet she won't want you to do it again, either." Troy had no practice talking to challenged adults. He tried to say what he thought a child Dixie's age might understand. "Where's your daddy, boy? Does he know where you're at?"

"He's digging a hole on yonder side of the house for Mama's new rose bush. He don't care where I'm at." An anxious Rocky continued, "But can't I just see your big motorcycle, just once Mr. Troy? I won't bother you again if you let me see it. Oh, pleeeeezzzzze." Rocky was putting on his best show for Troy.

Troy figured if he allowed Rocky to have his way this one time, there would be no more recurrences. He gave in. "Okay, Rocky. Just this once, and then we ain't doin' this no more. You hear me?"

"You bet, Mr. Troy!" Troy showed Rocky how to put his feet between the wire squares of the fence to ascend, then drop his leg over the top and climb back down. "Rocky did it, Rocky did it!" the proud young man exclaimed.

Troy smiled and nodded. He led him into the shed and pointed him toward the black shiny motorcycle parked by the right wall.

"Wow, Mr. Troy! Wow! Oh man, this is what I wanted to see. It is so big and I bet it's noisy, too, right Mr. Troy? Can I sit on it just once? I won't hurt it, I promise." Rocky looked like a young man who had just met Superman. His face was filled with astonishment.

Troy was surprisingly patient in his response. "Okay, Rocky, but just for a minute. Then you need to go home." Troy helped Rocky get on the cycle without turning it over. Rocky was acting more like a six-year old, making sound effects while abruptly turning the handle bars left and right. Troy smiled and remembered how exciting his own life had been when everything was new to him.

"Okay son, it's time for you to go now." Troy tried to motivate Rocky to get off the bike and climb back over the fence.

"What's that over there? What's that book? Is it a comic book? I like Superman!" Rocky jumped down from the bike and lunged toward the bed where Troy had been enjoying his pictorials.

Rocky's eyes grew wide and exclaimed, "Oh no, this is NASTY. This book has women and men with no clothes on. That's a No-No. You need to throw this away, Mr. Troy. Not good for you, no, they're not. My mama says you look at bad stuff and you'll go blind like she is. Am I gonna go blind, Mr. Troy?" Rocky started to tear up. He was getting scared.

"No, boy, you ain't gonna go blind. You didn't look long enough to go blind, but don't ever look again, okay?" Troy was treading water with his response. He'd never been in this kind of predicament before.

"Come on, I'll help you over the fence, and you just forget about that stuff, now. You'll be fine. Just don't tell your mama and daddy about what you seen and everything will be fine." Troy took Rocky's hand and led him through the shed door toward the fence.

"To climb the fence back over into your yard, just do everything you did before except do it in reverse, okay?" Troy told him.

"What? You mean do what I did to come over but go backwards?" Troy nodded yes.

Rocky turned his back to the fence and started to try his ascent with heels first in the wire squares.

"No, no, Rocky. Face the fence like you did before, but just go over to your house this time."

The light bulb went on in Rocky's head and he scrambled over the fence like a pro. He waved to Troy and put his pointer finger vertically against his closed lips, giving Troy a "don't say a word" signal. Troy returned the signal and waved goodbye to Rocky.

* * * * * *

Within fifteen minutes of Rocky's departure, Marvin Morgan was charging up the Tucker driveway yelling for Troy. Still behind the garage locking up the shed, Troy stepped around to the side of the garage and started walking toward the outraged man.

Mr. Morgan couldn't control his fury. "What the hell were you doing with my son in that shed? What did you do to him, you bastard! I oughta call the police right now and report you for child molestation. No, actually, I oughta knock your lights out first, you freak!" He took a step forward and Troy started backing up.

"Hold on there, Marvin. Your boy came to my shed and started yelling like a crazy person. He said he wanted to see my motorcycle and wanted to sit on it for a minute. That's all." Troy was telling the truth.

"Yeah, he told me that, too, but then he said you showed him naked people in books and he didn't want to go blind like his mother. What in the hell was that, huh? You wanna take me back there and show me there are no magazines, huh? You want to prove your innocence? Let's go right now and see what's in that place." Mr. Morgan started to walk briskly toward the direction of the shed, but Troy tried to stop him by reaching for his arm. Mr. Morgan halted and jerked his arm from Troy's reach.

"Yeah, I got magazines in there because that's my private place. I didn't show the boy nothin'. He's the one wanted to come over here and see my motorcycle. He saw the back cover of the magazine and picked it up before I could get to him. I swear that's the God's honest truth. I took it away from him and told him never to look at nothin' like that again. I swear. I didn't touch him. I'm married, for Christ's sake. He said if he could sit on the motorcycle he would never come back again, and I believed him. I don't want him over here, anyway."

Mr. Morgan gazed at Troy for a long time, maintaining a stern and hateful look on his face. He finally said, "All right, I'll give you the benefit of the doubt. THIS TIME. But if I ever find you near my boy again, I swear on my life I will cut your heart out." Mr. Morgan spit at Troy's feet and walked smugly back to his own yard to sit on the porch with his family.

Stunned, Troy didn't move for a few minutes, still trying to process everything that had happened within the last half hour. He had been accused of child molestation when the child was really the one bothering him. He had been called out about the magazines, even though he had every right to enjoy them in his private surroundings. He had been threatened by his crazy neighbor with a blind wife and half-wit son. What the hell had just happened?

Troy just wanted to forget about it for now. Anyway, it was all a misunderstanding. It would work itself out. He just had to pretend the Morgans didn't exist.

* * * * * *

Ma Rose watched the driveway confrontation between Mr. Morgan and Troy through the sheer curtains of her bedroom window. She smirked as she realized what was happening. She always thought her son-in-law was some kind of pervert, and now the yelling match confirmed her suspicions. As loudly as the two men were screaming out there, she surmised all the neighbors now thought the same thing about Troy.

As she dropped the sheer curtain and settled back in her overstuffed corner chair, she reached for her spit cup and held it closely under her bottom lip. Ma Rose let the snuff/saliva mixture roll from her mouth into the half full can that originally contained green beans. She shook her head, carelessly setting the can down near her feet. Ma Rose picked up her Bible and tried to recall the exact passage that would give her some direction on how Troy's horribly tainted soul might still be saved.

When she found it, her foot bumped the spit can and the awful brown liquid spilled on the wooden floor. She mischievously smiled and thought the accidental spill would probably push the jackass over the edge. She settled back with her Bible passage and promptly fell asleep in her chair.

CHAPTER 10

November 1955

On Dollie's fifth birthday in 1955, her parents got her a new red Radio Flyer wagon and a doll named Susie. The doll was almost three feet tall, wore a red-checkered blouse under a red jumper, and was supposed to be able to walk if its hand was held just right. Dollie had placed Susie in the new wagon and was running over everyone's toes as she zipped through the rooms of their Union Street home.

The Sunday afternoon before Thanksgiving was a perfect time to have LorAnn's joint birthday celebration with Dollie. The weather was crisp but beautiful, with autumn's paint still coloring trees that still had a few yellow or orange leaves hanging on for dear life. The fall had been unusually warm and the higher temperatures had delayed winter's approach. It seemed more like late September than November.

Miss Ruth, who had been with the Carter family for the past five years, volunteered—or rather, insisted—on making the cake for the two birthday girls. She also set up the dining room table for the guests. She believed she had proven to be a very valuable asset to the family. Even though she claimed she didn't do housework, she always picked up after the children and kept the house clear of clutter. She was a good cook, once she realized the Carters preferred meat, gravy and potatoes over pasta or exotic casseroles. She learned to be flexible with the comings and goings of Dixie to her grandparents' house, and she enjoyed her quiet time when Dollie took her afternoon nap. She believed she had fit in with the family very well.

Today, Miss Ruth was an invited guest to the joint birthday event, making her feel more like a family member instead of an employee. Standing with the aunts, uncles, and grandparents of the children gave her a sense of belonging. She was happy in her role as family nanny.

* * * * * *

After the traditional singing of the birthday song and blowing out the candles, Miss Ruth took the cake into the kitchen and carefully carved out the slices to be served to the crowd. A few of the family members remarked about how LorAnn had it made, having a maid and all. Not knowing how to respond, LorAnn just smiled and said Miss Ruth was a Godsend. They all agreed.

Without Miss Ruth, she wasn't sure how she would have survived that awful period that began right about the time Corb got the job with the City. Corb started coming home late, always blaming it on extra work he had to do at the City Garage. He also had more things to do away from home on Saturdays than he used to have. All these tell-tale signs led LorAnn to believe Corb might have slipped back into his old ways.

At first she thought he might have started seeing Nell Lambert again, but she soon found out differently. Her mind wandered as she recalled the hurtful events of the past three years.

* * * * * *

In early 1952, Miss Ruth had noticed that LorAnn hadn't been sleeping well during her normal day schedule. LorAnn also appeared to have lost some weight. She had circles under her eyes and appeared to be daydreaming a lot when she was awake. LorAnn couldn't seem to concentrate when Miss Ruth was talking to her.

Being a good judge of medical conditions with her nursing background, Miss Ruth began asking LorAnn how she had been feeling lately. When she was satisfied that LorAnn had no symptoms of illness, she concluded that something external to LorAnn's body was bothering her. Miss Ruth then inappropriately asked LorAnn about the state of her marriage.

LorAnn looked directly at Miss Ruth when she asked the pointed question. Without hesitation, she replied, "Miss Ruth, I don't know if there is anything wrong or not with Corb and me. A few years ago we had a rough patch and I thought he was gonna leave me for another woman. When Dollie was born, he seemed like a changed man. He's been real good to me and the girls since then, but I just think there might be somethin' else goin' on with him now."

LorAnn realized too late that she probably shouldn't have shared that concern with Miss Ruth. To date, she hadn't told anyone of her renewed fears, not even Roz. She had kept everything to herself on the hope that she was imagining the changes in her husband.

Miss Ruth studied LorAnn's face for a few seconds and then said, "Mrs. Carter, you leave it to me. I know how to find out what you need to know. And don't worry, I won't tell a soul what you told me today."

Miss Ruth patted LorAnn on the shoulder and left her alone with her thoughts.

A few days after LorAnn had told Miss Ruth her suspicions, an envelope was left on the dining room table with LorAnn's name printed on the front. It hadn't been on the table earlier that day. She wondered who had left it and when it got there.

As she reached for the envelope, Miss Ruth came through the dining room door and sat down at the table across from LorAnn.

"I see you found the information I got for you. Have you read it yet?" a curious Miss Ruth asked.

"You put this here? What is it?" LorAnn inquired.

"It's what you wanted to know about your husband. I have a friend I used to work with who does private investigation work on the side to supplement his income. He's very good at it, and he did this for free—as a favor for me." She paused. "You sure you want to read the report?"

LorAnn was stunned that Miss Ruth would do something so drastic without LorAnn's approval. She had immediate mixed feelings about reading the information. LorAnn's stomach started to revolt and for a moment she felt queasy. "I think I need some water," she managed to say while staring at the unopened envelope.

Miss Ruth went into the kitchen and returned with a glass of iced water. "Here you go."

LorAnn gulped the water and took a deep breath. Reaching for the sealed envelope, she wondered if Miss Ruth already knew the contents. Ripping it open, she read what she didn't want to believe.

According to the report, Corb had been seeing one of the secretaries in the City Manager's office. He met her when he went there to put in an application for the job he currently held. They had been meeting off and on for coffee and sexual encounters during the last few months. The report provided the woman's name, address, and detailed information about her husband and family.

Miss Ruth took the sheet of paper from LorAnn's hand and scanned it quickly. "Oh, dear. What do you think you'll do, Mrs. Carter? What can I do to help?"

As calmly as she could, LorAnn replied, "I don't plan to do anything yet, Miss Ruth. And I think you've done enough already." LorAnn abruptly left the dining room table and proceeded to get ready for her second shift job at the Rubber Mill.

Miss Ruth wasn't sure if LorAnn was pleased she had taken the trouble to acquire this private information through her professional source, or if she was angry that Miss Ruth took it upon herself to interfere. Regardless, Miss Ruth resumed her day's babysitting duties and LorAnn left the house for work at her usual 2:30 p.m. time.

* * * * * *

When LorAnn got home that same night, she had the single page report in her purse. Corb was snoring away in their bedroom, and the children were asleep in the front bedroom's double bed.

LorAnn sat on the side of the bed next to Corb and nudged his arm with her pointed finger. He moved slightly, readjusted his pillow, and turned his head in the other direction. LorAnn nudged him harder, this time on his shoulder. He awoke with a start.

"What's wrong LorAnn? What time is it?" Corb tried to get his bearings.

"It's 11:30 and everything's wrong, Corb." She held the report out to him, and he switched on the bedside lamp so he could see it.

"What is this? I don't know what this is... what is it? Where did it come from?" Corb asked.

LorAnn had to frame her answers carefully. "It was dropped off at the house today. I didn't ask for it, so I don't know why I have it. But you can read as well as I can, and it looks like you and that woman in the City Manager's office have been having regular dates. I know that woman's married, so maybe her husband wanted to know what she was up to. Maybe I just got a copy of what he's already seen."

Now sitting on the side of the bed, Corb put his elbows on his knees and ran his hands through his hair. He kept his eyes closed as if he were trying to think of the perfect words to get him out of the mess his randiness had once again created.

"LorAnn, I can explain all this. I think I have a sickness or something. I was pulled to her but only for sex. I don't love her or even care about her. It will be over tomorrow, I promise. Please don't make me leave. I made a bad mistake and I won't make it again. I love you, LorAnn, and I love our kids. Please don't make me leave." He started to cry. She tried to feel sorry for him but she was so devastated, all she felt was disgust and disappointment. For some reason, she wasn't afraid of losing her family like she had been before Dollie was born.

"Corb, move over. I have to get some sleep. My body's tired and my mind's even worse. Get on your side of the bed and give me some peace," she said unemotionally.

Moving over toward the window side of the bed, Corb made room for LorAnn to slip in the double bed beside him. She turned her back to him, and closed her eyes. She felt Corb reach around her small waist and try to pull her closer to him.

Through gritted teeth, LorAnn loudly commanded, "Get on your side of the bed and behave yourself, Corb. Believe me, this is NOT the night to try to be lovey dovey. I have to sleep on this and figure out what I'm gonna do."

Corb moved as far away from LorAnn as he could and stared at the ceiling. She was in the right, and he had it coming. Especially after all he put her through with Nell before Dollie was born. He had just let his little head overrule the big head again, like his mother always said men tended to do.

He had to straighten up and convince LorAnn this wasn't going to keep happening. He reached across the bed to touch her arm, but she shrugged it off.

It might be harder this time to get things back to normal. He was going to try again, though. Because now, *he* was the terrified spouse.

* * * * *

Miss Ruth never mentioned the report or their conversation to LorAnn again. She went on as if nothing had ever been said or done. LorAnn never said anything else about the report either.

Meanwhile, the bond of loyalty and friendship became stronger between Miss Ruth and LorAnn than either of them ever imagined it would.

* * * * *

Then in 1954, Miss Ruth observed LorAnn going through a similar episode with sleeplessness and lack of focus. Without discussing anything with LorAnn, Miss Ruth called her friend and asked for another favor. Within a few days, an envelope appeared on the dining room table with LorAnn's name printed on it.

This time, LorAnn immediately picked up the envelope and opened it, and once again was informed of a short-term extramarital affair between Corb and a waitress at Pope's Café. She tossed the report on the dining room table and went into the kitchen where Miss Ruth was doing prep work for the evening meal.

"Looks like rain tomorrow, Miss Ruth. Be sure to wear your rain boots and take an umbrella when you pick up Dixie at school." LorAnn commented as if she didn't have a care in the world.

"Thanks, Mrs. Carter. I'll certainly do that." Miss Ruth continued chopping vegetables while LorAnn circled back through the dining room, picked up the report , and stuffed it in her purse. She dreaded a repeat performance of the confrontation she had with Corb two years prior after the first report appeared. Then again, what difference did it make anyway? Maybe she should ignore it. She'd sleep on it and deal with it later.

* * * * * *

Snapping back into the present day, LorAnn realized just how far back she had let her mind wander. LorAnn attempted to shut out all the disappointing flashbacks, trying to focus only on today's birthday celebration.

November 20, 1955, was a good day. Everyone at the birthday party seemed happy and content. She believed Corb had been a faithful husband during the last year. He appeared to be comfortable and settled with his wife and family life. Dollie kept him on his toes, and he loved being her center of attention. He loved Dixie, too, but the older child seemed to be more attached to LorAnn. She supposed that was natural, under the circumstances.

* * * * * *

When the day was over and the dirty dishes had been washed and put away, LorAnn and Corb relaxed in the living room after the children had gone to bed.

"What 'cha want for *your* birthday tomorrow, LorAnn?" Corb asked as they watched *The Red Skelton Show* on their small television with the huge rabbit ears antenna.

"No need to buy me anything, Corb. What I want outta life can't be bought," She smiled and looked at Corb with a melancholy expression.

Corb got out of his overstuffed chair and moved to sit next to LorAnn. "Well, you'll be 34 tomorrow, same as me," he said as he put his arm around her shoulder. "You want to meet me at Pope's tomorrow for a birthday lunch?" he smiled easily as he said the words.

LorAnn had never told him she knew about the affair he had with the waitress there last year. She had hoped the fling would be a flash in the pan, and would have faded out without any help from her. Besides she didn't want to give away her information source, believing Corb would figure out that a second report wouldn't have also been generated by the spouse of his mistress. That would have been too coincidental.

LorAnn steadied herself and said, "I'd rather have lunch here at home with you. Just come by at your usual time, and I'll make sure I'm out of bed and ready by then."

Corb kissed her on the cheek, and they both settled in to watch Red Skelton's "Gertrude and Heathcliff" comedy sketch.

LorAnn knew deep in her heart that tomorrow's birthday would come and go just like every other one had over the last eleven years. There would be nothing special for her on the horizon. The only exception she could cite was her 28th birthday five years before. That was the year Dollie had been born. On her birthday that year Corb had sworn that their life together would be forever blissful. She wondered how Corb could so conveniently forget what he pledged to her that day.

CHAPTER II

Christmas 1955

The rest of 1955 came and went quickly like every other holiday season they had commemorated over the last few years. The Carters and the Hudsons held their separate Thanksgiving and Christmas affairs in the usual places. Only one incident occurred that could be considered out of the ordinary. Otherwise, all else seemed right with the world as the families enthusiastically approached the new year.

That bizarre incident happened during the Hudson Christmas Eve party.

After the family had finished eating and were milling around the Tuckers' spotless and heavily decorated garage, Rocky Morgan approached the fence line, leaned forward over the top of the wire fence, and called out to Troy through the wide-open garage door.

"Mr. Troy, can I have a piece of pie? I like pie," he stated happily. At least half of the Hudson family members turned their attention toward the young man at the fence.

Troy looked perturbed as he responded, "Boy, get your dumb ass back over to your own house. I ain't got no time to be messing with you."

Roz and LorAnn happened to be closest to Rocky from where they were standing sipping coffee near the door. Giving Troy a dirty look, Roz answered the Morgan boy, "Rocky, I'll get you some pie. You want to come over here and eat it at the table?"

An angry Troy raised his voice and said, "No, he don't and he don't get no pie neither." Directing his next comment to Rocky, he shouted his response. "Get your stupid ass back over there boy, and don't bother us no more."

By then, the whole Hudson clan was staring at the upset Troy, having a hard time believing how he had talked so brutally to such an innocent young man.

Out of nowhere, Marvin Morgan came to fetch his son. As he approached the Tucker property line, he shouted at his son, "Boy, get over here and leave that pervert alone. He didn't try to make you go with him to that shed again, did he?"

"No, sir. I just wanted some pie this time," a pouting Rocky muttered.

"Next time I see you talk to that nasty man, I'll beat your ass red, do you understand me, boy?" Mr. Morgan seemed to know something that Troy hadn't shared with anyone in the family.

"I know, Daddy. I won't talk to the nasty man no more. But can the nice lady give me some of that pie?"

Mr. Morgan was losing his patience with his childlike son. He grabbed him by the ear and started pulling the boy backwards toward their house. "Leave it be, Rocky. Your mama will give you somethin' to eat." Rocky shut his eyes and made a face that reflected pain as he half-walked, half-tripped along beside his daddy.

A clearly distressed Mr. Morgan called out as he retreated from the fence to his front door, "Troy Tucker, I told you to leave my boy alone. He don't need you messin' with him, and he sure don't need to see any more of them dirty magazines. Stay away from my boy, or I'll make you so miserable you'll wish you were dead."

All the listeners gasped when they heard the threat roll off Mr. Morgan's tongue. Troy shook his head and clenched his teeth. His fists were by his side, and his fingers were gripped so tightly there were fingernail indentions on his palms.

"That son of a bitch don't know what he's talking about. I wish him and his retarded son would disappear off the face of the earth. They ain't nothin' but liars and idiots, the both of 'em." He said to no one in particular through his still clenched teeth.

An embarrassed Troy looked at all the shocked faces peering out from the garage, and then left the assembly. He hurriedly made his way to the house and into his bedroom. He slammed the door behind him and tried to get control of his raging temper.

"God help me not kill him, God help me not kill him, God help me not kill him ....." Troy repeated.

* * * * * *

Soon after the disturbance, the family left and Roz joined her husband in the house. When she entered the bedroom, she found Troy lying on the bed, fully clothed, and gazing at the ceiling.

"What in heaven's name was that all about, Troy? Have you done something to that boy?" she asked with pained eyes.

Troy relayed the story of what occurred a month before when Rocky wanted to see the Harley-Davidson. Roz listened intently, but wondered deep inside if there was any truth to Mr. Morgan's claims. After all, she knew Troy had an elevated sexual appetite, and he was prone to scan through erotic magazines while he pleasured himself. She didn't care about that, but she certainly wouldn't stand for Troy abusing an innocent victim.

"Okay, Troy, but I think it'd be best if you didn't have anything else to do with them," Roz commented.

"For God's sake, Roz, that's what I was tryin' to do! You see how that crazy boy won't stop pestering me. They need to handle it on their side of the fence, not mine. If they'd keep that boy locked up or somethin', things might be all right around here," Troy preached.

Roz couldn't believe how irrationally Troy was talking. Maybe she didn't know the real Troy; maybe he had problems she never thought he'd had.

"All right. Just get yourself rested and calm down. I'll go start pickin' up the garage mess, and you come out and help me when you feel like it, okay?"

Troy nodded and turned on his side facing the wall. As she reached for the doorknob, she heard Troy's fist forcefully punch the pillow. "Damn them troublemakers. They need to disappear," she heard him mumble as she shut the door behind her.

* * * * *

In May of 1956, Dixie turned eleven years old and was in the final weeks of the fifth grade. She had proven herself to be a very responsible young girl, and was occasionally allowed to walk the few blocks to or from elementary school by herself, rather than have Miss Ruth transport her with Dollie.

From home, her path took her straight across the next door neighbor's backyard; then she took a sharp right turn onto a curving path that eventually led through about 15 feet of wooded area. The path came out in the rear parking lot of a church on the south corner of Elm Street, right across from the Red Ace gas station.

The elementary school was diagonally across the street from the Red Ace, and she knew how to cross Elm Street safely. After school, she took the same route back and was home within fifteen minutes of her class dismissal time.

The long one-story building where Dixie went to class was adjacent to the high school. Sometimes she saw Uncle Carl mopping or taking out trash, and she always tried to wave when he was looking her way. She was proud of her uncle, even though he wasn't one of the well dressed members of the teaching staff. She still thought he was a pleasant man who always smiled and talked to the students as if he was their best friend. Everybody liked Carl, and Dixie was proud that she knew him better than any one of her fellow students. After all, he was **her** uncle.

* * * * *

Dixie had become so precocious that she seemed older than her years. Her intelligence showed in everything she did. She had a special knack for figuring out how things were built or put together, and that made her daddy very proud. She often assisted him when he worked on car motors, washing machines, or when he built small pieces of furniture or mended anything wooden. She had insight as to how things should be assembled, and the skill to make it happen. Her common sense approach to solving problems was better honed than either of her parents'.

Her mental maturity was the very thing that made her appealing to many people. For example, Pap Stan loved to try to teach her how to handle simple store tasks. Before she ever made a sale, he made sure she knew how to count money and change, and could work the cash register. He gave her "junior salesperson status."

She was a joy to have in the store with them, and she was careful and efficient with every task they gave her. Pap thought it wouldn't be long before they could leave the store in Dixie's hands with confidence that all would go well. Pap took great pride in Dixie and her abilities.

The young girl spent as much time as allowed with Granny and Pap, which was where she always felt most at home. But those times had been restricted to one night a week now that she was older and their homes weren't as close. That meant she had to share her time at home with Dollie, who still acted like an actual baby at the age of five.

Dollie cried to get her way (often to the detriment of Dixie). She would tattle on Dixie when she did innocent little things that really didn't matter. Dollie would make those petty issues sound so awful that Dixie almost always got the switch. Dixie liked it better at Granny and Pap's than anywhere, especially when she had their full attention and there was no Dollie around to taunt her.

Several weeks before school was scheduled to begin in the fall of 1956, Dixie declared to her mother that she wanted to spend time that summer with her Aunt Roz. She believed Aunt Roz to be the kind of person who knew how to be independent yet still hold an equal partnership in the business of running a household. Dixie also admired her for wearing makeup and always dressing nicely. Aunt Roz had a strong personality, but she was also very patient and tender-hearted.

Dixie wanted occasional third-party guidance and direction from a more modern adult figure. Dixie thought her grandparents were much too old to understand the fads of the modern 1950's, but Aunt Roz was the perfect candidate.

Aunt Roz and Uncle Troy never had children, which was also a plus for Dixie since she would have her aunt's total attention just as she did with Pap and Granny. After dinner, she planned to ask her parents to work out a summer visiting arrangement with the Tuckers. School was going to end soon, and unless something changed, she would be stuck at home all summer with Miss Ruth and Dollie. She prayed something would be arranged so she could avoid her sister as much as possible. She thought Miss Ruth favored Dollie anyway, so Dixie didn't think her absence would be too disheartening to anybody in the Union Street house.

* * * * * *

Meanwhile, Miss Ruth pampered Dollie as if she were her own child. She spent as much time with her as she could, growing more attached every year. She had missed Dollie terribly when she entered first grade, but had managed to convince the Carters that her full-time employment was invaluable and still necessary.

Miss Ruth made it a point to arrive each school day morning in time to prepare breakfast for the children and Mr. Carter. She drove both girls to their appointed school buildings, and then came back to relax until time to make lunch for Corb. Her job was easy, plus it was steady.

As summer approached, Miss Ruth looked forward to full days again with Dollie and Dixie. With both of the parents working different shifts, she encouraged the girls to consider her as their primary guardian and advisor.

* * * * * *

On the last day of school in late May, 1956, Dixie was one of the students who ran out the doors, jumping up and down, celebrating the beginning of the summer holiday season. She had also been special given permission by Miss Ruth to walk home alone that day.

She excitedly crossed the street in front of the high school and stepped on the sidewalk of the Red Ace station property. There she saw Uncle Troy getting out of his brand new 1956 Chevrolet Bel Air about to fill it up with gasoline. Dixie went straight to him and gave him a hug. "School's out for the summer, Uncle Troy, and I'm so happy about it!" Dixie exclaimed.

"That's great, Dixie. Are you walkin' home by yourself these days? I'm surprised your Daddy or Miss Ruth would let you do that." Troy remarked as he removed the gas cap and started dispensing gas.

"Oh yeah. I been doin' that for a while now. I go down behind the church and through the wooded patch, and come out on the side road that runs behind our next door neighbor's house. It's not far and I can make it pretty quick."

Uncle Troy smiled. "You want me to take you home today instead of you havin' to walk? I'll buy you a 7 Up too, if you want."

Dixie smiled even bigger. "I sure would like that, Uncle Troy. Let's go inside and get my drink and you pay for your gas, and then let's drive around first."

"We can't ride too far, 'cause your Miss Ruth will be calling the police if you ain't home about when you're supposed to be." He took her hand and the two walked inside the gas station.

When Dixie got her 7 Up and Troy had paid for everything, he helped her get into the broad bench seat from the driver's side door. Dixie settled in and kept her drink firmly between her knees when she wasn't holding it up to her mouth. She tried to sit straighter so she would be able to see better out of the side windows as Troy drove out of the gas station and turned on Elm Street in the opposite direction of the Carter home.

Uncle Troy was smiling broadly and was happy to have something to do to kill a few minutes before going home. He dreaded the emptiness of the house when Roz was at work. Even with Ma Rose there, it was still like a tomb. The old woman didn't come out of her room even to go to the bathroom, opting instead for her own private chamber pot. As long as she emptied it and cleaned it herself, Troy didn't give a hot damn.

They turned on Main Street and traveled toward the city square. They both noticed faded flyers in store windows and on telephone poles depicting the missing Wendy Wilson's image, but neither spoke of what they saw. They, like the town, had filed the tragedy away in their minds' recesses, and concentrated on the present.

They circled around the Court House square, and then headed down Depot Street past the Princess Theater. "You ever seen a movie, girl?" He asked as they passed the theater.

"Nah, Daddy won't let us go to anything like that," she said calmly. She took another drink of her 7 Up and replaced it firmly between her knees.

"Seems like your daddy don't let you do a lot of stuff," he commented.

"Yeah, he believes we'll go to hell if we wear makeup or shorts or anything normal like that. I don't know why he thinks that, but he sure believes it," Dixie stated matter of factly.

"Well, I hear you might be comin' to stay with us some this summer. Is that right?" Troy wanted to know.

"Yeah, I would like to visit some. I already asked Mama but she said she'd have to talk to Daddy about it. So I guess I don't really know if I'll get to or not." Dixie shrugged as if she expected her Daddy to quash her plans before they could be implemented.

"Well, if you do get to come, we can go ridin' around every afternoon when I get off work and maybe even go to a movie now and then, if you don't tell your mama or daddy." Troy liked to push the limits. He also liked to be the good guy. He was trying to earn Dixie's loyalty.

"Wow, Uncle Troy, you'd do that for me?" Dixie asked as if doing those simple things could make the difference in her eternal happiness or sadness.

"We can do all kinds of things," he laughed as he was thinking of the many things he could teach this sweet young girl. "All kinds of things," he repeated to himself.

He turned left at the National Guard Armory onto Thompson Street and then found his way back to Elm. Dixie rode in silence, contemplating the potential excitement she might get to experience if only her Daddy would let her have summer visits with the Tuckers.

He turned off Elm and made his way down a side street, then turned on Union Street and pulled up in front of the house. Miss Ruth was standing on the porch as if she had been watching for Dixie's arrival. Nervously, she walked down the sidewalk toward the car to help Dixie out of the vehicle.

"Howdy, Miss Ruth. I ran into Dixie as she was walking home, and we decided to take a little ride 'cause this was her last day of school. I hope you didn't get worried or nothin' 'cause we didn't go far enough to be too late," Troy thought the woman looked mad, and he was trying to make his unscheduled trip with Dixie sound like a little deal, not a big one.

"Mr. Tucker, we do have a telephone in this house. It would have been nice if you had called to tell me you had Dixie with you. She's almost fifteen minutes later than usual, and I was getting very worried about her." Miss Ruth was trying to hide her anxiety and her mounting anger.

"Don't worry, Miss Ruth. This was the last day of school and it won't be happenin' again. I just thought she might like a little treat to make it a special day." He paused. The silence between them was deafening.

"Well, bye Dixie. I'll be seein' you some this summer. Tell your mama and daddy 'hi' for me. See ya, Miss Ruth." Troy got in his turquoise and white Chevy and drove off without a response from the irritated Nanny.

Dixie skipped into the house and spied Dollie sitting in the floor with her doll, Susie. Dixie continued skipping past her sister and intentionally kicked the doll across the floor. Dollie looked up with an unhappy expression, and Dixie simply said, "I'm sorry. That was an accident."

Dixie continued skipping into the kitchen to find a snack, but overheard Dollie tattling to Miss Ruth: "Dixie is mean. She kicked my doll. She needs to go get a switch for when Daddy gets home."

Realizing that Dixie probably did it, but also trying to keep peace between the girls and their parents, Miss Ruth said, "I'm sure it was an accident, Dollie. Why don't you come up here and sit in my lap, and we'll watch some television. Bring your Susie and we'll all watch together. How would that be, darling?"

Eavesdropping from the kitchen, Dixie thought she was going to puke.

* * * * *

The next day after overhearing Dollie tell Miss Ruth that her mean sister needed a spanking, Dixie decided to shut Dollie up once and for all.

Miss Ruth was in the kitchen and Mama was sleeping in the back bedroom when Dixie saw Dollie go into the front bedroom with her doll. Quietly, Dixie tiptoed in behind Dollie who was busy trying to take the shoes off of Susie. As Dixie silently closed the door, she leaned back stiffly against the door frame and quietly engaged the lock. She opened her eyes wide and made her best demonic face, waiting for Dollie to notice her.

Dollie turned around and was startled when she saw her sister there, who was apparently overtaken by some evil spirit, or so it appeared. Dollie's face was beginning to morph into the shape of a screaming victim when Dixie approached her slowly—still holding the same horrific facial expression. Dixie placed her hand over Dollie's mouth and said in a very low and deep voice:

"Shut up little girl....

    "I am not your sister ....

        "I am the devil ....

            "You will be nice to your sister or I will get you ....

                "You will tell NO ONE about this ....."

Wide-eyed and stricken with fear, a shrieking Dollie managed to move out from under the Dixie monster's hand and darted around her toward the door. It wouldn't open, no matter how hard she pulled at it. Dollie started to pee in her panties while she struggled and cried. Dixie smiled and moved behind the terrified girl to unlock the door.

Dollie yanked on the doorknob so many times, it made a commotion. They could hear Miss Ruth's fast footsteps moving toward the front of the house. When the door finally opened, Dollie ran straight to Miss Ruth, who by then was only a few feet away.

"Goodness sakes, child. What's wrong with you?" Miss Ruth inquired.

Before answering, Dollie looked straight at Dixie, who widened her eyes momentarily while Miss Ruth was looking at Dollie's tear-streaked face.

"Nn-n-nothin's wrong, I just peed my pants," was all Dollie could stutter.

Dixie looked at Miss Ruth then and shrugged her shoulders in an "I don't know" response.

"Well, let's get you cleaned up before your mama wakes up and finds you in this mess. Child, you don't have to cry about wetting your panties. It happens sometimes. It's okay." Miss Ruth's voice trailed off into inaudible sounds as she left the front part of the house, taking Dollie for a quick bath and change of clothes.

Dixie closed the door once again, this time trying not to laugh so hard that she would pee her own pants. That would definitely be hard to explain.

"I got that little brat real good this time," she whispered to herself. "Bet that's the end of her messing with me. I'm the big sister, and I AM IN CONTROL!"

Dixie giggled and thought this might be the best summer yet.

* * * * * *

Except it wasn't the best summer for everyone in Shelbyville. On Saturday, June 9, 1956 another young girl disappeared without a trace, and the unsolved disappearance case of Wendy Wilson was sure to be resurrected from its unofficial cold case status.

CHAPTER 12

Summer 1956

As the afternoon of June 9th faded into early evening, Sarah Beth Keller was getting ready to leave her house on Baker Street for her scheduled Saturday night babysitting job with Mr. and Mrs. Holloway. For three and a half hours, she would be in charge of two very obedient preschool children who were never any trouble and always went to bed promptly at 9:00 pm. Considering anything in the refrigerator was fair game, this was one of the very best babysitting gigs a teenager could get.

The Holloways' duplex home was located two streets over on West End Circle, but Sarah's parents always drove her there a few minutes before the preset 7:30 p.m. summer arrival time. Mr. Holloway would later drop Sarah off at her home when he and his wife returned from the American Legion dance around 11:00 pm. Last fall's disappearance of Wendy Wilson made most parents paranoid about tracking their children's whereabouts, so it had become standard procedure to avoid having a child walk anywhere alone if an alternative was available.

Sarah Beth was a very responsible fifteen-year old, and would be returning to Central High School as a sophomore in the fall. She had a boyfriend named Ryan Farrar, and she was popular with all of her classmates. Sarah Beth never skipped classes and always had her homework done on time. She enjoyed music and singing, and attended church with her parents at the neighborhood Pentecostal church on West Lane Street.

To the Kellers, Sarah Beth was a model daughter. To everyone else, she was the epitome of the sweet girl next door.

* * * * * *

Sarah Beth tried to clasp together her engraved identification bracelet, but she was struggling to get the chain to reach. "Mom, I can't get this bracelet hooked. Would you help me with it, please?

Mrs. Keller entered her daughter's bedroom and noticed how much Sarah Beth now looked more like a young lady than a little girl. "Honey, you are going to have to stop growing up so fast. You look like a young Grace Kelley with your hair pulled back like that!" Mrs. Keller took the bracelet ends and quickly clasped it in place on Sarah Beth's slender left wrist

"There. Now let me look at you," Mrs. Keller commanded. She moved a few steps back from her daughter who was wearing a navy and white striped blouse with solid white pedal pushers. "Oh, Sarah, I'm going to have to have a talk with that Farrar boy. He doesn't know what a prize he has with you as his girlfriend," Mrs. Keller said as she moved forward again to embrace her daughter. Sarah Beth blushed, patted her Mom's back, and her Mother released her hug.

"Come on, Sarah Beth, we're going to be late for the Holloway's and we don't want them to miss their regular Saturday night date," declared Mrs. Keller.

They drove the short distance in less than five minutes. When her mother pulled up in front of the Holloway home, Sarah Beth opened the car door but turned toward her mother before exiting the car.

"Mom, thank you for everything. I love you and Dad, and I hope I'll always make you proud." Sarah Beth blurted out on the spur-of-the moment.

"We love you, too, darlin'. Now get in there before you make the Holloways miss the first dance." She blew her smiling daughter a kiss as she shut the car door. Sarah Beth smiled broadly and blew a kiss back.

* * * * * *

When Jason and Marie Holloway turned into West End Circle, they were harmonizing along with the music on the car radio. Marie laughed at her husband for completely messing up the lyrics to "Be-Bop-A-Lula," a popular rockabilly song by Gene Vincent. Both smiled and giggled, feeling like teenagers again after an evening of listening to a live local band and dancing on the polished wood floor at the American Legion. Jason pulled the car into the right side driveway of their duplex (the first one on the right) and leaned over to kiss his wife. As Marie leaned toward Jason to meet her husband's lips, something unusual caught her eye and she leaned back abruptly.

"Wait, Jason. The side door is half open. Sarah Beth knows better than that. We better go inside right now," a concerned Marie stated. They both jumped out of the car and approached the door calling Sarah Beth's name.

Hearing no answer, they eased open the door and entered their kitchen, and found nothing out of the ordinary in the small room. Glancing toward the open area living room, they saw a bowl of popcorn and an opened Coca-Cola bottle on their coffee table. Sarah Beth's small beaded purse was lying on the couch. The television was turned off, but the lamp perched on top of it was shining brightly. Everything looked normal.

Proceeding down the short hallway, they passed the open-doored but empty bathroom. The two puzzled parents entered the children's room to find their children fast asleep. The Mickey Mouse nightlight was softly glowing from the wall outlet, and the little ones were snoring lightly.

Jason opened the master bedroom door and flipped on the lights. There was no one inside and the room didn't appear to have been entered since they closed the door upon departing that evening.

A perplexed Jason took a flashlight from the kitchen drawer. He told Marie he was going to look around outside the house for Sarah Beth, and Marie suggested he also check with their adjoining duplex neighbor in case she was there for some unknown reason.

Once outside, Jason repeatedly called Sarah Beth's name, getting louder each time he shouted. He checked the back yard, the side yard, and then approached his duplex neighbor's door. He rang the doorbell multiple times before a light came on and an elderly woman answered the door in her housecoat.

"Miss Sophie, I'm sorry to disturb you but our babysitter, Sarah Beth Keller, wasn't in our house when we came home. Our kids are asleep, they're all right, but we can't find Sarah Beth. I was really hoping maybe she was here with you," Jason said as his hands began to visibly tremble.

"No, I haven't seen her since about 8:00 pm when she was outside playing ball with your kids," a bewildered Sophie answered.

"Did you hear anything going on in our side of the house? You have any idea where she might be?" Jason sounded upset.

"Why, no. I went to bed soon after I saw them playing, and haven't been up until now. I wish I could help you, but I don't know where the girl might be," Sophie remarked.

Jason wasn't sure what was happening. His anxious thoughts were now feeding him hypothetical scenarios about what could have happened to Sarah Beth. He recalled Wendy Wilson's face smiling from a weathered flyer on a utility pole he and Marie passed on their way to the dance. Jason shuddered and prayed there was some other explanation for an unaccounted for teen.

* * * * * *

He had to let Marie know that he hadn't located Sarah Beth, and the girl wasn't with Sophie. Perhaps Marie had already located her. If not, she would know what to do next.

He trotted back to his own kitchen door and saw Marie standing in the living room with the telephone at her ear. He heard Marie respond, "No, Jane. She wasn't inside when we came home and the side door was wide open. We were hoping you came to get her early and she accidentally left the door like that. But … but … I know that doesn't make any sense, though. She would never leave the kids without someone here to take over," Marie's eyes were getting wider, and tears were beginning to roll down her cheek.

Marie listened intently and agreed with something Jane Keller was saying on the other end of the phone. When she hung up, she stared at Jason with a befuddled expression. "Sarah Beth isn't with her mother. Jane was expecting us to drop her off as usual, and she'd been waiting up for Sarah Beth. Jane's on her way here to help us look." As an afterthought, Marie asked Jason, "I guess you didn't find her out in the yard?"

"No, and Sophie hadn't seen her since 8:00 p.m. either. Oh God! What should we do? It's like the girl just vanished! Oh Jesus, help us!" Jason fretfully commented as he paced up and down the short hallway.

* * * * * *

In less than five minutes, a visibly upset Jane Keller pulled up in front of the Holloway's duplex, the very place where she had happily departed only a few hours before. This time she had her husband, Bradley, in tow. The worried parents jumped out of the car and sprinted to the Holloway's side entrance. The minute Marie opened the door, Jane fell into her arms sobbing loudly.

* * * * * *

The past eight hours had been a nightmare for both Detective Brian Martin and his partner, Harry Woodson. The two men, plus teams of other officers, had been on overtime duty since they converged on the Holloway's home shortly after midnight.

Neither detective had slept in the past 24 hours. Throughout the wee morning hours, each had struggled to stay focused and alert with strong black coffee and gum.

They had returned to their offices at 3:30 a.m. on the morning of June 10th, a day predicted for sunny skies and mild temperatures in the middle Tennessee area.

They sat at their respective desks clad in wrinkled suits, the same outfits they had been wearing when they arrived on the scene of the Keller girl's disappearance.

Detective Martin flipped page after page of the initial report taken by the responding officer, Jeff Cooper, who regularly patrolled that section of Shelbyville's west area. Officer Cooper had briefed the two detectives when they arrived, but the official report contained a plethora of details about the missing girl, her habits, her friends, family and more.

Detective Woodson was reviewing the Wendy Wilson file trying to find similarities between the two cases. So far, the only thing he recognized the girls had in common was that they both attended Central High School. Both girls were well-liked, outgoing, but at different grade levels with different cliques of friends. They lived miles apart. There were more things that differed about the girls than were alike.

Chief of Police Arnold Taylor had been briefed by phone after the initial call came in to dispatch. He appeared on the scene shortly after Martin and Woodson arrived, but stayed less than an hour, turning over the lead to the detectives. He asked to be briefed again at 9:00 a.m. in his office. The Detectives still had about an hour before the Chief would be grilling them about their progress. Each silently dreaded the meeting, knowing that what they had to say would not be what the Chief wanted to hear.

* * * * * *

When the Chief's black sedan pulled up outside their offices, both detectives left their desks to gather the newly opened file, additional notes and their writing pads. They stood solemnly as the door opened and the Chief hastily walked in, his own coffee cup in hand.

"My office. Now." was the greeting barked by Chief Taylor. The detectives followed the Chief into a corner office with awards and certificates decorating the plastered walls. A few golfing trophies adorned a bookcase, but the rest of the office was furnished with old, worn furniture that was probably older than the Chief himself.

Each detective took a seat in the green vinyl padded chairs facing the Chief's desk. Expecting the Chief to start the meeting with comments or questions, they organized their papers while they waited.

"Well, are you gonna tell me what's going on, or are we here to have coffee and talk about golf? DAMMIT, speak up. I don't have all day!" The Chief wasn't happy about a mandatory Sunday morning meeting, and he certainly wasn't pleased that his city was losing its peaceful reputation.

Detective Martin cleared his throat and began, "Chief Taylor, there was immediate questioning of the girl's parents at the scene. Also, the people who hired the girl to babysit gave a full accounting of what they did when they realized the girl was not in the house.

"Reports were completed by the parents at their residence, and the girl's room was searched for anything that could provide a clue of where she might have gone.

"There was a neighborhood canvass last evening on West End Circle and surrounding areas, where the alleged abduction occurred. No one saw anything or anyone suspicious. There were ground searches that have continued throughout the night. We have a list of other individuals to question, and we'll be starting that today.

"There were no signs of forced entry, but the door was left open with two preschoolers asleep inside. That, in itself, is not the kind of behavior that the missing girl would exhibit under normal circumstances. We believe the sixteen year old is at risk, and we are comparing this case with the Wilson one. If we have a serial kidnapper on our hands, we might have to call in additional help from other agencies." Detective Martin recited to a visibly flustered Chief.

Detective Woodson added his input, "So far, this case is similar to the Wilson case only because both girls vanished without any witnesses. Both girls were well liked and attended Central High School. But, that's all the similarities we've found."

The Chief looked at the files and notes that were passed to him when the detectives sat down in front of him. He said nothing for a long time, studying the information before him. "I'll call in the State Police to help. We'll try to get information out to the public to be on the lookout for the girl, some flyers too. Carry on with your good work, officers. I want another briefing here at 6 p.m. or before if anything changes," a weary Chief Taylor said to the only two officers who had any experience in missing persons cases.

Unfortunately, their experience was gained through their investigation of the Wilson girl's disappearance. There had been no such cases in Shelbyville that he knew of, and definitely not since he'd been running the police department.

If there were future abductions, the Chief would be forced to establish a specialized department just to handle missing persons. He realized that the world was getting crazier every day, but he never thought his calm city would join in.

* * * * * *

The two treasured souvenirs rattled when the kidnapper dropped them into the empty cotton drawstring tobacco pouch.

The charm bracelet from the first girl was fascinating. The wide linked silver chain had a total of three dangling charms that signified the girl liked cheerleading. The tiny megaphone didn't look realistic, because one had to inspect it closely for detail. However, there was a delightful flat silver disc with "**SCHS**" engraved on one side and "*W°W°*" engraved on the other. The final charm was supposed to look like a cheerleading girl in a jumping position, outstretched arms skirt flared, but it was so small it had no great definition. The bracelet was a nice souvenir, anyway.

The other bracelet was obviously a little more expensive, but it was very plain. It was just a thin rectangular piece with a name engraved on it. "Sarah Beth Keller." That was it. The chain was nothing special, either. There was absolutely nothing elaborate about that trinket, except it probably was real gold. Otherwise, it was just an easy trinket to collect.

There really was no good hiding place for these treasures, so a temporary spot under the sink would have to do—far enough back and perhaps disguised in some unique way so as not to attract attention from snoopers. Yes, that would have to do for now.

CHAPTER 13

1956

As the two city detectives plodded through all the "kidnapper" paperwork and files now piling up on their desks, Harry Woodson made a comment that got Brian Martin's attention.

"Brian, I just realized something. There may be one more thing that the Wilson and Keller girls have in common." Woodson waited for Martin to stop flipping pages and look up at him.

"Did you hear me, Brian? I said –"

"Yes, I heard you Harry," Martin interrupted his partner as he stared at Woodson. "I expected you to say what you were going on about. I'm all ears ."

"Well, it's just this…and I don't know why I didn't think of it before. It's Carl Brown. Yes, they're both students and would know Carl Brown. Plus Carl was the last one to see Wendy before she disappeared."

Martin shook his head. "Every kid in that school probably knows Carl Brown. What does he have to do with Sarah Beth Keller?"

Woodson smiled, "He just happens to live on Central Avenue, which is the street right in between Baker and West End Circle. That's a real coincidence, isn't it, Brian?" Woodson started to smirk.

"And how long ago did you figure this out, Einstein?" Martin sneered at his partner.

"I was going over case similarities once more, and read the interviews again. It made me think that maybe Carl knew Sarah Beth as well as he did Wendy. But when I looked into Carl's demographics and his school personnel file, his address just popped out at me. It was right there all along.

"And you'll never guess what else I found. This guy has a record: DUI and resisting arrest, with 30 days served in the county jail. Think we should go pay old Carl Brown a visit?" Woodson was already looking for his jacket.

"Yes, that's a great idea. But this time, let's try to catch him at home. See what kind of environment he lives in. See if maybe his home life makes him need a little diversion or some excitement, you know?" Martin suggested.

"OK, how's this for an alternative? Let's drive out Madison Street to the Honeyland Drive-In, next to the Oldsmobile dealership. They have the best cheeseburgers in town and their milkshakes always put me in a good mood. What'd you say to a nice break—a late lunch—then you can belittle me all you want for the rest of the day." Woodson made Martin smile as he reached for his jacket, too.

Talking to Carl Brown could wait an hour. Questioning Carl at his home might allow them to talk to Mrs. Brown, too. The delay could prove worthwhile if it meant speaking to additional persons and once again surveying the surrounding areas of the recent crime scene.

The detectives left their office for the much needed break and a chance to fill their empty stomachs. For the moment, both the old Wilson case and the new Keller case were on an hour's hold, and the Chief could like it or not.

* * * * * *

Carl Brown had been in the kitchen washing the lunch dishes and running after his 4 ½ year old son, the miracle baby Stevie. Dora was sleeping, the last part of her daily routine on scheduled workdays. She would have to be up by no later than 10:00 p.m. to get ready and be at her work station by the start of her 11:00 p.m. shift. The Rubber Mill didn't care what their employees looked like when they got to work, they just expected them to be there punctually. Dora didn't care how she looked, either. Often she didn't bathe or wash her hair before leaving for work. She wasn't trying to impress anyone, not even her husband. Carl feared that Dora might be slowly slipping back into a bout of depression.

* * * * * *

During the summer months, Carl had no job or paycheck with the Bedford County School System. If he were called in to help with a maintenance emergency, he would be paid. But Carl couldn't remember ever having been called in for an emergency during summer break. His nine month steady job with the schools provided a comfortable income during the school year, but the summer breaks prompted Carl to find other ways to supplement his family income.

Carl often bought discarded whiskey barrels from the Jack Daniels Distillery in Lynchburg, and fashioned decorative yard planters out of them. He sold them around town for $10 each, a good price for 1956. That income, plus the steady wages Dora earned at her Rubber Mill job, kept the family going through the otherwise lean summer months.

He was thinking about obtaining used large tractor tires and painting them bright colors. Many people wanted instant flower beds, and he believed this idea would serve the purpose. He figured he could make an extra hundred dollars or more with the tractor tire project if he kept his mind right. Any extra income helped during these difficult post-war times.

* * * * * *

After stuffing themselves with the calorie-loaded delights served by the Honeyland Drive-In, the detectives drove silently toward the west side of Shelbyville to Carl Brown's neighborhood. With bellies full and weary from lack of sleep, both suddenly felt like napping after their carbohydrate overloads.

The unmarked police car traveled down West Lane Street and made the left turn onto Baker Street, stopping in front of a rock house with whiskey barrel planters by the front steps. The front curtains moved as if someone had been peeking out the window to observe the strangers' approach.

As they stepped onto the wooden front porch, a young pre-school boy greeted them from inside the screen door.

"Who are you? Are you from the church? We don't go to church. We stay home so Mama can sleep," said Stevie.

Carl appeared behind the boy, and immediately told Stevie to get out of the doorway and go play with his toys. When the boy left the living room, Carl spoke to the detectives through the screen in the door.

"What's this about? I already told you everything I know about that missing girl. Why are you bothering me again?" The detectives were not invited to enter the house, and awkwardly stood on the porch.

"Carl, do you know Sarah Beth Keller?" Detective Martin asked.

"Everybody around here knows that girl. She babysits for some people, and she's helped us out before with Stevie. Somethin' happen to her, too?" Now Carl was curious. He hadn't heard anything about the weekend events.

"Carl, would you step outside to discuss this privately on the porch?" Detective Woodson asked.

"No, I don't think so. My wife's asleep and Stevie don't take real kindly to strangers. He gets upset real easy," Carl looked over his shoulder to make sure Stevie was still in the adjoining room playing with his cars.

"Your boy seemed just fine when we came up on the porch, Carl. Are you sure you won't come out for just a minute?" Detective Martin asked.

"Yeah, well it's Sunday and he knows it's church day for most of the neighbors. He probably thought you were sent by the preacher to get us to start going regular. If he thought you were police telling some scary story, it'd make him have bad dreams and such. I don't want to get the boy worked up." Carl protectively stated.

The detectives gave each other a questioning glance, and Woodson continued his probe. "Now Carl. We can do this one of two ways. You can talk to us here on the porch or downtown at the station. But if you come downtown, we'll have to make it a more official interview. You pick."

Carl considered his choices. He suddenly became belligerent. "You assholes are pestering me. I don't know nothin', I told you already. I don't even know what this is about. I'm trying to keep my boy from getting upset and y'all don't even care that he's prone to goin' into fits. My wife's tryin' to sleep for her night shift job, and you wanna bother us at my house and upset everything to Hell. You ain't getting on my property again without a proper warrant; don't think I don't know my rights. You can just get back in your fancy car and get the Hell out of here. I ain't telling you twice, neither." Carl's threatening demeanor made both the detectives suspicious.

"I'll tell you what, Carl. We *will* be talking to you under OUR terms. You got it, big man?" Detective Martin relayed, as the two officers turned and made their way to their car. As he opened the car door, Detective Martin turned back toward Carl and curtly said, "Don't leave town, Carl."

At that point Carl responded, "Go to hell," and slammed the wooden front door so hard the window panes rattled.

* * * * * *

"What the hell was that?" a perplexed Detective Woodson stated as they traveled back to their office.

"I don't have any idea, but Carl sure was defensive, wouldn't you say?" Detective Martin reflected. "Should we really try to get a warrant and check out his property?"

"What for? We don't have any probable cause. Now we've just pissed him off and he won't ever be cooperative." Detective Woodson wasn't looking forward to confronting Carl again. The man seemed to have one too many screws loose.

Brian Martin agreed with his partner; yet, he thought most of what Carl was saying was true. The Brown child seemed to act younger than his real age, and maybe his father was trying to shield him from some kind of health episode. Brian Martin had no children of his own by whom to judge, so he tried to give Carl the benefit of the doubt on the child's expected reaction. He also knew

Mrs. Brown worked the third shift at the Rubber Mill, but didn't think she'd have to work Sunday nights. That was a surprise.

Maybe they should give Carl a break, especially since the two showed up unannounced at his residence, and they weren't exactly nice to him.

Still, Carl never asked what had happened to Sarah Beth--at least he didn't ask for details. That single aspect of the conversation seemed to nag at Detective Martin. Wouldn't he want to know the story behind the inquiry, or did he already know what happened because he was there? Detective Martin mentally filed away his concern, and tried to concentrate on what he and Woodson would report to the Chief when they briefed him in three hours.

* * * * * *

A few minutes after the detectives left her front porch, a sleepy Dora stumbled out of the master bedroom making her way to the bathroom. She had heard loud conversations somewhere outside, and the disturbance jolted her awake enough to realize that she wouldn't be able to go back to sleep until she relieved her bladder. She managed to do just that within two minutes, then exited the bathroom still groggy from being awakened.

She saw Carl kneeling on the living room floor hugging Stevie. They weren't talking to each other, so Dora stepped in the room to see what was going on. Her bare feet made no sound on the linoleum floor.

Stevie noticed his mother first. "Mama, there were bad men here and Daddy ran them off," a proud Stevie told his mother.

Dora looked questioningly at Carl, who clarified, "No, there must have been something goin' on around here and two cops came by to see if everything was okay. That's all it was. Go on back to bed, Dora."

Not quite understanding why Carl was comforting Stevie for something like that, Dora turned and obediently went back to the bed. She dismissed the interruption as "probably nothing" and immediately fell back into deep slumber.

Meanwhile, the doting Carl left Stevie playing alone with toy cars and trucks on the living room rug.

With nothing else to do that day, Carl decided to reorganize and relocate his toolbox which was currently stored underneath the kitchen sink.

CHAPTER 14

1956 - 1957

The small town of Shelbyville, nationally known as "The Pencil City" and "The Walking Horse Capital of the World," was now being called something much more sinister: "Kidnapper's Paradise."

The Chief of Police, Arnold Taylor, was battling the townsfolk and the news reporters to stay as popular and positive as he could under the dire circumstances. He wanted calm in the city again, but by now tempers were flaring and parents were terrified. No one felt safe anymore.

Chief Taylor was receiving bad publicity and was generally referred to as "That Do-Nothing Police Chief." He foresaw his career ending on a low note without the promised gold watch. Instead, he expected to be tarred and feathered if something didn't break soon in the active kidnapping cases.

The unsolved Wendy Wilson case was spotlighted once again, and more and more pressure was being placed on law enforcement officials, regardless of rank or standing. Even school crossing guards were occasionally verbally accosted about not paying close enough attention to the city's innocent children.

The citizens desperately wanted someone to blame for all the recent disappearances. Without a suspect in custody to vilify, the next target for blame went directly to the very people trying to find the perpetrator.

* * * * * *

Corb and LorAnn Carter were two of those city citizens who became paranoid about their children's whereabouts. With the new school year beginning in a few weeks, LorAnn was concerned about the ongoing safety of her daughters. This was Dollie's first year at Tate Primary, situated across the street from the elementary school where Dixie attended.

Miss Ruth had offered to transport both children to and from school, and the Carter parents agreed that this solution had worked well in the past with Dixie. Actually, Miss Ruth had insisted on assuming this responsibility, which in her mind justified the necessity of her continued employment with the Carter household.

* * * * * *

In September of 1956, the school doors opened to welcome a new year for the city and county students. Principal Phillips kicked off the '56-'57 school year with special assemblies reminding all students of their scholarly responsibilities, school policies, and of the importance of being aware of their surroundings at all times.

Posters of both recently missing girls were prominent on bulletin boards throughout the high school hallways. A remembrance wall board was created for exhibition in the main lobby, which displayed both girls' pictures and was embellished with personal tributes written by the staff and saddened students. Even though hope remained in the hearts of everyone, most of the written messages referred to the missing girls in past tense, as if their dead bodies had already been discovered.

Dixie had heard about the disappearances, but her eleven year old mind didn't quite grasp the significance of what had happened. She had spent most of her summer with Aunt Roz and Uncle Troy, shielded from bad news and concerns for personal safety. She had experienced the best summer ever in her short years of life. She even preferred staying at the Tuckers' house even better than staying and playing at Granny's and Pap's store.

While at the Tuckers', however, she did feel uncomfortable about having to sleep with Aunt Roz and Uncle Troy. Their second bedroom was occupied by Ma Rose, so there was nowhere else for Dixie to sleep. The couch was not an option, since Dixie had a fear of sleeping alone in the dark. She didn't want to chance having a night terror and then embarrassing herself by crying and waking everybody up. She chose to sleep with her Aunt and Uncle.

She didn't mind being crowded in the bed, but she felt a little strange when Uncle Troy would drape his arm over her and hold onto her slender leg as he drifted off to sleep. Sometimes his hand would slide down toward her abdomen, and she would have to gently push it away. Almost always he subconsciously moved it back to her hip or leg, and eventually she would succumb to sleep under the heavy weight of his arm.

Uncle Troy always let her nap during the day when he was around, though. Sometimes he would let her sleep on the cot he had in his private shed behind the garage. He would tell her that he'd protect her, and she could lie there as long as she wanted without anyone bothering her. He was happy to just watch her sleep. He usually had something to read, anyway.

When she woke up, she always felt refreshed and Uncle Troy would take her to get their afternoon ice cream treat. Dixie was happy being the sole object of Uncle Troy's attention, and she loved that he seemed to like having her with him so much. She thought they were becoming very close—she might even be his favorite niece--and she didn't mind that a bit.

* * * * * *

By Christmas break, the fickle town grew less focused on the unsolved disappearances, and the upcoming holidays became the town's new center of attention. However, this was not the case for Detectives Martin and Woodson, or anyone who had been working feverishly to solve the kidnappings. The officers, especially the two detectives, became more frustrated with every passing day as case leads became nonexistent and hope faded for finding the girls alive. The "state boys" had left months ago, throwing up their hands and abandoning the city police to solve their problems alone. Still, the local police force members persevered, and fretted over every possible scenario that could lead to a break in the mysteries.

* * * * * *

When spring finally arrived in the early months of 1957, the township once again turned its attention toward re-growth and renewal. However, this year ushered in a new revitalization project in Shelbyville. The Big Springs Urban Renewal Project was officially kicked off during the latter part of 1956, and was now fast becoming a visible reality to the townspeople.

The "Urban Renewal" initiative planned to buy over 52 residential acres in the Big Springs area of the central city. Coincidentally, Corb's and LorAnn's Union Street house was right in the middle of the proposal area. In March of 1957 the Carters and their neighbors were approached by representatives of the Housing Authority to sell their property to the city in support of the $8 Million project. By the time the initiative would end, over 200 families would be relocated.

Corb wanted to move away from the city limits in an effort to shield his family from city crimes. Recent events provided him with enough justification to consider purchasing a piece of property a few miles out of the city. LorAnn agreed, but recalled the problems they would face in getting the children back and forth to school. They studied alternatives and eventually came to agreement that a rural area could work for them.

"Corb, we gotta move. But I don't want to move too far away from everything. I want to be able to go to the store to buy groceries when we need 'em, and not have to wait till the weekend to go into town for supplies. It's got to be close but not too close, if you know what I mean."

Corb knew exactly what LorAnn was trying to say. He promised LorAnn he'd be checking out potential residences that were close enough to town to accommodate their lifestyle. She approved.

* * * * *

April Fools' Day fell on a Monday in 1957. The students in Miss Jones' freshman English class laughed hysterically at how the conservative teacher crazily reacted to a fake spider hanging in the classroom's doorway. Instead of scolding the giggling group, she picked up a bucket of "water" and doused confetti over the heads of the surprised group. For the next few minutes, a boisterous Miss Jones had everyone scampering around under their desks gathering the small pieces of paper from the floor to be reused on her next unsuspecting class. Seems Miss Jones had been the owner of the fake spider, and the joke was on her students.

That was only one part of the day that Peggy Sue Overcast had enjoyed. She had tricked her friend, Nancy Weaver, by slipping into her purse a fake note which was supposedly written by the boy of her dreams, Joe Claxton. When Nancy discovered the love letter, her face turned bright red with excitement. Peggy Sue had to calm her down and admit that the note was her own April Fools' joke, even if it was in bad taste. They both laughed it off, but Nancy wasn't nearly as amused as Peggy Sue.

That evening, she would be studying with Nancy and she planned to make the prank up to her. Peggy Sue's mom was making homemade brownies, and she was going to take some to Nancy as a peace offering when she visited later.

* * * * * *

Gripping a book satchel and a small brown bag filled with warm brownies, Peggy Sue left her Shelbyville Mills Village rental home to cut across a few of the neighbors' backyards. Three houses down, she would cross into her friend's backyard and meet Nancy on the rear porch of the Weavers' duplex.

"Aren't you scared roaming around in people's backyards? Aren't you afraid they'll shoot you or something?" Nancy asked her friend.

"Are you kidding? With all the nosy neighbors around here, there'd be too many witnesses. Besides, I think all the neighbors like me." Peggy Sue was a very friendly person, and the neighbors knew her well. She didn't think anyone would harm her, accidentally or otherwise.

For the next two hours, the two girls proceeded to eat brownies, drink milk, share gossip, and study just enough to keep from blatantly lying about the reason for their evening social visit.

* * * * * *

When Peggy Sue wasn't home at 9:15 p.m., her mother decided to walk over to the Weavers' house and drag the absent-minded girl home. It was close to Peggy Sue's bedtime, and Mrs. Overcast had been lenient enough with her that day. In fact, she was aware that the so-called study session was just a ruse for the two girls to talk about boys and schoolmates. She didn't mind as long as Peggy Sue obeyed the curfew and made it home and in bed by 9:30 p.m. She sighed as she moved toward the Weavers' residence, wishing Peggy Sue had paid more attention to the time.

When Mrs. Overcast approached the Weavers' back door, she saw no lights on in either side of the duplex. Alarmed, she rushed to the back door and started loudly beating on the paned glass.

In less than a minute, a sleepy Herb Weaver opened the door, followed closely by his wife Alice. They both appeared to have been roused from bed, with Herb in light blue pajamas and Alice wrapped in a thin pink housecoat with her head wrapped in a scarf to cover the hair rollers underneath.

"What's wrong Lisa? What's the matter?" Herb Weaver squinted toward the upset woman.

"Please tell me Peggy Sue is still here. Please… please say she is," Mrs. Overcast slowly crumpled to the wooden porch floor and began to sob hysterically as the Weaver couple stared down at her in shock. At that precise moment, all three feared the dreaded kidnapper had struck again.

* * * * * *

By 10:00 p.m. the Village community was brightly lit by red flashing police lights, and every porch light in the small neighborhood was shining brightly. Sidewalks were lined with people trying to catch a glimpse of what must be yet another crime scene. Yellow police tape cordoned off the Weavers' back yard, and it appeared the barrier might be extended through other neighbors' properties, as well. Tense-looking police officers were milling about, talking to anyone who was in their line of vision. Other policemen were scanning ground areas with flashlights, looking for something that only they knew to be valuable.

Mr. and Mrs. Seth Overcast were sitting on the top step of the Weavers' porch, each appearing as if they were in some kind of stupor. Detectives Martin and Woodson approached and stood nearby. They were met by Patrolman Jeff Cooper, the same policeman who had briefed the two at the Keller abduction scene ten months earlier.

The efficient patrolman provided quick and precise information. "Sirs, we have initiated the same investigative protocols that were used in the prior disappearance of the Keller girl. We have everyone available on the scene, and more men will be available to provide relief in no less than six hours.

"The missing girl is Peggy Sue Overcast, 13 years old, last seen wearing a white blouse, a blue plaid skirt, and carrying a dark blue book satchel with a pink rabbit's foot attached to the zipper. She departed the Weavers' home through the rear entrance at approximately 8:50 p.m., according to Mrs. Weaver. She was supposedly going straight home, some 100 yards or less away. However, the missing girl's mother, Lisa Marie Overcast, appeared at the Weavers' home at approximately 9:30 p.m. looking for her daughter who had not yet arrived home. Approximately ten minutes later at 9:41 p.m., Mr. Weaver made the initial call to police dispatch, and we arrived on the scene at 9:56 p.m. We are about to interview both sets of parents, and an official report will be forthcoming."

"Thank you, Officer Cooper. Please carry on," said Detective Martin. He had to call the beleaguered Chief, who had recently been contemplating early retirement.

******

What an extraordinary pink rabbit's foot, the kidnapper thought. It was soft and warm, just like little Peggy Sue. The kidnapper believed this was the best souvenir that had been collected so far. Its bulk caused the tobacco pouch to bulge, which made the thin cotton bag appear half filled with goodies. Too bad the good luck charm didn't work for the whimpering girl. Maybe if the fur had been its natural shade instead of dyed such a girlie color, it would have retained its power. *Too bad*, the kidnapper thought. *That was just too bad.*

CHAPTER 15

1957

Everyone in town had a theory, but no answers for the disappearances of three young girls within a nineteen month period. Many tried to blame the parents for not having enough oversight of their children. Others blamed the school for having lax accountability procedures for students on school grounds. Most blamed the children for not being careful or for being prone to "run away" from home. Everyone blamed the police department for a plethora of reasons. No one knew the real truth behind any of the vanishings, but everybody thought they could figure it out better than those charged with that responsibility.

Chief of Police Arnold Taylor had suffered a heart attack the day after the last kidnapping. It was serious enough that he was immediately placed on medical leave until the Chief was officially released by his doctor to return to his stressful job.

The Shelbyville Police Department was now being led by the Deputy Chief of Police, Peter Stewart, who had not let up for a minute since the Overcast girl disappeared. He had to merge all three cases for similarities, but treat all three as individual events. The Deputy Chief was eager to catch up and make progress toward nailing the perpetrator. He would do it with however much manpower or time it took—he'd "get that slimy bastard and throw him under the jail."

Deputy Chief Stewart also made it a point to step in front of any camera that was filming a newscast about the three missing Shelbyville teens. He stopped short of calling Chief Taylor incapable of handling the pressure, and instead said that the Chief was resting comfortably after experiencing a medical setback which was "generally brought about by stress and other mitigating medical factors." His comments implied that the Chief had a nervous breakdown, but he never actually said the words. The *Nashville Tennessean* posted a front page picture of Deputy Chief Stewart in his formal uniform with the caption reading, "*The New Face of Hope For Shelbyville,*" as if Chief Taylor had failed miserably at rekindling the town's lost trust in the police force.

In every store window were now three separate posters depicting the innocent faces of the missing teenagers. "Have you seen this girl?" the posters' headlines cried out. Each flyer provided information on who should be contacted in case of a sighting or newly unearthed information. It seemed unlikely that the posters would do much good, but they remained on display as a symbol of Shelbyville's optimism and faith.

Politics were beginning to get dirty, and Bedford County residents' tempers again flared easily. Two weeks after Peggy Sue Overcast didn't return home, there was a town hall meeting to discuss what should be done to solve the current cases and to prevent further disappearances. The meeting had been in session for only a few minutes before disagreeing attendees began to take swings at each other; several attendees were arrested and transported to jail. Everyone else in attendance walked out following the arrests, leaving the moderator, Deputy Chief Stewart, alone behind the podium. He realized how volatile the town had become, and he decided a different strategy was needed to get the county residents to calm down. Otherwise, he feared the municipal executives would not consider him effective enough to be appointed as the next Chief of Police.

* * * * * *

Mr. Jack Tune, the previous City Superintendant of Public Works, finally retired prompting the City Manager to select his replacement. Corb's past performance as Assistant Superintendant of Public Works indicated that he was the most qualified person to fill the position. In early spring of 1957, Corb had been promoted. Thus, Corb got a hefty raise, a new job title, and new responsibilities, which included his elevated status within the city government ranks.

The timing of the Urban Renewal Project couldn't have been better for Corb and LorAnn. Not only did Corb now earn more money from the city, but the Project would buy his home at its fair market value, allowing him to reinvest in another home—maybe even in a safer area than mid-city.

Early on, when thinking about safer areas, he realized the Unionville Highway area hadn't been spotlighted in any recent crimes. The small Bedford County community seemed relatively peaceful. He was already acquainted with a few of the El Bethel residents. He thought it was a stroke of luck when he discovered a small house and acreage for sale in the area. He had already driven by the property without LorAnn for a quick preview. He had no idea if LorAnn would consider the location close enough to city conveniences, but far enough away from the city's corruption. A purchase would be her final decision, and he was hopeful she would approve after their first viewing.

He had also been thinking about how the girls would be able to ride the bus to school that fall, solving their transportation problem. Also, he knew Miss Ruth would be crushed when she found out the Carters wouldn't need her after LorAnn quit work.

He understood that the best part of the whole relocation effort was LorAnn's resignation with the Rubber Mill. She had never been able to stay home full-time with the kids. His new promotion had led him to drop hints about this potential scenario to LorAnn, but she still had her doubts that it could or would ever happen.

LorAnn dreamed of the day she would be on the same sleeping schedule as everyone in the house, and assume her role as full-time mother and caregiver. She was hopeful that this part of the relocation plan would come to fruition. Until Corb gave her the go-ahead to give her notice, she was better off putting this idea out of her head.

* * * * * *

LorAnn and Corb drove down a county road just a few car lengths behind their newly-appointed real estate agent. They traveled without speaking of the daily news events or local newspaper stories. The radio was switched to a country music station, and they listened to Marty Robbins sing about going solo to the prom in a white jacket with a pink carnation. The two hummed along as they passed by the few houses already erected on El Bethel Road.

The realtor turned right into the long driveway, coming to a stop around and behind a simple white house with a wide front porch and a built-on enclosed back porch area. There were rickety outbuildings for chickens and goats situated to the rear and parallel to the house, with a big fenced-in acre on the left side of the house for livestock. The other fenced-in area on the right side of the house was what remained of the previous owner's garden.

There were a total of eight acres that accompanied the residence. There was also a small pond somewhere on the land which wasn't visible from the house or driveway.

The interior of the house was most certainly inhabitable. There were two large bedrooms, a good sized kitchen and an extra wide living room. The house sported an indoor bath with an oversized claw-footed bathtub. There was a linen closet for towel and sheet storage, and it was certainly large enough. New wallpaper or paint might brighten the place up, but to Corb and LorAnn, the house was nice enough to move right in without much fixing-up.

They inspected all they could and spent nearly two hours wandering around the structures and acreage. Afterwards, Corb stood next to the kitchen counter and asked the realtor to show him where he should sign the contract to buy the property. The eager realtor steered him through the paperwork, and the deal went down smoothly. The transaction would be officially complete after the banking details and necessary legal business were handled, but the realtor assured the Carters that the place was now theirs.

The happy realtor left to go back to his office and start the paperwork chain. Corb and LorAnn remained behind to do more residential exploring and planning. The Carters wandered the rooms, envisioning how their furniture would look and how to set each piece in which room. It was beginning to be fun for LorAnn. She thought she might be able to make some delightful curtains and do some low budget decorating to make it look like an updated house. She was finally getting excited about moving.

* * * * * *

It took almost six weeks to get the sale of the Union Street house initiated and processed through the Urban Renewal Project management group. Afterwards, it took another week to officially close the deal for the El Bethel Road house.

Now some two months later, the house was ready for their arrival and the moving truck was scheduled.

Miss Ruth had been suspicious about what was happening with the Carters and their house-hunting efforts. She had not been filled in by LorAnn or Corb on their immediate plans. Her hope was that the Carters would move somewhere outside the Urban Renewal boundary, but still stay within the city. She felt certain she could convince them to continue her school transportation duties for the children. Also, she'd be willing to pick up extra housework (maybe some washing and ironing) if her back would allow it. She would remind Mrs. Carter that as a working mother, she would definitely need the extra help. She wondered if this would be a good time to ask for a salary increase.

* * * * * *

On Monday, July 8th, LorAnn gave her two weeks' notice to the Rubber Mill when she arrived a little early for her second shift position. She would work through July 19th and then assume her full-time position as wife, mother, and caregiver. She was ecstatic after the notice was accepted, and couldn't hide her excitement from her co-workers.

On Tuesday, July 9th at noon, LorAnn asked Miss Ruth to sit down and have coffee with her so they could chat for a few minutes. Expecting LorAnn to share the family's mysterious relocation plans, Miss Ruth accepted and hastily sat down at the dining room table.

Miss Ruth was going to prompt LorAnn into begging her to stay with their family wherever they moved. She had, of course, been the children's only permanent nanny since Dollie was born nearly seven years before. Miss Ruth believed the children would be absolutely lost without her. She smiled broadly and put on her friendliest face, waiting for the opportunity to hesitantly but graciously accept LorAnn's offer of continued employment.

"Miss Ruth, I guess you know everyone in this area is gonna have to move so they can start building the Housing Project, right?" LorAnn said, as Miss Ruth nodded with a fake smile still on her face.

"Well, Corb and I have bought a place out in El Bethel. The kids can ride the bus to and from school—door to door—since I'm going to be at home all the time now. I've turned in my notice at the Rubber Mill, and I only have this week and next week left to work there. Then I'll leave to take care of the children and become a full-time housewife."

Miss Ruth didn't quite get it. This didn't sound like what she had thought LorAnn was going to say. "Mrs. Carter, what are you saying?" Miss Ruth managed to ask.

"Well, after this week and next week, we won't need you anymore, Miss Ruth. I'll be taking care of the family from here on out. I'm giving you a two week notice to find another job, I guess." LorAnn wasn't very good at this, and she was uncomfortable looking at Miss Ruth, who appeared to be extremely confused.

"Well, now, Mrs. Carter, I expect I can still be of some assistance with the family. I will be glad to drive the children to school ... and..."

"There's no need," LorAnn interrupted. "It's all settled, and we've figured everything out. This is for the best. We sure have been blessed to have you here all these years. You've fit right in with the family, and I think the girls both think you're real special. We appreciate all the hard work you've put in 'cause it's sure helped the girls and Corb and me. You've been so good to us. We hope you were happy with us, too. We really will hate to see you go."

Miss Ruth stood up in front of her chair, "You will regret the decision to let me go, Mrs. Carter. It won't take long for you to see how valuable I am to your household and to your children. " Miss Ruth huffily walked out of the room.

LorAnn assumed Miss Ruth would settle down in a little while, since she had just been told her job would be gone in two weeks' time. Had it been LorAnn who was being fired, she probably would have handled it much worse.

LorAnn tried to sympathize with Miss Ruth, and left her alone to work through the unexpected news. Before leaving for the Rubber Mill, LorAnn said her usual "Goodbye," but this time no perky response was heard from Miss Ruth.

At the end of their two weeks' notice, one lady left her long-term employment believing her new life was just beginning, while the other believed hers was ending.

* * * * * *

While the Carters moved their household goods from Union Street to their rural home, the Carter children had been handed off to relatives for babysitting: Dixie went to spend the weekend with Uncle Troy and Aunt Roz, while Dollie took charge at the counter of Pap Stan's and Granny's store. Each girl had her own place in paradise for the weekend.

Dollie was terrorizing Pap Stan while he sat shirtless atop the Coca-Cola cooler dispenser. She wanted up on the cooler, too, but when she got there, she promptly squeezed his nipple and made him howl. She screamed with delight until Granny emerged from the back of the store and called down the two playmates.

Meanwhile, Dixie was helping Aunt Roz make a chocolate cake with chocolate icing, sprinkled on top with pieces of crushed hard candy. When that was finished, Uncle Troy was going to buy some ice cream to serve with it. Then they all were going to play cards. Dixie was thrilled she was being treated more like a grown-up at the Tucker house than she was at her own home.

Dixie honestly believed her parents didn't have a clue about how mature she had become. She was twelve now, and some girls her age had already started their menstrual cycles. Maybe she'd be lucky enough to be at Aunt Roz's house when it finally happened for her. She prayed she would. She thought she would need to get a bra soon, too, because she was feeling self-conscious about the little buds that were taking bloom under her shirt. Maybe Aunt Roz could help her with that this weekend, too, so she wouldn't have to bother her Mama with it.

* * * * * *

For the household move, LorAnn and Corb had enlisted the help of Uncle Buck (who now worked directly for Corb in the Public Works Department) and one of Corb's childhood friends to help with the move. The strong men did the lifting and placing as LorAnn directed traffic. It was going smoothly and much faster than anticipated.

By Sunday night, the Carters were in their new home. Beds were set up and made, the television was hooked up to the tall rooftop antenna, and food was in the refrigerator and on the built-in pantry shelves. All the kitchen dishes, cookware, and utensils could easily be located and used, and the stove worked great. They still had to pick up the girls to show them around the house and their rooms. The parents believed the girls would settle in quickly and grow to love rural life.

Corb and LorAnn were happy to be far enough away from the city to once again feel safe.

* * * * * *

LorAnn fell into the full-time homemaker role as if she had been doing it all her life. During the '57-58 school term, she woke the children by 6:00 a.m., fed them breakfast, and helped them get ready for school. She stood on the front porch with them as they all watched for School Bus #31 to come up the road toward their house. She always waved at the girls and the bus driver as the girls stepped up and into the long yellow school bus. It was always a relief seeing them wave back through the bus windows and watching the bus amble toward Unionville Highway on its route to Central Elementary.

During the day she did everything on her own schedule, with the exception of having a noon meal ready for Corb every work day. Although she didn't cook like

Miss Ruth, she was still a pretty good cook in her own right. Regardless, Corb always ate her food without complaint, and that was proof enough for LorAnn. In addition to perfecting her cooking, she found herself to be a decent housekeeper, too.

Corb believed they had made the right decision for LorAnn to quit her Rubber Mill job. Life was so much more pleasant now between the two of them. The girls had grown accustomed to having LorAnn around during their waking hours and they loved it. As a bonus, now they had lots of safe space to play in outside.

Part Three

Revenge and Other Life Lessons

CHAPTER 16

1957

The Carter girls had been on their routine school bus schedule for about two months. They knew exactly what bus to get on, and they knew where they were supposed to get off. The bus driver's father was the owner of a small store at the intersection of Unionville Highway and El Bethel Road, so the families knew each other well.

The girls knew not to talk to anyone they didn't know, or even someone they did know if that person was acting suspicious. They were well educated in scoping out a strange situation and how to avoid danger. But on this particular day, both girls got a curve ball thrown in their innocent little faces.

On Friday afternoon, November 15th, Dixie and Dollie were walking together toward the gym where they were to board Bus #31 in another ten minutes or so. It had been a long school week, and both girls were ready to get their weekends started.

While they waited for the busses to arrive, the girls spied a lady waving at them from the other side of the large parking area. Her head was wrapped tightly in a scarf, and she had on bi-rimmed sunglasses. Vehicles were allowed to short-term park against that side of the elementary school building, so this person was standing next to a parked car. She waved again and called Dixie's name.

The two girls held hands tightly, wondering if this person might be a relative of their Mom (she had so many brothers and sisters it was possible). They stepped cautiously across the parking lot, looking both ways for oncoming busses. The two sisters got within ten feet of the person and then stopped.

"Children, don't you recognize me? It's Miss Ruth! I haven't been away that long, have I? Now come give your Auntie a big hug!" she said as she reached for the girls and pulled them toward her.

"We're supposed to ride the bus home every afternoon. We gotta go stand in line or we won't get a good seat," Dixie said in her most responsible tone.

"Oh, girls. I have some bad news. Your daddy got hurt on the job today—not real badly, he'll be all right—but your mama asked me to pick you up and keep you for a few days until your daddy is released from the hospital."

Dixie looked questioningly at Dollie and then back at Miss Ruth. "Why did they call you, Miss Ruth? Couldn't Granny Rogers or Aunt Roz come?"

Miss Ruth smiled as if she understood the turmoil Dixie's mind was experiencing. "Sweet girl, your family members have jobs and they didn't have time to make arrangements. Since I'm already unemployed, it was easier for me. Especially since you girls have been in my constant care for so many years."

Dixie considered Miss Ruth's explanation and looked again at Dollie. Without hesitation, Dollie started to get into the backseat of Miss Ruth's 1949 green Plymouth sedan. Miss Ruth took Dixie's hand and pulled her toward the car, urging her to get in the back seat next to Dollie.

After quickly shutting her door and backing out of the parking area, Miss Ruth kept looking through the rearview mirror at the two girls sitting behind her.

"Where are we going exactly, Miss Ruth?" Dixie wanted to know.

"Why, first we're going to my sister's house for the weekend, and she's going to make us some homemade ice cream. You're going to love it. She uses fresh peaches and strawberries in her recipe. It's absolutely yummy!" Miss Ruth answered enthusiastically.

"Miss Ruth, I don't think we ought to go. Please stop and let us out. I think we should tell Aunt Roz where we're going," a concerned Dixie pleaded.

Miss Ruth looked at Dixie's face through the rearview mirror and remarked, "Sweetie, your mama already talked to everybody in the family, and they all know where you will be. They are all planning to help your mama with things while your daddy's in the hospital. He might have to have an operation, and it would be hard for your family to keep up with you girls if he has to go through all that."

Dixie still didn't really understand. She didn't think anybody in the family would want her spending the weekend with Miss Ruth or her sister. Dixie and Dollie never even knew she had a sister. She had a funny feeling in her gut that she should be on the bus with Dollie, and not in this car.

They drove for about an hour south of Shelbyville and through Fayetteville, then crossed the Alabama state line. When Dixie saw the *"Welcome to Alabama"* sign, she silently panicked. The clever little girl began to have doubts about Miss Ruth's intentions and suspected there was nothing wrong with her daddy. She tried to figure a way out of the alarming situation, but nothing was coming to her yet. She was beginning to believe the worst was yet to come.

* * * * * *

When LorAnn saw Bus #31 pass her house without slowing down or stopping, she ran from the porch to the end of the driveway and watched it motor around the curve going toward its next stop. There had to be a mistake, and surely the bus would be backing up any moment to drop the Carter girls at their house.

LorAnn waited for a few minutes more, then trotted back toward the house. She grabbed the keys to their newly-acquired second car, a used 1950 Ford, and revved up the motor. Gravel flew from the rear wheels as she exited the driveway in pursuit of the school bus.

By the time she caught up with the bus, it was crossing Unionville Highway to its nightly parking spot behind the neighborhood store. LorAnn screeched to a halt behind it, and ran up to the driver as he stepped down to the ground and closed the folding bus doors behind him.

"Mr. Sutton …Billy, where are my girls?" LorAnn asked as her anxiety-filled heart beat out of rhythm.

"Mrs. Carter, they didn't get on the bus today. I thought maybe you or your husband picked 'em up," Billy answered, now appearing concerned.

"Oh, God, no. They were supposed to come home on the bus. You were supposed to bring 'em home like you always do," LorAnn told him as she started crying loudly.

"Come inside the store and let's call Mr. Carter. Let's try to get this cleared up," Billy said as he took LorAnn's arm, supporting her limp body while they slowly made their way into Sutton's store.

* * * * * *

The green Plymouth had cautiously obeyed all speed limits while they traveled south through Tennessee. Miss Ruth had been careful not to attract undue attention from other travelers or law enforcement officers during the journey. They had moved slowly and carefully through a winding Highway 231 traveling towards Huntsville, Alabama.

"Miss Ruth, can you stop at a gas station and let me use the bathroom? I need to go real bad. Please." Dixie begged. "I didn't go before we left school, and it hurts."

Not knowing if this was a ploy or a real need, Miss Ruth answered, "It's not much farther. You can hold it, Dixie."

Dixie thought fast. "No, I don't mean number one. I have to do number two, and it feels like it's gonna be messy. I need to go in a hurry. Please stop. I don't wanna mess up your nice car. Please?" Dixie started to whine, and a frustrated Miss Ruth pulled into the next Texaco station in Hazel Green, Alabama to allow the frantic young girl to potty.

* * * * * *

As soon as Dixie made it out of the car, she sprinted toward the office inside the door of the station. The attendant looked up, startled to see such a sweet little face look so terrified.

Miss Ruth quickly appeared behind Dixie before the child had time to utter a sound. Dollie's upper arm was held stiffly by Miss Ruth's tightly gripped hand. "We need to use your facilities, sir. This child has an urgent need," The business-like Miss Ruth addressed the middle-aged attendant with authority.

"The key is hangin' on the wall next to you, Ma'am. The Ladies' room is on the right side near the back of the building. If you need gas, you should pull your car up to the pump and I'll fill 'er up for ya'." he stated as he looked back down at his *Popular Mechanics* magazine.

"That won't be necessary. Thank you, sir. We'll return the key momentarily." Dixie closed her eyes for a brief second, wondering how she could conjure up diarrhea on a moment's notice.

* * * * * *

When Corb took the call from Mr. Sutton, he was getting ready to leave the City Garage to go home. Mr. Sutton told Corb what had transpired with LorAnn, and reiterated that he was certain the Carter girls were not in line to board their bus when it arrived at school around 3:15 p.m..

Corb froze. For a moment he couldn't think clearly as his greatest fear was turning into a nightmarish reality. He told Mr. Sutton to keep LorAnn there at the store to make sure she was all right. He said he'd be there as quickly as he could.

He paused for a moment at his desk, trying to decide the most logical thing he should do next. He took control of his emotions long enough to pick up his phone and call the police.

Upon hearing Corb's brief summary of the unfolding events, the dispatcher patched him through directly to Detective Brian Martin, who agreed to meet the Carter family immediately at Sutton's store.

By 4:40 p.m., the fearful father and two apprehensive detectives were speeding down Unionville Highway to face whatever horror would present itself that evening.

* * * * * *

It was nearly 6:00 p.m. when Miss Ruth pulled her Plymouth into the driveway of a medium sized brick rancher-style home in Gurley, Alabama. Neither girl knew exactly where they were, except Dixie knew they weren't in Tennessee. She had read the sign when they crossed the state line, but she knew nothing about Alabama or how far they had travelled from their home town.

A lady who looked a lot like Miss Ruth came out the side door which was sheltered by a car port. Stepping down two concrete steps, she walked along side a late model blue Chevrolet to greet Miss Ruth as she exited her car. The two women embraced, and Dixie heard Miss Ruth say something about having a surprise for the other lady.

Just then, Miss Ruth turned and pulled the driver seat forward, clearing a path for the two Carter girls to exit the vehicle. "Dixie and Dollie, I want you to meet my sister, Mrs. Abernathy. Millie, these are the Carter girls I've told you so much about."

Mrs. Abernathy bent forward, smiled and waved to the young girls. Neither girl made a move to get out of the car.

"Don't be shy girls. My sister has already made homemade ice cream for me, but she didn't know I was bringing guests. But, don't worry, girls. There'll be plenty enough to go around," a cheerful Miss Ruth stated.

The girls reluctantly exited the car, holding each other's hands as if they feared they would be separated. Dixie was skeptical, but for the time being, she made herself appear to be a willing participant. She wanted Dollie to remain calm, as well. She hoped her efforts to remain collected would provide silent encouragement for Dollie to relax.

When they went inside, Dixie asked a pertinent question, "If you are Mrs. Abernathy, where is Mr. Abernathy?"

Miss Ruth immediately answered, "Dixie, mind your manners. That is a very personal question. But to answer you, Mr. Abernathy passed away a few years ago. My sister is a widow. Now go into the hallway and find the bathroom. You girls need to wash your hands, and be ready for supper in a little while. And Dixie, while you're in there, see if you can do number two. I'm afraid you mistook symptoms of constipation for diarrhea when your stomach was hurting earlier. Now, go."

Miss Ruth turned to her sister, sighed, and said, "Children. They only grow up to be snotty teenagers, so I prefer them when they're young and trainable." The two woman laughed, and proceeded to set the table for supper. They were having fried chicken, mashed potatoes and green peas. Miss Ruth would have to remind the girls to save room for the scrumptious ice cream.

* * * * * *

Detectives Martin and Woodson arrived at the same time Corb pulled into Sutton's store parking area which was adjacent to Unionville Highway. The three men converged on the store's screen door with the diagonal "Kerns Bread" sign affixed across its middle.

The second Corb stepped in the door, he could hear LorAnn sobbing in the corner near the cash register. He moved quickly toward her and embraced his inconsolable wife with a hug so tight she felt his heart beating.

"Oh my God! The girls! The babies! Oh God, where are they. We've gotta find 'em, Corb. Please go find my babies and bring 'em home!" a heartbroken LorAnn pleaded with her distressed husband. She broke down in tears and body-shaking sobs again, and all Corb could do was hold her.

Detective Martin stepped forward near the worried parents and started to introduce himself as the lead investigator for the recent child abductions. Before he spoke, he thought about the terror his descriptive introduction could provoke in these parents. He carefully revised his words before speaking.

"Mr. Carter? I am Brian Martin. We spoke on the phone when you called the police department earlier. Is there someplace private we can talk? Detective Woodson noticed that his partner didn't go into great detail about who he was and what his experience was with child abductions. He understood the sensitivity Detective Martin was feeling for the terrified parents. Woodson would be sure to use this technique when he introduced himself to the Carters in the next few minutes.

* * * * *

The girls politely ate dinner and showed off the table manners Miss Ruth had taught them. The women laughed and talked, but mostly they talked in some kind of code when the girls were around.

"Edith, what is this? Why do you have this 'company' with you?" Millie asked early in the evening when the girls were washing up.

"Shh. They'll hear you. It's a sad story, really. As you know, these girls have been in my care ever since the little one was born. I was her neonatal nurse, and soon afterwards, I resigned my position at the hospital to become the children's nanny. You know all this, of course.

"But, what you don't know—and they aren't yet aware—is that their parents were killed earlier today in an automobile collision. It was instantaneous, and they didn't suffer. So the grieving relatives called me and requested that I take care of the girls for a few days. I thought it best to take them far enough away that they wouldn't possibly suspect the fate of their parents until their relatives make the decision to inform them. So very tragic, such sweet little girls." Miss Ruth sniffled into a tissue.

"Oh, my goodness. Those poor things. You can stay here with them as long as you like, Edith. I'll help you in any way I can. Those poor babies. So sad," Mrs. Abernathy remarked.

* * * * * *

By 8:00 p.m., Detectives Martin and Woodson had heard everything pertinent from the parents and the bus driver, Billy Sutton. They now knew the last time the girls were seen by them, the clothes they were wearing, their usual routines, and their bus schedules.

When the Detectives departed, both Corb and LorAnn felt drained and numb without their children by their sides. The family doctor had been notified of the situation, and he made a personal house call to the Carter's house to provide some medicine to help LorAnn relax and rest. Corb declined any medicinal help.

* * * * * *

When the detectives returned to Police headquarters, Deputy Police Chief Stewart had gathered all available policemen, Rescue Squad members, and civilian volunteers together in one large briefing room. Detective Martin took the podium and began to disseminate the known information. He also answered questions posed by the audience.

"Who saw the children last at school and at what time?" was the first query from the group.

"We have talked to the teachers of both Dollie and Dixie Carter, and those instructors verified that each girl was dismissed with the rest of their classes to make their way to the bus pickup area between 3:00 and 3:15 p.m.," said Deputy Chief Stewart.

A civilian volunteer asked, "Did anyone see the girls together at the bus stop?"

Again, Deputy Chief Stewart answered. "No one has come forward with any information to confirm or deny that the girls were in the bus waiting area."

"So, who have you been able to talk to from the school, then?" another volunteer wanted to know.

"We have talked with the principal, a few teachers, the girls' bus driver, and a few other drivers. These people had neither seen the girls nor were they aware of any pertinent information about the girls during the 3:00-3:15 p.m. time span.

The audience was buzzing in low tones, but no one had a specific question to ask. The Deputy Chief tried to fill in some gaps. "Let me remind you that the circumstances surrounding these two missing girls have few similarities to the previous kidnapping cases we recently investigated.. These children are much younger than the other victims (who were teenagers), and the two were supposedly together when they were abducted. The other three cases involved kidnapping one child at a time. Today's abduction apparently happened in the middle of a crowded area, with people and cars and buses all around. The other victims were alone in secluded or non-public areas when they were abducted. We don't know if the cases will be related or perpetrated by the same person until we get farther along in our information gathering process.

"Let me also say that classmates of these two children were already on their way home by the time we were called in to investigate. Therefore, the school Principal will provide us with the names and addresses of students who would have been waiting in the bus area to determine if we can find anyone who might have seen the girls leave. This will take some time.

"We have also closed off the parking area, known as the bus pickup area, from public traffic so that the police can comb through the gravel and surrounding vicinity to find any potential leads. We have nothing to go on, at least not now; but we will be interviewing more people as the weekend progresses, and we hope to bring the Carter girls safely home to their family."

He paused. After spending a few moments scanning the quiet and somber faces of the audience, he humbly added, "We will not stop until these little girls are found and brought home safely."

The Deputy Police Chief stepped down from the podium and walked directly to his office. Before he shut the door behind him, he yelled, "Martin, Woodson, get in here."

The two detectives did as they were ordered.

* * * * * *

It was approaching 9:00 p.m., and Dollie was getting sleepy. Dixie was still wide awake, but feigned sleepiness so she could be put to bed. There she would be left alone to think of ways they might make their escape.

Miss Ruth looked at both of them as they sat on top of the double bed. "Girls, are you comfortable in the pajamas I bought you before I picked you up? Do they fit well enough? You know, I had to guess your sizes."

"Yes, Miss Ruth. They fit okay. But what clothes will we wear tomorrow? The clothes we wore to school are all dirty now," Dollie innocently asked.

"Don't worry, child. You also have some new pants and tops and a skirt or two. You have almost a whole new wardrobe. You'll be excited when I show your new things to you tomorrow, I'm sure. Now give me a good night kiss and it's lights out for my girls," Miss Ruth said as if she were their mother.

Both girls pecked her on her cheek without emotion, and then turned their backs to Miss Ruth while she lingered on the edge of the bed. As they closed their eyes and settled in to get comfortable, they heard Miss Ruth quietly walk out the door and close it behind her. There was no nightlight in the dark space, and Dixie began to tremble. Dollie moved closer to her and whispered, "It's my turn to protect you tonight, Dixie." The homesick girls eventually fell asleep in each other's arms.

CHAPTER 17

1957

The weather in Alabama on Saturday, November 16th, was unseasonably warm for that time of year. The temperatures were mild with no rain in the forecast. It would have been a lovely day for enjoying outdoor sports such as tennis or golf, but the Carter girls were not allowed to go outside for any reason. Miss Ruth had told them that they had to stay inside in case someone called about their daddy's condition. They just couldn't afford to miss such an important call.

"What's wrong with my daddy? Is he very sick? Is Mama with him?" Dollie started to whine.

Miss Ruth gave Dollie a stern look. "Child, I told you it all happened in a hurry and we don't know the details. Now shush, and don't ask again. We will know more as time passes."

Dixie asked another obvious question: "Can't Dollie and I go outside and play ball or something? You will be here to answer the phone, so why do we have to stay inside?"

Mrs. Abernathy looked at her sister and said, "If you're expecting a call, Edith, why don't you stay in here by the phone and I can take the girls out for a little exercise. I'm sure they're tired of being cooped up in this old house."

"No, Millie. They are my responsibility and I won't put that burden on you. We are all fine right where we are," Miss Ruth said with a lilt of authority in her voice.

"Do you girls like to play bingo? I have cards and numbers we can draw out of a bowl and make up a game. Would you like to do that?" Mrs. Abernathy thought this might be the solution to everyone's boredom.

Both girls clapped their hands and began clearing the small round breakfast room table to make way for the game. Mrs. Abernathy came back holding a box that rattled, obviously holding many game pieces inside.

As she opened the lid, she found most of the cards chewed around the edges and the pens dried up. The plastic number discs were faded and were dirty from rodent droppings. "Oh no. This won't do. This box has been put away in the garage for decades, but I thought it would be usable if I ever dug it out. Guess I was wrong. Children, we can't play bingo today. I'll have to get a new game for another time." Mrs. Abernathy appeared to be truly sorry that the game was not suitable for their afternoon fun.

"Could we go buy one now? We could play for the rest of the afternoon and maybe even tomorrow. Please? It would make us both happy," a convincing Dixie pleaded her case.

"Edith, you have a problem if I go get a new game down at the Five & Dime? It won't take a minute and we could be enjoying ourselves in just a little while."

Miss Ruth was not happy that her sister was inadvertently disrupting her plan of laying low with the children. However, her sister didn't know the whole story, either. Believing she had to provide some slack to her helpful but ignorant sister, she threw her a crumb. "I think that would be a good idea, Millie. Why don't you run on out and we three girls will try to find something to watch on television."

"I suppose I could do that, but why can't I take the girls with me? They may see some game they like better. Bingo is an old game anyway," Mrs. Abernathy stated.

Miss Ruth tried not to show her irritation, and started to repeat her previous 'no' answer. Then she decided perhaps that was not a bad idea. She could be checking the local news to see if any stories had spread. She was curious to know what was going on in Shelbyville right about now.

"Millie, you must promise to take them to the store and then come right home. No stops. They must not wander off, and you must not lose sight of them at any time. Do you understand? Do you think you can do that?" Miss Ruth inquired.

Mrs. Abernathy laughed. "Of course I can, dearie. These children are so obedient and mindful, there wouldn't be a problem anyway. We'll be back in two shakes."

Dixie reminded the adults that both children always went to the potty before they went anywhere in the car. The girls excused themselves to go to the bathroom and shut the door.

Dixie whispered into Dollie's ear: "I am gonna try to sneak away and find a phone to let the police know we are here but shouldn't be. If I see a phone, I'll let you know. Then you start throwing a fit for Mrs. Abernathy to buy a toy while I try to use the phone. Keep her busy with your acting out for as long as you can, okay?"

Dollie shook her head to indicate "okay" and winked at her sister. Dixie rubbed the top of Dollie's head and told her to do her best at acting like a spoiled brat, and Dollie said she'd been practicing since she was born. The two girls giggled as they exited the bathroom and held hands as they walked through the kitchen and toward Mrs. Abernathy's blue car.

* * * * * *

The Five & Dime was about two miles from Mrs. Abernathy's street. It was a plain concrete block building next to a hardware store, also fashioned from concrete blocks.

The places didn't look very fancy. Both girls walked in holding hands with Mrs. Abernathy tailing closely behind so she could watch their every move. When Dixie spied the phone behind the counter where the cash register was, she knew she had to get to that side of the store and try to connect with someone. She squeezed Dollie's hand and motioned with her eyes toward the phone across the room. Dollie understood and winked at Dixie.

Dollie broke away from holding Dixie's hand and reached for Mrs. Abernathy's. As she touched her wrinkled skin and polished nails, Dollie thought how much the woman's hand felt like Granny's. She wished she was with Granny Rogers, but she couldn't think about that now.

"Come with me, Mrs. Abernathy, I want to show you something in the toy section!" Dollie jumped up and down as if she were impatient and excited.

"Where's your sister? I can't leave her alone to wander around," the obedient Mrs. Abernathy inquired.

"Even I can see her head from here. Come on, we won't lose her. She would never leave me, anyway. I just want to show you something, please?" Dollie whined a little louder this time.

"All right child, but just for a minute. We aren't supposed to stay here very long, you know."

* * * * * *

Dixie went by the counter where the phone was sitting, then passed by it again, trying to be certain no one would approach her or would need to ring up a sale. A few seconds passed and it seemed clear to make the call.

As she slipped behind the counter, she picked up the phone and put it in the floor behind the counter's wooden back. Now seated in the floor, Dixie scooted as close to the center back of the counter as possible. She could not be seen unless someone came behind the counter and looked down.

Now that she felt safe, she nervously dialed "0" for Operator. When the operator answered, a very mature Dixie told her the story, "Miss, my little sister and I have been kidnapped. Miss Ruth has us somewhere in Alabama but our home is in Tennessee. My name is Dixie Carter and my sister is Dollie Carter, and we live in Shelbyville. We need help to get home. Can you tell my daddy to come for us? I don't know where we are except it's Alabama. Wait... there's a phone book on this desk. It says it's for Gurley. We are with our Nanny at her sister's house. Her sister is Mrs. Abernathy. I have to go now. Please help us." Fearing she had taken too long, she hung up the phone abruptly. She eased herself out of her hiding spot and put the phone back up on the desk. As she walked across to the next aisle, she saw Mrs. Abernathy glancing around as Dollie was gearing up to throw a fit for some trinket that she really didn't want. Quickly Dixie stepped around the aisle and said, "Stop acting like a baby, Dollie. You know Miss Ruth wouldn't be pleased if Mrs. Abernathy tells her how you were about to throw a fit."

Dollie straightened up and acted just like the sweet little girl she had been prior to the visit at the store. Mrs. Abernathy was amazed at how well the little girl listened to her older sister. She was pleased they had avoided a scene in the local store.

Walking to the cashier stand, Mrs. Abernathy was about to pay for the new bingo game in her hand. She added two bags of M&Ms, one for each girl, as their reward for being so good while shopping.

Afterwards, they all happily took their seats in the blue car headed back to Mrs. Abernathy's house. They sang *"Row, Row, Row Your Boat"* all the way back to the house.

* * * * * *

LorAnn had been sedated for the past fifteen hours. Corb was pacing about the house like a zombie, waiting for some word about the children's whereabouts. Each minute seemed to linger for five. Time was standing still for him.

Troy and Roz were with him in the living room of their El Bethel home. LorAnn was in the front bedroom, sleeping and whimpering throughout her bad dreams and grief. Granny and Pap Stan had been there earlier to drop off some food, but no one felt like eating. The food was still untouched and sitting where they left it hours before.

The television news was carrying the story with the same speculations they had made about the three teenagers' unsolved disappearances. They were tossing around words like "serial kidnapper" and "serial killer" which upset everyone even more. Finally, Troy turned off the television and sat back down on the couch next to Roz.

They stared at each other for the longest time. No one knew what to say. Anything that could be said was not what anyone wanted to hear. They silently prayed their individual prayers, hoping for the miracle that three other missing children had been denied.

* * * * * *

The operator who took the call from Dixie had written down everything the girl said. Sandra Haskins wrote it in shorthand and transcribed it for her supervisor. She left her seat and found her supervisor reading some technical paper inside his office. She cleared her throat at the door, and her boss looked up at her saying, "Yes, Miss Haskins, what can I do for you?"

The young lady handed the transcribed conversation to her supervisor who read it over at least three times. At first they discussed the possibility of some prankster, but Miss Haskins assured him that it was the voice of a child, very clear and precise, and she believed there was a problem. She asked her supervisor to reach out to the Shelbyville Police Department and verify that there are children missing.

He told her he would consider her request dismissed her. He placed the paper containing the transcribed message on the edge of his desk. Later when he cleared his desk to leave for the evening, the paper accidentally slid off into the wastebasket that sat adjacent to the desk. The supervisor left for the rest of the weekend, and never thought again about the message.

Later, Sandra Haskins wondered if the supervisor ignored her request for follow-up on the little girl's call for help. She left her work station and entered his office through the open door. The first thing she saw was the pink note slip on top of his wastebasket trash. She retrieved it and took it back to her desk. She would take matters into her own hands. The supervisor would never know, anyway.

Locating the phone number for the Gurley, Alabama Police Department, Sandra Haskins placed the call.

* * * * * *

Back in Shelbyville, Detectives Martin and Woodson still had no leads in the Carter children's case. They talked to children who rode the bus with the Carter girls, but none of them remembered seeing them that Friday afternoon at the bus stop. They talked to other students who rode other buses but congregated at the same place every afternoon. There were still no sightings. However, one of the elementary school teachers remembered looking out her window and seeing a tall lady in a scarf standing by some old car parked outside the teacher's window. She didn't really see anything else except she said the lady was waving at someone toward the bus stop across the parking lot. The teacher walked out of the room before she saw anything else. When she came back in her classroom, the woman and her car were gone. She didn't remember what kind of car it was or its color.

Basically they were facing another dead end with nothing to go on, whatsoever.

* * * * * *

While Detectives Martin and Woodson shuffled papers and followed dead end leads, the Police Chief in Gurley, Alabama was listening to what Sandra Haskins was reading to him over the telephone. The Chief took notes and thought he had nothing to lose by following up on this strange message.

After several minutes, his telephone call to the Shelbyville Police Department was put through to the detective in charge of missing persons. Brian Martin answered the phone.

"Detective, this is Chief of Police Hal Carson from Gurley, Alabama. I received a notification from our local phone company that a young girl and her sister were in Gurley at a residence, but the caller indicated the girls had been kidnapped from your area."

Brian Martin stood straight up at his desk. He grabbed a piece of paper and started taking notes. "Chief, do you happen to know the name of the caller? We have several active missing persons cases right now."

The Chief cleared his throat. "Dixie Carter. The girl said she and her sister were taken by their babysitter to the home of a Mrs. Abernathy here in Gurley. We haven't done any surveillance. Thought we'd better find out if this was a hoax or the real thing before we made any moves."

Detective Martin explained the events of the past twenty-four hours to the Chief, and they both excitedly planned an extraction of the girls from the kidnapper. They were not sure if the woman was armed and dangerous, or what the situation was.

They agreed that the Chief should send a unit out on the pretense of a wellness call. A backup would be positioned outside. If the officer saw two children in the house, he would alert the backup for assistance. If anything out of the ordinary started to erupt, additional backups would be dispatched.

Meanwhile, Brian Martin would wait to hear if the children were there and if they were rescued. He would alert the Carters once he knew the situation was under control.

"Hot Damn" he thought. "Thank you Jesus and Amen."

* * * * * *

As the arriving officer reached the front door of the Abernathy home, he could already see through the front picture window there were two young children in the living room playing a board game with one of two elderly women also in the room. The other woman was lounging in an overstuffed chair, reading a newspaper.

When the officer rang the doorbell, all activity stopped inside the room. It was evident that company was not expected. The lounging lady sat straight up in the chair with an anxious look on her face. The other lady stopped playing the board game, stood up and proceeded toward the front door. The lady in the chair started to argue with the other lady, and it sounded as if she was telling her not to answer the door. The officer signaled the backup that there might be trouble.

When the door finally opened, the smiling officer stated, "Good evening, ma'am. I'm Officer Johnson with GPD. We are canvassing the area due to a rash of break-ins over the past few days, and wondered if you had experienced any of these sorts of crimes. I'd like to check your house for safety while I'm here, if that's all right." He stepped inside the door.

A stern looking Miss Ruth stepped around the corner and found herself eye-to-eye with the handsome officer. "Nothing's happened here. This house has all the safety features it needs. You can move along, officer."

The officer looked at his note pad. "And which of you ladies is Millie Abernathy?"

Mrs. Abernathy raised her hand to shoulder level, indicating she was Millie.

"So, who is this other lady, Mrs. Abernathy?" the officer asked innocently.

"She's my sister from Tennessee, Miss Edith Ruth. She's here visiting for the weekend with two tots who just lost their family." By now Miss Ruth had started to move toward her unsuspecting sister to shut her up before she said too much.

"Millie, dear, why don't you get the officer a nice cup of coffee. I'm sure he could use a little break since he's been working so hard," Miss Ruth practically insisted.

"Oh, dear me. Where are my manners. Come on in, young man," Millie said as she quickly moved toward the kitchen and away from the front door.

"Where are the children Mrs. Abernathy referred to, Ma'am? If they're here, I'd like to talk with them."

"What on earth for, young man? They certainly haven't done anything to be questioned about," Miss Ruth told him.

"Can you give me the names of the children, Miss Ruth?" the officer persisted.

A huffy Miss Ruth replied, "I can't see as how that should concern you."

The officer became firm.. "Ma'am, I am going to call in my backup officer, and I believe we need to have a discussion about what you are doing in Alabama with two children who don't belong to you." The second officer came through the front door just as Mrs. Abernathy brought in three cups of coffee. She motioned the officers toward the living room where she planned to serve them coffee. No one moved except Mrs. Abernathy.

Miss Ruth was beginning to feel panicky. She asked to be excused for a moment to get her identification and guardianship papers. She swiftly turned and headed toward the kitchen.

"That's not where your room---, hey, where are you going, Edith?" her sister shouted as she heard the storm door slam on the carport side of the house. The policemen rushed past Mrs. Abernathy and gave chase. By the time they reached the carport, the extra backup officers already had Miss Ruth stopped at the edge of the lawn. As they put handcuffs on her, she sneered in the direction of her ignorant sister.

"Now may I meet those little girls, Mrs. Abernathy?" Officer Johnson asked.

"Why of course, officer. They are delightful girls and so much fun to have around. So very sad about their parents." Mrs. Abernathy still didn't have any idea what was happening, but she thought the nice officer should have the pleasure of meeting the two orphaned girls.

CHAPTER 18

1957

Gurley Police Chief, Hal Carson, notified the FBI the moment the Carter girls were identified, confirmed as abducted from Tennessee, and located in Alabama. The federal agency's response was immediate and precise. They took custody of the arrested Miss Edith Ruth, who was now temporarily sheltered in the women's section of the Madison County Jail in Huntsville awaiting transport to Tennessee.

By 3:00 a.m. on Sunday, both Carter girls had been routinely but carefully questioned, medically examined, and released for transport to their parents. The girls would be delivered by Special Agents Eva Cortner and Phillip Houston to the prearranged Tennessee meeting place. The Shelbyville Police Department would officially receive the girls from the FBI agents, and hand them over to their anxious parents and family. The FBI agents would also interview the parents as soon as the children were delivered.

News outlets had been alerted by Deputy Chief Stewart when he was notified of the safe recovery of the missing girls from their captor. The police department parking lot was overflowing with press members, news teams, and cheering citizens, all waiting to get a glimpse of the family reunion and discover the details of the children's horrible experience.

When the black sedan turned down the street in front of the police station, Special Agent Cortner muttered to her partner, "My God, look at this circus. You'd think that it was 4:30 in the afternoon instead of 4:30 in the morning. With all these lights, it's as bright as day out here."

* * * * * *

The government sedan nudged through the celebrating crowd and managed to parallel park by the building's front steps. When the car stopped, the two groggy girls roused in the back seat where they had been sleeping soundly for the past hour. Dollie's sleepy face popped up and peered through the rear passenger window of the sedan, recognizing the familiar surroundings. Then Dixie's head appeared next to hers, and the two girls smiled broadly when they spied the faces of their waiting parents. They struggled to open the door, but Special Agent Cortner had exited the vehicle and was already reaching for the outside door handle to help them get out of the car.

It was a poignant reunion—tears streaming down the faces of friends and strangers alike—when the two children ran from the car to embrace their parents for the first time in almost 48 hours.

Flash bulbs exploded. Cheers erupted. The sobbing but relieved Carter family slowly made their way into the building, closely followed by the two FBI Special Agents and Detectives Martin and Woodson.

In the same public room where weary policemen and volunteers had been briefed on the case only hours before, the happy family now gathered to embrace the children they so recently feared were lost forever.

* * * * * *

Deputy Chief of Police Peter Stewart was eager to address the press and the cheering citizens who had patiently waited for hours at the station to welcome the children home. He made a point to compliment the FBI and acknowledge the fine work of the Gurley, Alabama police force.

Then he blatantly accused the perpetrator of this "foiled plot" of having involvement in the three previous unsolved abductions in Shelbyville. He made these surprising claims as if he had solid evidence or a signed confession by the woman in custody, but the truth was hidden to the audience. However, he led the gullible crowd to believe that this case was the pivot point for solving what the public had thought were inactive cases. He reassured the citizens that justice would prevail for those still missing victims just as it would for the Carters.

Stewart stepped backwards from his makeshift platform to raise both arms and unashamedly urge the crowd to cheer. He was wallowing in his unjustified glory, feeling as though the town was in his pocket. The Deputy Chief placed his palms together with fingers pointed upward as if he were praying. He looked skyward and said, "Thank you, sweet Jesus," and the crowd went wild with applause.

He smiled and walked through the glass doors of the police station with more confidence in his step but less faith in the force's ability to solve the outstanding cases. It took a country bumpkin Alabama Police Chief to solve the Carter case while his own people were twiddling their thumbs. Martin and Woodson were going to have to make up for this.

But that was tomorrow's business. For now, he was mentally replaying his great performance for the appreciative crowd still milling around outside. He had them in the palm of his hand.

The Deputy Chief was whistling as he passed Chief Taylor's temporarily vacant corner office. A quick glance toward the poorly decorated walls reminded him that Taylor was only a figurehead in a position that needed active involvement. The old man's office reflected his dull personality. Deputy Chief Stewart – soon to be Chief Stewart, thank you very much-- already knew exactly how his executive office would be furnished.

* * * * * *

Detectives Martin and Woodson were overjoyed that the two little girls had safely rejoined their family. There was no doubt that the swift response by the Alabama policemen was ultimately responsible for the apprehension of the suspect and recovery of the children. However, the sweet victory in this quickly-solved abduction only made the detectives' failure to crack the previous cases much harder to swallow. They were reminded every day, either verbally by some inquiring person or visually by the flyers posted everywhere, that they had failed to bring justice to these innocent victims and their families.

Days had turned into weeks since the FBI Special Agents delivered the little girls back to their well-publicized homecoming. Deputy Chief Stewart had soon after assigned Martin and Woodson to find any and all connections between Miss Edith Ruth and the three victims in the outstanding abduction cases. The Deputy Chief ordered them to dig as deeply as they had to, since he thought they might be able to nail Edith Ruth on the old cases, too. Neither Martin nor Woodson thought this approach would yield anything useful, but they both delved into the newly-defined assignment with enthusiasm. They were happy to be tracking leads again.

* * * * * *

As the detectives delved into the background of the woman who had taken the Carter girls, they found that there was nothing special about the spinster Edith Catherine Ruth. She was born in 1900 in nearby Rutherford County. Her parents passed away many years ago.

The report stated that her only sibling is a widowed sister, Millicent Loraine Ruth Abernathy, who currently resides in Gurley, Alabama. She is two years older than Edith. Both Edith and Millicent were well-educated. In 1918 Edith enrolled in a two year nursing program, receiving her nursing degree in 1920 from Bainbridge School of Nursing in Nashville.

A few months later, Edith started working in the Rutherford County Hospital maternity wing, her first job after graduating from nursing school. She was there about ten years. It was rumored that she had to relocate with her parents from Murfreesboro to Winchester, because she wanted to put them both in a nursing home run by the State. Her sister had married by then and declined to have any say in the decision.

In 1930 Edith took a job in the maternity wing of the Coffee County General Hospital as the Deputy Supervisor of the entire floor. She was not well liked, was never promoted to Supervisor as she had expected, and eventually decided to resign in 1939 after both of her parents died that same year.

Miss Ruth then moved to Bedford County and was hired by the Bedford County General Hospital as the maternity ward head nurse. Her duties also included attending the new mothers. She resigned in 1950 and a few months later went to work as a nanny for the Carter children.

All this information had been gleaned from official records. Admittedly, it was a good start. However, there was still work to do to learn more about Miss Ruth's behavior and personality traits. That information, when meshed with the demographics and facts, turn a black and white picture into a colorfully detailed painting. The painting was what Martin and Woodson hoped to bring to light.

Each believed the best place to start would be to work their interviews from the most recent employer backwards. They would skip the Carter family for now, and begin with Bedford County General Hospital. They were hoping it wouldn't take long to learn the facts about Miss Edith Ruth's job, people skills, quirks, or habits. On the outside, it would be hard to imagine that this woman was anything but boring, but one never knows. "You can't judge a book by its cover," someone very perceptive once said.

* * * * * *

Because the Carter girls were abducted from their home town in Tennessee and driven across the state line into Alabama, the crime became a federal case. Thus, the FBI was now officially in charge of the kidnapping case levied against Miss Edith Ruth. They were responsible for the jailing, arraigning, prosecuting, and punishment if she was found guilty. They were building their case on the evidence collected through the investigations by both the Shelbyville and Gurley police investigations.

However, in the Carter case, the children were found unharmed and returned to their family. The previous mysterious Shelbyville kidnappings were still in the sole jurisdiction of the local law enforcement agency. But when local cases appear to have connections with federal cases, sometimes jurisdictional protocols tend to muddy the proverbial water. It becomes unclear who should be interviewing whom and why.

The detectives in the unsolved cases were ordered by their Deputy Chief to pursue whatever avenues they must in order to link the Carter case with the others not yet solved. Fearful of stepping on federal toes, Detectives Martin and Woodson proceeded with caution when they started their interview process with Miss Ruth's former employers.

They made an appointment with Mr. Jesse Johnson, the Administrator of the Bedford County General Hospital where Miss Ruth had worked from 1939 until 1950. They were scheduled to be at the Hospital by 3:00 p.m. on Friday December 13th to glean any information Mr. Johnson could give them to connect Miss Ruth to the open teenagers' cases. Mr. Johnson appeared eager to help when they spoke with him over the phone.

Detectives Martin and Woodson pulled up to the parking area immediately right of the front entrance. Adjusting their wrinkled suits, they went straight to the nurses' station a few feet inside the door.

"We're here to see the Hospital Administrator, Mr. Johnson. He is expecting us," Woodson volunteered.

"Yes, sir. He's expecting you. He should be here any minute to take you to his office. I hear it's about Edith Ruth. Glad somebody brought that witch down a notch or two," the nurse remarked. Her name tag read "Vicky."

"So you didn't care for Edith Ruth, ...uh, Vicky?" Detective Martin read her first name from her name tag and smiled as if he were in on the big secret.

Vicky rolled her eyes and answered, "Are you kiddin'? She was a horrible person. Nobody could get along with her. She acted like she owned the hospital and even put a few doctors and rich patients in their places a few times. The staff, including the doctors, dreaded having to work with her. She intimidated everybody. That woman was so rigid I bet she couldn't have stuck a pine needle up her butt." Suddenly Vicky's face flushed.

Detective Martin cleared his throat and tried not to smile. "Any other input that would help me understand Miss Ruth a little better?"

Vicky Lawson shook her head and made direct eye contact with Detective Martin. "Not only has she cost this hospital a lot of money and donors, I heard she got fired for hitting a kid a while back. We all thought there was something wrong with her, but we thought we had to tolerate her. They wouldn't fire her because she was the best nurse they had in the whole hospital. But, we were all happy when she left. I'm not surprised she went nuts and took off with those poor little girls. I think she was well on the road to psycho-land long before she reached her destination, if you know what I mean."

Detective Martin wasn't exactly sure what she meant, but he wanted to know more. Unfortunately, before he could question Vicky further, Mr. Johnson came down an adjacent hallway and stopped at the entrance of the reception lobby to introduce himself. He came forward to shake hands with the officers, and proceeded to show them to his office. Detective Martin looked back over his shoulder and mouthed "Thanks" to Vicky, and she nodded her head.

Mr. Johnson's office was nicely appointed, with leather chairs, a mahogany desk, and custom made curtains on the windows. It looked more like a wealthy person's den than an institutional office setting.

They made themselves comfortable, declining coffee or water, and got to the point. Detective Woodson started the questioning.

"We are following up on the investigation of Miss Edith Ruth, a former employee of the Bedford County General Hospital. We are trying to learn more about her as a person, rather than as an employee number or a badge number. We hope you can give us some insight into what Miss Ruth, the person, is like. She worked for you for some eleven or more years. That must give you some insight as to what she liked, disliked, her disposition, her moods, and so forth. We would appreciate anything you can tell us about her that might be helpful." Detective Martin nodded in agreement with what his partner had just recited.

Mr. Johnson rubbed his chin, and then picked up a thick file that had been resting on the corner of his desk, separated from other documents spread there. "This is her personnel file. There were a few times that management thought she was adhering a little too strongly to the rules, and maybe she should have been willing to bend rules a little more by using good judgment and more common sense."

Wondering if this was what Vicky was referring to, Detective Martin encouraged Mr. Johnson to go on.

"We had an incident in the mid 1950, June or July maybe, in which Nurse Ruth was accused of assaulting a ten year old girl. It was a big mess and it cost us some donors and funding opportunities when it leaked out. We also thought we were going to be sued by the girl's parents. That could have resulted in having to close down the hospital, and we desperately wanted to avoid that," Mr. Johnson cleared his throat and for a moment he seemed to be getting angry.

Detective Woodson asked Mr. Johnson to start at the beginning of the incident and verbally paint a vivid picture of what happened.

* * * * * *

"In the summer of 1950, Miss Ruth had been complaining that too many children had been trying to sneak up to patients' rooms during visiting hours. The hospital's policies restricted anyone 13 or younger from visiting any person admitted as a patient. She had caught a couple of sneaky children trying to enter a room, and she promptly threw them out without incident, I might add.

"But one day Miss Ruth caught a little girl trying to find her mother's room. The mother had a miscarriage, a baby boy, and the mother had been in a thoroughly depressed state. The daughter, who was about ten at the time, had a small box of candy and a few colorful flowers she had picked from their home garden, and she wanted to cheer up her mother with those gifts. She confidently walked up the stairs to the maternity ward area and asked the first nurse she saw where her Mother's room was located. The gracious nurse told her it was a few doors down, and the little girl turned to walk in that direction.

"But then, Miss Ruth rounded the corner finding herself face to face with the child. Everyone at the nurses' station stopped what they were doing and listened to what was going on. The child had her back to them and was facing Miss Ruth, so they could see and hear everything Edith was saying. I happened to stop by just as the child left the nurse's station, so I saw the whole thing.

"Miss Ruth must have been trying to make an example out of the policy abuse, and maybe she even wanted all of us to see she meant business. She immediately screamed at the little girl, and told her she wasn't supposed to be on this floor because she didn't meet the age requirement for visiting. The little girl told her that it was only this once, because her Mother was so sad that her baby brother was born dead. Miss Ruth had no sympathy: Rules are Rules. But the girl persisted. She started to cry because she thought her mother was going to be sad forever if she didn't get some help. Again Miss Ruth told her to leave the floor or she would call the police. The girl told her to go ahead, that the police helped people and she needed help to see her mama. That infuriated Miss Ruth. She started yelling that if the girl didn't leave, she would take the candy and flowers and put them in the trash and her mother would never get them. The little girl supposedly (according to Miss Ruth) stuck her tongue out at Miss Ruth, and then Miss Ruth slapped her. She didn't slap her hard, but she did knock the girl off balance and she crumpled to the floor. I suppose it scared her more than anything. She started crying loudly, and of course, we all rushed to her aid.

"As Administrator, I watched Miss Ruth's interaction with the child and she absolutely had no social skills in that situation. In fact, she looked overpowering and threatening. When she slapped the child, none of us expected that. She just stood there after it was over as if she couldn't believe she'd done it, either. The Mother heard all this from her open room, and had been trying to get out of bed to rescue her daughter. She made it to the door just in time to see the slap.

"The unsteady mother immediately tried to attack Miss Ruth. It took several of us to pull her off the nurse. Needless to say, the father came by soon after all this occurred and threatened to sue the hospital and everyone in it. That was when we called Miss Ruth in for disciplinary action and put her on her final probation. This was her last chance, especially after she had other warnings in her file relating to insubordination and several patient complaints. From the date of the final probation, she had to spend six months without incident or she would be terminated. Unfortunately, the incident with the Carter baby put her out of a job."

The detectives had listened intently to the detailed story told by Mr. Johnson, seeing a side of Miss Ruth that clearly showed her to be rigid and potentially violent.

"Tell us about the Carter baby incident that cost Miss Ruth her job," Woodson requested.

"Well, it's a little embarrassing, I must say. But Miss Ruth had never had children of her own, and we all believed she really had no maternal instincts herself. Don't misunderstand me. She was an excellent neonatal nurse. She knew everything backwards and forwards that was required to keep a baby healthy and strong. To her, the babies could just as well have been little crying and wiggling machines. She just didn't get close or attached, you see.

"But when the younger Carter child was born, for some reason Miss Ruth really took to the child. She claimed she even helped name the baby, but I don't know if that's true. Anyway, she was always holding that baby when it was supposed to be in the nursery, or she would try to feed it whenever the Mother was asleep. That way she could tell Mrs. Carter that she slept through the feeding time. Miss Ruth even suggested that the baby would be better off on formula so the baby wouldn't be dependent on breast milk.

"But the baby was about three days old when it happened, the final straw. One of the other nurses went into the nursery and found Miss Ruth in a chair, somewhat secluded in a corner, pretending to breast feed the Carter baby. She had shoved her exposed breast toward the Carter baby's mouth and was trying to urge the hungry baby to latch on. That action was despicable and a complete violation of our policies, not to mention how morally wrong the woman was in trying to do that. That was Thanksgiving morning of that year, and the child and mother were able to go home that day. We never told the Carters about the incident. We still don't want to, either.

"We let her go after her shift ended that day. We told her she could resign or we could fire her; by then it made no difference to us. She chose to resign.

"I heard later she went to work for the Carters. That frightened me a little at the time, but I didn't really think she'd hurt either child. Looks like she got more attached to both girls as time went by."

Detective Martin shook his head and said, "I didn't realize she was such a volatile woman. Maybe we should interview the child she slapped back in 1950. Would you give me her name and address?"

Stumbling for words, Mr. Johnson finally said, "I can give you her name, but no one knows where she is."

The puzzled detective asked, "I don't understand. Did she move away?"

Mr. Johnson lowered his eyes and solemnly said, "Her name is Wendy Wilson. I don't think you or anyone else knows where that poor child is."

CHAPTER 19

1958

For the first two months after the Carter children were reunited with their family, both Corb and LorAnn became increasingly overprotective of their daughters and their whereabouts. Dixie and Dollie were only allowed to be away from their parents when they were at school or when spending a few brief hours with Aunt Roz, Aunt Tessie, or Granny and Pap. Even then, the two parents were overwhelmed with worry until their children were safely home.

Billy Sutton, the driver of Bus #31, had taken it upon himself to instigate an accountability program for all the children who were assigned to his bus route. He required the children to count off as they exited the bus every morning at school. In the afternoons he never pulled the bus away from the loading area until the children counted off again. He made sure he had everyone on board before leaving the school grounds. Any child boarding his morning bus who planned not to ride the bus home was required to present a parental note to Billy explaining and approving the absence. He was doing everything possible to be more alert and careful of the children in his charge. Other bus drivers began to employ similar accountability measures, and soon it became the norm in the county bus system.

Meanwhile, many people secretly hoped that the apprehension of the Carter girls' captor had ended the crime spree of abductions that had overtaken the town during the past two years. Most assumed the worst was over, and tried to enjoy a more relaxed environment. Others, who were not readily convinced that the jailed perpetrator was also involved in the teens' disappearances, persevered with their protective temperaments intact when it came to the town's youth.

* * * * *

In late January of 1958, Dixie was allowed to spend her first full weekend with Aunt Roz and Uncle Troy.

It had taken her parents this long to believe she was finally ready to spend the night somewhere besides her own home. Dixie had been having frequent nightmares again, and more often than not she would wander into her parents' bedroom in the middle of the night to seek the security of their arms and their bed. Dollie never seemed outwardly affected like Dixie, but Corb and LorAnn assumed she never really understood how much danger she could have faced had things ended differently.

Dixie, of course, recognized the potential peril; and, as the older child, felt responsible to keep Dollie safe. Dixie developed and engineered a rescue plan using her precocious thinking and ability to stay calm. Perhaps the night terrors were her way of playing out the many "what if" scenarios had her escape plan failed.

Eventually Dixie began sleeping through the night free of bad dreams and without interruption. When she asked her parents when she would be able to visit Aunt Roz, they told her she could go whenever she thought she could handle it. Thus, she made plans with her aunt and uncle, and LorAnn delivered an excited Dixie to her sister's front door the next Saturday morning.

* * * * *

It seemed as though Uncle Troy was happier to see Dixie than Aunt Roz. After his niece settled in, he took her for a ride down Fishingford Pike while Aunt Roz did some backlogged laundry. He wanted to get them both out of the house for some well-deserved ice cream, and perhaps while driving the back roads, he could secretly scout potential rendezvous spots for future use with his lady friends.

He hoped the private car time with Dixie might help him gauge the twelve year old girl's state of mind after having gone through the disturbing events of

November past. Neither he nor Roz had spoken with her about what happened, with the exception of a few passing comments inquiring about how she or Dollie were doing.

At the end of Troy's driveway, he turned right. Dixie had never travelled in this direction. They had always gone back toward town when leaving the Tuckers'. She intently watched from her front seat as unfamiliar houses and vacant lots passed them by.

"Where are we going, Uncle Troy?" Dixie asked with wide eyes. "I've never been this way before."

Only then did Troy realize that Dixie might be apprehensive about traveling unknown routes. Troy reminded himself that the girl was still sensitive to her surroundings, and tried to calm her apprehensive mind.

"Dixie, I'm gonna show you the back roads to get to your house. I don't think you ever thought you could get home any other way than the way you always go. We're gonna stop at Sutton's store for our ice cream treat, and then we'll come back. We're gonna make a big circle, and I think you'll enjoy the ride. Is that all right with you? If you don't want to, we can turn around," Uncle Troy answered.

"No, it's all right. Would you just please keep telling me where we are while we're on the way? I think that will make it better," Dixie remarked as they kept driving.

"Sure will. See that bunch of buildings behind the trees over here on my side of the road? That's the Southern Rendering place. They take dead animals and make glue or dog food or something over there. Smells rank, most of the time. I've seen 'em haul dead horses down this road in the back of a truck, and them horses would be laying on their backs with their feet straight up in the air, deader'n a doornail." Uncle Troy laughed, but Dixie kept a straight face.

"Uncle Troy, that's disgusting. I can't believe you laughed at that. It's sad," she said in her most adult-sounding voice.

"Dixie, you can't tell me it wouldn't be funny if you saw a truckload of horse legs going by, now could you, girl?" He chuckled again.

Dixie just shook her head and said, "Uncle Troy, you got a warped sense of humor."

That remark made them both chuckle.

As they veered toward a side road on the right, Uncle Troy announced this was the split that would put them on the road that came out next to Sutton's store. "This is Troupe Road, see the sign? You just follow this road and it leads you straight home."

Dixie looked at the road sign and the surrounding landmarks intently. "So someday I will be old enough to drive this shortcut to your house, right Uncle Troy?"

"You'll be old enough to drive before you know it, Dixie. Time goes by quicker'n you think."

They drove in silence, looking at the small homes and pastures that were parallel to the road. Finally the road dipped downward--a short but steep decline—and Uncle Troy halted at the STOP sign. This was the intersection of Troupe Road with Unionville Highway. As Uncle Troy had promised, there was Sutton's Store on Dixie's right. El Bethel Road was just across the highway.

"Look Uncle Troy! There's Suttons, and there's our road. You were right. I didn't know it was so easy to go the back way. It's a shortcut, for real." Dixie smiled while Uncle Troy turned to the right and slowed to a stop in the store's parking area.

"Run on in there and pick us out something real good. Don't forget I like chocolate ice cream. I'll be in 'fore you know it. I'm gonna smoke a little of this cigar first." He reached in his overall bib pocket and extracted a short stub of a cigar.

Dixie took off running toward the door, and Troy could hear her greeting Mr. and Mrs. Sutton as she entered.

He wondered if Dixie might be attempting to memorize everywhere she was taken—a new defensive tactic, perhaps. He would be careful to keep his scouting thoughts to himself. She might inadvertently recount to someone the places he took her on this or future joyriding trips. It could backfire on him if he wasn't alert. Plus, he didn't want to upset the child or make her think she was being kidnapped again. He'd never want to harm that child physically or mentally.

He smoked his cigar, or what was left of it, and threw the stogie on the gravel drive. When he entered the store, Dixie and the Suttons were laughing at a joke she had told. Troy hadn't seen the child laugh in months, and he smiled right along with them. She pointed to the ice cream freezer and told her Uncle she found an Eskimo Pie he'd like because it was filled with chocolate ice cream. She licked the popsicle she was holding before it dripped down her hand. In two more bites, it was gone.

"Uncle Troy, can we go back home the way we came? I want to see those roads again and try to learn the shortcut. I can show it to Mama and Daddy and they can use it, too," she exclaimed, happy that she had discovered something she could share with her parents.

"Yep. You ready to hit the road, Dixie? " he said while finishing his Eskimo Pie.

"Let's hit the road, Uncle Troy. Bye, Mr. and Mrs. Sutton. I liked talking to you."

The Suttons waved back and said their goodbyes, and Mr. Sutton told Uncle Troy, "Be mighty careful with that child. I'm surprised she's not scared to get in the car with anybody but her Mama and Daddy. She must really trust you, Troy."

Troy nodded his agreement, and felt proud that someone else noticed that Dixie trusted and loved her Uncle Troy.

* * * * * *

They were almost home when Dixie pointed out the pretty rose bushes growing at the side of the Morgan's house. They were planted on the side that didn't face the Tucker property; and since she had never travelled in this direction, she was pleasantly surprised when she spotted the beautiful bushes. Troy remembered Rocky telling him when his daddy was planting roses for his Mama, so that must have been when he put those in. Silently, Troy wished Mr. Morgan would take better care of the house, because it needed painting more than the yard needed flowers. He started wondering why that boy-adult kid of his couldn't do some work around the yard, but he decided he was too dumb. He'd probably mess everything up.

Troy let his Morgan family thoughts fade into new thoughts about what they could all do for entertainment during the afternoon. Today should be a special day for Dixie. He wanted her to have some fun. She deserved it, and he could use some, too.

When the two of them entered the house, Aunt Roz was about to take some wet clothes out to hang on the clothesline. They had recently purchased a dryer, but she liked the way the clothes smelled when they dried outside. Troy picked up the heavy laundry basket for her and followed her to the clothesline in the backyard. He set it down, looking over his shoulder to see if Dixie was still inside.

"Roz, I think Dixie was nervous riding around just now. At least, she was at first. I told her we were gonna find a new way to go to her house and that we'd end up at Sutton's store. She was okay with that, but before she knew that she seemed kinda jittery. You think she's okay to be spending the night away from home so soon?"

Roz looked at him with a soft smile. "Troy, you're a good man. Sometimes you're not so smart, but you're good just the same. You prob'ly shouldn't have taken her down roads she'd never seen before. But looks like it turned out all right." She pointed to Dixie who was opening the back door to come outside. When Dixie spotted her Aunt and Uncle, she smiled broadly and asked if she could go next door to visit Mrs. Swing for a minute, since she hadn't seen her in a long time. Mrs. Swing always gave peppermints to visiting children, and Aunt Roz suspected this was the real reason Dixie wanted to visit.

Aunt Roz nodded her permission to Dixie, but also held up five fingers, indicating how many minutes Dixie should stay. Dixie responded with a thumbs up and started running across the field that divided their residences.

"Well Roz, since you're busy with this stuff, I guess I'll go out to the shed and work on my motorcycle. I need to do a little work on the fuel pump, so let me know when lunch is ready. Just send Dixie out to tell me." Troy started walking toward his shed. Roz kept hanging up wet clothes and wondered how long he'd be in that damn shed today.

Within her allotted five minutes, Dixie managed to say hello to Mr. and Mrs. Swing, get a handful of peppermints, drink a short glass of fresh lemonade, and tell them about her new house in the country. They were delighted to see her, and let her talk her full five minutes' worth. They understood that Dixie had to be back immediately, but were happy she made time to visit.

* * * * * *

"What are you doing out here, Uncle Troy?" Dixie asked as she hesitantly peeked around the shed door.

"This is where I keep my motorcycle so no one can steal it. It's also where I work on it, so I don't have to be outside in the sun tryin' to fix it. All my bike tools are in here." Troy paused and then asked, "You here to tell me lunch is ready?"

"Yep. Then Aunt Roz wants me to go to the grocery store with her. I'd rather stay here with you, though, if you don't care."

When Troy looked at the doe-eyed girl, his heart melted. He preferred to work in the cramped shed alone. It was big, but when he spread out his tools, plus turning the cycle where it could be easily reached, it took up a lot of space. If Dixie would stay on the cot and not get in the way, he figured it would be all right.

"Only if your Aunt Roz says it's all right. She might be wanting to take you to get clothes or something. You better ask her." Troy replied.

"Okay, now let's go eat before Aunt Roz gets pissed," Dixie giggled as she looked at Uncle Troy for a response to her dirty word.

"Girl, what did you say? You better watch that mouth! I'll have to get my belt after you if you keep that up!" Troy said while trying to suppress his laughter. He knew what Dixie was doing. She was trying not to laugh, too. The two walked through the backyard to the house holding hands and giggling.

* * * * * *

Roz left to do her grocery shopping right after lunch, and Dixie sat in a patio chair beneath the poplar tree in the side yard. She was flipping through a beauty magazine Aunt Roz had left on the couch. She liked to look at the pictures of the beautiful women, their makeup, and their clothes. She liked their shoes and purses, too, but could only imagine what it must feel like to be so gorgeous. Even though she really was a pretty girl, she didn't have that image of herself. She felt ugly most of the time, especially when everybody talked about how beautiful and cute Dollie was. Dixie felt like she must have never been pretty because she couldn't remember when anyone said nice things like that about her.

She dreamed of being a lovely girl who had a handsome boyfriend—one that thought Dixie was the greatest person on earth and would love her until eternity. She hoped someday she would meet that boy who would be her forever love.

Maybe Aunt Roz could help her pick out a little bit of makeup someday soon, and she could become more glamorous that way. She still thought she needed a training bra, but she hadn't gotten up the nerve to ask Aunt Roz for help. Aunt Roz could give her advice on lots of things Dixie would be too embarrassed to ask mama about. Even Uncle Troy might know some stuff that daddy wouldn't ever talk about with her. Sometime soon she'd ask him what she should be expected to know at her age. She would believe anything either of them told her. She trusted them.

* * * * * *

Dixie threw down the magazine, frustrated that she couldn't identify with anybody or anything in it. She stomped her way to the back yard so she could talk to Uncle Troy while he worked. She approached the shed's door and asked if she could come in. Uncle Troy told her to enter, but stay on the cot so she wouldn't get in his way. She did as she was told, trying to remain quiet so as not to disrupt his work, but she just couldn't keep her thoughts from coming out of her mouth.

"Uncle Troy, I want you to talk to me about things." Dixie blurted out.

"What kind of things, Dixie? I'm not real educated, so you prob'ly know a whole lot more than me." Troy answered her without taking his eyes off the tools in his hand.

"Good grief, I am twelve years old. Next year I'll be a teenager, and they still treat me like a little girl. Mama and Daddy, I mean. They don't think I'll ever grow up, but I already am growing up. I know lots of things about stuff...I mean, I've heard some things. I don't know the difference in what's real and what's made up. But I'm old enough to find out the truth about things, about life. I want you to promise me that you'll teach me things, Uncle Troy. Things I'll need to know—really know—when I get to be a woman. I don't think I'd ever be able to ask my Daddy or Mama about this stuff. Will you help me, Uncle Troy?" This time Dixie's face looked more mature than before when she giggled about using a dirty word. Now she seemed intent on knowing what the world was really going to be like for an older Dixie and what she could do to fit in it the best way possible. Troy was still thinking over his reply, but before he could get any words out Dixie interrupted.

"Uncle Troy, I don't want to just be Dollie's big sister. I want to get attention in my own way. I know I'm not as cute as she is, but that doesn't matter to me. I want to be the kind of person who everyone likes because I'm likeable." Dixie wrinkled up her nose and asked, "Did that make sense or did it just sound stupid?"

Uncle Troy leaned away from the motorcycle and looked directly at Dixie. "No, it didn't sound stupid, and I know what you mean. Never hurts to have a guide when you walk down a new path, you know. Maybe when I finish here we can start your first "Life Lesson." That's what we'll call our talks. So the first life lesson will be whatever you want to talk about. So, get outta here and let me finish this, or I'll be out here all night and we won't get to talk about anything." He turned back to his repair work. "Go pick some grapes for your Aunt Roz."

Dixie hurried out of the shed and raced to the kitchen to get a plastic bowl. Aunt Roz had grapevines along the backyard's rear fence. Those grapes were juicy and dark red and delicious. Dixie picked a grape, ate a grape, and repeated the process. By the time the bowl was full, Dixie needed a nap. She took the grapes inside and set them on the kitchen counter. Then she went back to the shed, silently got on the cot, and napped while Troy finished cleaning the fuel pump on his Harley.

* * * * *

When she returned from shopping, Roz walked out to the shed and peeped around the open door. She watched her husband cleaning the detached parts of his motorcycle and carefully laying them on a white rag on the floor. He was concentrating hard and apparently didn't hear her approach. She leaned to her right and saw a sleeping Dixie lying sprawled on the cot next to the far wall. She looked comfortable, and it was warm enough, so Roz backed out from the shed and silently went back to the house to put away the groceries.

Troy knew Roz was watching him and Dixie, and didn't move while she did her spying. He wanted her to see that he used the shed for exactly what he told her. She had only been to the shed one other time, and that was when he was trying to get his sparse furnishings inside and arranged. After Roz helped him find the most efficient placement, she left him to enjoy his shed alone. That was the way he preferred it, too. Alone.

As Troy finished up, he picked up several tools to deposit them in the tool box drawer. The sound of tools clanking against the metal side of the box woke Dixie.

"Sleeping Beauty's awake," chuckled Uncle Troy. "I thought you were gonna lay there all day."

Dixie sat up and yawned. As she blinked repeatedly and wiped her eyes, she realized she had slept better in that short while than she had for a long time at home. She felt comfortable, secure and safe there with Uncle Troy standing guard. She smiled a genuine smile.

"Uncle Troy, I'm ready to talk if you're finished working on your motorcycle. Do you want to start?" Dixie didn't want to waste any time with her life lessons.

"Yeah, we can start, I guess. This time you get to ask questions. Next time maybe I will, I don't know. But let's start this way for now. Go ahead. Ask me a question," Troy directed.

"Okay, but you have to tell the truth and not make up answers, okay?"

Uncle Troy smiled and said he agreed. Then Dixie began the first life lesson.

"When do people start kissing?" an absolutely innocent but puzzled Dixie asked her Uncle.

"Whoa. I thought you were gonna ask me why the chicken crossed the road or somethin'. This is kinda "out there" for a kid your age, ain't it?" Troy was shocked.

"Please, Uncle Troy. Be serious. These are things I think I need to know, or I wouldn't ask you. Now come on. When do people start kissing?" Dixie stubbornly repeated.

"Okay. Whew. Well, I think it depends on the people. I think people start kissin' when they go on dates and stuff. For sure, they kiss when they're in love." Troy was proud of his answer.

"How do you know when you love someone? How do you know if they love you back?"

Troy exhaled loudly. "Jeez, you're not holdin' back anything, are you, girl? Good God, I don't know. I guess you think about that person all the time and want to be with them all the time. Uh, maybe you would even die to save that person.

Shit, I don't know. That's a hard damn question. I don't think you'll have to know that answer for a few more years, so gimme some time to work on it. Next question." Troy was beginning to regret his agreement to go through with this.

"Okay, but if you don't answer this one honestly, I'm just gonna have to ask someone else this stuff. I intend to get the answers outta somebody, and I'd rather it be you than anybody else. But anyway, here's the next question: What is sex and how do you do it?" Dixie looked at him with a blank face.

"Dammit, girl. Why are you askin' me this stuff? Your mama should tell you about this crap. Okay, okay. Just gimme a minute here. Okay. Sex is when two married people take off their clothes and fit their parts together real close. That is sex and that's how you do it." Now Uncle Troy was sweating and absent-mindedly wiped his brow with a dirty oil rag.

"What do you mean fit their parts together? Like what parts?" Dixie wrinkled her brow as if she were trying to imagine how that worked.

"Look, you remember when you were little and your Aunt was changing little Stevie's diaper over here at one of our family dinners?"

Dixie nodded but her brow stayed wrinkled.

"Well, he had a part ...down there... that little girls don't have. When he grows up that will be the part he uses for sex." Troy muttered to himself before he resumed his explanation. "Where little girls don't have that part, they have a place where that part can go in. Oh, Jesus, I can't do this. Dixie, I think it's time we go in for supper. Get off the cot and let's go. We'll finish this up another time."

Dixie didn't move. "But Uncle Troy, I think what you said must be right. It makes sense to me. I just can't imagine my mama and daddy doing something like that, though. Maybe you can get me some pictures to look at so I can understand better? Maybe sometime before too long?"

Uncle Troy closed his eyes and breathed deeply. "Let me think about this, child. But don't go talking to anybody else about this kind of stuff. AND don't be telling anybody about the life lesson we had today. They wouldn't understand. Is that a deal?" Troy looked befuddled.

"Okay, Uncle Troy. Let's pinky promise." Dixie held up her crooked little pinky and Troy linked his into hers. They smiled at each other, Dixie proceeded into the house, and Troy stood there for a minute shaking his head and mumbling, "Now what have I gone and done? She's too smart for me."

He entered the back door, kissed Roz on the forehead, and watched Dixie pop one of Mrs. Swing's peppermints in her mouth just like the kid she was. Troy wondered how she could switch back and forth so easily from innocent little girl to demanding adolescent.

He figured she took after Roz.

*** ***

Later that afternoon Roz went outside to take down her dry laundry from the clothesline. When she finished, she picked up the basket of crisp-smelling clothing and began her trek back inside. As she neared the back door, she noticed one of her magazines laying in the grass next to the popular tree in the side yard. She set the basket down on the porch and walked the few extra steps to grab it by the rustling pages flapping in the breeze.

As she stooped over to retrieve the magazine, she peripherally saw a figure move toward the neighbor's fence. The she heard Marvin Morgan's upset voice. "Ms. Tucker, you need to talk to Troy about what he's doin' with that little girl back there in that shed. My boy went to get kindling and firewood for his Mama today, and heard him telling that girl about S-E-X. Rocky said they was talkin' about kissin', too. That man ain't right when it comes to kids. You better watch that girl when she's around Troy. He'll mess with her if you ain't careful. I already told Rocky never to be around that pervert when he's by hisself. Just a friendly warnin' to y'all." Marvin turned and retreated to his house without further conversation.

Roz stood there wondering what the hell she had just heard. She couldn't believe Troy would do such a thing, especially considering how he seemed to love Dixie.

Maybe he loves her too much? Have we all just been looking the other way and not paying attention to the signs? Was Troy actually capable of doing what the retarded boy said he did?

She recalled the Christmas incident with the Rocky and the pie. She tried to remember exactly how Troy had explained that to her when they were alone in the bedroom. She remembered that he sounded sincere, and it was easy to believe that the mentally unstable Rocky had just made the whole thing up.

Roz had not responded to Mr. Morgan while he said his piece. He had left her speechless and stunned. She felt for the arm of the chair and eased into the seat. She sat there collecting her thoughts and steadying herself for facing Troy again.

When she went inside, Troy and Dixie were on the living room floor playing marbles. Ma Rose was in a corner chair with her Bible in her lap and spit cup in hand. She had made one of her rare appearances outside her room in honor of Dixie's visit.

Still unsure of what to believe, Roz bypassed the group and headed toward the bedroom where she could fold the clean laundry in solitude. She wanted to be left alone with her tumultuous thoughts for a while. She needed to find a way to trust Troy with Dixie, even though she knew he certainly couldn't be trusted around other women. *Damn you, Troy.*

CHAPTER 20

1958

Detectives Martin and Woodson sat in the front row of Deputy Chief Stewart's mandatory briefing held on Monday, January 27th. Any person who had gathered information about the three yet unsolved kidnapping cases was in attendance. The Deputy Chief had spent weeks reviewing every tidbit of information available, and was making a case for pressing charges against Edith Ruth for kidnapping the Shelbyville victims.

The Deputy Chief held up three slim files before the audience. "The meager contents of these files are disturbing to me and to all the citizens of Shelbyville. I realize that you all believe you've done your best, but in this situation, apparently that hasn't been good enough. The only viable link to these missing children turns out to be sitting in a Nashville jail waiting for trial in the federal court system.

"At first, we had our suspicions when the Carter case was closed. Now, I feel confident that Miss Edith Ruth is either responsible for or was instrumental in the disappearances of Wendy Wilson, Sarah Beth Keller, and Peggy Sue Overcast.

"All victims were attended by Edith Ruth when they were born in the Bedford County General Hospital. When Wendy Wilson was ten years old, she was slapped by Edith Ruth in the presence of the maternity staff and the Hospital Administrator. Miss Ruth was placed on probation and eventually fired when she was found trying to nurse an infant in her ward. That infant was none other than her future kidnapping victim, Dollie Carter. That particular incident, which followed the Wilson girl's assault, without a doubt provide a solid link to all the Shelbyville kidnappings.

"Interviews with the parents of the kidnapped teens all confirmed what we first suspected. Miss Edith Ruth, as attending nurse to the new mothers was stern, cold, and hateful. Witnesses report that she despised dealing with any children other than infants, and she was not really fond of babies. She tolerated them because she was once overheard to say that they were too young to complain or report her to her supervision. She held a dim view of children, in general.

"We have yet to understand her attachment to the Carter children, unless it fed some sort of late onset maternal tendencies. Regardless, she has confessed to the Carter kidnappings, and we believe with enough perseverance, we will be able to get her confession regarding the other unsolved cases.

"Tomorrow afternoon I have scheduled a news conference and will announce our intention of charging Miss Edith Catherine Ruth with three additional counts of child abduction. We believe there is enough circumstantial evidence to make a strong case against Miss Ruth.

"However, you all have twenty-four hours to gather any last bits of evidence to support these charges or bring me another suspect. Good luck, gentlemen."

The Deputy Chief turned and exited the room without taking questions from the officers.

Detective Woodson turned to his partner and remarked, "I don't think she did it. I don't think the links are anywhere close to a motive. Everything he said is circumstantial, at best. Besides, we don't really know what happened to those kids. There aren't any bodies, so there's no murder to investigate. The parents say the kids weren't the types to run away, but what do parents really know about their kids anyway? I think Stewart's blowing hot air, and he wants to do all he can to make his job permanent. He's been getting too much flack recently, and he can't stand to fail. He's rushing to judgment, if you ask me."

Brian Martin held his mouth tensely closed. He picked up his notepad and then turned to look into Woodson's eyes. Quietly he muttered, "Stewart's got his head up his ass. He's ignored everything we've told him, and he's let his imagination work overtime. All he wants to do is mark these cases "Closed" so he can go join the country club and hobnob with the rich people. He knows if he doesn't get this right, it's his neck. He's just praying Edith Ruth will admit to everything because she's a spinster with nothing left to lose." He made no move to leave and then added, "The country club would black ball him anyway. He's a prick."

The two peeved detectives left the building and drove to the Rebel Maid for a few minutes of uninterrupted peace and strawberry milkshakes.

* * * * * *

When Tuesday's press conference began, Deputy Chief Stewart confidently faced an audience of media representatives and concerned citizens. He spoke of bringing justice to the sick person who committed the horrendous kidnapping crimes. He carefully avoided disclosing the links to each case and kept his statement brief. When he cut to the chase, the audience fell solemnly silent.

"Edith Catherine Ruth is currently remanded to the Davidson County Jail, and has confessed to illegally abducting minors Dixie and Dollie Carter. She now awaits federal sentencing for the Carter children's kidnapping and other related federal charges to which she has pled guilty.

"We now also intend to provide evidence that Miss Ruth was also involved in the local kidnapping cases of Wendy Wilson, Sarah Beth Keller, and Peggy Sue Overcast. Therefore, we will be bringing additional charges of kidnapping against Miss Ruth for these three previously unsolved cases. We will keep the press and the good citizens of Shelbyville apprised of developments as they occur. Thank you."

Again, he took no questions and walked directly to his office. The audience members were left to mill around for a while, discussing the impact of Deputy Chief Stewart's statements. One reporter tried to question Detective Martin, but he gracefully answered "No Comment," and managed to get away and join Detective Woodson as they exited to their offices.

"You know, Harry. I think there's more to this little act by Deputy Chief Stewart than meets the eye. My gut tells me he's hiding something or knows something important that he's not sharing. Maybe we should be watching him, too."

Woodson agreed. "Wouldn't it be great if we had an internal leaker or informant or whatever role an internal rat could play? Then we could take down the bad cop, too. We'd be heroes." He laughed and continued, "I'm just shitting you, man. Don't look so surprised. I just don't know if that fairy tale will work out for you, Brian. I don't think cops slip up when they've perfected being bad cops. I'd think it takes a long time to catch them."

"Eventually, everybody gets caught. If there's something fishy with Stewart, I want to be the one to find it,' Brian uttered.

* * * * * *

In Nashville, the Davidson County Jail held both men and women who had allegedly committed murder, drug trafficking, robbery, assault, and a host of other crimes that none of their mothers would be proud to hear about.

Miss Edith Ruth, who had been placed in the Davidson County Jail pending her federal court sentencing, had no mother who would be concerned about her daughter's fate. Her Dad was gone, and her hair-brained sister might as well be checked off the list, too. Nobody was there for her. She had no support system, and she knew she would never have visitors. She didn't make friends--they were too much trouble. So, the proper Miss Ruth sat in a holding cell with a filthy dirt bag of a woman who clearly abused some drug that rotted her teeth. Miss Ruth was hopeful this woman would not be her cell mate for long because the woman was so utterly disgusting. Her putrid body odor nearly made Miss Ruth gag.

Then one day in early February, Miss Ruth was taken from her holding cell and escorted by an unfamiliar jailer to a cell in the rear of the building. She was placed in solitary confinement, but she had done nothing to warrant the change. The jailer was silent as she escorted Miss Ruth from one cell to the other, leaving her repeatedly asking, "Why am I being moved? What did I do? Can I speak to my lawyer?" There was no response. Even when her meals were brought to her, the jailer never talked. She thought she was due an hour of daily outdoor exercise, but after three days in the "hell hole," she'd never been taken out of the cell for any reason.

After a miserable few days with no contact or conversation with anyone, Miss Ruth was not holding up well after. She certainly had no sunshine or exercise. She was despondent by then, and hardly moved from the corner of the cell where she sat staring at her bare feet. She had to get out of this mess. She hoped she could withdraw her guilty pleas and reenter a plea of temporary insanity, but she thought that was impossible now.

Before she was moved from her original cell, another inmate in an adjoining cell predicted that Miss Ruth would probably get the death penalty because she took so many minors' lives and tried to take those little girls away to do who knew what. Miss Ruth didn't believe that would be her fate, even though she had been told Shelbyville was pressing additional charges against her for the teenagers' disappearances. She didn't understand.

On the fourth day of her solitary confinement, another female was ushered into her cell by a jailer she didn't recognize. Eager to talk to anyone, Miss Ruth sat on the side of the bed eagerly awaiting the company.

When the jail door shut and they were alone, Miss Ruth smiled and introduced herself. The big woman smiled back, then rammed her fist straight into Miss Ruth's nose. She punched her face again, this time breaking her jaw. Blood was pouring down Miss Ruth's face. She was mentally stunned and instantly terrified. She tried to get up and run toward the door, believing the jailer was close by. Instead, the woman tripped Miss Ruth and she fell on her hip, causing horrific pain in her back and leg. She could hardly move.

The terrifying woman stood over Miss Ruth as she lay on the floor in a fetal position. "You are expected to admit to whatever kidnappings your hometown throws at you. You got that, Babe Ruth? You do this right, and you won't ever see me or any other unfriendly face again. You deny those charges, and you got about 20 members of my gang just waitin' to get you alone in the shower when they send you to the federal prison. You ain't been fucked till you get fucked by the prison crew." She kicked the fearful Miss Ruth in the stomach as she walked past her, whistling loudly as a signal for the door to open.

Miss Ruth knew she could never identify who allowed the monster in or out, but it wouldn't have made any difference. She knew she was doomed no matter what she chose to do.

She cried and nursed her swollen nose and broken jaw as best she could without proper instruments or bandages. Her hip hurt, but she soon found she could limp around. When the familiar jailer came to deliver supper, she spoke to Miss Ruth.

"What'd you do? Run into a wall?" she snickered.

"Do you think I might be able to go to the hospital, please? I need to have my nose looked at and my jaw set...from when I ran into that wall," she meekly asked.

"I'll check with the Sheriff and see what we can do. Eat your food, you're gonna need your strength," the jailer said as she winked.

Miss Ruth was now afraid that all the county jailers and federal guards were dirty and for the right price, would allow the more powerful inmates to do anything they wanted to the weaker ones. She anticipated being beaten to death by some big bully with tattoos, ugly dyed hair, and earrings through her nose and tongue. She knew the type. She wouldn't last long if all her future beatings were given with the same force as this first one.

Not expecting to ever see a doctor, Miss Ruth decided her best course of action would be to control what was left in her power, and not let others have that control. *Strike first*, she thought. *Take all the pleasure out of it for them.*

* * * * * *

The sheet on her cot was old and thin. It was easy to tear it into strips and braid a strong enough rope to hold at least 150 pounds. She did it with ease, and when the rope was about five feet long, she stopped braiding and tied it off.

The only tiny window in the cell had bars on it, and it was about six feet high. Thankfully, the bars were on the inside and the glass was on the outside of the window frame, supposedly to ensure no glass could be broken and shards retrieved for use in cutting wrists or cutting others.

Her cot was light and moveable. With minimal effort, she slid it under the window, then stood atop the lumpy mattress as she stretched to thread the sheet/rope between the bars. She knotted it securely, and then fashioned a serviceable noose.

Once she thought she had the perfect setup, she pushed the bed about a foot away from the wall. Carefully standing on the edge of the bed, she slipped her head through the noose. If she pushed the bed with her feet, she'd be at least six inches off the floor. That would be enough height that she wouldn't be able to back out.

While she stood perched on the side of the bed, she thought about how all she ever wanted to do for Dixie and Dollie was to care for them. Their father wasn't a good man; he had too many women and that showed no respect for his gentle and kind wife. She thought that Corb never gave the girls—or LorAnn for that matter—what they needed most: love and affection. He was too busy getting his kicks with trashy women. She just wanted those girls to be in a home where they were truly loved. Miss Ruth would have sent for LorAnn after settling the girls in Alabama, because she believed the mother truly did love her daughters. She just wouldn't have been able to do it very soon, because she would have been risking getting caught.

Well, look how that turned out for you, she thought and smiled a sad smile.

She took a deep breath and stood absolutely stiff as she positioned herself. She silently counted to three and pushed the bed away from her with the balls of her feet. She hung from the window by the braided cotton rope, feet dangling and eyes bulging, until the early morning hours when it finally gave way and her lifeless body fell to the floor.

* * * * *

At 7:00 a.m. on Saturday, February 8, 1958, the familiar jailer opened the door slot in Miss Ruth's solitary confinement cell to slide her breakfast through. The guard saw what appeared to be Miss Ruth sleeping on the floor, but the slot was not large enough to provide a full view. She didn't think much about it since all the cots in solitary were lumpy, hard, or so worn out that inmates often preferred the flatness of the floor for sleeping. The unconcerned jailer continued with the breakfast rounds. Miss Ruth's body was not discovered until twelve hours later during a wellness check.

* * * * *

When Deputy Chief Stewart received the call informing him of Miss Ruth's death, he stood up behind his desk and shouted "YES!" so loudly, people in surrounding offices came to see what was happening. Embarrassed, he directed those curious few to tell all officers to be in the briefing room in ten minutes. He would fill everyone in on the important news he had just received from the FBI. Monday was not usually his favorite day of the week, but this day was about to become stellar!

Martin and Woodson showed up, along with the rest of the kidnapping case officers, and seated themselves near the front of the room. Shortly thereafter, a beaming Deputy Chief Stewart entered and immediately went front and center of the group.

"We were in the process of completing the required paperwork to officially charge Edith Ruth for the kidnapping of the three local missing children we've so diligently tried to find. Well, apparently Miss Ruth took her own life while in solitary confinement in the Davidson County Jail sometime during the night of February 7 or morning of February 8. She managed to tear a bed sheet into strips and weave it into a strong rope. She then tied it through a window bar and hanged herself. We've heard, although not officially, that she believed she would receive the death penalty if convicted of all the kidnapping charges. It is not confirmed if that was her motivation to prematurely end her own life.

"What we do know is that now we will officially close the three kidnapping cases we have worked so hard to resolve over the past three years. Our primary suspect is now deceased, and we have no other suspects or leads. Explanations of how the kidnappings were executed and the location of the victims is irretrievable. The only person who knew that is now dead.

"We will announce to the press that the three previous kidnapping cases will be closed based on collected evidence clearly implicating Miss Ruth as the perpetrator of those crimes. I will talk to the parents of the victims in a separate venue before the announcement is made to the newspapers.

"Thank you all for your dedication and efforts on these very difficult cases."

Deputy Chief Stewart then worked the room, stopping to shake hands with happy officers who saw this turn of event as less overtime and more time at home with their families. Congratulations were exchanged and laughter was loud and boisterous.

Detectives Martin and Woodson didn't smile at the news. They both thought it inappropriate for the officers to be laughing as though the woman's death was something to celebrate. It just seemed wrong to both of the men.

When Deputy Chief Stewart approached the two detectives, he extended his hand first to Martin who reluctantly shook it. When he extended his hand to Woodson, the detective turned away and said, "Excuse me, I have some work to do." Stewart looked puzzled but shrugged it off.

"He's been under a lot of pressure, sir. He's emotional right now," Martin told Steward, trying to make excuses for his friend.

"Hey, it's understandable. We've all felt that pressure. You boys did fine work on these cases, fine work indeed. I'll remember that, 'cause I don't forget the dedicated folks that work the hardest." He slapped Martin on the back as he joined another group of officers. Martin subconsciously wiped his shoulder where the Deputy Chief had just placed his hand. Then he went to find Woodson.

* * * * * *

Woodson was ranting when Martin found him pacing in the alley behind the station. "Stewart is hiding something, I *know* it. You can call it gut instinct or pure dislike of the man, I don't care. He's pushing too hard to close these other cases without actually proving they've been solved. We never even found the bodies of those kids, for Christ's sake! There's only circumstantial evidence against that woman, if that. Stewart's trying to make it sound like that woman confessed to everything, and we both know that never happened." Harry caught his breath before continuing. "Maybe I ought to just resign. I don't think I can work with that son of a bitch much longer," a frustrated and angry Woodson told his partner.

"Look, man. I told you I thought something was fishy with Stewart, too. Maybe now we just might found out why if we go about it the right way. Don't you think it's squirrelly that this lady commits suicide over being in jail? I think there's more to it; I just don't know what or where to look," Martin said to a fuming Woodson. "And, while we're at it, we have to play the part. You can't be refusing to shake the boss's hand when he offers it to you. He'll think we don't trust him—which we don't—or suspect him of something—which we do. Otherwise, he'll start being more careful and cover his tracks if he really is up to something. Come on, man. Help me out here. Help me get that prick."

Woodson seemed to calm down after Martin said his piece. "All right, I'll give it a shot, but we're probably running into another dead end here, too. And I still want to work on those kidnappings. They're not closed as far as I'm concerned. They're just taking an official break."

Martin shook hands with his partner, and threw his arm around his shoulder as they walked back into the building and toward the conference room.

"Deputy Chief, I'm sorry about that. Congratulations on closing those cases," a now smiling Woodson said and reached out to shake Stewart's hand. As Woodson gripped a little too hard, he glanced at Martin and then quickly faced his boss. Woodson sincerely commented, "I hope you get everything that you deserve and more, sir."

CHAPTER 21

1958

When the local newspaper published their exclusive story about Miss Edith Ruth's apparent suicide, the town had mixed reactions.

Almost everyone believed that the Deputy Chief of Police was right when he promised there would be no more child abductions because the perpetrator was dead.

Others weren't so quick to assume everyone was safe just yet. And of course, the victims' parents still wanted to know exactly what happened to their youngsters. They needed answers.

* * * * * *

On the following Saturday, Carl Brown awoke next to his feverish wife. Dora had felt headachy and had a sore throat for the past twelve hours or so. She believed it was the beginning of her winter cold, but soon she realized her ailment was much worse than a common seasonal cold.

By mid-afternoon, Dora had no appetite and was too lethargic to leave her bed. Carl called the family doctor to see if he could come by to check on Dora, or at least call in some medicine at the drug store for her.

After asking about Dora's vitals and symptoms, the doctor called in two prescriptions for Dora at the Rexall Drug Store not far from the Brown's home. Since the pharmacy offered delivery services, the prescription should arrive at their Central Avenue home within a short time.

* * * * * *

The pharmacist at the Rexall Drug Store had Dora's medicine ready within 30 minutes of the doctor's call. However, the delivery boy was out on another run, and wasn't expected back to the store for another hour. The pharmacist had intended to call Carl to see if he could pick up the script, but the busy man was interrupted by several counter customers. He forgot all about the courtesy call until Joe Claxton returned to the drug store.

"Joe, I'm glad you're back. We have one last delivery to Carl and Dora Brown over on Central Avenue. You can deliver this one as soon as you can get on your bike and take off. Oh, and since it's late, you can go on home from there and I'll pay you for the rest of the day. No sense coming all the way back here just to turn around and go back the way you came. How's that work for you?

The smiling fifteen year old gave his boss a thumbs up signal, and then picked up the white bag filled with Dora's medicine that had been set aside on the counter.

"Thanks, Mr. Cook. I'll see you Monday after school," the cheerful boy said.

Mr. Cook nodded his farewell to Joe while answering the ringing phone next to the cash register.

* * * * *

Richard Joseph Claxton (known as "Joe" to his friends and family) was a handsome young man who was a sophomore at Shelbyville Central High School. He was on the lean side, but certainly not skinny. He had blue eyes that sparkled, deep dimples in his cheeks, and wore his hair in a butch waxed flattop, the fad in 1958. He wasn't in the popular clique at school. However, he was known to be friendly but a tad introverted when it came to joining up for extracurricular school activities. His girlfriend, Roseanne, had been in love with him since they met the summer before they both entered high school as freshmen.

Joe was devoted to his family. He wanted to help supplement their low income by paying for his own indulgences through his after-school and weekend job at the drug store. He paid for his bike, which he used to make store deliveries, and anything else he wanted to buy for himself or his girlfriend.

Last Christmas he had made enough money to buy Roseanne a ring at Henning's Jewelry store. The design was of two ornate interlocking hearts, and the ring was pure white gold. He was proud of the gift, and Roseanne always teased him, saying it was their pre-engagement ring. Joe knew she was right. He definitely wanted to marry her some day.

That same Christmas, Roseanne had given Joe a twin set of identification dog tags on a beaded silver chain. They were made to resemble military dog tags, and they were the recent fad among teenagers. Of course, Joe gave one of them back to Roseanne who proudly wore the extra "Joe Claxton" dog tag as a further symbol of their commitment as a couple.

Joe and Roseanne were two of the happiest teenagers in Shelbyville. They planned to spend a glorious lifetime together.

* * * * * *

Joe was pedaling as fast as he could when he made the turn onto Central Avenue. He planned to start the evening as early as possible, and wondered if now he'd have enough time to take Roseanne to a movie at the Princess Theater.

When he arrived at the Brown household, he knocked on the door but didn't wait for an answer. Instead, this time he opened the screen door and placed the bag of medicine next to the closed wooden front door. He knocked quickly and turned to race toward his bike. He heard the front door creek open, and a weak female voice said, "Thanks, Joe." He mounted his bicycle and headed toward Jackson Street. "You're welcome, Miz Brown," he yelled over his shoulder as he hurried toward home.

* * * * * *

On Saturday nights, Joe's parents knew he would be working until 5:00 p.m. and then would have a scheduled date with Roseanne. They weren't surprised when he hadn't made it home as the family prepared to leave for the church's 5:30 p.m. hamburger supper. The Claxton's two other children were already in the back seat of the sedan when the mother stopped. She glanced down the road looking for Joe, just in case he wanted to join them at the last minute.

"Let's go, Margaret. Get in the car. I want to make sure we get a piece of egg custard pie before it's all gone. Joe's not interested and wouldn't go with us even if he was here. Get in the car and let's get going," an insistent Nolan Claxton pleaded.

"I don't know why, but I feel like I need to talk to Joe. He's been on my mind all day, but I can't figure out why," Margaret said while closing the car door behind her.

"Maybe because you think he's growing up too fast and he spends more time with Roseanne than he does with you," said her teasing husband.

Margaret smiled and leaned over for a quick kiss from Nolan. "EEWWWWW," came the response from the back seat audience members, their nine-year old twins.

The family laughed in unison as they backed out of their driveway and without a care in the world, headed toward Sister White's house for their weekly feast of hamburgers and pie.

* * * * *

At about the same time as Margaret Claxton was peering down the street for sight of her son's bicycle, Joe was in the process of being bound and gagged. His eyes were blindfolded and he had trouble catching his breath. By the time his dog tag was ripped from his neck, he was unconscious.

* * * * * *

The two Shelbyville Police Detectives were finally able to enjoy Saturday nights with their families since the kidnapping cases had been closed. The overtime and the constant attention required on the cases had reached a colossal amount of time spent away from their friends and families.

On Saturday, February 15th, Detective Brian Martin had made a reservation for himself and his wife at a nice restaurant in Murfreesboro, about 25 miles away in Rutherford County. They were going to simultaneously celebrate a late Valentine's Day and their fifth wedding anniversary.

The bachelor Detective Woodson had planned a weekend of hunting in the Normandy area, a small little town in Bedford County located on the outskirts of Shelbyville. He and some of his old high school buddies scheduled at least one hunting outing each year, and he was more than happy to finally be available. By Saturday morning, he was anxious to exchange his cramped paperwork-filled office for the open and relaxing outdoors.

* * * * * *

After the Martins returned from their evening out, Brian and his wife relaxed in their cozy living room with wine and chocolates. The two sat close together, not talking but reading each other's minds about an evening of anticipated intimacy. As Brian leaned over to kiss his wife, the phone rang loudly.

"Don't answer it, Brian," Jenny pleaded as she pulled his face toward her waiting lips. She kissed him with passion as the phone continued to interrupt their moods. "I'm not," he said as he returned her kiss with tenderness.

When the phone stopped ringing, the two gathered their wine glasses and headed toward their dimly lit bedroom. Before they made it to the bedroom door, the phone started ringing again. Brian looked as his wife and with defeat in his eyes, turned to answer the call.

* * * * * *

When the dispatcher gave him directions to the Claxtons' home, Detective Martin recognized the street address. He and Woodson had been called to a home on West End Circle two years before when Sarah Beth Keller disappeared. His stomach was feeling uneasy at the thought of a new kidnapping spree—or worse, a continuation of the first one.

The Claxtons' home was located in the center lot of the street's cul-de-sac, five or six houses down from the Holloways' duplex from where the Keller girl vanished. Nolan and Margaret Claxton were waiting in their living room for the policeman to arrive. Sitting alone in a side chair was an obviously worried teenage girl, soon identified as the girlfriend of the missing boy.

When the detective entered the house, he introduced himself and started the interview process. He realized this situation mirrored those of the other three missing children: no witnesses had come forward, no one had any reason to believe the child ran away of his own volition, and the teen did not seem to have any enemies. Nothing. Not even an idea of where the boy was last seen.

As he had done so many times before, he attempted to soothe the worried parents and girlfriend. He promised a full investigation, and pointed out that several patrolmen were already canvassing the neighborhood for potential witnesses.

When he assured them that he and the police force would throw all their resources into solving the disappearance, the angry father stood up from the couch.

"Full investigation? Just like you all did when the other kids went missing?" said Nolan Claxton. His anger and his voice rose. "The police was quick to point a finger at the woman who's dead now. Nobody found out what happened to those missing kids, though. Stewart just said the files were closed. I guess your boss will say the dead woman was involved now, too. Huh? And he'll try to push this one off on her, too? I don't think the police can help anybody anymore. Margaret and me can probably do a better job ourselves." A furious Nolan Claxton abruptly sat down by his wife. The two were now sobbing uncontrollably. Roseanne held her head in her hands while the Detective stood there, feeling chastised but understanding why Mr. Claxton felt that way. It was very much the same way he and Woodson felt about Stewart's leap to judgment on the previous case closures.

He left the house and met with Patrolman Jeff Cooper to let him know he'd talked with the Claxtons and the girlfriend, but learned nothing solid yet. Patrolman Cooper looked despondent, realizing that the detective must be feeling the same déjà vu he was since they both investigated the same type of crime in this neighborhood a few years before.

Detective Martin knew he would have to inform his partner about another disappearance, but he wasn't exactly certain he would be able to locate Woodson in the Normandy woods. He decided to give his partner a break--one more night of worry-free relaxation and then Martin would drag Harry back into their own recurring nightmare.

* * * * * *

The following day, Detective Woodson found a note on his door when he got home from his hunting trip. He could tell his partner had written the note as soon as he opened it. When he read the contents, he closed his eyes and said to himself, "Shit, shit, shit, shit, shit. Dammit, Brian. Dammit to hell."

He dumped his gear and took a quick shower before he reported to the Police Station. When he entered the building, he saw Brian Martin getting a cup of coffee down the hall, and yelled through the corridor, "I knew it wasn't over. I knew it, and you did, too. Damn crazy people. What have we got so far?"

Brian Martin nodded his agreement with his partner. "Come on back and I'll fill you in. And, by the way, you're welcome. I could have tracked you down last night right in the middle of your Kumbaya ceremony, but I decided to give you a break. Don't tell Stewart though. That would probably get my ass in trouble."

Woodson smiled as he filled a cup with hot coffee and said, "Thanks buddy. Your secret is safe with me." They each took their coffee and walked solemnly toward their offices, better known as "Kidnap Central" to the entire city police force.

* * * * *

In Gurley, Alabama the Police Chief was looking over his notes for the departmental morning briefing. When the phone rang, he expected his wife to be on the other end of the line, reminding him of his doctor's appointment that day. Instead, the voice belonged to someone he didn't recognize.

"Chief Carson, this is Millicent Abernathy, you know? I'm the sister of the woman with the little orphan girls from Tennessee?" she reminded him of how she had met him before.

"Yes, ma'am, what can I do for you Miz Abernathy?" he responded graciously.

"Well, I'm not sure, to be honest. You know about the unfortunate and untimely death of my sister, Ruth? Well, her body was released finally, and her remains came in to the local funeral home."

"Yes, ma'am, that's normal procedure," the patient Chief remarked.

"Well, when the Funeral Home Director called me to tell me she was here, he said the police told him I should come by and formally identify the body and then we could start making funeral plans. So I went over there, and Lord, her head was all beat up, black and blue. Now I just don't understand how she did that to herself if she committed suicide. That's not normal, is it?" Mrs. Abernathy asked, clearly agitated.

"Well, ma'am, why don't I go by there later today and have a look for myself. Would that be all right with you?" Chief Carson offered.

"That's what I had hoped you'd do, Chief Carson. I'll just wait until you let me know you've seen her before we start the funeral arrangements. Thank you, thank you. I didn't know who else to call."

The Chief had hoped the quickly-resolved kidnapping case was history to Gurley. He wasn't looking forward to seeing a dead body, either, but sometimes it couldn't be avoided. He would go by the funeral home sooner rather than later so he could put this case to rest.

* * * * * *

Detective Martin answered the phone, and scribbled down everything Chief Carson was saying. He motioned to Woodson to stand near the phone and read his notes as he wrote them. Woodson eagerly awaited each word's appearance on the paper as the message became clearer. There were still questions about the cause of Miss Edith Ruth's death, and now they were hearing about it from someone outside their state.

CHAPTER 22

1958

When the school year ended in May of 1958, Shelbyville citizens had grown hostile toward the police force and its management. Ads seeking applicants for a new Police Chief were taken out by private citizens in the classified section of the *Times-Gazette*. Moving vans had been maliciously sent to the homes of the City Manager and the Mayor.

The unrest had grown to its pinnacle by the time the school year ended. Frantic parents wanted solid answers and explicit instructions on how to best protect their children. Citizens wanted justice and closure on every unsolved kidnapping that had occurred since Wendy Jo Wilson vanished in September of 1955. For three years, the town had been on a roller coaster of fear and relief, and the public expected the police to act, not react. They wanted off the ride.

Police Chief Stewart had received his official promotion the day before the Claxton boy was reported missing. The ironic timing of the recent kidnapping and Stewart's appointment as Chief did not go unnoticed by Martin and Woodson. Almost all the police force had questions about the timing, but no one was stupid enough to voice a concern.

* * * * * *

On the first Saturday of June, Corb and LorAnn planned to take a day trip to Tullahoma to do some shopping and get a foot-long hotdog at the drive-in near the city limits. LorAnn liked to shop for the girls' clothes in Tullahoma's Castner-Knott store, because she never seemed to find what she liked in the Shelbyville stores. Corb's mouth watered at the thought of the foot-long chili dogs at the drive-in. They both looked forward to getting what they wanted in this one combined trip.

Dollie had been granted weekend privileges with Granny Rogers and Pap Stan, and she was making the most of her time by helping store customers and trying to sell a new shipment of flip flops to prospective buyers. Pap Stan sat on the Coca-Cola cooler and watched as the girl worked her magic. She had more of a salesperson aptitude than Dixie had, but she lacked Dixie's ability to accurately count money and make change. For a seven year old, Dollie did well enough-- provided Granny or Pap helped her with the cash register duties.

Occasionally when Dollie would stay at the store, she was allowed to go next door to the Bishop residence and play with Rodney, the nine year old son of the black pastor and his wife. The children seemed to have no awareness in the differences in their race. The Rogers' store was situated in the center of the black section of town. The Rogers loved all their customers, regardless of race or income. Just like Dollie, they never met a stranger.

During this particular weekend visit, Dollie and Rodney decided to walk to the end Cooper Street to the Lipscomb Street intersection, then made a right down Quarry Street. They proceeded a short distance to a chain linked fence that enclosed an abandoned quarry owned by the City. The quarry hadn't been functional for many years. What was once a deep body of clear blue water had now turned murky and uninviting.

"I betcha can't throw a rock through the fence and get it in the water," Dollie challenged her friend.

"That's easy. Stand back and watch this," Rodney quipped as he backed up and tossed a rock toward the top of the fence. The rock bounced off and landed a few feet from where the two were standing.

"Told 'ja. I bet I can do it. Watch me." Dollie attempted the same thing, but her rock also hit the fence and bounced backward.

Rodney thought for a second and then made a suggestion. "There's a cut place in the fence over there. My brother showed me once. I bet we can wiggle through it and get close enough to get lots of rocks to hit in the middle and sink."

Rodney quickly looked around to make certain there was no one around, then he took off running toward the back section of the fence. After scanning it briefly, he found what he was hunting.

"Dollie, c'mere. See if you can get through this hole," he called. Dollie ran to him and got down on her knees, preparing to crawl through.

Before Dollie made forward progress, she heard a man's voice screaming from her left.

"What the hell ya'll doing!" yelled a terrified and angry Pap Stan. "Git away from that right now! You'll drown in there! Dollie, you get your butt back to that store and don't let me hear you say nuthin' till I talk to your Granny. Rodney, get home. NOW." Pap Stan was filled with anger and fear. He was mad at himself for letting Dollie so far out of his sight before he noticed her missing. He was afraid Viv would knock the hell out of him for being so careless with the girl. He was mostly afraid Corb would find out about this incident and stop the girls from visiting again.

* * * * * *

A shameful Stan Rogers mounted the steps of the store's porch and upon entry, found a crying Dollie holding on to her Granny's apron with one arm, and clutching Granny's upper leg with the other one. When Pap came through the door, Dollie buried her head in the apron's side, and started wailing even louder. When she peeked out, her reddened cheeks showed the evidence of blotted dirty tear streaks.

"Stan, what's wrong with this girl? She was cryin' so hard when she came in here, she couldn't talk. Is she hurt?" Before Pap could answer, Granny looked down at Dollie and asked her the same questions. Dollie only wailed louder.

"Hell, old woman, I caught her and Rodney down at the quarry tryin' to sneak through the fence. They had piled up some rocks, so I guess they were gonna try to throw 'em in. Hell, I don't know what they were doing. But, I yelled at 'em as soon as I seen what they was up to, and I told Rodney to get home and Dollie to get back to the store."

Granny gave Pap a vicious stare. Her blood was boiling and her face was turning red. "What the hell was she doin' all the way down at that quarry? Corb is gonna be hot to trot when he hears about this. Dammit, old man, don't you have any sense? Wasn't you watchin' this girl? Go on in the back and get me a wash rag so I can wipe her face."

Pap did as he was told, thinking he was getting out lightly. He heard Granny telling Dollie never to go off Cooper Street again. She wasn't allowed past the Bishop's house anymore. Stan arrived with the wet washcloth as a pitiful Dollie looked up at them with a pouted bottom lip and said, "I won't, Granny. I'm sorry--please don't be mad at me. Don't tell Daddy I went down to the big swimming hole. Please don't tell him 'cause he won't let me come back over here. He'll whip me with his belt, too." Dollie started squalling again.

Granny took the wash cloth from Stan's hand and gently wiped the girl's face. "Hush, girl. This'll be our secret. Now go get yourself a candy bar and get in the back to watch television with Pap." Looking over her wire rimmed glasses at her husband, she said, "I think Pap can handle somethin' as simple as watching television with you. Now scat, the both of ya."

A relieved Pap and a pacified Dollie went toward the back residence rooms and entered through a heavy curtain hanging over the open doorframe. As they settled on the small couch, Dollie took a big bite of her Zero candy bar. She chewed quickly and told Pap, "I hope y'all are good at keeping secrets."

Pap chuckled and turned the channel to an episode of "Father Knows Best."

"Me too, girl," Pap said as he leaned back and helped himself to a big plug of tobacco.

* * * * * *

While Dollie was with Pap and Granny, Dixie had chosen to visit with Aunt Roz and Uncle Troy again. It seemed to her that Aunt Roz was acting a little bit strange lately. She was always hovering around a lot, and often asked Ma Rose to sit in the living room while she and Uncle Troy played marbles or jacks on the floor.

During her last few visits, the only time she was with Uncle Troy alone was during their ice cream runs. They started going through the back roads to Sutton's store, but they had lengthened their trips back home by going the long way through town. Their Life Lesson sessions had to be given while they drove through the roads and streets of Bedford County.

Roz had mentioned to Troy that it might not look so good to Corb if he ever found out Troy was spending time alone with Dixie in the shed. Troy considered this good advice, plus he wondered if Roz had caught on to what he and Dixie discussed. He decided to heed the advice and keep his growing relationship with Dixie low-key.

Dixie hadn't said anything about their not visiting the shed. Instead, she was getting closer to her Aunt Roz, which had been her original intention when she started regular visits to the Tucker's house.

Aunt Roz had been giving Dixie beauty tips, even though her parents didn't allow her to wear makeup. Instead she showed Dixie how to accent her eyes by styling her hair a little differently. Aunt Roz also gave her a small bottle of cologne for "special occasions." Last fall, Aunt Roz had secretly taken her shopping and bought Dixie her first bra. Wearing the bra made her blooming adolescent figure look more proportioned, and Dixie liked the way wearing it made her feel more secure with her body. Little by little, Dixie was becoming a beautiful thirteen year old young lady.

* * * * * *

As soon as Troy and Dixie pulled out of the driveway to go on their ice cream run, Dixie started the session with a question.

"Uncle Troy, I think I've learned a lot during our last few sessions, don't you?"

He nodded while he watched the road ahead.

"Well now that I'm thirteen, do you think I'm ready to have sex?" she asked, in a clinical tone.

He tried to keep the car positioned in the center of the road as he turned his head to look at her serious face.

"Who do you want to have sex with? You don't even have a boyfriend yet, do you?" he asked in a concerned, fatherly sort of way.

"No, of course not, silly. I'm not asking TO have sex, I just want to know when a girl CAN have sex."

Relieved, Troy began his answer. "You got all the body parts that you have to have to do it. You just don't have the love part in your heart. I wouldn't go trying to find anybody to have sex with just yet." Neither said a word. He wasn't sure she heard him or understood what he meant to say.

He drove further down the road, taking the right fork to Troupe Road. He broached a new idea for a lesson plan topic. "Maybe sometime I can tell you about what it's like to have sex. Would that be somethin' you think would help you understand better?" Troy's heart was pounding harder.

"I guess so, Uncle Troy. Maybe if you don't get into too much detail, it'd be okay."

They drove on in silence, got their ice cream at Sutton's, and took the shortcut back home. Troy wanted to be absolutely sure about what he was going to say to Dixie next time they had their Life Lesson. Thankfully, Dixie didn't ask any more questions of Troy during the remainder of the weekend.

During the next week, Troy spent a lot of time in his shed trying to gather his thoughts for the revised Life Lesson plan. He had to look through several of his stashed magazines to get a feel for the next stage of his teacher role.

Part Four

Corruption, Cover-up, and Confirmation

CHAPTER 23

1958

Brian Martin leaned back in his desk chair, stretched his arms above his head and yawned. He looked at the clock and realized for the tenth night in a row he wouldn't be home until midnight or later. He wondered how much more patience his wife had left.

Harry Woodson came through Martin's door with a bag of Krispy Kreme doughnuts, swinging it in front of his face in an attempt to lure his partner to take a break.

"You know, Brian, maybe the answers we've been looking for are right in front of our noses. You know K-I-S-S really means "keep it simple, stupid." Maybe we're trying to make these cases more complicated than they really are." Woodson took a bite of a chocolate glazed doughnut as he sat down on the corner of Martin's desk.

"Exactly which answer are you referring to, Einstein? The one about the Ruth woman's death, the one about the four unsolved kidnappings, or the one about why you can't get a date?" Martin sneered as he reached for the bag to grab himself a treat.

Woodson smiled, and answered his sarcastic partner, "Right now, I'm thinking about the Ruth woman's death, but the same theory probably applies to everything."

"Please enlighten me, Harry. I'm too tired to play guessing games," said the weary detective as he reached for his half-empty cup of cold coffee.

"Well, I started thinking about the late Miss Ruth. Nobody at the jail admits to knowing what happened to her face and the bruising on her body, and apparently her sister was the only one curious enough to ask about it. When you and I talked to the Sheriff, he said maybe she was so out of her mind she banged herself up trying to kill herself, and when that failed, she took the sure-fire hanging route. Besides, the autopsy ordered by the Feds didn't make much of those injuries.

"And remember when we told Stewart about our interview with the Sheriff? Remember how upset he was and reamed us good for not talking to him first before we questioned anybody in Nashville ?"

Martin finished off his doughnut and reached into the bag for another. "Yeah, go on," he urged his partner.

"When I think back on it, he looked angry and guilty as sin, to me. We let it go because he was new and we figured he wanted us to bow to his authority. You know how power affects some people."

"Yep," Martin stated while he licked chocolate frosting off his fingers.

"Here's where we didn't keep it simple, or maybe kept it too simple. If we had followed our gut, we wouldn't have stopped there. We would have interviewed other people from the jail and tried to find out who caused the injuries to that woman before she died. We got sidetracked with another kidnapping—and rightly so—but now that I think about it, we didn't go about our job right with any of it."

Martin looked as though he had been insulted. "Look Harry. That so-called suicide happened in another jurisdiction. We didn't have any control to begin with. What could we have done differently?"

Woodson answered immediately. "All I'm saying is we should have let our gut lead us to what really happened in ALL the cases. We were pretty sure that Miss Ruth didn't have anything to do with the teenagers' disappearances, yet we let Stewart close the cases and get his promotion. We did what everybody else did, and we followed like sheep. We accepted what was in front of us and hoped for the best. That hasn't worked out very well for anybody...except Stewart."

Martin now looked as if a light bulb had come on in his head. "So you think it all leads back to Stewart somehow?"

"Maybe not everything, but I think he's dirty and has too much ambition. Maybe he found a way to get himself into the Chief's saddle without buying the horse." Woodson smiled as if he had made a profound statement.

Martin crumpled up the empty doughnut bag and threw it at his partner, barely missing his face. "Worth looking into a little more, I'd say. Okay, partner. Let's do some "what if's" for a while."

The two detectives left their office lights on and went directly to their best thinking spot, the Rebel Maid. They ordered their favorite strawberry milkshakes and waited for their treats to arrive.

In their unmarked car in the crowded lot of a drive-in, they batted their hypothetical scenarios back and forth. Both men believed they were on to something. Without being able to explain why, both men believed in their "gut" they were about to put themselves in danger.

* * * * * *

Performing a covert investigation involving a fellow employee is difficult. Even when your assistants are loyal and sworn to secrecy, there's always a chance that the person being investigated will learn about it and sabotage the outcome.

The detectives still weren't positive about Chief Stewart's possible connection with the Edith Ruth case, but they believed they would always wonder if they didn't make some attempt at finding the complete truth.

Detectives Martin and Woodson determined that the best way to handle their unauthorized sleuthing would be do it alone, with no outside help from anyone. Official trips to Nashville would be questioned and would not be approved if Stewart thought the two were trying to find out anything more about the Edith Ruth case.

The most logical way to continue with their clandestine work and keep suspicions to a minimum required Brian Martin to ask for time off to take his wife on a much-needed "surprise" vacation. If this worked the way he hoped, his wife wouldn't know the real reason behind the adventure.

* * * * * *

When Chief Stewart stopped by Martin's desk on the afternoon of June 27, 1958, he noticed that the detective had cleared his desk of the normal clutter.

"What's up, Martin. You planning on resigning?" The Chief chuckled. "I don't think I've ever seen your desk so clean."

"Well, sir. I was hoping I might be able to take a few days off next week before the Fourth of July holiday and take a short trip with my wife. We were interrupted during our anniversary dinner when the Claxton boy disappeared. She's been very patient with me and my long hours, and I was hoping I could find a way to make it up to her."

The Chief stalled for a minute, recalling how the backlash from all the disappearances had calmed down a little since the initial uproar in February. "Can Detective Woodson fill in for you if anything comes up?" the Chief asked hesitantly.

"He knows everything I know about our work. He asked me the other day when I was planning to take Jenny for a second honeymoon. I think he knows how all that time away from home has affected her. I don't think he'd mind covering for me for a few days."

The Chief smiled, trying to earn points with his lead detective. "Why not? Go ahead and take the whole week… that is, if you're sure Woodson can single-handedly take care of everything that comes in while you're gone." The Chief smiled his most gracious fake smile.

"Thanks, Chief. Jenny and I really appreciate it. I'll go make sure Woodson's fully on board with next week, and brief him with anything left hanging before I leave today." Brian smiled broadly as the Chief patted him on the shoulder and returned to his office.

* * * * * *

The bustling city of Nashville was a delight to Jenny Martin, who had not had her husband's undivided attention for years. She would have preferred going to Gatlinburg to visit the beautiful Smoky Mountains, but she was content with Nashville—anywhere alone with Brian and away from the reach of his office.

Brian had already mentioned he had to do some research at the main library in the city, so she volunteered to spend a day sightseeing and shopping in the busy downtown area while he took care of his errand. When she finished, she planned to walk to the Hermitage Hotel and relax in their room until it was time for dinner.

* * * * * *

When Brian dropped Jenny off on Fifth Avenue, she waved goodbye and threw him a kiss when she was safely on the sidewalk. He watched her start walking toward the Ryman Auditorium, feeling confident that her day would be filled with enough adventure that she would forgive him if his research took more time than planned.

He made his way toward West End Avenue to meet a friend who was a Detective with the Metro Police Department of Nashville. His college buddy, Aaron Caldwell, had spent most of his career as a homicide detective, but he also had experience with the narcotics division. Early in his career as a patrolman, Aaron received a broken nose when he tried to break up a rowdy domestic dispute.

Brian looked forward to seeing Aaron again after so many years, but today was not as much about reliving memories as it was establishing a motive for a suspicious death.

* * * * * *

Brian parked under the shadiest tree he could find, hoping to fend off the summer heat as much as possible. He had arrived early, so he rolled down the car windows and turned on the radio. He sang along with Elvis when the radio played "Jailhouse Rock," thinking how appropriate that song was for him and all the guys from the office. He was beating out the song's rhythm on the steering wheel when he heard a familiar voice coming from behind him.

"You still got it, swivel hips," his friend Aaron laughed. Brian got out of the car and greeted his buddy with a quick handshake and an even quicker hug. They walked for a short distance in the shadow of the Parthenon, talking about their families and their careers, and their baffling caseloads. They settled on a park bench under a sprawling oak tree that must have been a century old. They laughed and joked, and lamented friends lost too soon. Eventually they got to the subject they were meeting about.

"Brian, I asked around about the woman who was found hanged to death in the Davidson County Jail. I have a few department friends who I exchange information with on various occasions, so I went to them first.

"There are gangs in the women's jails, just like in prison. Some of them offer protection to paying inmates, while others will beat the hell out of anybody if they have something they want. You know what it's like. But there's this one crew specifically in the Nashville Women's Prison that's run from the outside by a big hefty cow of a woman. She is the one person everybody's afraid of, even the prison guards and county policemen. She's out on parole now, but she has active connections in both the state prison and the county jail.

"It's been said that she spends a lot of time talking to the Deputy Sheriff. They get along real well, if you can believe that. Supposedly, she gets paid for informing on other criminals, and sometimes that might include roughing up a target for whatever reason. Some guards and jailers have been told to look the other way whenever "Big Mama" has a tantrum or wants something special. That kind of treatment has to be the result of an arrangement from higher up in the towers. From the way it sounds, the Sheriff may not even know what's going on."

Brian was taking notes as Aaron talked, but he stopped to ask a question. "So who is this Deputy Sheriff and how did he get so cozy with Big Mama?"

Aaron shook his head. "I don't know how he got under Big Mama's spell, but I can give you the name of the guy." Aaron took his own note pad from his chest pocket, flipped a few pages, and then said, "The guy's name is G. Howard Wilson. I did a little digging on him, too, 'cause I figured you'd ask."

Brian nodded with complete understanding. He and Aaron had the same work ethic and always seemed to think along the same lines. "Let's have it, Buddy."

"George Howard Wilson was born in Davidson County in 1908, making him roughly 50 years old now. He attended high school in Nashville, college at MTSU, and went on to Vanderbilt Law School. He practiced law in Franklin, Tennessee for a while. In 1946 he accepted a job with the Davidson County Sheriff's Office as Deputy Sheriff and relocated from Franklin to the Belle Meade area here in town."

Brian stopped writing and commented, "He doesn't sound very interesting to me. Got anything else?"

Aaron's smile broadened. "Maybe this will be interesting to you, maybe not." He just looked at Brian and didn't say anything.

Brian's curiosity was getting the better of him. "Okay, I give. Spit it out, Aaron."

Aaron theatrically flipped another note page in his little black book. "It says here he married a pretty little girl from Shelbyville in 1933. Let's see, what was her maiden name ...hmm... can't seem to locate it. Let me keep looking."

Brian couldn't tolerate the playful pause. "Who'd he marry, Aaron? Who'd he marry?"

"Miss Mary Ellen Stewart, sister to Geraldine Stewart and Peter William Stewart." He snapped his note pad shut and put it back in his breast pocket. He looked pleased with himself.

"Holy Shit, Aaron. Do you know what this could mean? That prick, Peter Stewart, probably *did* have connections to the Ruth woman's death. And that meant he could pin all the other disappearances on that poor woman. It helped him get the Chief's job and it permanently shut up the only person who knew what he claimed was bullshit. Damn, you do good work, Buddy." Brian stood up and for a minute, Aaron thought Brian would break out in a victory dance.

"Hey man, don't draw attention to us. I had to call in some favors to get this information, and I expect anonymity," Aaron reminded his friend.

"Don't worry, man. I got your back, 'cause you may have just saved me and the whole town from a dirty cop running the show. I'll work this with my partner and we'll be very careful as to how it goes down." Brian couldn't hide his revived optimism. "Now how about we get some lunch? It's on me, of course."

"Absolutely! If you're buying, I'm gonna hit you up for a good steak," Aaron teased.

Brian was feeling generous. "Just point me in the right direction and I'll get you the whole cow. You deserve it, man. You really came through for us. I can't thank you enough, so I'll buy you the best damn steak you've had in a long time."

* * * * * *

Brian returned to the Hermitage Hotel feeling more confident than he had in months. Jenny hadn't returned from her shopping and sightseeing yet, so he turned on the shower and jumped in. He was happy to have some time to himself to let everything sink in that he had found out today. He knew the powerful impact of revealing what he knew, and he also recognized the risk of sharing the information too soon. He would have to talk with Woodson. Between the two of them, they'd figure out how to get everything into the public spotlight nice and neat.

Before he turned off the water, he heard the bathroom door open. Jenny jerked back the shower curtain and revealed Brian's drenched naked body. "Oh my goodness, sir. I'm from housekeeping and I didn't know a big, strong, handsome man like yourself would be standing in the shower without anything to cover his gorgeous body. I do declare, sir, you make me blush," Jenny stated in her best Scarlett O'Hara voice.

"That's all right, miss. I was just about to dry off and take a nap. Or maybe you'd like to inspect the towels and the sheets with me?" Brian kissed his wife with renewed passion. His focus had shifted to Jenny. Only Jenny.

* * * * *

After a romantic dinner in the hotel's dining room, Brian asked Jenny if she would go ahead to their room to prepare for the late night dessert he had ordered. It would be arriving in an hour, and he suggested that she slip into her lounging pajamas ahead of the scheduled delivery time. Jenny left Brian alone at the table, and sashayed through the maze of tables toward the lobby. Brian paid the check and then made his way to the lobby to find a phone.

* * * * *

When Harry Woodson answered the call, he was sitting at his desk and preparing for another long evening of paperwork. He had expected to hear from Brian during the day and wondered if he had learned anything that would provide fresh leads on the Edith Ruth cause of death.

"Harry, you're not gonna believe what I found out today," an excited Brian Martin told him from the other end of the line.

As Martin repeated what Aaron Caldwell had learned, Harry became more motivated with every revelation. When he finished, Martin calmly asked, "So what's our next move?"

Harry replied, "You and Jenny enjoy the rest of your vacation, and leave everything else to me. I have an idea about how we can move forward without disrupting anything from here--at least for now. I expect when the shit hits the fan, this office will be covered with flying turds." The two detectives laughed together for the first time in a while.

Woodson began to plan his next move.

So did Martin, but his plan didn't concern the police department. He took the hotel elevator to the third floor, and entered his room to discover his beckoning wife lounging on their bed.

* * * * *

Woodson was kept busy while Martin was away. Not only did he competently handle his routine detective duties, he kicked off the clandestine implementation of his plan to further the investigation of Miss Ruth's beating and eventual death.

As soon as he hung up from Martin's informative call, Woodson opened his center desk drawer and pushed away loose paper clips and scattered office paraphernalia looking for a business card he'd taken almost a year before. He finally located it stuck in the seam of the wooden drawer. With renewed enthusiasm, he picked up his desk phone and dialed the number prominently displayed on the card's bottom corner. Silently, he hoped the call would be answered, even though it was early evening when most people would have already left for the day.

When a female voice answered, Woodson breathed a sigh of relief.

"Agent Cortner, this is Detective Harry Woodson from the Shelbyville Police Department. Do you have a few minutes to chat about a former case that you worked on that concerned the abduction of two young children from our town? You and another agent drove the girls to Shelbyville from Alabama in November of '57."

FBI Special Agent Eva Cortner remembered the case vividly. She thought everything concerning the case had been tied up in a neat package and put to bed. She was surprised that the Shelbyville detective still had questions.

"Of course, Detective. But I have to tell you that I'm late for a banquet that I'm required to attend. If this is going to be a lengthy conversation, it might be better to have it in person somewhere that's convenient to both of us. I'm temporarily assigned to the Nashville office this month. Perhaps we could arrange lunch in Murfreesboro in the next couple of days? The drive would be basically split between our two offices."

Detective Woodson was elated. "It would be my pleasure to meet with you and tell you what I'm concerned about. And for your trouble, I'll personally treat you to lunch—this isn't formal and doesn't officially concern the city.

Agent Cortner smiled on her side of the phone, remembering her first sight of Woodson and how she had thought he had a certain charm about him. "That sounds good, Detective. Let's tentatively plan for Wednesday at 1:00 p.m. I can meet you at the Big Boy Restaurant on Murfreesboro Road near the Highway 231 intersection. I don't know anything about restaurants there, but I do know where the Big Boy is located. Nothing extra fancy, since you're treating."

Woodson was also smiling. "That's a deal, Agent Cortner. I'll look forward to it. Enjoy your banquet," he remarked as he hung up the phone.

He was happier about this prospect than he should have been. He remembered the exact moment when the attractive and shapely Agent Cortner exited the car that brought the Carter kids home. He remembered how his heart started beating faster immediately afterwards.

CHAPTER 24

1958

As Corb drove through town on his way back to work from lunch with the family at their El Bethel home, he noticed that all the storefronts displayed newly printed flyers of all four unfound kidnapped victims. He thought back to when his own girls had vanished from the school grounds, and thanked God for his daughters' safe return. The long hours before they were recovered had been hell on earth for him and LorAnn. The whole family silently suffered, too. He shook his head with sadness and imagined that surely those unfortunate children on the new posters must already be dead.

When he turned down Pencil Street on his way back to his office at the City Garage, he saw Marvin Morgan pass him going the opposite way in the city's Animal Control truck. Even though Marvin didn't work directly under Corb, the vehicle he used to retrieve strays and road kill was housed in a warehouse type building on the same grounds as the City Garage. Marvin was an hourly part time worker for the city, and was only paid for trips he was called upon to make. Somebody must have reported a dead dog or deer somewhere around the area for Marvin to be leaving the warehouse around lunchtime.

Those thoughts led Corb to remember the altercation between Marvin and Troy during Christmas a few years back. He chuckled to himself at how Marvin's weird son apparently caught Troy with his pants down. He didn't really think Troy had fooled with the Morgan boy, but he was well aware of Troy's penchant for dirty magazines and jerking off, not to mention the occasional extramarital fling. Corb just figured Troy was interrupted by the "retard" and was so flustered, he didn't handle it well when Marvin confronted him about his upset son.

Corb didn't care for Marvin Morgan anyway, and was thankful he had no supervisory duties associated with the man. Corb didn't want to be in the middle of the Tucker-Morgan mess, either, so he avoided Marvin as much as he could during work. It was a blessing that Marvin appeared to avoid Corb, too.

* * * * * *

One thing Corb always tried to do when he was near the City Manager's office was to visit other municipal offices and get acquainted with the town's representatives. He made it a practice to stop into the Police Department offices occasionally because he liked the feeling of camaraderie those particular visits inspired.

After seeing the new posters of the missing teens in passing window fronts, he felt overcome with gratefulness to those individuals who had worked so hard to find his girls. Before leaving the city limits to go home for the day, he made a special trip to see the Police Chief and the two detectives. He wanted to once again thank the people to whom he was obliged for saving his daughters.

* * * * * *

Dixie wasn't aware that there was a spot of blood in her panties until she took them off before her bath that night.

Oh no. It's here. I wanted Aunt Roz to help me when this happened, and now look what's happened. I'm stuck down here in the country and she's at work by now.

Dixie had no choice but to call for her Mother. LorAnn answered outside the bathroom door when she heard Dixie call her name.

"Mama, I think I might need some help. I got blood in my underwear," Dixie calmly responded.

LorAnn had been expecting this for a while, so she tried to open the bathroom door, but it was locked.

"Wait a minute, Mama. Let me put my clothes back on," a modest Dixie explained to her mother.

When LorAnn entered the bathroom, Dixie stood there with her dirty dress on awaiting her mother's assistance.

"Dixie, do you know why you got this blood?" LorAnn quizzed her precocious daughter.

"Mama, they showed us a movie in school about it. I know it'll come regular now, but I don't know how to keep it off my clothes. Can you help me fix that?"

LorAnn smiled and hugged her daughter. "I sure can, and if there's anything you need to ask, just let me know."

Dixie stated solemnly, "That's okay, Mama. After this, Aunt Roz can help me if I need it."

LorAnn attempted to conceal her hurt feelings and carried on with the mission at hand. Once Dixie had learned about sanitary belts and napkins, LorAnn left her to get it right and put it on. Dixie never asked her anything else, except where to dispose of her used pads.

* * * * * *

LorAnn was still feeling sad and hurt about Dixie's preference for Aunt Roz over her own mother. For a while, she sat on the front porch in her rocking chair, watching Dollie chase a stray dog around the front yard. The dog had appeared overnight, and Dollie was already attached.

In a while, LorAnn stood up and solemnly walked back indoors and picked up the phone. The party line was occupied by Mrs. Harris, a widow who lived up the road and had nothing to do except talk to her relatives on the phone. LorAnn put the occupied phone down and waited for Corb to get home. At least he could empathize with her. He sometimes believed Troy was Dixie's favorite male adult, and he had voiced his concern to LorAnn once or twice before.

She picked up the phone again, and this time she heard the familiar hum of a dial tone. She dialed the number just when she remembered Roz would be at work by now. She hung up, relinquishing the phone to Mrs. Harris, who had already picked up again before LorAnn hung up.

* * * * *

It was six o'clock before Corb arrived home that evening, and a hot supper was waiting on the table. Dollie wanted to bring the stray dog in to eat with them, but Corb unequivocally said no. LorAnn finished setting the table while the girls were washing up, and Corb sat at the head of the table while they finished.

"Dixie started her monthlies today," LorAnn whispered discreetly to her husband. "Don't you say a word about it, though. She don't even wanna talk to me about it. Says she'd rather talk to Roz."

Corb looked at LorAnn with a puzzled look on his face. "Why would she do that?"

"I don't know. Maybe they're getting' too close. You think maybe we oughta slow down their visits or maybe cut 'em off all together for a while?" LorAnn responded.

Before he could answer, both girls entered the kitchen and found their places at the table. They reached for cornbread, acting as if they were both starving. Corb looked at LorAnn and shrugged his shoulders in a silent response to her question.

Later that night when the parents were lying in bed, Corb turned to LorAnn and rekindled the discussion about the Tuckers.

"LorAnn, maybe you oughta talk to Roz and let her know how Dixie's acting lately. It could just be that she's embarrassed to talk to you about this stuff. I admit, I think the girl's got real close to both Roz and Troy, and I'm beginning to wonder about that. But I don't think it's worth stopping their visits all together."

Always adhering to Corb's wishes, she agreed that she'd explain things to Roz and maybe she would start acting more like an aunt than a substitute mother to Dixie.

* * * * *

When mid-morning rolled around the next day, LorAnn was ready to call Roz and have the dreaded chat with her Sister. She waited until she was certain Roz would be up from her late morning slumber and ready to start her day. There were only a few hours left before Roz would have to get ready to report to the Rubber Mill.

Roz answered the phone on the second ring. When she heard her sister's voice, she sat down in the seat that was made into a part of the phone table. She tried to get comfortable, anticipating a lengthy catch-up call.

"Roz, I need to talk to you about Dixie. She started her period yesterday, and she wouldn't talk to me about it. She said she'd wait and talk to you," LorAnn blurted out without thinking. That was not how she had planned to start the conversation.

"What are you saying, LorAnn? Are you concerned about that? Don't be. When we bought her that bra, she asked me about getting' periods. I told her when that happened, we'd talk about it then. I sure wasn't tryin' to step on your toes." Roz meekly replied.

"Maybe it just hit me wrong. You know she's spending so much time with you and Troy, I just wonder if that's a problem. I know you didn't mean anything by it. You're just tryin' to help, s'all," LorAnn said as she wiped silent tears from her eyes.

Roz hoped LorAnn was just feeling emotional considering everything that had happened to the family, along with the depressing mood of the town after the other missing kids had not been located.

Roz brought up a topic she had been hesitant to broach. "While we're talkin' about Dixie, has she said anything about spendin' time with Troy?"

LorAnn remembered that Corb had also wondered if Dixie was becoming too attached to her doting uncle. "No, she don't talk much about what goes on when she's with y'all. Do you think somethin's happenin'?" Now LorAnn's internal alarm was going off.

"No, I don't. It's just that Marvin Morgan came outside one day and told me Troy had taken Dixie out to the shed. He said his retarded son heard 'em talking about kissin' and stuff. I shrugged it off 'cause they ain't been out to the shed since and Dixie don't seem like she's been scared or anything. Only time they've been alone since is for ice cream trips, and it don't seem to take too long to do that. After Marvin and his boy caused the ruckus during Christmas that time, I guess I got my imagination all worked up when he told me about the shed. I really don't think there's nothin' to it. Troy loves your girls too much to ever cross that line. He knows Corb'd kill him if he ever touched a hair on their little heads, too." Roz got it all out in one fell swoop.

LorAnn contemplated what she had just heard and tried to decide if she should tell Corb about Marvin Morgan's insinuation. Finally LorAnn spoke again to Roz.

"Let's just leave it be for now. I don't think Troy would do anything like that to Dixie, either. I guess we're both getting' over-protective, and it's hard to know what to do. I don't hardly know how to deal with a teenager, 'cause I ain't had much practice. I guess we're all learning as we go." Unless she knew for certain there was a concern with Troy's behavior toward Dixie, LorAnn wanted to keep her head buried in the proverbial sand.

They ended the call on a pleasant note and made plans for the girls to visit soon.

Roz got ready for work while Troy was washing his motorcycle.

LorAnn went to her bedroom, shut the door, and prayed for guidance.

* * * * * *

Corb was still at work when he got the call from LorAnn. After her talk with Roz, she had tried to determine if Dixie might be in some danger with Troy or whether she was overreacting. She eventually concluded that only Corb could set her mind at ease. He always easily discerned what should be handled and what should be ignored.

When he answered the phone, LorAnn repeated to him the full conversation she had with Roz earlier that afternoon. She explained how she'd prayed over it, hoped for a release of anxiety, but still had a sinking feeling in her gut.

Corb listened carefully and when she finished, he tried to calm her feelings. "LorAnn, Roz and Troy are good people. They been good to us and our girls. I think Dixie has felt left out a lot since Dollie's been born, and she used to spend a lot of time with Ma and Stan. When we moved to Union Street, she started goin' to Roz and Troy's then. It's like she's had three sets of parents. She's just acting natural toward them and to us. She'll come out of that."

LorAnn reluctantly agreed but still had questions. "But what about the shed? What about Rocky hearin' Troy talkin' to Dixie about that kind of stuff?"

In his mind, Corb was upset about that, as well. However, he knew Troy better than a lot of people and couldn't believe he would ever do or say anything inappropriate to Dixie. "LorAnn, that crazy boy told his dumber'n shit Daddy a made up story, that's all. I don't believe it for a minute. If it'll make you feel better, I'll talk to Troy about it. At least we'll be makin' a full circle and gettin' everything out on in the open that's botherin' us."

Again, LorAnn listened to Corb's reasoning and allowed herself to relax. She knew Corb would take care of Troy if he ever made a move against either of their daughters. She was confident he would protect them at all costs.

She was more certain of what their girls meant to him than she was of how he felt about her. After all, he continuously had affair after affair. She was content with that as long as it didn't break up her marriage. That, she couldn't tolerate-- she wouldn't tolerate.

CHAPTER 25

1958

The first time Harry Woodson entered the Big Boy Restaurant in Murfreesboro, he scanned the booths and tables searching for FBI Special Agent Eva Cortner. He spotted a raised hand waving in the far right corner. Sporting his best suit and brightest smile, he eagerly strolled toward the restaurant's nearly empty back section to find a stunning woman awaiting his arrival.

It was apparent that the two were glad to see each other again. After small-talk and a brief perusal of the menu, they placed their lunch orders, and then gazed at each other shyly before the official conversation began.

"I've been looking forward to this for many reasons," a bold Harry Woodson stated. He caught her blush and when they made eye contact, she flashed him a timid smile. She looked toward her lap at her nervous hands and decided she shouldn't be acting like a silly school girl. She raised her head and told him, "Well, I certainly hope there's something I can help you with today. You know— "justice for all."

Harry wasn't disappointed in her response. In fact, had he been in her place he would have said something like that, as well.

"Well, then. Why don't I give you the basics now, and after we eat we'll discuss strategy. If there is a strategy, I mean."

Harry recited the history of the kidnappings that had occurred in Shelbyville since 1955. When he finished the overview, she gazed to her right as if she were visualizing and reviewing everything that the detective had just said. She remained silent for several minutes, causing Harry to think he had lost her attention.

When she turned her head to face him, the serious look of her expression told Harry that she had heard everything and was processing the spectrum of information. He had mentioned all his suspicions about the new Shelbyville Chief of Police and his Davidson County Deputy Sheriff brother-in-law. She had the total overview of the story, but still needed details to fill in the gaps.

"Look, Harry. I think you may be on to something, but I'm not sure how the FBI can help. I think I need to know everything, every detail, every suspicion. Maybe we should table that discussion for now and meet again later to firm it up."

Harry was agreeable to another meeting, and quickly accepted the offer. "Sure, Agent Cortner. Whatever you say. I'm just thankful you're willing to listen."

Eva was pleased to have another opportunity to see Harry again, albeit under semi-official circumstances. However, she planned to do a little digging of her own before they met next time, and she didn't want the detective to know that just yet. Harry had given her names that she could start with, and she believed he was onto something. She knew she would have to bring her boss on board if her suspicions were to lead to an official investigation. Eva silently hoped what she might preliminarily find would warrant just that.

Eva looked at her watch, and took a final bite of the strawberry pie they were both sharing. "I'm sorry, Detective Woodson. I've gotta run." She started gathering her purse and notepad to leave.

"Please call me Harry. And I'd like to call you Eva if you don't mind," he remarked as he extended his hand to help her to her feet.

"I'd like that...Harry," she responded as she took his hand in hers.

Harry felt his stomach do a somersault. He released her hand and motioned for her to lead the way out.

As she reached for the door handle of her sedan, she called across the car's roof to Harry, "I'll call you when I'm ready to talk more. I've got your card."

Harry gave her a silly little salute and got into his car. *That was stupid. A salute? She must think I'm a bumbling idiot.*

Eva chuckled as she got a glimpse of the detective sitting behind the wheel of his parked car. She could tell he was kicking himself for that silly salute.

As she pulled out onto Murfreesboro Highway and headed toward Nashville, her mind shifted to what must be done to prove there was something in his story that warranted an official federal investigation. She had several ideas, and she made up her mind to pursue them all.

* * * * * *

Eva and Harry met again, but this time she met him at his garage apartment on the north side of Shelbyville.

She had contacted Harry on Thursday evening to arrange another restaurant meeting, but he said he feared their private conversation would be overheard in a public area. Instead, he suggested that he try to cook spaghetti for her. She agreed, and consented to be there Saturday evening at 7:00 p.m.

When she pulled in the white fenced, winding driveway she thought she was at the wrong place. She started to back out, but then she saw Harry waving to her from the second story porch of the detached garage. She put the car in drive and headed toward the handsome bachelor's apartment.

"You live in a swanky area, Harry. I'm impressed," Eva laughed as he met her at the door.

"Just wait till I show you my vast art collection, madam. They're all originals, and collected by my mother during the first decade of my life. There are some watercolors—excuse me, finger paintings—and others were done with crayons, but I assure you the artist will someday be discovered." Eva thought he was hilarious.

"I can't wait. But for now, do you rent this place or what? It's really neat up here," she said as her eyes took in the full scope of the living space.

"I rent it from a very nice couple. He's a horse trainer and she's his bookkeeper. They're down-home folks and they don't really need the money. My rent is ridiculously low, which is something else this apartment has going for it."

* * * * * *

Harry served his guest a heaping plate of spaghetti, which was his specialty. She found it surprisingly good. He served a red merlot with the meal, and had bought a strawberry pie from Whitman's Bakery for their late evening dessert.

They both ate second helpings and admittedly overindulged. They took their glasses of wine to the small private back balcony outside Harry's bedroom. Eva glanced toward the neatly made bed as they passed through the room, but Harry acted as though it wasn't there. He proceeded to open the sliding glass door and ushered his guest outside.

The view was pastoral with horses running through the beautiful grassland, romping with each other and tending their foals. The sunset was beautiful as they peered beyond the green trees and distant rolling hills.

Their conversation was limited, but their thoughts were overflowing. Neither wanted to acknowledge the feeling of closeness they were building. Both were career-minded people, and attempted to remember the reason they were meeting in the first place.

Eva broke the spell when she emptied her glass and said, "Well, let's go get 'em. I have some new information to share, and I think you'll be pleased."

She left Harry standing alone on the small balcony. He downed his remaining wine and followed her through the bedroom to the cleared small kitchen table where they sat during dinner.

He pulled a chair out for Eva to take, and he took the seat next to it. She opened her briefcase and extracted two inches of paperwork and laid it on the table.

"Now I'll show you where your little suspicion has taken me. Hold onto your horse, Harry. We're about to take a wild ride."

* * * * * *

It took almost three hours for Eva and Harry to get through all the information Eva had collected over the past 48 hours. Harry was impressed and overwhelmed.

"How did you get all this accumulated, Eva? I didn't know you had that kind of power," a stunned Harry said.

"It's easy when you've got the resources, Harry. Also, federal agents have more available to them than city cops," she casually stated.

"Kinda' makes me want to join the federal forces. I'm amazed at all this." Harry flipped through a section of papers.

Eva had uncovered a huge discovery. She started with a closer look at the Deputy Sheriff, G. Howard Wilson, the brother-in-law to Shelbyville's Chief of Police. She managed to get access to his bank account and immediately found monthly scheduled withdrawals in the amount of $100. Tracing the checks to their destination revealed a regularly scheduled deposit to a bank account in the name of Irene Simpson, also known around law enforcement circles as "Big Mama."

When Eva realized a state government employee was funding a non-family, former inmate's bank account, she brought her boss on board. The Special Agent-In-Charge gave her the go ahead to proceed with her probe, and also supplied Eva with additional manpower and resources to launch a covert investigation into the Deputy Sheriff's activities.

A look at the phone records from the Deputy Sheriff's office also showed several incoming and outgoing calls to Police Chief Stewart, with eleven or more calls during the period that Miss Edith Ruth was held in the Davidson County Jail.

From all appearances, there could have been collusion between the brothers-in-law to solicit the strong-arm services of Big Mama. Perhaps she was told to convince Miss Ruth to confess to everything. There was no way to tell from the gathered information. There would have to be more effort invested in the investigation to find out anything definitive.

Harry and Eva agreed to work together and include Brian Martin in their joint collaboration.

* * * * * *

Brian Martin returned to his office on July 7, 1958 after more than a week of much-deserved vacation with his beautiful bride of over five years. Not only did he refresh his relationship with Jenny, he had revived his enthusiasm to move the Shelbyville Police Department back on track.

After turning the light on over his desk, his venture through the office maze was to discover an unattended, empty glass coffee pot simmering on the warming element. He swirled cold water around in the browning glass pot and carefully filled the machine to brew another pot. While he waited, his partner rounded the corner and welcomed him back enthusiastically.

"Martin, old man! Good to have you back. Did you and Jenny kiss and makeup? Is everything happy in paradise now? Should we expect any little Brians running around in the Martin household in the near future?" Woodson laughed as he slapped his partner on the back.

"Go to hell, Harry," Brian chuckled. He sipped his steaming coffee and turned to mosey back toward his office. He looked back at his partner and asked, "You got anything you want to share about what you been doing this week, Harry?"

Woodson eagerly responded, "It just so happens I do, Lover Boy. Why don't we get together in about thirty minutes to talk about it. I believe the amount of progress I've made –while you were off having a grand old time, I might add--will make your first day back at the grindstone easier to tackle.

CHAPTER 26

1958

FBI Special Agent Eva Cortner walked toward the entrance to the Davidson County Jail in Nashville with Special Agent Phillip Houston, her partner for the past three years. Their gaits were measured and sure, and they entered the facility with confidence.

When they stopped at the sign-in desk, they flashed their badges, introduced themselves, and informed the desk sergeant that they had an appointment with the Sheriff, Roland Kirkman. They stood patiently by the sergeant's station awaiting entry and directions to the Sheriff's office.

As they were led toward a small hallway, the Sheriff himself greeted them. He was a tall man with a bald head and a charismatic smile. "Good morning, agents. I'm Roland Kirkman, but please call me Rollie. I have my office set up with some coffee and pastries, and I've arranged for my Deputy Sheriff to join us later, as you requested. Please follow me to my office."

After they entered his oversized office, he seated himself at a small round table in the corner, leaving three chairs vacant. The two agents joined him there, while the secretary offered them coffee and a cinnamon roll. The agents declined, but the sheriff accepted both.

The sheriff appeared to be eager to get the conference started, still not quite understanding the reason for the impromptu meeting. However, he tried to make the agents comfortable and gave his secretary explicit instructions on the meeting's privacy. He reminded her, "No interruptions. Not even from my wife."

"Mr. Kirkman ... uh, Rollie. I am Special Agent Eva Cortner and this is my partner, Special Agent Houston." The Sheriff nodded to acknowledge the formal introduction. After flashing their badges and identification, the agents took a moment to give the sheriff their business cards, which he accepted and stowed in the breast pocket of his jacket.

"First of all, we'd like to thank you for arranging this meeting on such short notice. I'm sure you're wondering why the meeting was called, so we'll get right to the point," Eva stated in her most official voice. The sheriff nodded.

"Well, sir, we're here because of suspicious circumstances surrounding the death of one of your previous inmates, a Miss Edith Ruth."

The sheriff looked puzzled and asked, "Yes ma'am, but that was a suicide. What exactly are you looking into?"

Agent Houston took over for Eva. "Were you aware that Miss Ruth sustained injuries consistent with a brutal and near-fatal beating just prior to the time of death?"

"No, of course not. I wasn't ... haven't been made aware of any such thing. How do you know this? Has it been confirmed?" a flustered Sheriff inquired.

Agent Houston continued, "Yes, sir. Even though there was a rushed autopsy performed in Nashville indicating strangulation as the mode of death, we now have postmortem photographs taken by a mortician when her body arrived at the family funeral home in Gurley, Alabama. The mortician alerted Miss Ruth's only surviving relative, a sister, and the sister eventually made contact with us through local law enforcement. A second and independent autopsy was performed, additional photographs taken, and the final autopsy report indicated that the injuries and bruises were sustained ante mortem. That means ..."

"I'm aware of what that means, agent. But what I don't understand is why I wasn't informed of this. If what you're implying is true, this woman was assaulted by one of our own people or someone that was able to bypass the jailer and illicitly enter the cell. That's not possible. We have a strict accountability protocol in place to..." The Sheriff's words trailed off to silence.

"Sir, you were saying you have protocols?" Eva asked.

The sheriff inhaled deeply and with a stern facial expression asked the agents, "Exactly what do you think happened here? Do you have something you want to share? I assure you it will not be disclosed by me. What exactly can we do to help clear this up?"

The agents revealed their proposed plan to the sheriff, who emphatically agreed to assist. He told his secretary to ask the Deputy Sheriff to join them in his office.

* ** * ** *

G. Howard Wilson walked confidently from his office and down the hallway to the sheriff's office.

Wonder what His Highness wants now? He has to have somebody to agree with him about everything. I'll bet he doesn't take a shit unless his bitchy wife gives him permission.

As he entered the secretary's office, she motioned him to go right in to see the sheriff. He sauntered toward the door and opened it quickly, surprised to see the sheriff with two other law enforcement types sitting around his small conference table.

"Come in, Howard. I'd like you to meet a couple of FBI Agents. They need some assistance from us and you're just the man who can help. Take a chair here at the table, but first help yourself to the cinnamon rolls and coffee on the credenza over there. Might be the only chance you get to eat today," a cheerful Rollie Kirkman said while stuffing the last bite of his roll into his mouth.

Howard hadn't been informed of any federal visitors. He bypassed the offer of food, and sat down in the only vacant chair at the round table. He found himself situated between the two federal agents and directly across from the sheriff.

"Of course, sir. I'll be happy to help. How can I assist you?" Howard asked as he swallowed hard.

Once again, Eva made their introductions, flashed their badges and identification, and gave him a revised version of why the agents were there.

"We recently had involvement with a case that concerned an inmate who we had remanded here awaiting federal sentencing. She had already confessed and waived her right to trial. However, the inmate killed herself before she ever made it back to Court for sentencing.

"We've been trying to reconstruct how she was able to hang herself with only a ripped up sheet. So, Agent Houston and I have been placed on a special assignment to assist the Corrections Department with assessments of all state jails and federal prison layouts, and perhaps interview some county inmates and federal prisoners about facility conditions. It's an independent committee, through which we will be assessing all Tennessee lockups."

Relieved, Howard Wilson smiled broadly. "Of course, that's a very important mission. I'll clear my calendar and join you back here in about fifteen minutes, if that's agreeable to you both. I have a few loose ends, but it shouldn't take me long."

The sheriff smiled, "Sure Howard. I'm sure these agents have lots of time to wait on you. Take your ever-lovin' time."

Howard shut the door behind him and gruffly told the secretary, "Don't you ever surprise me like that again. If there's somebody in there with him, you tell me before I go in." The petite secretary looked over the top of her horn-rimmed glasses and smirked as Howard rushed down the hall.

* * * * * *

Howard picked up his desk phone and with trembling fingers, dialed the number of his brother-in-law, Shelbyville Police Chief Peter Stewart.

The Chief picked up the phone and before he could say anything, an angry Howard Wilson was yelling at him.

"Did you know the damn FBI are here today snooping around about that Ruth woman? Is there something I should be concerned about, Pete? You promised this wouldn't come back on me. And, oh yeah, you promised me a job in the City Attorney's Office, too. How's that comin' along, you lying son-of-a-bitch!"

Chief Stewart stretched the phone line as far as he could so he could close his office door. "Now listen to me, you ignorant piece of shit. That woman's dead and buried. That's all over. They must have something else they're looking for. Where are these people right now?"

"They're in with the sheriff, and they just told me they're on some special committee to inspect jails or prisons or something. I don't know—I got confused because I was about to piss my pants. They made it sound innocent enough, but I got my doubts," Howard retorted.

"Look. Howard. Calm yourself down. You don't have doubts, you got paranoia. Now get over that. You'll give yourself away when they're not even looking at you. Just be nice and polite and follow orders. Don't give 'em any reason to think you're trying to be anything but accommodating. But above all, don't jump to conclusions. Call me tonight when you get home and let me know how it went." The Chief hung up on his brother-in-law.

Howard was desperate to leave and let the sheriff handle those snoops. He knew he couldn't, though. He agreed with Pete. He had to be calm and not act suspicious or they'd start asking him questions he wouldn't want to answer. He wiped his sweaty brow with a handkerchief and left his office.

He had his best fake smile plastered across his face as he entered the sheriff's secretary's office again. In an attempt to make up for his outburst when he left the office a few minutes earlier, he blew the secretary a kiss. She shot him a bird. He smirked at her, replaced his artificial smile and faced the sheriff's closed door.

As he entered, he said, "Okay agents, my calendar is clear and what do you say we start with a little tour. How's that sound?"

"That sounds fine, Mr. Wilson. But could we also see the cell that Miss Edith Ruth was in at the time of her death? That might give us a better idea of the questions we should be asking," Eva asked. She thought she saw Howard's jaw twitch when she mentioned the woman's name.

"Sure. Right this way, please." Howard was beginning to perspire again, and he took out his handkerchief to wipe his brow.

"Are you feeling ill, Mr. Wilson? You look a little faint," Eva said as they walked down the long hallway to the awaiting cellblock.

"Gosh, no. I'm fit as a fiddle. I just think the sheriff keeps his office too hot because of his arthritis and all. I usually try not to stay in there too long when he's not running his fans. I'm real hot natured." Howard thought his response was reasonable.

Eva smiled and nodded. Howard wasn't sure she'd bought it.

* * * * * *

By the end of the day, the three had walked though the facilities, spoken with random policemen and several inmates about jail conditions, and toured the solitary cells and the famous "Hell Hole" that no one ever wanted to occupy. According to Howard Wilson, they didn't use the "Hole" anymore because it was just too "inhumane." The agents nodded again—something they had done repeatedly that day--took more useless notes, and kept moving.

They had planned to spend the first full day with Mr. Wilson to gain his confidence in what the purpose of the "assessment" was. On the second day, they wanted him relaxed and at ease when they threw surprise questions at him.

So, when the agents mentioned they hoped to finish their assessment by noon the next day, Mr. Wilson gladly volunteered to continue his tour guide duties for them. He wanted to make sure the entire visit didn't veer off in an unfortunate direction, and he believed the best way to keep that from happening was to escort them at all times.

Pete told him to handle it, and he would. Then he'd think about why he hadn't been offered a job by the City of Shelbyville's Attorney's Office.

Just for the hell of it, I won't be calling Pete tonight after all. He can sweat this out, too. The bonehead deserves to squirm, just like I squirmed this morning when I first saw the feds with the Sheriff. It was even worse when they mentioned the suicide woman. I shouldn't have to feel all this anxiety alone. I'll give ole Pete a little bit of my anxiety, and he can't say a damn thing about it to anybody.

* * * * * *

It was a beautiful hot August morning when the two FBI Agents drove for the second day straight into the jail's parking lot of the Davidson County Sheriff's Department. They hoped this day would not be as boring as the day before when they had to listen to Howard Wilson spout out numbers that didn't mean anything to them, or when he acted like a regular Barney Fife, proud of his lofty position yet insecure in what he was talking about.

Their arrival was expected by the sergeant on duty, so they entered the facility with ease. They were told to go straight to the Sheriff's office. The Agents assured the sergeant that they were able to find the office themselves, so they were allowed to walk unescorted to their destination.

Upon their arrival they spent a few minutes with the Sheriff alone. They gave him an update on their tours and conversations from the previous day. They also asked him if there were three side-by-side interrogation rooms that might be available by late morning. The Sheriff could make that happen, or so he said. Rollie Kirkman would have his secretary find three connecting offices, if necessary, and run the occupants out for the day if they couldn't find anything else. Agents Cortner and Houston left that request in the capable hands of the sheriff and his secretary. As soon as she could, the secretary would let them know about the location and what time the offices would be available.

* * * * * *

A chipper Howard Wilson brought a filled coffee cup to the sheriff's office the next morning, just in time to see the sheriff shut his door with the two Agents inside. Howard started to approach the door, but the secretary told him he was to wait outside. This pissed Howard off again, but he managed to conceal it.

All he wanted was to get those FBI people out of his hair, once and for all. He hoped he could rush them through whatever questions they had left. The sooner they were out the door, the better he'd feel. And so would Pete. He was nervous all right. Pete called him at almost midnight last night to find out what happened at the jail. Howard told him it was nothing to worry about and go to bed. That pissed Pete off, too. There's no pleasing some people, he thought and chuckled to himself.

* * * * *

When Eva and Phillip exited the sheriff's office, they greeted Howard Wilson with handshakes and smiles. He returned the courtesies.

Eva started out first, saying, "Mr. Wilson, I think we've seen enough of the jail and infrastructure to make a pretty good assessment report. The only thing we lack is more responses from actual or previous inmates on their perception of incarceration accommodation. You know, the usual stuff. We want to interview in separate rooms, and we'd like it if you would coordinate retrieval of the interviewees and bring them to the separate rooms."

"No problem at all. Where are the interview rooms set up?" Howard asked.

Phillip answered him this time. "The Sheriff's secretary is supposed to let us know when they're ready. She said she'd call your office and inform us of where to be. They'll be in the Administration Building somewhere."

Howard did not want the federal agents in his office, even though there wasn't anything in there he wouldn't want them to see. It just made him uncomfortable for some reason.

"Well, let's go on down there, and wait for her call about which rooms to use." Howard tried to make the two comfortable, but his office was very cramped and nothing like the sheriff's. He wasn't embarrassed, but he was nervous.

The FBI Agents pretended to be going over their notes from the previous day, as Howard pretended to be looking for something in a drawer. All were using diversionary tactics while hoping the phone would ring with the room locations so they could get out of Howard's office.

Howard answered the phone before it had time to ring twice. "Ok, that's great. Thank you very much," Howard said into the phone as he hung it up.

"They got three conference rooms together, but they don't have connecting doors. There are windows with window blinds that can provide a little privacy if you think you'll need it." Howard was being accommodating. He offered to take the lead to get the agents to the right spot through the quickest route.

Within a few minutes, they arrived in the administrative wing of the building. Eva took one conference room while Phillip took the other. The third was left vacant. Howard wondered who would be in the third room, but the agents never disclosed that information.

When it was time to start the interviews, Eva asked Howard to fetch a visitor who was waiting by the desk sergeant's station. He waited patiently for the visitor's identification; but when she said "Irene "Big Mama" Simpson," he thought he would vomit right there.

He returned within ten minutes with Irene "Big Mama" Simpson at his side. He ushered her in Eva's conference room and stood there as if he thought he'd be invited to join in the session.

Eva smiled at him and said, Thank you Howard. I believe Agent Houston has someone in mind that he needs to see, as well. Would you check with him please and close the door on the way out?"

Howard followed orders. He stuck his head in the next conference room to ask Agent Houston who he needed to interview. When Agent Houston told him to go find a jailer named Betty Kingree, Howard nearly lost control. Instead, he turned and tried to be as unruffled as possible as he left Houston's conference room to go get the jailer. His knees were shaking. When Howard and the requested jailer returned, Agent Houston thanked him politely. She then asked him to wait in the empty conference room.

He went in the vacant conference room and sat at the head of the oval table. He tried counting off the minutes he was in there, but time went by more slowly doing that. He got up once to find a water fountain. He wanted a Pepsi Cola, and his throat was getting dryer by the minute. He would have to make do with water. When he made his way back to the conference rooms, Howard was surprised that both interviewees were still in the rooms with the agents. In his opinion, they had been meeting too long to simply be discussing warmer showers, better food, or whatever they bitch about.

He watched for movement through the nearly closed blinds. Occasionally he would see someone move around to a chalk board and he could hear the scraping sound when the chalk skipped. He believed neither of the interviewee had left her chair. He nervously wondered if Big Mama was ratting him out.

He was beginning to think about Miss Ruth's surprise visit from Big Mama. The jailer who slipped Big Mama the cell key was being interviewed right now. From what he could see, Betty Kingree didn't appear to have lost her composure.

Howard thought he might be about to have diarrhea, and silently prayed that it was just gas. When he was anxious, he did tend to get bad cases of gas.

Finally Eva came out of her room, shutting and locking the door from the outside while leaving Big Mama inside. She tapped on Phillip's door, and he followed the same procedure. The two stood side by side for a moment, then walked toward the conference room where Howard was anxiously sitting.

Howard stood up and asked, "Are you ready for me escort the visitor back to the lobby?"

Eva and Phillip stood silently for a moment and Phillip turned to shut the door. They both took seats directly across the table. They said nothing for minutes, while staring intently at the physically shaking Howard Wilson.

"Howard, why don't you just come clean with us and tell us what we want to know? We've heard some interesting stories from your buddies in the other room. They've thrown you under the bus, I'm afraid," Eva stated.

Howard was sweating again, and Eva knew that the temperature in the room had nothing to do with it. "I don't know what you mean," he said meekly.

"Sure you do, Howard. You'll feel better when it's all out. They'll go easier on you if you go ahead and admit what you did," Eva added.

"I don't know what you're talking about," Howard said as he wiped his brow again.

Eva said to Phillip, "Agent Houston, would you like to give him a hint as to what we'd like for him to explain?"

Phillip picked up his notepad and scanned the first page. "Okay. Let's start with you subsidizing Irene Simpson's bank account every month for $100. You've been doing this for several years, and she's been paid quite a sum. Now why don't you tell me about that."

Howard looked as though he was about to cry. "Please. She needed help. She asked me to help her because she said she couldn't get a job on the outside with her record."

Eva looked Howard straight in the eyes and smirked, "That's so sweet, Howie. And what do you get in return for that generous gesture? A blowjob here and there? An old lady gets beat up on your say-so? What are you paying for, Howard?"

While Howard contemplated his answer, Phillip interrupted. "Or maybe you'd like to talk about all the phone calls you made to your brother-in-law who just so happens to be the Shelbyville Police Chief. You remember Shelbyville? It's been in the news a lot lately. Your brother-in-law has been taking some heat over closing three kidnapping cases based on the fact Miss Edith Ruth was apprehended for taking some little girls across the state line for a visit with her sister. Maybe your brother-in-law needed someone to convince the old lady to confess to the kidnappings she didn't do, making certain someone's career would remain secure. Does any of that sound about right to you, Howard?"

Howard broke down under the pressure and laid his head on the table, sobbing. "Oh, God. I just want this to be over. I didn't mean anything by it. The old woman wasn't supposed to die." He sobbed loudly and emotionally.

Eva whispered to Phillip that perhaps the Sheriff should join them. Phillip left and returned with Rollie Kirkman in tow.

"Howard, start from the beginning and tell us everything. Maybe we can help you out with some leniency if you will cooperate," the sheriff suggested.

Howard lifted his head up off the table and stared at his boss. "You knew? You knew they were going to do this to me? This was a set up."

The fatherly look on the sheriff's face seemed genuine. "No, Howard. I didn't know. They brought it to me, and I was secretly hoping that they were wrong. I'm sorry to find out they were right. But if you'll tell us who's behind all this, maybe we can help you out. Maybe even give you immunity if the right people sign off on it. I can't promise that, but I can promise I'll try to help you in any way I can if you just cooperate with these agents."

"Okay, I'll talk. I'll tell you about everything, but you gotta promise before God as your witness you'll do everything possible to keep me out of prison. You know what it's like when inmates have a new cop brought in with them. They don't last long. I don't want to go to prison." Howard started crying again.

The agents left the room while the sheriff stayed with Howard. The sheriff was trying to comfort the defeated Howard Wilson.

Each agent opened the doors of the conference rooms where the interviewees still sat. They had been completing a personality assessment form which was 80 pages long, usually taking the average person over three hours to fully complete.

Neither Big Mama nor Betty Kingree had been questioned about Howard Wilson. They thought they were assisting with some part of the jail/prison assessment the agents were handling.

The Interviewees were instructed to put their pencils down and turn over the assessment forms. The jailer was then instructed to escort the visitor back to the lobby before reporting to her work station. In five minutes, two of the three conference rooms were clear.

Howard Wilson was now in handcuffs. Sheriff Kirkman sorrowfully escorted him to the same holding cell that the doomed Edith Ruth once occupied.

It would still be a while before Chief Stewart felt the ramifications of his brother-in-law's confession. It would take time to get statements, verify information, and start another leg to the investigation. But the investigation would come and it wouldn't take long for Chief Stewart to start dodging flying turds when the shit really did hit the fan.

CHAPTER 27

1958

Shelbyville citizens were on the down side of the roller coaster ride once again. They were in despair because it had been six months since Joe Claxton had vanished. Vendors were posting new flyers of the previous victims, and it was another sad reminder that not one, but four innocent teenagers were lost, probably forever.

Joe Claxton went missing in February, and now it was late August. The police department always alleged the same thing: no leads, no witnesses, and no ideas. It was frustrating to live in fear for the lives of your babies. It was unacceptable to allow it to go on forever. Citizens kept pointing fingers at Chief Peter Stewart for being ineffective and disinterested.

* * * * * *

In mid-August the FBI had taken Chief Stewart in for questioning for something that was going on in Nashville, but everybody was "hush hush" about it. He was whisked off to the capitol city in the back of an unmarked black sedan. People assumed he was on his way to join some special task force team the FBI couldn't talk about, or that perhaps he was being arrested for something major. It was hard to tell, considering how fast it all happened and how no one was giving out details.

There was one very good thing that happened after the Chief took his "involuntary" leave of absence. The Mayor called Brian Martin and asked him to assume the position of Acting Chief of Police. It was a great honor, but he turned it down. He suggested that his partner deserved that promotion and would he be proud to serve under him. The Mayor then called Harry Woodson, and by the next afternoon, the City Policemen were reporting to new Acting Chief Woodson. There was rejoicing in the station when the announcement was made.

* * * * * *

Acting Chief Woodson wanted to go back to square one on all the cold kidnapping cases and reopen them with fresh eyes. He wanted to figure out if there were common denominators that were somehow missed before. "K-I-S-S," he would say. "We've got to keep it simple. Sometimes the answers are staring us right in the face and we just ignore them."

A new investigative team, headed by Brian Martin, was formed by the Acting Chief on the second day of his elevated job. Martin was eager to review every detail of the four files, and directed his teammates to study the files with microscopic effort. "Anything could spark a new lead," he told the team. "Nothing is too small to be examined."

The team used a rolling black board and developed an elaborate diagram of the victims and their contacts. Again, Carl Brown's name popped up as one of the common denominators that magically appeared within the schematic.

Brian looked over the intricate diagram and shook his head. *Carl Brown just doesn't fit the type.*

* * * * * *

The new school year was set to start on September 2, the day after the 1958 Labor Day holiday. The students would start school after the Tennessee Walking Horse National Celebration ended. The walking horse attraction brought tourists and visitors from all over the country and often enticed international visitors, as well. The convergence of the multitude of tourists on the small town of Shelbyville caused excessive traffic and congestion, and the school system authorities strategically avoided throwing school buses and pedestrian students into the mix by slightly delaying the start of the school year.

Both Dixie and Dollie pleaded with their parents to spend some additional time with their relatives before having to go back to school. Each girl considered those visits to be escapes from the boring rural setting of their El Bethel home.

Corb and LorAnn realized the gap in the girls' ages prevented them from being compatible playmates, and eventually relented, allowing their daughters to spend one last weekend away from home before they went back to school.

Dollie would be picked up by Granny and Pap Stan on Friday night, August 29th, and Dixie would be dropped off the next morning at the Tucker's home. Corb and LorAnn would have a free weekend to do last minute school shopping for the girls. They planned to drive to Tullahoma or Murfreesboro for a wider selection of clothing choices. They would decide where they were going when they got on the road.

* * * * * *

On Saturday morning, Dixie had a small overnight bag ready to take with her to Aunt Roz's house. She packed the small bottle of perfume her aunt had given her, as well as some headbands and hair clasps adorned with small fake rhinestones. She hoped Aunt Roz would help her find a new hairstyle for her as she entered the eighth grade.

Corb and LorAnn pulled into the Tucker's driveway and heard Marvin Morgan's voice when they exited the truck.

"Boy, I told you to get away from me. I told you I'm gonna work in the yard awhile, and I don't want you botherin' me. I can't get nuthin done with you jabberin' all the time. Go ride your motorbike and leave me be," Marvin shouted, clearly irritated.

A pouting Rocky came around from the other side of the Morgan house and stomped up the steps to the porch. He slammed the screen door behind him and the shouting was over. Corb and LorAnn looked at each other, hoping the argument between the Morgan men was over for the day. Dixie walked ahead of them to enter the Tucker's house.

When the Carters entered the back door, Aunt Roz was standing at the kitchen counter finishing up her last cup of coffee for the morning. She greeted her sister and brother-in-law and reached out to receive Dixie's embrace.

"I forgot all about my hair appointment this morning over off West End. I hope you don't have a problem with Dixie being here with Ma Rose and Troy while I'm gone. It'll just be for a couple hours, 'cause I'm s'pose to get a permanent," Roz told them.

"Yeah, it's all right," Corb hesitantly stated. LorAnn's facial expression turned somber.

Feeling as though she had just dropped a bomb on the parents, Roz quickly offered to take Dixie with her if they'd prefer. Dixie looked at her parents with a questioning expression.

"Why would I have to do that? I'd rather stay here and look at Aunt Roz's magazines so I can pick out a hairstyle I like. What's the big deal, anyway?" Dixie wanted to know.

"No big deal, sugar," Aunt Roz answered.

"You can stay here with Troy and Ma. Just don't get into any trouble while your Aunt Roz is gone," LorAnn remarked, trying to look unconcerned.

Dixie again looked questioningly at the three adults, and shrugged her shoulders. "Okay, I'll be in the living room talking to Ma Rose. Y'all figure out what you want me to do and I'll do it. But I still don't know why y'all are actin' so weird."

Dixie left the room and greeted Ma Rose who was sitting near the fireplace in a rocking chair. She had her Bible in her lap and motioned for Dixie to come toward her for a hug.

LorAnn told Roz that they would be back the next afternoon to get Dixie. They embraced and the Carters left Roz standing in the same place as when they first entered. Roz emptied and rinsed her coffee cup, turned off the percolator, and ran her fingers through her hair. She picked up her purse and called to Dixie, "I'm leaving, Dixie. Take care of Ma Rose while I'm gone. Your Uncle Troy is working on his motorcycle, and I expect he'll be in before long."

"'K, Aunt Roz. Bring us back some beauty tips," Dixie answered, as she picked up the latest edition of *Glamour* magazine from the coffee table.

* * * * * *

It only took fifteen minutes for Ma Rose to fall asleep in her chair. She had her finger pointed at a Bible passage when her chin dropped toward her chest and her light snoring started.

Dixie had thumbed through the magazine and was about to pick up another when she noticed Ma Rose's change of position. The young girl tiptoed toward her slumbering Grandmother and tried to adjust her head to a more comfortable pose. When she touched Ma Rose's face, she quickly opened her eyes and snorted.

"I didn't mean to wake you up, Ma Rose. It just looked like your neck could be hurtin' with your head down like that," Dixie explained.

"That's all right, child. Why don't you help me get to my room and I'll just take a little nap on top of the bed." Ma Rose started to stand, but she grabbed the chair arms as if she were about to lose her balance. Dixie helped ease her out of the wooden rocker. She assisted Ma Rose across the living room and through the short "heater hall" to her room.

When Ma Rose was settled, Dixie covered her frail legs with a blanket. She kissed her Grandmother on the cheek as Ma Rose closed her eyes and drifted back to sleep.

Dixie closed the door behind her when she left her Grandmother's room, then went into the kitchen to look for a snack. As she peered into the refrigerator, Uncle Troy came through the back door.

"Where's your Aunt Roz?" he asked.

Dixie responded without taking her eyes off the filled refrigerator. "She's getting' her permanent. She won't be back for a couple of hours." Dixie selected a leftover chicken leg and moved toward the kitchen counter to get a napkin.

Troy looked around the kitchen and through the wide doorway to the living room. "Where's your grandma?" he wanted to know.

"She's asleep in her room," Dixie replied between bites of her snack.

Troy carefully worded his next question. "You wanna do the next lesson while it's quiet and we can talk without anybody hearing us?"

"Okay, Uncle Troy. Let me get a drink of water and we'll start it if you're ready." Dixie commented.

"I'm ready, girl. I hope you are," Troy grinned as he led Dixie to the shed.

* * * * *

Uncle Troy rounded the corner to the shed, and Dixie was a few steps behind him. He moved the rusty can near the door, retrieved the key, and quickly unlocked the padlock. He dropped the open lock on the ground in his usual fashion.

Dixie followed him into the shed and plopped down on the cot. Uncle Troy walked toward the girl and decided he could best be heard if he sat close to her. He took a seat on the cot leaving about a foot's distance between them.

"Before we start, you got any questions you want me to answer since we talked the last time?" Uncle Troy asked his niece.

"Well, I don't think so. I still can't figure out how this sex thing works. I remember when I looked at Aunt Dora's baby when she changed his diaper. His little thing didn't look much like it could be stuck anywhere. It was too little and too droopy. That part still doesn't make any sense to me." Dixie responded, obviously perplexed.

"Well, that part of a boy changes when he gets to be growed up. His privates grows bigger and when the man is excited, it gets harder." Troy answered.

"You mean getting excited about something makes a man's privates get big? I still don't get it."

Troy cleared his throat. "Maybe you could understand it better if you saw it for yourself. I got a few magazines that show what I'm tryin' to tell you." Troy got up and opened the bottom drawer of his tool chest, removing several "educational" magazines for Dixie to view.

He placed one on her lap and instructed her to look through the pages. If she had questions about anything she saw, he offered to explain.

"Uncle Troy, these are grown men and women. The men's private parts don't look anything like a baby's." She continued studying the pictures, turning each page slowly.

As Troy watched her examine the pictorials, he was becoming increasingly aroused. As he sat next to Dixie on the cot, he shifted in his seat in a failed attempt to hide his erection.

"Good grief, Uncle Troy. This looks gross. Do you and Aunt Roz do this stuff? Do my parents do this? Is this what having sex looks like?" Dixie blurted out.

"Yeah, all grownups do it. You will too, someday. But only after you get married. It ain't proper for an unmarried woman to have sex." Troy was getting anxious, feeling like he was doing something immoral by providing sex education to his niece. It also made him feel horny and aroused.

"So this is how babies are made, right?" the innocent girl asked.

"Yeah, the man shoots off into the woman and that's how a baby starts." Troy wasn't feeling as confident about branching out into this educational area.

"So, if you wanna have a baby, you have sex. I guess my Mama and Daddy only had sex twice, since they got two kids. But if you and Aunt Roz have sex, why don't you have babies, too?" Dixie had clearly missed this part when she had her "period" education at school. Either that, or she ignored it. She was too bright to not catch on.

"Well, the man shoots out cum, and it's got little things in it that go into the woman's part. The woman has eggs inside, and if the cum stuff hits 'em just right, they make a baby. Makin' a baby don't happen every time you have sex. But sex is the only way you can get pregnant and have a baby. And some people just never have babies because of different things. A man can wear a rubber that catches his cum and the little cum things don't ever get the chance to find the woman's egg." Troy wiped his brow with a handkerchief he pulled from his overall's side pocket.

Dixie nodded. "Oh, I get it. What does this rubber thing look like?"

Troy reached into his bib pocket and pulled out a shiny package. He ripped it open, extracted the prophylactic and handed it to Dixie.

She inspected it and handed it back. "How do you get that thing on?"

This was the moment Troy had anticipated. He stood up, looked outside the door of the shed and scanned the area. He could see that Roz's car wasn't in its usual parking spot in the driveway and Ma Rose never took walks outside the house, being too frail.

Troy reentered the shed and asked, "Are you sure you want me to show you? You can't never tell anybody."

Dixie considered his question, then nodded.

Troy didn't take a seat; instead, he stood behind the shed's closed door and unzipped his overalls. He reached inside the opening and pulled out his purplish, fully erect penis. He stood there for a moment and Dixie's eyes got wide.

Without saying anything, he placed the prophylactic on the head of his member. He carefully and slowly rolled it down snugly around his shaft. He stood there for Dixie to inspect his work.

"Wow, Uncle Troy." Dixie said as she looked with amazement. "Is your private part always that big?"

Troy's heart was beating fast. "No, just when I get excited about sex. Mostly it's little and droopy like you said about the baby's part."

Dixie looked him in the eyes and hesitantly asked, "Are you excited about sex right now? I thought you were just trying to give a Life Lesson. I don't want to have sex with you."

Troy quickly said, "No, girl. I wouldn't try to have sex with you. It's just 'cause I was lookin' at them magazines, too, and sometimes I get excited by the pictures."

He quickly pulled off the rubber and put it in his pocket. He adjusted himself and zipped his overalls.

He sat next to Dixie on the cot again. She scooted a few inches farther away, then turned to face her Uncle.

"Okay. Just so you know, I am *not* gonna be having sex 'til I'm older and with somebody I love."

"That's the way it oughta be, Dixie. That's good to hear." Troy was still trying to settle his nerves.

"But you can tell me about what it feels like to have sex, if you want to." Dixie had resumed her role as student.

Troy began relaying what it was like for him, and trying to imagine what a female partner must experience. He got bolder and bolder with his examples, telling her of girlfriends he had even after he was married to Roz. He told her explicit details about the affairs, and left her with the impression that all adult men were prone to wanderlust. He ended his recitation by giving her details of his one and only experience with a male partner. Dixie was astonished at her Uncle's sexual exploits and wondered if her own Daddy had ever done the same things.

"Uncle Troy, I don't think I can listen to anymore today. My mind's full of all this stuff. I need some time to sort it all out before our next lesson. Let's go get some ice cream or something. I think we should talk about other things for a while." Dixie got up to leave the shed, and Uncle Troy stood up to follow.

When Dixie went ahead to check on Ma Rose, Troy put the padlock back on the door and locked it. He didn't notice Rocky crouching behind the fence on the Morgan's side of the property. Rocky had witnessed everything. The boy-man was holding his hand over his mouth to make sure he wouldn't make a sound as Troy and Dixie made their way back to the house.

* * * * * *

The next morning, Shelbyvillians awoke to reports of a newly crowned champion from Saturday night's finale of the Walking Horse Celebration.

The town's local radio station, WHAL, also broke with their regular Sunday morning gospel program to report the apparent disappearance of a teenager last seen at the Horse Show grounds after the championship horse was crowned.

* * * * * *

Linda Diane Adcock was an outgoing fourteen year old girl who dreamed of owning her own horse one day. She looked forward to the annual horse show, and loved to walk through the stables during the day and visit with the horses. The horse trainers and owners recognized the girl when she would come by, because she always brought a bag of carrots and apple slices to feed the horses. She had been a regular visitor to the stables since she was eight years old.

When the horse show came to town in 1958, Linda's routine didn't vary from her previous years' customs. Other than the fact she was a year older, her look never seemed to change. She would still hear the stable staff call out her name when they saw her across the way, just as they had over the years. She always wore khaki colored riding pants tucked in brown riding boots, and wore her red hair in a long pony tail hanging past the collar of her tan and white plaid shirt. She always wore a blue ribbon tied around her pony tail, copying the symbol of a walking horse's championship status. Sometimes she would change to a blue and gold ribbon during high school athletic seasons, but never during the annual walking horse celebration. She liked wearing the famed "blue ribbon."

After the champion walking horse was crowned that year, she hurriedly tried to make it to the stable area where she knew 'Setting Sun', the new world grand champion, would eventually return. She knew the trainer well, and felt certain he would allow her to mount the horse and maybe even ride the chestnut stallion around the stables.

When she walked through the individual stables, she heard a sound that made her believe there was a wounded horse nearby. She took a detour toward the sound and stepped around a dark corner.

She never witnessed Setting Sun's arrival at the stable.

* * * * * *

Acting Chief Woodson and his 'Kidnap Central' crew studied the black board with the new entries for the missing Adcock girl. Members of Brian Martin's team were on the scene, canvassing the few witnesses left on the horse show grounds, and doing everything possible to assuage the shock and misery of the girl's parents.

"I still see Carl Brown as a link, even though I doubt he attends the Horse Show. I don't see any other possible connections except that she's a local student. This is a very public place with potential witnesses from all over the world. Most of them cleared out of town after Saturday night. We can talk to horse show personnel, of course, but we have no way of knowing who the last person was that laid eyes on this girl," Brian Martin said to his team and the Acting Chief.

Acting Chief Woodson agreed. He knew that he was going to face the same public scrutiny as his predecessors had if these cases weren't solved quickly. He knew the first 48 hours after a disappearance were critical hours. There might be a slim chance that they could find the Adcock girl alive if they could find anything to go on. Judging by the past cases, he doubted if any promising flags would pop up within the next day and a half.

* * * * * *

Carl Brown was getting sick and tired of being one of the first people the police talked to when a kid disappeared. Sure, he understood that being a school janitor made him an easy target, especially when the first girl had been talking to him right before she vanished. He didn't even really know the others that well. Still, the police came right to him and asked him questions that made him feel like he was a criminal. It was just a coincidence that Dora happened to be the last person to see the Claxton boy. He felt like God must be trying to punish him for something by putting him in a position for the police to harass him.

Even the school staff members had started looking at him a little funny. They seemed to be trying to keep their distance from him, too.

And now another student had vanished. He expected to be visited by that Martin fellow again, only because he was the janitor at the school. He had been out all summer and school wasn't even in session yet. He still knew they'd be at his door, regardless.

* * * * *

Brian Martin gave interview assignments to his team members, decided to hold back the one for Carl Brown. Martin was undecided about talking to him, and made a mental note to check out some other things first and maybe get around to speaking with Carl later.

CHAPTER 28

September 1958

On Labor Day, the Carter family had no special plans and opted to spend the beautiful day at home. Occasionally, the family would walk the acreage and sit by the murky small pond west of the homestead. Corb and LorAnn thought it would be a great day to take a picnic lunch to the pond site and let the girls do some exploring.

Corb walked ahead of the group, chopping back obstructive branches or low lying vines with the machete he kept in one of the outbuildings behind the house. LorAnn carried the picnic basket and trailed the eager girls. The whole family was enthusiastic to wander through the undeveloped property.

After a while, they came upon the pond area, and were disappointed when they saw the bottom was dry and cracked. They laid out an old quilt on the ground nearby, deciding it was about time for lunch anyway.

They feasted on fried chicken (Dixie's favorite) and warm biscuits that LorAnn had taken from the oven only minutes before they left the house. They ate tomatoes from the garden, biting into the unpeeled skin and sprinkling salt on its exposed insides before taking another bite. They ate bananas and grapes and gorged themselves with sugar cookies. By the time they finished, Dollie lay down on her back, tummy extended, and rubbed her full belly. She looked as though she might take a nap. Corb laid down on his back next to his young daughter, and threw his right arm over across his face to shield his eyes from the overhead sun. It didn't take long for him to join Dollie in peaceful sleep.

* * * * * *

Dixie walked around the dry pond and absent-mindedly threw loose rocks into the center of the parched bed. LorAnn ambled around the pond area and approached her daughter, watching her gather more rocks.

"Dixie, you've got a pretty good arm," LorAnn commented when Dixie threw another rock, hitting dead center of her target.

"Thanks, Mama," Dixie answered as she dropped the handful of rocks she had just collected.

LorAnn asked her daughter, "Is somethin' botherin' you, Dixie? You seem to be quieter than usual."

Dixie pondered for a moment, wondering if she should ask LorAnn to clarify a few things she had heard during her most recent Life Lesson. She hesitated too long before answering, making LorAnn wonder if Dixie was holding something back.

"Mama, I was just wondering if you could help me understand a few things. I don't think we should talk in front of Dollie and Daddy, though. I don't want them to hear. It's kinda personal," Dixie stammered.

Relieved, LorAnn was happy to oblige her daughter with any motherly advice she could. She feared Roz was taking her place in that department.

"You can talk to me about anything, Dixie. Why don't we move back a piece to those tree stumps over yonder. We can talk there and nobody will hear but you and me."

Dixie nodded her agreement and followed her mother about twenty feet further from their picnic spread.

When they were situated comfortably on tree stumps that were under some shade, Dixie started with her queries.

"Mama, do you and Daddy use a rubber when you have sex?" Dixie asked her mother point blank.

LorAnn froze. She didn't believe those words were coming out of her daughter's mouth. "How do you know about such things, Dixie? Why would you ask that?"

Dixie suddenly realized she shouldn't have asked her mother anything about what she had learned from Uncle Troy. She tried to cover up her source. "Well, you remember when I saw that film at school about periods and stuff? I heard some people talking afterwards about things they'd heard, and I've been wondering, that's all."

LorAnn thought Dixie looked apprehensive. She took a big breath and answered her daughter. "Dixie, the answer is no, we don't. But I don't want you to be thinking about such grown up things. You're not ready for that, and I don't think you should be trying to figure that kinda stuff out at your age."

Dixie felt as though her mother was dismissing her, and didn't know if she should proceed with any other questions. Only a few minutes before her mother had told her she could ask anything, and now she'd changed her mind.

LorAnn's thoughts were all over the place when an important question occurred to her. "Dixie, how do you know about rubbers? I didn't think that movie would have mentioned that to a group of young girls."

Dixie felt trapped and didn't have a ready answer.

"Dixie, please tell me you haven't been messin' around with some boy!" LorAnn exclaimed.

"No, Mama, I wouldn't do that. You know I wouldn't. I don't even know any boys except at school. And I know Rocky, too, but he's crazy." Dixie was feeling more nervous and was hoping she could hold back her tears.

LorAnn thought more about how Dixie could have picked up on such a sensitive topic. She dreaded to ask the question, but didn't think she would have another perfect opportunity. "Dixie, I want you to tell me the truth, and don't make up no stories. Tell me, Dixie, has your Uncle Troy taken you out to his shed?"

Tears now streamed down Dixie's face. Her mother got up and moved toward her daughter, kneeling in front of Dixie's body. LorAnn took Dixie's hands in hers and peered into her tearful eyes. "Did he do something to you, Dixie? Please tell me what he did."

Dixie sobbed, and sniffed her running nose. "Mama, I love Uncle Troy. He wouldn't hurt me. He just wanted to help me understand life, so we've been having Life Lessons."

Trying not to let Dixie see how upset she was, LorAnn tried to smile and once again held her daughter's gaze when she asked, "And what happens in these lessons, Dixie?"

Dixie believed the truth would set her free. "I asked him some questions, and then later he told me things about sex, and we looked at some magazines. After that, he told me about what a rubber was and he showed me how he put one on. That was all, Mama, I swear." Dixie hung her head in shame and LorAnn stood up, pulling her daughter's head toward her body and embracing her.

"Did I do wrong, Mama? I didn't mean to, I really didn't," Dixie muttered through the cloth of her mother's blouse.

"Sshh, child. Everything's all right. You did right by telling me," LorAnn whispered as tears rolled off her cheek onto the top of Dixie's head.

* * * * *

LorAnn and Dixie sat quietly together and held hands under the shade tree until Dollie woke up and punched her sleeping daddy.

"Get up, Daddy. Mama and Dixie are gone!" A startled Corb sat straight up and looked around the pond area for his wife and daughter.

"Dollie, I see 'em over there under that shade tree. Go tell 'em to come back over here and let's get ready to go back to the house."

Dollie stood up and yelled, "MAMA, COME ON. DADDY SAYS WE'RE GOING BACK TO THE HOUSE!"

Corb laughed and said, "Dollie, I told you to GO get 'em, not yell at 'em."

By then, Dollie was already running toward her mother and sister. When she got closer she urgently said, "We gotta go, Mama. You and Dixie come on," and with that, she turned and ran back toward Corb.

Everyone carried something back which made the trek home easier. Corb stashed the machete in the tool shed high enough away from curious children. LorAnn stacked dirty dishes and utensils in the sink, while the girls went into their room. It was only mid-afternoon, but Dixie wanted to get her school clothes out for the next day, the first day of the school year. Dollie mimicked Dixie, and found an outfit she hoped her parents would approve of her wearing.

When Corb came into the kitchen, LorAnn seized the opportunity to privately suggest he take the girls to town for an ice cream cone. She hinted that Corb hadn't done anything alone with the girls in quite a while, and it might be good for them to have some daddy time. Corb had nothing else planned for the rest of the day, so he agreed with LorAnn's plan.

By 4:00 p.m., Corb and his daughters were licking ice cream cones in the parking lot of the Rebel Maid. A few cars over, Brian Martin was sipping through a wide paper straw, trying to get the last bit of his strawberry milkshake out of an orange striped cup with a pretty maid on the front.

* * * * *

LorAnn had kept her emotions in check all afternoon. She wanted so badly to repeat everything Dixie had told her to Corb, but she was hesitant. She feared Corb would get so furious that he would jump in his truck, find Troy, and kill him on the spot without thinking through what he was doing.

She picked up the telephone, surprised that Mrs. Harris wasn't talking with her relatives. She dialed the Tucker house. Roz answered.

"Roz, I gotta talk to you. It's real urgent. But first, is Troy there with you?" LorAnn asked anxiously.

"He's been out in that shed fiddling with that motorcycle all day again today. What's so urgent?" Roz questioned.

LorAnn started to cry and Roz realized her sister was very upset about something. "Has Corb been runnin' around on you again?"

LorAnn blew her nose on the other end of the phone. "Not lately, but that doesn't even matter to me anymore. It's worse, Roz. It's so much worse." LorAnn started sobbing.

"You want me to come over there? What is it?" Roz asked, feeling more concerned by the minute.

"You ain't got time to get here before Corb gets back with the kids. They went to get an ice cream in town, and I just got a few minutes to talk before they get home." LorAnn paused before continuing.

"Roz, Troy's been talkin' to Dixie about sex, and she said he even showed her how to put on a rubber. Dixie was upset this afternoon and told me all about it. I ain't even tried to talk to Corb about it, 'cause I'm afraid he'll kill Troy." LorAnn sobbed more and blew her nose again.

Roz sat there in silence on the other end of the phone. She didn't want to believe what her sister was telling her, but she had already suspected something had been going on with Troy. She had tried to dismiss her suspicions as being over-reactive, but her gut still told her there was something amiss. He hadn't been acting right for a while now.

"Okay, LorAnn, I understand. I've wondered myself about this. You know I have, but I never dreamed anything would come of it. I never thought Troy would cross any lines with Dixie. But, you listen to me, now. You don't say a word to Corb about any of this and I'll take care of this mess from here. Trust me on this, LorAnn. Swear to me you won't talk to Corb or anyone else about what you told me. That includes Dixie. Just act like it never happened, and let me work this out with Troy. I guarantee he'll never so much as cross his eyes toward that girl—or Dollie—ever again. Do you understand me?" Roz was fighting mad. She knew she was going to have to square off with Troy sooner rather than later.

"I understand, Roz. Please don't do anything crazy. But I trust you to get Troy back in line. I swear, I don't know whether I can ever look that man in the face again." LorAnn's sobs were back.

"Just trust me, LorAnn," Roz said and hung up the phone.

As Roz turned to go outdoors, Ma Rose stepped quietly into the heater hall adjacent to her room. She heard the back screen door slam and knew Roz was on a strike mission. Ma Rose smiled to herself, having eavesdropped on Roz's side of the conversation. *That bastard's gonna get it now,* she thought to herself, and wished she had the stamina to follow Roz outside and watch it happen.

* * * * * *

Roz pulled open the shed door to find Troy lying on the bed looking through a dirty magazine with his hand in his overall fly. He was startled when the door opened and sat straight up, penis in hand.

"What the hell, Roz?" Troy said as he tucked his member inside his pants. He turned his legs toward the side of the bed and slid his bare feet into his slippers. He was about to stand up with Roz advanced toward him and pushed him back down to sit.

"What the hell is right, you son of a bitch! What the hell have you been doing out here with Dixie and God knows who else?" Roz's voice rose and spit flew from her mouth with every other word.

"Who told you that shit? That's a lie. I don't know what you're talking about, you crazy witch. Have you been listenin' to that retard next door? Or maybe his stupid daddy? C'mon Roz. I thought you knew me better than that." Troy tried to present the first phase of his defense, but it wasn't working with his infuriated wife.

"I know you all right, you cheatin' bastard. You think I didn't know all these years that you ran around on me. You thought you was doin' this shit behind my back, but you didn't think about all the people that saw you, did you? You didn't think anyone would ever tattle on you, did you? Well, the joke's on you, you slimy cheatin' rat. I knew about every damn one of them whores, and guess what? I didn't give a damn. I hate going to bed with you anyway, and figured I'd rather they have to do it than me. How ya like that? Does that make you feel like a big man?

Well, Mister, the party's over. I'm gonna tear every board outta this shed and then I'm gonna have myself a nice bonfire. Might even invite the Morgans over for a weenie roast. You better watch out cause it might just be your weenie that gets roasted this time, you miserable fucker."

Roz started frantically kicking at the parked Harley on the opposite side of the shed. It fell back against the wall and almost tumbled over. The handlebars lodged against the window frame and served as a supporting prop.

Troy started to stand up, and Roz swiveled around. She picked up a stray wrench that was on top of the tool chest and threw it at him. He dodged the wrench, but it barely missed his head.

"Damn it, Troy, don't you move till I tell you to. I'll knock the living shit out of you if you even act like you're gonna get up off that bed." Troy sat motionless, afraid Roz had lost her mind.

Roz pulled out all the drawers of the tool chest one by one. From the top one she grabbed an even larger wrench and pointed it toward Troy. He stared at her as if he were watching a movie. She looked through all the drawers while he watched, finally pulling out the bottom one and saw his stash.

Roz dug through the pile and pitched filthy magazines in the air as she plowed further into the deep drawer. Under the publications she found several sex toys, prophylactics, Vaseline, and a set of handcuffs. Still holding the large wrench, she turned toward Troy with a sneer.

Roz's voice now took on the tone of a deep growl. "You really are a warped man, you devil. I want a divorce and I want everything. I want the house, the furniture... I want everything. And if you don't agree to it, I'll drag your ass to court and we'll be talking to the Judge about your little adventure with my niece." She kicked the motorcycle again. This time it fell, and the unbuckled saddlebag spilled its contents.

Roz reached down and picked up a small tobacco pouch. She opened it and peered inside. "What the hell is this, Troy? You been collectin' stuff from your whores?"

Troy looked surprised. "I don't know what that is. Let me see," he said as he reached toward Roz to take the bag.

"You ain't seeing nothin' till I look at this stuff," Roz said as she swiped the wrench through the air with her other hand. "You just sit right there and let me see this stuff," Roz ordered.

Roz moved closer to the toolbox and spilled the bag's contents out onto its top. She saw a charm bracelet, an ID bracelet, a rabbits foot, dog tags and a blue ribbon with long strands of hair with something sticky in it. Her eyes got bigger as she read the name on the dog tags.

"Troy, no. No, no. Tell me this isn't what I know in my heart it is. Oh God, Troy. Why? Why did you do it? How could you?" she moaned as she took a weak step backwards almost tripping over the motorcycle's extended tire. Tears streamed down her face as she leaned against the shed wall and sobbed.

Troy started to stand, but Roz screamed, "NO. No, don't come near me. I told you not to move." Roz attempted to control her sobs as she tried to understand the implications of all she had discovered that day. She wiped her mouth with her hand, sniffed, and then wiped her eyes. She ran her fingers through her freshly permed hair and gripped a handful of curls. She locked eyes with her husband who appeared to be dumbfounded by his wife's outbursts.

Roz carefully slid all the treasures back into the tobacco pouch and put it in her dress pocket. She held the big wrench in front of her and made her way to the door. She slid outside the door and shut it, leaving Troy imprisoned in his private sanctum. She picked up the padlock from the ground and locked the door securely in place.

"You stay in there, Troy and let me do some thinkin'. I gotta clear my head. Don't you move," she ordered.

Troy weakly responded, "Roz, please listen to me. I gotta explain."

"DON'T YOU DARE TRY TO COME OUT OF THAT SHED, OR I'LL GO GET YOUR SHOTGUN AND FIX YOU FOR GOOD!" Roz screamed through the door.

Troy sat back down on the cot and stared at his Harley that was now sprawled on its side. He had never seen Roz act this way. It was as if some demon had taken control of her body and wanted to destroy everything in its wake.

He tried to determine if he should try to get out of the shed or wait for Roz and the consequences she brought with her. He feared she may have left to fetch the shotgun. She knew how to use it to protect herself-- he had seen to that. But who was going to protect him?

He heard her coming back toward the shed. It was too late now, regardless. He'd have to defend himself against whatever demon she happened to be hosting.

* * * * *

Corb answered the phone while LorAnn was washing the dirty dishes and cleaning up the kitchen. Both his daughters were in front of the television watching a game show.

"Hello?" he said as he sat down on the edge of the couch occupied by the girls.

"Corb, this is Roz. I need some help from you. Is there any way you can come by tonight without telling LorAnn?"

Roz had never asked Corb to come to their house without LorAnn. Her request puzzled him.

"Well, I guess so. What exactly do you need?" he asked, trying to determine just what he might be facing.

Roz paused for a long time before she spoke. "I told Troy I wanted a divorce. He's gone and I need some help getting' some of his stuff outta here. It's gotta be tonight before I change my mind."

Corb was happy to help, but really didn't want to get in the middle of a family dispute. "Are you sure you don't need to wait awhile before doing all that?"

Roz quickly retorted, "No. Now. It's gotta be now. Can you help me? You're the only one I know with a truck. And don't say anything to LorAnn. I'll tell her later about Troy leavin' but I don't want her to know you're helpin' me clean out. Just say you gotta go to work or somethin', okay?"

"Yeah, I'll be there in about half an hour," Corb said and hung up the phone.

When LorAnn appeared in the living room doorway, she looked at Corb with a questioning expression.

"LorAnn, I gotta run by the City Garage for a few minutes. I hope I won't be too long, but don't wait up for me." He stood up from his perch on the couch arm and moved toward his wife. He kissed her forehead, then turned back to his daughters. "If I ain't home before you go to bed, I'll see you first thing in the mornin' before you get on the bus."

Intently watching their television show, both girls said "bye, Daddy," without moving their eyes from the screen.

LorAnn watched him leave through the back door. She wondered what woman he was rushing off to see in the early evening hours of Labor Day.

Part Five

Vengeance Is Mine

CHAPTER 29

1958

On Tuesday, September 2, 1958, Brian Martin received an unexpected phone call that changed the lives of all Shelbyvillians, but especially those of the Shelbyville Police Department employees.

When Brian picked up the phone, the person on the other end said only a few words, "Marvin Morgan is the kidnapper. Start checkin' him out." The caller hung up the phone.

Brian had written Marvin Morgan's name on a piece of loose paper, and picked it up as he headed toward Acting Chief Woodson's office.

Woodson was on the phone, but motioned Brian to come in. The detective sat down in the green padded chairs that had been there for at least ten years. He was anxious to talk with the Acting Chief, and showed his impatience by leaning toward Woodson's desk in a stiff position, drumming his fingers on the desktop. Woodson noticed and quickly ended the call.

"What's got you so worked up, Lover Boy? You look like you want to tell me Jenny's pregnant or something." Woodson laughed as Martin just shook his head.

"Maybe something better than that, Chief. Someone just called and gave me the name of our kidnapper." He leaned back in his chair and looked for Woodson's reaction.

"So you don't know who called you, or why, and you believe this person?" the Chief asked with a smirk.

"Right, Chief. We've run down all sorts of dead ends. We have no real leads. Never have. So I suggest we at least check this fellow out. At least it's a positive move. Right now all we seem to be doing is writing on a black board and clapping chalk out of erasers at the end of the day. I'm ready for some field work. You approve of that?" Brian asked.

Chief Woodson smiled. "Course I do. I'm just messin' with you, Lover Boy. What's the name of the suspect?"

"Marvin Morgan. I haven't run anything on him, so I don't know anything about him yet. But I guarantee we'll know his whole life story in just a few hours." Martin got up to leave.

"Keep me updated, if you find out anything good right away. Otherwise, I'll be here till 6:00 p.m. tonight. Got a date with an angel, and she's heavenly," Woodson said and theatrically swooned with the back of his hand against his forehead.

"You mean you were able to get a third date with Miss FBI? You amaze me, Woodson. I thought you were a confirmed bachelor," he asked.

"Well, you were wrong, for once. I plan to marry that girl someday. She's everything I've ever wanted, and I think she feels the same way about me."

Brian Woodson looked at his friend and sincerely said, "If all you want is happiness, you probably got the right girl. She seems to be real nice, Jenny likes her, and so does everyone else. She's way too good for you, you know." Brian said and left the Chief's office.

* * * * * *

When Detective Martin stepped into 'Kidnap Central,' he coughed loudly to try to get the team's attention. They all looked at Martin and stopped what they were doing.

Martin started his briefing. "Listen up, everybody. We've just received an anonymous telephone tip. Our unidentified caller said only a few words, and I quote: 'Marvin Morgan is the kidnapper. Start checkin' him out.' The caller disconnected the line after making that statement."

"We are not going to ignore any tips, so I'm going to assign duties to all of you so we can find out if this person should be placed under active surveillance.

"We'll need to get his background, the names of his family members, find out where he lives, and where he works. Talk to neighbors, employers, or anybody who knows anything about the man. See if he has a police record or military record.

"We may be looking at his personal finances, too, but we may wait on that. Just get started and report back here at four o'clock for a briefing to me and the Chief.

"Get going and good luck." Brian dismissed the team and returned to his desk.

I've heard that voice before, but I just can't place it. Maybe he'll call back and I'll recognize it.

* * * * * *

Roz called LorAnn on Thursday after the Labor Day phone call. LorAnn picked up the phone thinking it was Corb calling to see when supper would be ready or to tell her he would be a little late getting home. She was relieved to hear Roz's voice on the line.

"I've been dying to know what happened with Troy. It's been so hard not telling Corb about any of this. So, tell me what happened?"

Roz cleared her throat and began her tale. "Well, I went out to the shed and caught him jerkin' off to a magazine. I was already mad, but I think that pushed me over the top. I accused him of trying to fool around with Dixie, and I told him I knew about all his other women. Then I told him I wanted a divorce, and told him to leave. I said I never wanted to see his ugly face again, and I don't. He's gone now. I don't know where he went, and I don't care. I got all his stuff together and that's gone now, too. Guess I'll be a single woman again before long, and I'm kinda happy about that part. I just hate that it had to take him being such a nasty person to get to this point. LorAnn, he said he didn't do anything to Dixie, but I believe he did have his dick out and he showed it to her. I think that was the worst of it all. So don't worry about her innocence. I'm sure it's intact."

LorAnn felt relieved and sad at the same time. She had always thought Roz and Troy made a good team, but she didn't know everything that went on in that house. She always thought if Roz was able to tolerate Troy—like she tolerated Corb's flings—then she guessed everything was all right.

"I think we should try to move on and forget about it. I ain't gonna say nothin' to Corb about any of it, and you can tell him yourself about Troy leavin'. You can make up whatever you need to that'll make him understand. But I don't ever want him to know what Troy did or said to Dixie. That would break his heart. Dixie's been through enough in her short life. I don't want her daddy looking at her different now. It just needs to go away and stay away, far as I'm concerned." LorAnn responded.

Roz agreed with LorAnn and told her she'd call Corb that day and let him know about Troy. She felt a little guilty over telling her that lie, but it would be better for everybody if Roz just let the story go as she and Corb had planned. She was thankful that she didn't have to tell Corb about Troy and Dixie having Life Lessons. What she **had** shown Corb was enough to convince him that she had done the right thing.

The sisters hung up. Both felt a heavy weight lifted off their shoulders.

* * * * * *

When the team reported for their four o'clock briefing session with the Chief and Detective Morgan, they were excited with their findings. One of the team members turned the rolling black board around and started filling the clean side of the board with newly obtained information.

When it was all written down, Brian Martin stood in front of the board, reading the new info to the group.

MARVIN JACKSON MORGAN, Born 1910

<u>Married to</u>: Geraldine Stewart Morgan, Born 1930,

Disabled since 1947 (Legally Blind) Insurance Payout

<u>Children</u>: Rocky, born 1932, Lives at Home (Mentally-Challenged)

<u>Employer</u>: City of Shelbyville, Animal Control (Part-time)

<u>Address</u>: 631 Fishingford Pike in Bedford County

<u>Relative</u>: Former Chief Peter Stewart, (Brother-in-law)

No other known living relatives yet identified

"Well, folks, we have quite a story to figure out, don't we? Tomorrow we need to go see Mr. Morgan and interview him thoroughly. We'll see if he has something he wants to share with us." Acting Chief Woodson commented.

"Chief, I'd like to talk to his employer, too. I know Corb Carter who works as the Superintendant of Public Works. Maybe Morgan works for him or under one of his sections. I'm sure he'd help us if he could. He is the father of the two girls kidnapped by Edith Ruth and returned by the FBI," Detective Martin volunteered.

"Good idea, Detective. Why don't we go see them both together? I remember Mr. Carter, too. I'd like to see him again anyway." Acting Chief Woodson said.

"Sounds fine to me. Let's say we roll out of here around nine o'clock tomorrow morning," Martin suggested.

Woodson replied, "Just like old times, right buddy?"

They laughed and went back to their office to clear up their desks for the day.

* * * * *

The following morning, Detective Martin and Acting Chief Woodson were riding down West Lane Street on their way to the City Garage. They looked forward to seeing Mr. Carter again, since they believed he would assist them in any way possible to help solve the kidnapping cases. His daughters were also kidnapped once, but that story had a much happier ending than what either of the officers predicted for those yet unsolved.

When they pulled up in front of the City Garage, they parked in one of the two open spaces near the door. They entered the building, seeing two offices built into the side of a warehouse-type building, a small open break area with a coke machine, and the remaining space that reminded them of an airplane hangar. This building didn't house planes, but it did store a variety of heavy equipment including a garbage truck, a road grader, a roller truck for tamping pavement, and at least one bulldozer. The remaining equipment was in use around the area.

Corb Carter was sitting at his desk in the first office that the officers saw when they walked in. He came out to see what he could do for the gentlemen. He knew they were the detectives that had helped to get Dixie and Dollie home, and he would go out of his way to do whatever they needed if they asked for his help.

"Mr. Carter, so good to see you again," Brian Martin said while Acting Chief Woodson shook Corb's hand.

"Can I get you guys something to drink?" Corb asked politely.

"Nothing for us, thank you. We were wondering if there is some place private we can talk?" Acting Chief Woodson inquired.

"Why don't we talk in here. It's my office and it's the most private spot we have around here." He motioned the officers to follow him.

"We're here to get some information about a Marvin Morgan who is a City Employee in charge of Animal Control. Can you tell us anything about him? Does he work directly for you?" Martin asked.

"He don't report to me, but he's got a small outfit across the street--you can see it from the front door--and his truck stays parked over there. When he gets a call to pick up road kill, he leaves his house, comes here for his truck, then leaves to go do his work. Brings the truck back, empties the dead animals into barrels inside in a small freezer, and when he gets a barrel filled to the top, he puts 'em on his forklift and dumps 'em in a hole in the back section of the property near the dump. We come along behind him and fill up the hole. Then he starts all over. The job ain't hard; it's just nobody wants to do it." Corb explained.

"Is Mr. Morgan on-site today?" Detective Martin asked.

"I can see the truck over there, so he's at home. Guess he ain't got any calls today to pick up strays or dead critters." Corb replied.

"Is there any way that you could show us inside the small outfit that he works from? Do you have a key?" Chief Woodson asked.

"I have a key to just about everything," Corb laughed, pulling a large key ring from his pocket that had at least 50 keys hanging from it.

The three men crossed the road from the City Garage parking area and moved diagonally across the graveled property. When they reached the front door, Corb had to try several keys before he found the right one.

Corb opened the door to a relatively neat office set up on one side of the small warehouse. On the other were stacks of empty 50 gallon drums, a stockpile for future road kill deposits.

They walked around the area, flipping papers, but generally just eyeballing the entire set up. Acting Chief Woodson walked down the right side of the building toward a big door that looked like it might open a walk-in freezer. He looked at Corb and pointed to the door.

"It should be open. Go on in." Corb walked quickly to catch up with them. He was standing less than a yard away when Woodson opened the door.

There were two pallets, each holding four upright barrels, and they appeared to be sealed. "Like I said, he keeps these barrels in here until he fills 'em full of road kill. Then they get sealed and buried." Corb repeated.

"So if these aren't sealed, can we look in them?" Detective Martin asked.

"If you want to, go ahead. It's not somethin' most people want to do, and the smell is awful. Might make you lose your breakfast. But go ahead and give'r a whirl." Corb stepped a few feet back in order to avoid the putrid smell as much as possible.

Detective Martin took one end of a crowbar and tried to pry open the top on the first barrel he came to. He finally flipped it, and the lid fell to the floor. Martin looked over the rim to see a large pile of dead smelly animals ready for burial. He closed the top and moved to the next barrel.

He did the same maneuver with the second barrel that he did with the first. The crowbar helped him get leverage, and when he pressed down on the bar, the top flipped off and scooted to the side. He picked it up and held it while he peered inside the partially full barrel.

He saw something he wasn't expecting to see. It looked like a small human hand cramped against the side of the barrel. It was underneath the carcass of a dead dog, which had to be removed before the remaining barrel contents could be examined. Once free from the carcass obstruction, the detectives clearly saw the small crumpled body of a young girl.

"Mr. Carter, I'm afraid I am going to have to ask you to leave. This is now an active crime scene. There will be special investigative units arriving momentarily, and we may have to look at the burial site if there is a chance our kidnapping victims might have already been buried in barrels. We have to positively identify that this body belongs to one of our kidnapping victims," Brian Martin said.

Acting Chief Woodson chimed in, "And you are not allowed to disclose to anyone the nature of what we found or were looking for when we entered the building. We will be notifying your superiors who have a need to know. Do not contact

Marvin Morgan. We'll be sending a squad car out to pick him up within the next few minutes."

Detective Martin's face lit up as he said to Corb, "We appreciate everything you've done to help us. Without you, I don't think we'd be standing here right now, would we?"

Corb smiled, "Well, I do have a lot of keys," he replied as he held up the heavy key ring in front of the Detective.

They shook hands and Corb went back to his office in the City Garage. He occasionally peeked out the window to see how much further along the police had gotten in cordoning off the area. He thought they might be there for several days, and Corb pledged to be on hand to assist if it would help get that nosey Morgan out of everybody's hair.

CHAPTER 30

1958

Deputy Chief Woodson and his former detective partner, Brian Martin, stood outside the yellow police tape at the Animal Control building, observing the Crime Scene Investigators come and go through the steel door.

"I gotta tell you, Brian. I had lost all hope on these cases. It just felt like we were never going to get any fresh leads to help us find those kids," the Acting Chief sighed.

"Me, too, Harry. This whole thing has dragged out for way too long, and every trail we thought we should follow got cold before we ever got to it. At least we may have some closure for the kids' parents when this is all said and done." Brian and Harry always seemed to share the exact sentiments on police matters.

"Harry, why don't we join the officers at Morgan's house? Don't you think we deserve to be there to pick up that piece of slime? You realize we started this thing together, and it's only fitting for us to be the guys who nail him," Brian asked his boss.

Harry looked at his long-time friend and partner-in-crime. "You're absolutely right, Lover Boy. Let's hit the road. Maybe we can get there before they arrest him."

As Martin drove, Woodson radioed central dispatch to ask the status of the Morgan apprehension. He was told the squad car was just about to turn onto Fishingford Pike. Woodson told dispatch to give the officers his direct order to wait at Bart's store before proceeding, even if it meant they had to turn around to get there. He would arrive momentarily with Detective Martin to personally apprehend the suspect.

With that handled, Brian accelerated and sped toward their destination.

* * * * * *

Geraldine Morgan sat in front of their television, listening intently to someone trying to name a tune with only three musical notes. She couldn't see well enough to distinguish the features of the excited contestants, but she enjoyed the show because she often knew the name of the song before the participants could blurt out the title.

Marvin Morgan walked between his wife and the television, knowing that it wouldn't bother her to have her viewing area obstructed. He passed through the living room to the kitchen and stooped down in front of the sink. Opening the cabinet's double doors, he rearranged the various kitchen products to make room to retrieve his small household toolbox. He slid the small box through the cleared path and set it on the floor in front of him. He opened the lid and scanned the contents.

"ROCKY! Where's my plumber's wrench?" he shouted when he realized the tool he needed was not in the top in the box's removable shelf. He lifted the shelf and peered into the bottom section of the metal box. "ROCKY! GET IN HERE RIGHT NOW!" Marvin Morgan shouted to his son.

Rocky entered the room and saw his father squatting in the floor in front of the opened toolbox. "Daddy I needed to fix something so I borrowed that wrench. I know where it is, though. I'll go get it," the nervous son stated.

"What in the devil did you need a plumber's wrench for?" Marvin's breathing was getting deeper and faster. "Did you take somethin' else outta here, too, boy?" an agitated Marvin demanded of his son.

"I saw a little bag of purties and I played with 'em for a while. I know where to git them, though. You want me to go git 'em now?" the compliant Rocky asked.

"Where are they, boy? I'll git 'em myself," Marvin said.

"I put 'em in a secret hiding place, Daddy. One of Mr. Troy's secret hiding places. C'mon and I'll show ya." Rocky started to leave the kitchen through the back door.

"Wait a minute, Rocky. You went over there when I told you not to? Did Troy ask you to come over there?" Marvin was getting angrier by the minute.

"No, Daddy. I know where his shed key is and I used it. It was dark when I went over there and nobody saw me. I put the key back under the can like Mr. Troy always does." Rocky smiled a confident smile.

Marvin Morgan was getting frustrated, but tried to maintain his composure while he questioned his immature son. "How'd you get over there? Did you walk straight up the driveway? Didn't they see you comin'?"

"Only Miz Roz, but that was later. She's a nice lady. I went through a hole in the fence near the woodpile. I fixed it so's you can't tell it was cut through." Rocky grinned with satisfaction at his father.

Marvin studied his son as his mind whirled with thoughts of possible discovery. He finally spoke to Rocky in the calmest tone he could muster. "Son, Miz Roz is prob'ly asleep right now. Troy's at work, I guess. Maybe now's a good time for you to go fetch that little bag."

"Okay, Daddy and I'll fetch the wrench, too. I left it in the shed, I'm thinking." Rocky took off on his mission as Marvin sat down in the floor, legs spread. He closed his eyes and hoped Rocky didn't come back empty-handed.

* * * * * *

Two parallel squad cars waited patiently with engines running in the parking area of Bart's Store. When Detective Martin and the Acting Chief passed the waiting officers, Woodson held his arm out his open car window and motioned for them to follow. The three cars formed a caravan as they drove rapidly down Fishingford Pike toward the Morgan home.

Two squad cars pulled into the Morgan driveway, while Woodson parked in front of the house on the roadside. When Martin and Woodson exited their vehicle, they signaled the officers to stay behind as backup.

Woodson knocked on the door with badge in hand and shoulder holster unclasped, ready for use if needed. Martin stood a step behind, ready to cover Woodson should Morgan feel threatened enough to try to evade arrest.

The door was opened by a middle-aged woman who was having trouble focusing on the two officers. They spoke clearly so the woman would understand that they represented the City Police Department and they were there on official business.

Mrs. Morgan opened the door wider to allow the officers entry into her home. Over her shoulder, she called for her husband.

"Marvin, there's some men here to see us," she said as she led the men toward the living room couch. As an afterthought, she asked, "Are you here to give me an update on my brother?"

The two officers looked at each other with confusion. "Your brother, Mrs. Morgan?" Woodson asked.

"Yes, my brother, Pete Stewart. He was the Chief of Police for a while and now he's up in Nashville on some special project? How's he been doin'?" Mrs. Morgan inquired.

"Uh, ma'am, we're not here to talk about that. I'm sorry, but I'm sure he's doing well," a baffled Brian Martin answered.

"Well, we haven't had a check in a while. I thought maybe you men were here to give us the money he usually sends at the end of the month ," she casually said.

The officers realized their case may have gotten even more expansive than originally assumed.

As the three of them sat down in on the couch, Marvin Morgan came into the living room with apprehension all over his face.

"Who are you and what do you want?" Marvin barked.

"Mr. Morgan, I am the Acting Chief of Police, Harry Woodson. This is Detective Brian Martin from the Shelbyville City Police Department. We would like to ask you a few questions, and I think it would be best if we went downtown for the interview. Would you mind coming with us, sir?" Woodson said with authority in his voice.

Marvin sneered at the men. "I ain't going nowhere. What's this about? You never said."

"It's regarding the separate disappearances of five teenagers over the past few years," Martin said as he started to rise from his seat on the couch. Woodson stood, as well.

A perplexed Mrs. Morgan said, "You mean you think Marvin had somethin' to do with that?" She turned her head toward Marvin. "Marvin, is that why Pete was givin' you regular money? I don't understand all this." Mrs. Morgan's hands were shaking now, and she was clearly upset.

Marvin Morgan turned abruptly and darted toward his bedroom. Once inside, he shut the door and latched it behind him. Woodson and Martin followed closely, ordering Mrs. Morgan to lie on the floor and stay out of harm's way.

With pistols drawn, Woodson and Martin stood on either side of the door frame. Woodson shouted, "Come on out, Marvin. We just want to talk to you. There's no need for any of this. We just want to talk."

At that moment, Rocky Morgan entered the back door excited that there were cop cars outside. He wanted to play with the siren and pretend he was the driver.

"Hi, I'm Rocky. Can I look at your cars?" the boy asked the two men standing in his home with guns ready to fire.

"Rocky, get out of here!" his frantic mother shouted from her spot on the living room floor.

"Mama, what's wrong? Did you fall?" Rocky questioned as he quickly moved toward his mother.

"ROCKY! Git the hell out of here now," his father screamed from the other side of the locked bedroom door.

Confused, Rocky went to his mother's side and squatted next to her outstretched body. She motioned for him to lie down next to her, and he obediently followed her direction. He snuggled close to his mother, holding a small bag and a plumber's wrench tightly close to his chest.

At that precise moment, Woodson charged at the bedroom door, attempting to burst through to apprehend the suspect. When the door crashed open, Marvin Morgan was sitting on the edge of the bed with a rifle wedged between his knees and the barrel in his mouth. The desperate man pulled the trigger, leaving brain matter and pieces of bloody hairy tissue splattered on the walls and the white chenille bedspread. Mrs. Morgan could be heard screaming from the living room.

The officers holstered their guns as the backup officers rushed the scene. Mrs. Morgan was now in a sitting position, but Rocky still lying on the floor.

"I got Daddy's wrench and the purties, too, just like he told me to," Rocky smiled at his mother, oblivious to the dramatic events unfolding around him.

Detective Martin walked to the living room spot where Mrs. Morgan and Rocky remained. "Can I see your car, Mr. Police? I'll let you hold the treasures if you let me sit behind the steering wheel. Maybe I can turn on the siren, too?" Rocky inquired as he handed the tobacco pouch to Brian.

Brian peeked into the cotton drawstring sack and immediately saw Joe Claxton's dog tag. He cinched it shut and turned toward the Acting Chief.

"I think this boy deserves a ride in a police car. Let's see if one of the men can accommodate him while we get this scene under control," Brian commented as he waved the small pouch at Woodson.

Woodson nodded agreement and directed one of the patrolmen to give Rocky the royal treatment, including a few alerts with the siren. A happy Rocky grabbed the patrolman's hand and rushed him out the front door. He could be heard jabbering to the officer as they left the front porch. "Mr. Police, can I drive the police car?"

Woodson and Martin heard the patrol car pull out of the driveway, and a few moments later heard the familiar "Blurp" of a short siren blast. Within a few seconds, a long siren blare could be heard in the distance.

An ambulance was called for Mrs. Morgan who clearly was suffering from shock.

The crime scene investigation unit had to divide their crew, leaving half at the Animal Control scene while the other half immediately reported to the Morgan house.

The county coroner would handle the official autopsy, and most likely rule the cause of death to be suicide. Once satisfied that no further examination would be necessary, the coroner would release the body to the family. Eventually, Gowen-Smith Funeral Home would make the final arrangements for Marvin Morgan's closed casket funeral.

CHAPTER 31

1958

It took nearly five more weeks for the excavation team to discover the other four bodies buried in fluid-filled barrels in the segregated Animal Control section of the landfill. With the City Garage within view of the burial site, Corb watched every day as more barrels were extracted and taken back to the cordoned area for internal inspection.

All the teenagers' bodies were examined for signs of torture or sexual violence, but none were found. Each had the pinky finger removed from the right hand, and some showed signs of puncture wounds in various parts of their bodies.

Tissue samples from all the victims were rushed to the crime lab in Nashville. All samples showed traces of etorphine plus a synthetic opiod, the basic ingredients used for tranquilizing animals. Often these mixtures are loaded into tranquilizer gun darts.

* * * * * *

The investigation expanded and revealed the ghastly dealings Morgan had with his brother-in-law, former Chief of Police Peter Stewart.

Investigators discovered that the then-Deputy Chief Stewart had offered his brother-in-law a monthly stipend if he could help elevate his career into the Chief of Police position. Together, they plotted what they believed to be a fail-proof plan that resulted in the kidnapping spree that began in 1955.

Morgan was to scout around the city in the official Animal Control truck, stopping when he noticed a discreet opportunity to abduct a child.

* * * * * *

During his first kidnapping of Wendy Wilson, Morgan was nervous. He had parked his truck on a side street corner near the football field. When he saw the cheerleader pass the field and turn toward her home on Woodbury Street, he climbed out of the truck and retrieved a small baby cat that he had picked up earlier. As the girl got closer, he stood behind the open van doors of the truck, soothing the tabby kitten.

He called to the girl when she was within a few feet of the truck's rear and asked her if she wanted the cat. He begged her to take it home, since it would have to be put to sleep if an owner wasn't identified. The girl happily took the cat in her arms, and when she looked down at the furry bundle in her arms, Morgan pulled a tranquilizer gun from the back of his belted pants. He aimed it at the girl's leg, being at close enough range to definitely hit his target.

When the girl realized what had happened, her wide eyes started to roll back in her head as she succumbed to the potent tranquilizer. He swept her off her feet and laid her limp body inside the truck, leaving the fallen kitten free to scamper off. He slammed the doors and immediately drove to the uninhabited Animal Control building.

She stirred in the back of the truck before he got there, teaching him a valuable lesson about future abductions. He carefully backed the truck up close to the rear door of the building. When he opened the truck's back door, the girl was sitting up and ready to leap for escape. Morgan already had the tranquilizer gun drawn and shot her again, this time hitting her chest near her heart. When she dropped back down on the truck floor, he scooped her up and carried her inside the building. He went directly to the freezer.

He already had a barrel ready, partially filled with dead animals scraped off the roads during the past week. But before he stuffed her still-breathing young body into the barrel, he sealed her mouth with industrial duct tape, then bound her ankles and hands. He snipped off her little finger and removed her silver charm bracelet. He put the finger aside in a jar, and stuffed the bracelet in his pocket.

When the container was topped off with the day's fresh road kill, he filled the barrel with an odor-killing liquid, then sealed it permanently. With a hand dolly, he managed to move it to the pallet of barrels that would be ready for burial on Monday.

He set the temperature of the freezer to well below its normal range when he closed the thick door and locked the compartment behind him.

After he cleaned up after himself and ensured there was nothing visible in the building or the vehicle that could alert anyone to his atrocity, he moved the truck to the front of the building in its usual parking space. By then it was past supper time, and the workers at the City Garage had already clocked out for the day. He felt confident that he had been unobserved throughout the entire ordeal. He got in his car and headed for home.

Later he dug a hole at the side of his house to give the teenager an official memorial spot. He threw Wendy's tiny detached finger into the dirt and buried it under the beautiful red rose bush he had bought for his wife.

* * * * * *

The second abduction was easier than the first one, mainly because nine months had passed since Wendy Wilson went missing. No one had ever questioned him about the first abduction, as he'd been careful to cover his tracks and perfect the kidnapping process during those months. As every day passed, he grew more confident that he and Stewart had come up with the perfect plan: a crime that would be nearly impossible to solve, but would still reflect badly on the current Chief of Police.

In June of 1956 when Stewart called him with his next assignment, Marvin felt ready to face a perfected challenge. He spent the designated afternoon buying a second red rose bush, and later he prepared another hole for the upcoming memorial.

Late in the afternoon he stopped in at the empty Animal Control building and prepared a fresh barrel. He layered its bottom with a healthy portion of the week's road kill harvest, With the exception of a flattened raccoon, he put the rest of the recovered dead animals aside to later top off the barrel holding the future victim.

He had his snippers laid out and a jar handy. His tranquilizer gun was loaded and a roll of duct tape was right inside the truck's rear door. He was ready.

* * * * * *

He drove the Animal Control vehicle around town and scanned the streets for his potential next victim. He traveled through the streets slowly, as if searching for stray dogs or cats. He saw a small terrified puppy wandering near the Willow Mount Cemetery, and he stopped and picked him up. He placed the shaking animal in the empty cage he kept ready in the truck.

He continued his drive down Jackson Street and turned into West End Circle. There he spotted a teenage girl playing ball with two children no older than seven, if that. They were running in the yard of the first duplex on his right. He deduced that the girl must be a babysitter. He made a mental note to check back after dark. Marvin circled the cul de sac and waved at the children as he passed the house to leave the subdivision.

Sometime around 9:30 p.m. he returned to Jackson Street and found his scouted parking area near the entrance to West End Circle. He backed his truck into the abandoned driveway of a burned down house located to the rear of the duplex's property boundary. He surveyed his possible path to the side door of the targeted duplex, then took his raccoon road kill from the back of the truck. He tossed it into the center of Jackson Street and then retrieved a plastic bag and shovel out of the back of the truck. He left the vehicle's rear doors open as he leaned the shovel against the side of the truck, carefully placing the plastic bag on the ground under the shovel's blade.

He looked up and down Jackson Street. Seeing no one, he took the puppy from its cage and made his way up the driveway of the burned house. He peeked through the dividing overgrown brush and clearly saw the side door of the duplex. He jogged forward with caution and stood on the side porch, peering through the kitchen door.

He watched the teenager enter the room with a bowl of popcorn and a soda. The other children were nowhere to be seen. She was about to move toward the television, but he interrupted her as he knocked lightly on the door.

She approached the side door trying to squint to see who was behind the window. She recognized the face of the man who had driven by the house in the dogcatcher truck. She looked through the glass and saw him holding a trembling puppy.

She opened the door slightly, and he asked her if the puppy belonged to the household. She said no and he just stood there for a moment. He looked disappointed and then asked if he could use the phone to call his boss about what to do with the mongrel.

Because he was a city representative, she didn't hesitate to let him in the door. She took the puppy while she showed him the phone. When she turned her back to go to the couch and comfort the puppy, he drew the tranquilizer gun and fired a dart into her arm. The puppy leapt from the couch and ran out the partly open kitchen door.

He picked up the limp girl, stepped toward the door and stuck his head out to see if anyone was outside. Believing he was safe, he stepped through the door not bothering to shut it. He carried the limp girl as fast as he could to the bordering underbrush, then cautiously proceeded to the rear of the truck. Marvin pushed her limp body inside the cargo area and applied the tape to her mouth, wrists, and ankles. He left the truck's rear door open, casually taking the shovel and black bag to the center of the road. He scraped up and bagged the raccoon carcass for the second time that day, waving to a scattered few passing motorists as he deliberately did a good job.

The next morning, there was an additional frozen barrel on the pallet ready for the Monday burial process. He had a new identification bracelet to add to his bag of souvenirs. There was also a new rose bush memorial planted at the side of the Morgan house, with a freshly buried finger intertwined in its roots.

* * * * * *

By the time he captured Peggy Sue Overcast, Marvin Morgan had the process down pat. All he had to do was snare a child into his abduction web and the details would fall into place.

He received another call from his ambitious brother-in-law during the last week of March, 1957. He wanted a third abduction completed within the next week. He thought Police Chief Taylor was hopelessly depressed and frustrated enough to consider early retirement if he had to face the angry township over another scandalous abduction.

Marvin's previous abductions had occurred on Friday and Saturday nights. He wanted to change things around a little bit, so he chose Monday, April 1st as his next timeline. *What better way to shake things up than with an April Fools' joke*, he thought to himself as he drove around the Village community in his official vehicle.

He again waited until twilight to start actively scanning for his victim. He backed his truck into the driveway of a house that had a "FOR RENT" sign in the yard. He had picked up another stray kitten that he had caged in the rear of the truck, so he went to the rear of the vehicle to get it out.

As he stood there between the two open doors, he noticed a young girl with a blue book satchel waving goodbye to someone inside a house two doors down. She walked almost to her own back porch when she glanced across the adjacent back yards. She stopped and watched the dogcatcher holding and stroking a little kitten. He smiled broadly and beckoned her to come over and pet the kitten.

She met the same fate as the other two victims. It was easy as pie.

Marvin was so proud of himself and the expanding rose garden that he was planting for his wife.

Happy April Fool's Day to you, Stewart, you piece of shit.

* * * * * *

After the third abduction, Chief Taylor had a heart attack, and Peter Stewart was unofficially promoted to Acting Police Chief. Things were apparently working out well with the kidnapping scheme, at least for Stewart and Morgan.

Meanwhile, 1957 moved steadily along, and the abduction of the two young Carter girls once again rocked the town. Marvin was puzzled, wondering if Stewart had anything to do with it, but he doubted it. *Maybe it's a copycat thing. Imagine that. Someone tryin' to copy me.*

When the girls were caught and the babysitter was charged, Stewart told Morgan he could stop the kidnappings now. He was going to solicit their brother-in-law, the Deputy Sheriff at the Davidson County Jail, and get him on board with a new plan. The two of them would ensure the incarcerated woman would take the blame for the previous abductions, leaving Marvin and Stewart in the clear.

Marvin was proud of his work and all the effort it had taken to carefully plan and execute the yet unsolved crimes. Still, as long as the Deputy Chief was supplementing his family income, Marvin had no reason to buck the system. Unfortunately, since Stewart didn't need Marvin's assistance any more, the supplemental income stopped abruptly when Stewart was officially promoted to Police Chief.

By early February of 1958, there was still skepticism among the citizens about why Chief Stewart so quickly closed the three teenagers' kidnapping cases without complete resolution. They still wanted answers.

Marvin took it upon himself to execute a lone-wolf plan. He would shock the town once again with a fresh new abduction. He wanted to prove to himself and Stewart that he was still needed. He wanted to earn back his routine supplemental income checks from the Chief.

That's when it occurred to Morgan that a young boy would be a nice change in his abduction protocol.

Buried Sins

* * * * * *

Often, Marvin's wife had medicine delivered to their home. There were such frequent deliveries that all Morgan family members knew the delivery boy by name. Every time Joe Claxton came by the house for Saturday deliveries, he had been pleasant and courteous, and even tried to converse with Rocky about bikes and motorcycles. The whole family liked him.

On Saturday morning, February 15, 1958, Marvin had to run a couple of errands in town. Marvin was in the family car and was on his way home when he passed Joe riding his bike toward his delivery destination. They waved to each other as they both proceeded in opposite directions.

Marvin turned around and went back toward town, proceeding to the Farmer's Co-op. He picked up another rose bush...this time a white one...and drove home before noon.

That afternoon he dug another hole and told his wife he had some things to do in his office. He would probably be back before supper, but he instructed her and Rocky to eat without him if he hadn't made it back by then. He explained he had forgotten to do some paperwork, and he needed to get it finished before Monday morning. They never questioned Marvin about anything concerning work.

Marvin left his home by 3:00 p.m., and went directly to the Animal Control building. There he made his preparations, going through the same established routine as always. By 4:00 p.m. he was on the road in his official truck and scanning the route that Joe Claxton would be taking to go home from his drug store route.

When Marvin saw Joe riding down Baker Street, he pulled up alongside him while he pedaled. Joe glanced to his right and caught sight of his frequent customer. He smiled as Morgan yelled out the window, "Could you use an extra $10 bucks, Joe?" Joe slowed a little and so did Marvin as they approached the end of the street. At the Baker Street stop sign, Joe sat astride his bike and chatted with Marvin through the open passenger window of the Animal Control truck.

"Maybe. What do I have to do, Mr. Morgan?" the young boy asked.

"Just help me move a few barrels down at the Animal Control building, that's all. Shouldn't take but a few minutes and I've pulled my back out. I don't think I can do it by myself." Marvin feigned a stiff back as he moved around in his seat.

With no one near and no traffic around them, Joe rolled his bike to the rear of the truck as Marvin got out to open the two back doors. Marvin helped Joe lift the bike into the rear space, and Joe got in the front passenger seat, ready to make a few extra bucks.

From there, it was a piece of cake.

* * * * * *

Chief Stewart was infuriated with his lame-brained brother-in-law. He was certain any credibility he had built as Chief would now disappear since another teen had vanished. When he called Marvin, he let him have it, admonishing him for acting on his own.

Marvin calmly replied, "Well, if you hadn't stopped sendin' us checks, I might have been more inclined to follow *your* plan. Now I've got *my own* plan."

The Chief begrudgingly wrote another check to Marvin, wondering how much longer he could afford to keep this up. His resources were running thin now that he had to pay off his other brother-in-law for that "Miss Ruth fiasco" in Nashville. He had fewer sources of income since he had taken the Chief position, finding his kickbacks for dismissing various charges for the town's elite were less frequent. He didn't have any other slush funds, and his salary wasn't large enough to keep diving into.

Unfortunately, the checks stopped again when Chief Stewart was spirited away to Nashville on his "secret mission." The town hadn't been officially advised of the reason behind his swift departure, but they were glad to see him leave under any circumstances. The citizens believed the new Acting Chief Woodson would do a much better job than the troll who held the job before him.

Marvin began to feel nervous again about his family, and it didn't help that his pervert neighbor kept things hopping. He was afraid that Rocky would get into trouble with Troy Tucker. He tried to figure out a way to kidnap or kill Troy without ever being a suspect, but they'd had too many arguments with too many witnesses for Marvin not to be the primary suspect. Marvin had to find a way to relieve his pent up tension.

* * * * *

All that led to abduction number five, Linda Adcock.

In his heart, Marvin knew he couldn't hold off for long. He was itching to do something to get back at Stewart, his other jackass brother-in-law in Nashville, and the Troy Tuckers of the world. He thought maybe he'd make this one his final masterpiece. He believed he'd been pressing his luck, and it would be a good time to quit this foolishness.

He knew there'd be no more money coming from his relative. He also figured the cowardly Stewart would run his big mouth and eventually blab to everybody about their joint effort to get Stewart securely in the Chief's job. Marvin assumed the new Police Chief might have more sense than Stewart and solve the cases anyway. The way he saw it, he didn't have much to lose if he got caught doing the crime or after it was over. He was still going to get caught sooner or later. The idea didn't seem to bother him too much.

So on the last night of the Celebration when the World Champion Walking Horse was selected, Marvin planned to select his own champion and the finales of both events would coincide. It would be a night to remember for so many visitors and citizens.

* * * * * *

Marvin slowly drove his Animal Control vehicle around the stable grounds outside the main stadium of the horse show. Cheerful people were coming and going, laughing and grinning, and it made Marvin sick. He wanted to give them something to cry about.

By twilight, he backed his truck into an area near the back row of stalls. Anyone who saw him might have thought he was visiting and the Animal Control truck was his only mode of transportation. They may have assumed he was there in case some poor animal dropped dead. He didn't care what they thought. He was there for a reason and it wasn't to watch some horse go around in circles.

Late in the night, he heard the commotion from the ring. The new champion had been selected. Marvin got out of his truck, armed with his tranquilizer gun, and started his stroll between the stalls.

It didn't take long for him to spot the young girl who he had seen visiting many of the stabled horses that day. She appeared to know a lot of people, and she was obviously a horse lover. That gave him an idea.

He moved stealthily toward the stalls in the direction she was headed. When she passed, he made a sound like a wounded animal. She stopped in her tracks and looked around. As she started to move forward again, Marvin made the same sound. She turned and entered the alley between the small buildings and Marvin grabbed her. She never even felt the tranquilizer dart.

* * * * * *

Marvin made it to his closely parked truck and put the unconscious girl in the same place four others victims had occupied. He went through his usual steps, and drove off into the night—ahead of the crowd but behind the eight ball.

It was so late that Saturday night when he got to the Animal Control building, he was tired and not thinking straight. He managed to get his prey prepared for the barrel, but he only had one dead animal carcass to lay across the girl's head. That wasn't enough to fill the barrel since the girl was so small. He needed a few more pieces of road kill to top it off. Thinking he'd have time the Tuesday after Labor Day to take care of it, he just tapped the metal lid closed and did his other usual clean up ritual before leaving for the long holiday weekend.

* * * * * *

After Marvin Morgan committed suicide in the presence of Chief Woodson and Detective Martin, his brother-in-law Peter Stewart made a full confession. As Marvin had predicted, the cowardly former Police Chief broke down and spilled his guts in an attempt to avoid a potential death penalty sentence for his "murder for hire" plot. Stewart voluntarily revealed every sordid detail of the abductions that Marvin had bragged to him about. The scandal rocked the state, and garnered national attention in the news. The *Shelbyville Times-Gazette* did weekly features for over six weeks. The *Nashville Tennessean* published a full section documentary of the detailed kidnapping stories in one of their Sunday editions.

The anonymous caller who tipped off the police to investigate Marvin never came forth to claim the recognition he deserved.

* * * * * *

Peter Stewart was eventually imprisoned for life without the possibility of parole. His brother-in-law, the former Deputy Sheriff, served fifteen years in the Nashville State Penitentiary for his illicit involvement with the Edith Ruth case.

Marvin's wife and Stewart's sister, Geraldine, had no steady income except social security for herself and her son, but Marvin had left her a life insurance policy that paid off, even in the event of suicide. She combined the proceeds with what was left of her injury settlement, and managed to live comfortably thereafter. She sold their home on Fishingford Pike and moved with her son into a duplex apartment in the nearby Cedars subdivision, not far from the house where Marvin ended his life.

Only Geraldine and Rocky attended Marvin's funeral.

Chief Harry Woodson became engaged to his FBI girlfriend, Eva Cortner. They set their wedding date for Saturday, September 12, 1959, three days past the fourth anniversary of the first kidnapping in the City.

Brian and Jenny Martin had a beautiful set of identical twin girls, and moved into their newly constructed 3-bedroom, 2-bath home. Brian became the Deputy Police Chief a year after he and Woodson cracked the unsolved cases.

The City of Shelbyville and its Police Department finally returned to a low-key status. Under the watchful eye of Police Chief Harry Woodson, the crime rate dropped and wouldn't steadily rise again until some 30 years later, well beyond Chief Woodson's retirement.

Part Six

Reconciling the Past

CHAPTER 32

Preparing for the Funeral

2001

Dixie Carter Edwards was exhausted. She had just recounted almost a decade of life-changing history in excruciating detail to her younger sister.

Dollie Carter Estes had been superficially aware of most of the events, but had lived in blissful, youthful ignorance throughout most of the period. Of course, she knew about the town's kidnappings and murders—there was too much publicity and talk throughout the years for that to be forgotten.

She vividly remembered the trip with Miss Ruth but never thought as much about the potential danger as Dixie had. Dollie thought of the trip more as an excursion, with the whole town ecstatic to see them when they returned.

Dollie never knew that Dixie had felt so detached from their parents, nor did she have any idea about Uncle Troy's sexual appetite. She only had a fleeting memory of the man, and it was certainly not anything negative. She knew he skipped town at some point, leaving Aunt Roz behind and without ever contacting anyone in the family again. She vaguely remembered Aunt Roz and Mama talking about how Aunt Roz could make it on her own without the help of a man.

Her father's escapades were common knowledge to most of the family in later years, especially after his divorce from Mama in 1984 and his two subsequent marriages. He always found a way to be away from home in the evenings and on weekends. Dollie remembered once when, as a teenager, she volunteered to drive Mama around town to see if they could catch Daddy with his proverbial pants down. There had been good times and bad times, but Dollie's recollection about the period Dixie had relived was fleeting at best. She had been too young to remember with clarity.

"So, tell me again why Daddy thought it was important that we should go through all this historical stuff?" Dollie asked as she got up from her comfy spot on the guest bed. She walked toward the door but didn't exit. She turned to her sister for an answer.

"I think Daddy wanted us both to remember the chain of events for some reason. He knew that you had no idea about the trinkets Aunt Roz found in the shed the day Uncle Troy left town. I didn't know that myself until a few years ago. That was when Daddy told me he was the anonymous caller to the police about the Morgan man. If Aunt Roz hadn't found that little bag and if Rocky hadn't appeared by the fence when he did, everybody probably would have thought Uncle Troy was the kidnapper. I'm glad he wasn't. He was a sick man, but he wasn't a killer."

Dollie started toward the door to refresh her drink, but stopped when Dixie started to speak again.

"I never knew why Uncle Troy left, at least not for certain. I always suspected it was because Mama must have told Aunt Roz about the Life Lessons. I was so ashamed of that, I asked Mama not to ever tell Daddy, and I still don't think she did. I believe Daddy died thinking Uncle Troy was always a good uncle to me."

Dollie turned from the door and seated herself next to her big sister. "I'm sure Mama wouldn't have told him. She was a little bit afraid of Daddy's temper like we all were. She probably told Aunt Roz hoping she'd knock some sense into Uncle Troy. I doubt he left her over that. With all his running around with other women, she probably reached her limit when the Life Lesson thing came up. I hardly blame her."

Dixie smiled at Dollie and shoved her with her shoulder. "I think we've talked enough for tonight, Sis. Why don't we check on Mama and then let's go to bed. I'm tired and I know you are. We'll have time tomorrow to rehash any of this stuff we want to. Besides, we have to get to the bank before they close at noon. I can't imagine what else Daddy left in his lockbox except for his Will. I know he made one when he married Phyllis."

They both stood up and shared a brief embrace. Dixie left the room ahead of Dollie who headed straight for the bathroom after the three hour talk.

It was close to midnight but Dixie wasn't sleepy. She tiptoed down the hallway on the other end of the mobile home. When she reached her mother's bedroom door, she paused. She turned the doorknob and heard quiet sobs coming from the darkness. "Mama? You awake?" Dixie whispered into the room.

LorAnn switched on the bedside table light. "I woke up a little bit ago and started thinking about everything you girls have been through. I was gonna go see if y'all were still awake, but y'all weren't in the living room. I could hear you talkin' back there in the back bedroom. You was telling Dollie about Troy and what he did to you. I hated that man after you told me that, and you know I tried to teach you girls not to hate anybody. But I had hate in my heart for him. I'm glad he left town. I always felt guilty about stirring that up. I prob'ly should have just told your Daddy instead of Roz," she said while she silently wept.

Dixie sat on the bed next to her mother's frail body. She was so small, Dixie thought she had shrunken from the feisty mother she remembered so well.

"Mama, I think we all did our best. I've always loved you for being there for me." Dixie leaned over and kissed her mother's soft cheek.

"I want you to know I never told Corb and I don't think Roz ever did either. I promised you, and she promised me. We had a lot of secrets from each other back then." Mama clutched at Dixie's hand.

"I know, Mama. I know. Now get yourself some sleep, 'cause we've got a busy day tomorrow. Good night," Dixie said as she pulled the cover over her mother's shoulders. She switched off the light and made her way back into the kitchen.

Dollie was standing at the kitchen counter with a piece of Aunt Tessie's sweet potato pie. As she stuffed a big bite into her mouth she asked her sister, "Want some? It's real good."

Dixie smiled and said, "Sure, Dollie. I've really missed country cooking."

* * * * * *

The next day came much too early for either of Corb Carter's daughters. They dressed and had breakfast with their mother who served them fried eggs, bacon and toast. She had the food spread out on the kitchen counter for the girls to serve themselves. The three Carter women took their filled plates to the small round kitchen table that was positioned next to the wall.

"Mama, Dollie and I are going up to the bank to get Daddy's Will out of his safety deposit box. When we get through, we'll come back here. We'll all get some lunch later at Pope's if you want," Dixie stated with a slight hint of authority. Dollie took a big bite of bacon and slurped down Mama's strong coffee.

"That's fine with me if you're driving. I don't like drivin' up on the square these days. There's too much traffic. But I do want y'all to see your daddy's brick in the Court House sidewalk. I ordered it a while back and when it come in, they laid it on the west side walkway. I seen it right after they put in down. It says "Pvt. Corbin Lee Carter, World War II."

Dollie reached across the table and patted her mother's hand. "We'll look at it this morning after we do our bank business and while we're still on the square, Mama."

* * * * * *

When Dollie entered the Peoples Bank lobby, she saw an old classmate who had graduated in her high school class. She crossed the lobby and greeted Gerald Smith, the President of the bank.

She told him why she and Dixie were there. He escorted the two women to the lockbox sign-in area, then took Dixie's key and led them to the vault. They stepped inside as he inserted the master key, taking Dixie's key to unlock the door. He left the small door open and disappeared from the vault to give the customers some privacy. Dixie pulled out the long box, set it on a small table, and lifted the top.

Dixie removed a legal document wrapped in a blue cover and folded by fourths to the size of an envelope. The outside said "Last Will and Testament," and Dixie handed it to Dollie without opening it.

There was one other item in the box with the Will. A long white envelope with "For My Girls" inscribed on the front in a shaky handwriting they both recognized as their Daddy's.

Dixie took it out of the box and looked anxiously at Dollie. Then Dixie unsealed the envelope and read its contents, passing it to Dollie as she sat and cried in the bank vault.

> To my girls,
>
> I never was to good at saying how I feel about things, so I hope you will both over look what don't come out right. I just want you both to know that I never been big on saying that I love anybody just ask your Mama. But if you girls hadn't been born I would have been lost for sure. Your mama is a good woman and I always have loved her. I guess maybe I just had a wild streak I couldn't get hold of when I was young. I learned that to late in life and then Lorann wouldn't have me back.
>
> When I left your Mama for Audrey, I wasn't thinking right. I hurt your Mama and you girls to. I am sorry. I wish I could take all that back, but I cant.

What I want you to know is I did something bad a long time ago. I was trying to proteck my family and things just went wrong.

Your Aunt Roz called me and said Troy left her that day. She wanted me to help move his stuff out with my truck but she told me not to tell Lorann. I went over there and found Troy dead. He was in the shed laid out on the little bed. Roz said they was arguing and he tried to hit her. She grabbed a rench and hit him over the head. She said he was dead when he hit the floor. She told me that when they was fighting she knocked his motorcikle and something fell out of the side bag. She picked it up and found stuff that somebody stole off the kids that had went missing. She thought Troy had done it. That's when she said he went for her and she hit him with the rench.

After dark I helped her load Troy up in his car. I drove his car over to the quarry and unlocked the big gate in the fense. I had the key sinse I worked for the City then. She followed me over there and help push the car off into the deep water. The City don't ever mess with that quarry since it got fensed in so I thought he would never been found. If you're reading this, I guess Troy is still in the bottom of the old quarry.

You know your Aunt Roz got the canser in '87. Sinse she is past on now, I thought it was time you girls know the facts. I didn't kill Troy, but I help cover it up.

I found out about the Morgan man being the one that took them kids cause their boy Rocky came looking for that little bag while me and Roz was trying to get Troy in the car. We told him Troy was sick and we was taking him to the doctor. Roz told him to put the bag back where he could find it again later. She told him it was safe here with her. That is when I decided I have to call the police. I was the one that tipped the police off back then but I never told anybody but you Dixie til now.

If you feel like you need to tell anybody about this go ahead. It can't hurt me or Roz now. I just wanted somebody I care about to know what happened. Do what you think is the right thing. I trust you both and I love you to.

Don't tell Phyllis about any this. She is a good woman to. She was just somebody to keep me company in my old age but she don't know it,

                                      Your Daddy

PS Tell your Mama I always love her. She is still in my heart.   C L C

* * * * * *

The Carter women sat in the back booth at Pope's Café eating chess pie after a filling lunch.

"I love the hot roast beef sandwiches they make here with all that good gravy, potatoes and slaw. Lord, how I wish they had something comparable to this in Knoxville," Dollie said as she tried to hide her burp. She took another bite of pie and pushed back the small plate. "That's it. I'm full."

Dixie smirked, "Sure you are, Dollie. Just wait till we get back to Mama's and you remember there's still some sweet potato pie in the refrigerator. I bet you get your appetite back then." All three women chuckled.

"Did you get your Daddy's Will ? Y'all ain't said nothin' about it. Was there somethin' else in there?" Mama asked shyly.

"We got the Will but we haven't even looked at it. We spent the rest of our time walking around the Court House and looking for Daddy's brick. We found it. It looks real nice, Mama," Dixie answered, avoiding the complete answer.

"Hey, what do you say about driving out to the old El Bethel house and looking at what the owners have done to the property? How long has it been since we've been out there? 40 years?" Dollie asked.

"Maybe longer than that for me. I bet Mama rides out that way sometimes, don't you Mama?" Dixie smiled.

"Sometimes me and Dora takes rides out there. You know she has a hard life since Carl died in that accident and Stevie overdosed on them drugs. We're the only two left in the Hudson family and we gotta take care of each other."

LorAnn stared out the window, thinking of how her life was about to change with Corb gone. He had remarried Phyllis Potts, but he would come by her trailer daily to chat for a few minutes and have a glass of buttermilk or cold water.

They both looked forward to those times, and Phyllis didn't mind. In fact, she encouraged Corb to visit LorAnn. She knew it made him happy to be able to check on the mother of his children. He would repair her washer, fix her plumbing, or do anything around the mobile home that he could to help her.

Often LorAnn would visit Phyllis and Corb at their house. They would sit on the screened-in front porch in the white metal glider and talk about anything and everything. It was good for them all to be friends with each other.

It was somewhat ironic that when Corb had his fatal heart attack in his driveway, it was Phyllis that called LorAnn to see if she would accompany her to the Emergency Room to wait on news of Corb's condition. When the doctor came out and told them Corb had passed, they sobbed in each other's arms. They were both good women with pure hearts. They both loved Corbin Carter.

* * * * * *

LorAnn Hudson Carter and Phyllis Potts Carter stood next to each other in the line to receive friends at Corb's funeral held at Feldhaus Memorial Chapel. Also there to greet the attendees were Dixie and her husband, Brax Edwards, and Dollie with her spouse, Samuel Estes. Corb's sister, Tessie Buckley, stood at the end of the line with her husband, Buck. Children, grandchildren, and other relatives watched the long procession pass by while they sat solemnly in the rows of pews facing the receiving line stationed in front of the opened casket.

Corbin Lee Carter's funeral was well attended. He had been a City employee for many years and many policemen, Rescue Squad members, and city officials were there to pay their last respects. There were people there whom neither LorAnn nor Phyllis had ever met, but they shared stories of Corb's kindness and willingness to help a neighbor. He was well-liked and well-respected, and the family was proud of this beloved man.

* * * * * *

Dixie had prepared a short tribute to read to the crowd before the Reverend Doug Whiteside "preached" her Daddy's funeral.

She stood up nervously and approached the podium, walking on shaky legs. Her husband Brax helped her get situated behind the podium and then returned to his seat.

Dixie cleared her throat, looked around the room and started to read from her prepared statement.

> "You all knew my Daddy, Corbin Carter. You may think you knew him, but you only knew one side of him: the side he allowed you to see.

> "This man had so many different sides. Yet he rarely revealed them to anyone but close family, and sometimes not even to them."

She paused for a moment and looked to Dollie for encouragement. Dollie nodded as a sign for Dixie to keep going.

> "He was a simple man, a proud man. He was a devoted father and good provider. He never met a stranger and he was well-liked by most everyone.

> "You knew all these obvious things about Corbin Carter, but did you know that he was an honorably discharged veteran of World War II? Our precious mother and wonderful stepmother made sure his service was commemorated on a brick in the Court House sidewalk. The next time you go to the square, look for it. I'm sure Daddy would be proud you came to visit.

> "Did you know that when he was a boy, he helped support his divorced mother and big sister by catching live snakes on Horse Mountain and selling them to the carnival for a nickel a piece? Again, he did that to help feed his family with the meager amount that he collected.

> "Did you know that as a young boy Corb wanted a Radio Flyer wagon so badly that he worked for months to try to save a few pennies at a time to

get the 60 cents he needed to buy it? He finally saved 50 cents but he could never quite get the other ten cents. He had more important things to buy—like food and clothing. Finally, he gave up and used the money for necessities. He never got his Radio Flyer wagon. But each of us girls, his daughters, got a wagon when we were young. We never realized what a wonderful feeling it must have been for him to be able to gift us with those wagons.

"And finally, did you know that the City of Shelbyville and all its citizens are indebted to Corb Carter for a reason they never even knew existed? During the mid-1950s there was a spree of kidnappings in our town. It lasted for several years without any break in the cases or the recoveries of any of the missing children. Finally, there was closure, the kidnappings stopped, and the grieving parents were able to finally have closure.

"By chance, Corb Carter found out who the kidnapper was and made the anonymous phone call to the police that days later broke the case wide open. He never took credit for that. He never wanted recognition. He only wanted the children of Shelbyville to be safe and secure in their home town. He did that for all of us.

"We may have never truly recognized this man for the hero he was, but today he deserves that honor.

"Daddy, I love you.

"Dollie loves you.

"Mama and Phyllis love you.

"And greatest of all, God loves you.

"May you rest in eternal peace and greet us with open arms when we meet you at Heaven's Pearly Gates. "

* * * * * *

 The pall bearers carried Corb's mahogany casket to the hearse, and a familiar song could heard resonating softly through the chapel.

As the mourners stood to leave the mortuary, they smiled when they heard Fats Domino singing *"Blueberry Hill."*

CHAPTER 33

2002

There were no storms clouds in sight from the bow of the boat. Breakfast had been served, food eaten, dishes cleared and now the two ladies sat back on thick cushioned lounge chairs drinking orange juice from crystal champagne flutes and reading fashion magazines.

"I love it here. I wish we could come as often as you and Brax do," Dollie commented as Butler brought her a juice refill with some fresh strawberries. She thanked him and he disappeared.

"Umm, I love it here, too, but it gets lonely after a few weeks, and three months is a long time to be away from home," Dixie complained.

"Maybe Sam and I should come with you and Brax every year and stay a couple of weeks. We can keep you company while the Meathead rakes in all the money," Dollie chuckled.

Dixie laughed out loud. "Every time you call him that, I think of how much Daddy was like Archie Bunker, excluding the racism, of course." Dixie looked up at the cloudless sunny sky. There was a cool breeze flowing across the deck of the boat, making their sitting area feel the way Paradise should feel.

"Would you and Sam like to walk around the Atlantis Resort? They have activities over there that you might like. They also have a casino with beautiful blown glass light fixtures and artwork." Dixie offered. "Or we could just wait and go over for dinner."

"Oh, I don't know. I've seen that place enough, but I do like to play the slot machines once in a while. On second thought, I don't have the kind of luck you do, Dixie. I always lose. You must have the magic touch." Dollie leaned back in her lounge chair and adjusted her sunglasses.

As Dollie began feel relaxation overtaking her, she was startled when Dixie said loudly, "I know! Let's see if one of the Atlantis tour guides can show us around the public sector. You said you'd never been to the public Market, and it's a lot of fun. Do you think Sam would want to go?"

Dollie thought about the idea of Sam tagging along while the two sisters chatted, giggled, and stopped to look at things that he would never be interested in buying. "Nope. He wouldn't like it. Why don't we all just relax for a little while longer and then go join Brax for lunch at the resort dining room. Then maybe we can all provide input on what would be nice to do during the afternoon."

Dixie looked disappointed. "Oh, come on, Sis. This is *your* vacation. Brax and I live here-- sorta."

"Believe me, my idea of a vacation is to lie around and do nothing. No ringing phones, no deadlines, no alarm clock, no schedules. I need a day or two to get that out of my system. Then maybe I'll climb a cliff or dive off a waterfall. Just not today," Dollie smiled, laid back, and closed her eyes.

Sam came around the corner and joined them on the deck. "You girls having fun?"

"Peachy, except your lazy wife just wants to lie around and she doesn't want to do anything that requires energy. I thought she'd be more fun than that." Dixie could pout almost as well as Dollie.

"How about this, ladies? Why don't I charter a small plane and we can island hop all day. There are several islands around here that are beautiful but they just aren't as commercialized as this island," Sam offered.

Both ladies shook their head. *Been there, done that*, they thought.

"Okay, ladies. I'm all out of suggestions for now. I think I'll go over to the shore and look at the yachts. Maybe I'll go sit by a pool for the beautiful view of the la..landscape," he chuckled.

Dollie slapped him with a magazine. "I know you want to see the views of the la..ladies. Just don't touch. I'll be right here waiting for you when you get back—IF you get back," Dollie said as she closed her eyes to try to nap again.

Dixie got up and went into her bedroom.

* * * * * *

Dixie stood alone in her stateroom clutching the letter that their Daddy had left in the safety deposit box. Neither she nor Dollie had said a word to anyone about the letter's contents. They believed they had been too emotional during the funeral period to make a well-thought out decision about the confession. Dixie had subsequently hidden the letter, not sharing with Brax. Dollie swore she had not told Sam anything about it. Dixie wanted closure on this, but the only person she could discuss it with was Dollie, who seemed to be uninterested.

Daddy's Will had designated that Dixie and Dollie equally share all real or personal property purchased prior to his marriage to Phyllis. Anything the two of them had accumulated together after marriage would belong to Phyllis. He left nothing specific to LorAnn, but Phyllis had allowed her to look through Corb's personal belongings and pick out anything she wanted to keep. Again, Phyllis was very gracious. Both daughters did the same with their mother. If she wanted something that the girls inherited, it was LorAnn's to take.

The Will was an easy document to comply with, but the letter required a hard decision to be made.

She almost wished there hadn't been a letter.

* * * * * *

When Dollie awoke from her nap, she looked for Dixie and found her sunning alone on the back deck. She had a drink in her hand and a tray of cold watermelon and cantaloupe pieces on the side table next to her.

Dollie sat down on an adjacent lounge chair and began the discussion she had tried so hard to avoid for months.

"Dixie, here's what I think. You want to talk about the letter, but I don't believe it should be my place to weigh in on it. However, I do feel strongly that Mama should never know what happened about Uncle Troy, Aunt Roz, and the quarry. Any decisions other than that, you have sole authority to make them. But, when you do make them, please tell me what you're going to do so I won't be shocked to read something in the newspaper. Deal?"

Dixie wanted to shake Dollie by the shoulders and make her take half of the responsibility for this. "Sis, listen to me. We can't tell ANYBODY Daddy's confession, 'cause if it hits the newspapers, Mama will find out regardless. Then Aunt Roz's name gets dragged through the mud. I don't think we should do anything. I do feel bad about Uncle Troy in the bottom of that quarry for all these years. But he's dead now, so what difference does it make anyhow?"

Dollie made a suggestion. "Why don't you do what Daddy did? Why don't we make an anonymous call to the police and tell them they need to search the quarry to find out what's been in the bottom undetected for years?"

"And when they do and they identify Uncle Troy, what happens then? They track it back to his disappearance all those years ago? They ask Mama questions and scare her to death? Don't you think we should leave well enough alone?" Dixie argued.

"I don't know, Dixie. There's a part of me that believes the man deserves a proper burial some day. There's another part of me that thinks he got what he deserved. Trouble is, I don't remember him well enough to have a strong opinion about it," Dollie said.

"You're not much help." Dixie got up and walked away.

* * * * * *

They took the water taxi to shore for lunch in the new Gulfstream. The ladies found Sam by the pool enjoying the view. He had a glass of chardonnay in his hand and a straw hat on his head. He looked like a typical tourist, and he was proud of it.

They went to one of the nicer dining areas to wait for Brax to join them. When he walked through the door, spied Sam's straw hat and made his way to the table.

"I've got great news. I just closed an investment deal with a new client! He won a mega- million dollar lottery jackpot and wants me to navigate the investment waters for him. Tonight he'll celebrate with us on the yacht. I hope you all want lobster and prime rib. Surf and turf is always a good entrée choice when there's something to celebrate. Dinner will be catered from Atlantis and it should be quite an exciting evening." Brax smiled and held up his water glass to toast the endeavor. Everyone simultaneously said "cheers." Then lunch was served.

* * * * * *

By the time the catered meal arrived on the boat, the sisters had had enough time to agree there would be nothing done with the letter Daddy had left for them. They would destroy it later, perhaps when they were together again back on the mainland. Dixie would keep it safely concealed until they chose the exact date to do the deed.

Meanwhile, both Sam and Brax were enjoying the appetizers of shrimp, crab legs, and fresh oysters with horseradish sauce. Brax expected his guest to arrive any minute, and had kept the mystery person's identity a surprise.

* * * * * *

When the water taxi pulled up in the Gulfstream to deliver the expected guest, Dixie, Dollie and Sam waited for Brax to escort the mystery investor to the temporary dining area on the yacht's front deck.

As the elderly gentleman made his entrance, a hauntingly familiar face shyly smiled at the group. Brax took over with the formal introductions.

"Sir, I'd like you to meet my wife Dixie, her sister Dollie, and Dollie's husband, Sam.

Everybody meet Mr. Rocky Morgan, my newest investor and soon to be my new 'partner-in-crime.'"

Dollie sat down mumbling, "Oh, Meathead," then gulped a full glass of champagne.

Sam grinned but looked extremely confused.

Dixie dropped her glass, swooned, and promptly fainted on the polished deck.

Brax was beaming as he draped his arm across his new client's shoulders.

An excited Rocky requested a glass of 'Bubbly Juice' and then asked his host,

"*Can I drive the big boat?*"

ACKNOWLEDGEMENTS

My sincere thanks to everyone who helped me stay motivated and encouraged me to publish this novel:

Dr. Suellen Alfred, family friend, novelist, and editor *extraordinaire*: **Dr. Sue,** you taught me so much about sentence structure and proper use of the English language. You helped me face the new challenge of writing fiction with confidence and an improved presentation. Thank you for taking me under your editorial wing!

Daniel Baker, novelist, former co-worker and friend: ***You*** inspired me to write this book. When I read your first book and the draft of your second novel, I was hooked. Thank you from the bottom of my heart for giving me your honest feedback and constructive criticism. After implementing your suggestions, I now take pride in my first novel! You have my lifelong gratitude.

Sandi Crowell, my best friend and beach buddy: I was on pins and needles while you read the very first draft of this book. Since you are an avid reader and lover of good mysteries, your overall opinion was the "go or no-go" verdict I was seeking. Your valuable insight kept me focused on how to make the writing better and improve the plot. As the self-appointed president of my fan club, you are *MY* hero! ☺

Jo Ann Kirkland, my dear sister and lifelong friend: Thank you for allowing me to pattern one of the characters after my childhood memories of you. Even though the events were fictional (*thank goodness*) I had 1950s' visions of you--my big sister--while writing the manuscript. Thank you for helping me to create a thrilling story line. I love you, and I am forever grateful for your encouragement.

Faye Crews , Keith Gaines, Jim & Liz Harris, my family members: Thanks to each of you for reading and commenting on my drafts. Your remarks were very much appreciated. **Faye**, you should write your own book, you're so talented! **Keith, Liz,** and **Jim**, I appreciate your pointing out the remaining editorial changes. You all have my gratitude for taking time out of your busy lives to help me.

Joe Finch, childhood friend and family friend: I am excited that you found the final draft to be so entertaining. Thanks for taking time to read it and providing me with your thoughts. Within the next few months, I hope to have a second novel for your review!

Thank you to **Amy Simpson,** co-owner of Pope's Café in Shelbyville, Tennessee, for allowing me to reference your legendary restaurant in my story. I'm looking forward to a piece of your chess pie next time I'm in town!

Dr. David Seay, family physician and friend, thank you for answering all my unorthodox medical questions! You are the greatest!

And lastly, to **Samuel Gaines, my love**: Your support and encouragement throughout this process was absolutely invaluable! You listened, edited, provided terrific plot suggestions. You tirelessly brain stormed with me and kept me interested in successfully finishing this project. You were as excited as I was throughout this whole process. I couldn't have started or finished this effort without you as my touchstone and my daily cheerleader.   I love you, Baby.

Mary

CPSIA information can be obtained
at www.ICGtesting.com
Printed in the USA
LVOW03s2250280218
568254LV00002B/2/P